FAR
Away

BRYAN T. CLARK

Published by Cornbread Publishing
Cover Art by Kellie Dennis at Book Cover by Design, http://www.bookcover
bydesign.co.uk
Layout by www.formatting4U.com

For more information on Bryan T. Clark and his works, please see www.btclark.com

Fiction / Gay & Lesbian / M-M Romance / Contemporary / Publishing

First Edition

Print ISBN: 978-0-9970562-5-9

There are times when fiction isn't exactly a tale,
but more like an exaggerated truth.

When the lines between imagination and reality are blurred,
only the author may know the truth.
— Bryan T. Clark

PROLOGUE
Somewhere over the Aegean Sea

It was the middle of the night, and yet Noah lay awake, staring out the plane's window. The weight pressing on his chest wouldn't afford him the comfort of sleep. In the dimly lit cabin, most of the other passengers were asleep as the small twin-engine plane made its descent over the dark Aegean Sea. Mesmerized, Noah stared down at the ruins of the Byzantine castle lit up atop the mountain on the tiny Greek island of Lemnos.

His stomach churned, not from the sway of the plane as it fought the crosswinds that attacked it, but because Noah was about to connect his past with his future. He was ready to bury his life filled with *what ifs* that prevented him from moving forward. This was the final step he needed to free himself from the turmoil that had plagued him for the past twelve years. This was a day he'd dreamed about for years.

Two days ago, he left his New York apartment in Greenwich Village in the middle of the night. Three flights and eight thousand miles across the world later, he found himself here. Good or bad, this was the trip that would answer his years of unanswered questions about a summer love when he was just eighteen years old.

If successful, the trip would end in a fairytale happily ever after—the stuff of which romance movies are made. He shuddered at the thought of any other ending.

Noah was chasing a lost love. A love born and suspended on the shores of Lake Winnipesaukee, New Hampshire, where he'd fallen in love for the first time. It was a love so brief, yet it still consumed him. A love he'd never been able to shake, so intense, he could think of nothing else. A love that left him stuck in so many ways.

The decade of pining over a person he hadn't seen in years was one of the few things Noah hid from his therapist. Sure, they talked about Noah's more recent relationships and the poor choices he was making.

1

However, with his aching for someone from so long ago, Noah was afraid she would say he was obsessing. He didn't want what was so true in his heart to be devalued as simply an obsession. He was in love and always had been since that fateful summer.

He stared at his reflection in the window, taken aback by how tousled his sandy blond hair had become. His sky-blue eyes were drawn past his own image, out to the plane's propeller in the middle of the wing as it cut through a patch of clouds. The whir of the blades as the wing vibrated drew him deeper into a hypnotic state. For a second, Spiro's face appeared in the reflection of the window. His long, shaggy black hair, hazel eyes, and smile that rose on the right side of his mouth was that of a Greek god's. A smile etched in marble: He had been cast in beauty for eternity.

Noah saw himself as the exact opposite. He was often the chameleon in the room. At five-eleven, his thin, lanky body had the muscle tone of a fifteen-year-old boy's. His run-of-the-mill blond hair blended into his pale skin. It was nothing he did specifically, but being an introvert, he was often mistaken as distant, unapproachable, or aloof. In reality, he was none of that. He enjoyed having fun, being with people, and taking risks; he just didn't know how.

Noah pushed his back firmly against his seat as the plane hit another patch of turbulence, sending his heart into his throat. He tried to focus on something other than the plane possibly crashing.

Maybe his therapist was right. Perhaps he was picking guys who would ultimately fail him, thus making them the bad guy and him the victim. But he wasn't convinced that he hadn't loved any of them or that the pain felt after each of those breakups wasn't real.

In retrospect, there was no denying the dysfunctional thread of trust and love woven through his entire life since childhood—emotional bruises and wounds that healed into deep emotional scars. He took a deep breath and exhaled years of failed relationships with men who, unbeknownst to them, probably never stood a real chance. Not because of who they were... *but because of who Spiro was.*

CHAPTER ONE
TWELVE YEARS EARLIER

Noah stood on the train platform in the little town of Concord, New Hampshire. Nestled in a forest of majestic white pines and red oaks, Concord had the majestic White Mountains as its backdrop. Concord was the closest the train could get him to his family's lakefront home on the shores of Lake Winnipesaukee.

A ray of sun warmed Noah's fair cheeks, causing him to look up. The sky above the mountaintops glowed in an array of hues from burnt orange to pale pink under the setting sun. About an hour and a half of daylight remained.

It was sixty-one degrees when he left New York this morning. In a couple of hours, Noah had gone from a cement and steel city filled with millions of people walking around in a world of their own to tree-lined streets and strangers smiling and greeting each other. The sound of taxicabs honking and buses roaring was replaced with a single mower. With a population of forty thousand, Concord was the big city for this area of New Hampshire.

His phone said it was seventy-seven degrees: too warm for the navy sportscoat that encased his slender shoulders. His pressed khakis, perfectly starched and ironed white dress shirt, and yarmulke easily identified him as part of the town's Jewish community. Aside from his taller than average height for an eighteen-year-old, he had a boyishly thin face, wheat-colored hair, and rosy cheeks resembling a young child.

Somehow, this day wasn't how Noah imagined it had been for his peers who had already celebrated their eighteenth birthday this year. Today, he should be smoking a joint, drunk off rum and Coke, or having wild sex in the elevator with the tall Cuban doorman in his building. He should be doing something wild and crazy that would mark his passage into adulthood. Alejándro, the doorman, would definitely work. Noah

3

chuckled under his breath. Who was he kidding? He'd done none of that stuff, but he could dream.

Instead, Noah spent the early morning of his eighteenth birthday sitting in a New York taxi en route to Penn Station. And tonight, he would dine alone with his eighty-one-year-old grandmother. He shook his head as his eyes rolled. He could hardly contain his excitement.

Noah had to get through the next eight weeks of summer. After that, he would be off to Harvard and out from under his homophobic, narcissistic parents. He had to hang in there for two months, and then he would be free to do his own thing. The thought did nothing to quell his churning stomach and the feeling that he could vomit at any moment. He swirled saliva around his mouth, trying to banish the metallic taste that coated it.

The stomach acid and metallic taste were what his mother said was an ongoing gastrointestinal issue. Well, actually, she used the words *Over-Imaginative Active Brain Filled with Irrational Worries*. According to her, the reason for the ten pounds he lost over the last year boiled down to anxiety.

The loud roar of the locomotive as it pulled away from the station was replaced with the sound of heels clicking, as the other passengers made their way across the wooden platform. Anticipating that his grandmother was in the parking lot, he followed the handful of people into the Norman Rockwell-looking train station.

Inside the old building, Noah paid no attention to the old photographs that lined the yellowed walls. Since he was thirteen, he'd been traveling from New York to New Hampshire on the train with his twin brother Nathanael, who was now deceased. When they were kids, his parents felt he and Nathanael were old enough to make the six-hour train trip north by themselves.

This year, Noah's parents were supposed to have come with him for the weekend so they could all celebrate his eighteenth birthday together. Somehow, he'd been gullible enough to think this birthday would be better than last year's. In all actuality, he shouldn't have been surprised when his parents had a change in both their work schedules and couldn't make the trip. The true surprise was how indifferent he'd become to their absence.

Inside the station, Noah's guileless blue eyes caught the gaze of the overweight middle-aged ticket agent behind the counter. *Yep, he still works here.* Dressed in a sloppy black dress coat and white shirt, the man's predatory, squinty eyes sunk into his fat, round face stalked Noah as he moved through the building. Noah had first seen the man at the end of the summer last year. His stare was creepy, an eeriness that unnerved him enough to remember him a year later.

Noah glanced over the head of the short woman rolling two suitcases and trying to move her little girls along out the front door. Rolling his bag, he held his phone in his other hand as he used his elbow to stop the glass door from closing on him. Outside, as he scanned the parking lot for his grandmother, Noah took in a conscious breath of the vibrant scent of pine from the giant evergreens surrounding the train station. Then, he slowly exhaled, accepting he was here.

With graduation less than a week ago, Noah spent the last few weeks of his high school years saying goodbye to his friends in the honor society and chess club. Now, the quiet kid with a nearly perfect SAT score was eager to escape to the next chapter of his life, Harvard University. The real upside of Harvard was that it was two hundred miles from his family's lavish apartment on the Upper East Side of Manhattan.

The woman and the two little girls stood at the curb as a large white Suburban pulled up and stopped before them. A short, chunky man jumped from the SUV and greeted the little girls who squealed with delight as he gathered them into his arms.

Noah couldn't watch the sappy, joyous reunion any longer and turned his head away. Never in his entire life had his parents welcomed him like that. They were much more restrained, leaning toward the dull side.

"Excuse me," a male voice called to him.

Noah turned toward the voice, seeing the overenthusiastic family guy now approaching him. "You must be Dr. Rothenberg's boy... I'm friends with your parents."

Noah knew the man was really referring to his mother as his *friend.* Noah's father, who was the best thoracic surgeon on the East Coast, didn't have friends, he had colleagues. His mother, who was equally respected as an OB-GYN, was the more sociable one of the two.

"I'm Dr. Dobrowski," the man stated as he extended his hand to Noah. "Is your mother here?" His bright blue eyes stared intently at Noah.

"Hi... um, no, she's still in the city. It's me and my grandmother, for now."

"Dr. Eidelman? Oh my gosh, I haven't seen your grandmother in years. How's she doing?" His voice was too damn bubbly. "Besides being one of the best OB-GYNs in New York next to your mother, your grandmother made the best lemon meringue pie on this side of the lake." He released Noah's hand. His portly belly was evidence of just how much he probably loved pie.

A car horn honked, Noah prayed it was his grandmother, rescuing him from further conversation with Dr. Happy. Relief washed over him as the black four-door Mercedes-Maybach rolled up to the curb. Noah cracked a half smile at Eros, her Greek driver and handyman, as he peered over the steering wheel and brought the massive car to a stop.

His grandmother lowered the rear window. "Dr. Dobrowski. What a pleasure running into you. I'd heard you and your family were up this summer."

Dr. Dobrowski approached the side of the car and stepped between the curb and the car before extending his hand to shake hers. "Good afternoon, Dr. Eidelman. I was just telling... your grandson—" the man's face frowned as if he realized he didn't know her grandson's name. "—that I was hoping to get the families together this summer. Peggy would love to see everyone." Releasing her hand, Dr. Dobrowski stepped back on the curb. "The girls are in the car, and I'm sure they're exhausted and want to get to the cabin. But I promise, we'll make it by... I promise."

Noah's eye shifted from Dr. Dobrowski walking away to Eros, who was holding the car door open for him. Eros's face was heavily lined with deep wrinkles, and his thick grey brows were longer and wider than the year before. He was now at least six inches shorter than Noah this year.

"Sir." Eros greeted Noah as he took his suitcase from him. Noah climbed into the back seat of the large sedan.

"My dear, you're getting skinnier and skinnier. You're nothing but bones." Noah's grandmother adjusted her own slender body to face him. Her hair was more gray than silver this summer, yet perfectly coiffed.

Noah rolled his eyes. If she was going to insult him, she could at least show up on time. "Thank you, Grandma. It's good to see you, too," he responded with little more than a grumble.

His grandmother, like his mother, had probably never given a compliment in her life. Over the years, Noah heard his mother on numerous occasions describe her childhood as difficult. According to her, his grandmother was restrictive, cold, and judgmental. She talked about his grandmother issuing severe consequences that weren't proportionate to her or her sister's behavior.

6

He settled into one of the two cushy seats in the rear of the sedan. He wasn't a car person, but this wasn't just a car. It was the ultimate in luxury. He'd overheard his father say she spent over two hundred thousand for the damn thing.

"How much do you weigh now?" she asked.

"I don't know. One forty, I think." Noah thought for sure she would've laid into him first about the length of his hair. His current experiment was to see how long he could let it grow before either his mom or dad said something. His classic crew cut had grown to the base of his neck with hues of butterscotch. He was surprised no one had said a word to him yet—their rabbi's noticeably unappreciative glance last week at Synagogue didn't count.

"I'm so sorry we were running late." Her face showed no reaction to the current weight he'd given her. "We had a storm last night, and several trees fell across the highway. We were stuck on the road for over an hour." Dressed in an ivory blouse with a ruffled neckband that climbed up her neck, it looked as if the blouse was about to swallow her head.

After his grandfather passed away, Grandma Maya had retired and turned over her medical practice to Noah's mother. His grandmother now split her time between the family's lake house during the summer months and her penthouse in Manhattan the rest of the year. At eighty-one years old, she maintained all her wits and mobility.

Noah, focused his attention on Eros as the car pulled away from the curb. He was a quiet man who seemed content taking care of everything and everyone at the house over summers. Noah could count what he knew about the old man on one hand. He was Greek, he was old, and Noah's family had employed him to tend to the lake house as long as Noah could remember. Oh, and he stayed with a sister in Boston during the winter months.

Tired of sitting, what should have only been a six-hour train ride today took ten hours because of repairs to the track that was being done just outside of Boston. A six-hour train ride was never fun, but being stuck in a train sitting on the tracks for an additional four hours was painful. Noah reclined his seat and shifted his bony ass onto one cheek. He tucked the small leather pillow behind his head for the hour-long drive deep into the New Hampshire forest toward the lake house. He occupied himself on his phone until it couldn't keep a signal.

Deeper into the woods, the car sped down the two-lane highway flanked by a forest of gigantic pines, maples, and oaks. Noah stared at the time in the upper right corner of the phone, waiting to see if his phone would reconnect. He'd made this trip so many times, he knew he had one or two more chances to grab a signal before he lost it for good. This was the beginning of two months of sheer boredom.

His body pushed against the door as the car sped around a curve and jolted him from his trance, enough to realize his grandmother was speaking to him. "... *and* he's only here for the summer. Try to stay out of his way."

"Mmm-hmm." Noah didn't know who she was talking about, but pretended as if he understood.

It was dusk when the car veered off the main road and onto the narrow gravel road leading to the house. The large sedan bounced along for several feet until Eros slowed to a speed that was less troublesome.

Noah wasn't sure his life with Eros driving was in any better care than if his grandmother had the wheel herself. Holding on to his seat, he closed his eyes, but that was worse. If they were going to hit one of the hundreds of birch trees that lined the gravel road, he wanted to see it coming.

The car slowed as they made the twists and turns down the half-mile of gravel driveway until the old three-story house and lake appeared. The massive house was like something from a Nicholas Sparks movie, where someone went either to hide or escape civilization. The house sat on five and a half acres of dense forest, wildlife, and crawling insects. This was where the change in season was welcomed in waves of orange, crimson, yellow, and golden-brown foliage. Lake Winnipesaukee was where time ticked by twice as slowly as the rest of the world. He used to love coming to the house as a child, but he hadn't felt the same since Nathanael died.

Out of the corner of his eye, Noah caught a glance at a strikingly good-looking young man walking toward the barn. There was just enough daylight left to reveal his long, black wavy hair and slender build. *Was this the guy Grandma was speaking of earlier?*

Noah peered out the back window as the car rolled past the young man towards the old, rustic barn, and stopped in front of the house. Like a ghost, the guy had disappeared, but Noah had seen enough of him to pique his interest.

The warm smell of a brisket cooking greeted Noah as he entered the old house. The housekeeper, Ms. Jimenez, met Noah. Short and plump, Ms. Jimenez wore her black hair filled with grey streaks pulled into a bun. Since his grandmother had been with Eros for the last couple of hours, he knew he was smelling Ms. Jimenez's brisket.

"Good evening, Mr. Rothenberg." Ms. Jimenez clasped her hands, seemingly waiting to see if Noah needed anything from her.

"Hi, Ms. Jimenez." He smiled at the overweight, middle-aged Hispanic woman who tended to them three days during the week. The aroma of dinner caused his stomach to grumble. His stomach, asking for food, clashed with the anxiety that accompanied eating. Increasingly, eating resulted in him getting sick. As recent proof, the frozen pizza he ate yesterday had wrecked his gut until almost two a.m. this morning.

"Why don't you head on upstairs and freshen up while Ms. Jimenez finishes up dinner?" Grandma Maya suggested, as she shrugged off her coat and handed it to Ms. Jimenez.

"Sure." Noah took his suitcase from Eros, who had scooted in behind them. He, too, looked as if age was finally catching up with him.

Exhausted from traveling all day, Noah trudged up the two flights of stairs that zigzagged up to the third floor. The last thing he wanted was to come back downstairs and eat. He would only get sick.

Come on! Quit being so lazy. I'm hungry. I want to eat! Noah could hear Nathanael's voice barking at him three steps above him. He rarely heard Nathanael yapping at him anymore other than here. It seemed like every summer when he arrived at the lake house Nathanael's presence was intense. Back in the city, things changed every day, like the new French bakery on the corner that sold the killer strawberry cream puffs, the new mall, the new movie theater, even Alejándro, the new doorman. These were all new memories that didn't include Nathanael. But here, life was exactly as it was four years ago. Here, every room held a memory. Anything Noah did, he'd done it with Nathanael already. He couldn't even use the bathroom without Nathanael walking in on him.

He took his time unpacking things from his backpack, laying them about his room before washing up and returning downstairs. At dinner, Noah and his grandmother sat at opposite ends of the table as Noah picked at what was supposed to be a birthday dinner. As delicious as Ms. Jimenez's brisket and cabbage normally was, after the pizza yesterday, he was a little worried he'd spend another night on the toilet. He overchewed the brisket as if swallowing it would cause him to vomit. The thought of vomiting killed what little appetite he could muster up. He now had more saliva than meat in his mouth, forcing him to swallow.

Bryan T. Clark

His grandmother had a different diagnosis for Noah's stomach problems. According to her, the fault lay with Noah's parents because they'd strayed from their kosher practices. She still kept a kosher kitchen, maintaining it was more important in today's world to choose meats that had been slaughtered according to Jewish law.

Unlike his grandmother, Noah and his parents dined in restaurants that coveted the Michelin star status but didn't necessarily keep with kosher practices. What neither his parents nor Grandma Maya knew was, when he was left to fend for himself after school, it was all about fast food for Noah. A big fat Burrito Supreme from Taco Bell was his heaven.

"The Alpersteins arrived yesterday," his grandmother said. "Chris will be happy you're here."

"I suppose." The Alpersteins, who owned the cabin across the lake from them, had been coming up every summer for as long as Noah could remember. He had mixed emotions about seeing their son, Chris, in the morning. Six months apart in age, his friend Chris was six inches shorter and likely thirty pounds heavier than Noah. By the end of summer last year, Chris was well on his way to having a mustache. *How different will Chris be this summer? Will he want to hang out anymore?* A quiver swelled in his stomach, a tingle that tightened the walls of his gut. As much as he wanted to blame his discomfort on the meal, perhaps this was the year Chris realized how lame Noah was and would no longer speak to him.

Noah grabbed a biscuit from the saucer in front of him; bread was always a safe bet to eat. He tore off an edge and popped it in his mouth. *Oh, my gosh, this is the best biscuit in the world*, he told himself as he gave himself a second to enjoy it.

He swallowed the moist, buttery biscuit and forced himself to hold off on another one. He had questions, burning questions that couldn't wait a minute longer. "Grandma, who's the guy who was in the driveway when we pulled up?" He'd barely seen more than a glance of the tall, obscure figure, but it was enough to trigger desire—the desire to know more about whoever it was.

Grandma Maya's steel grey eyes remained cast down at her plate. "That's Spiro, Eros's nephew I told you about. He's working with Eros this summer." She cast little more than a glance toward Noah. "He's from Eros's village. This is his first visit to the States."

Noah stared at the biscuit in his hand. He'd never heard the name Spiro. His short glimpse of the stranger intrigued him.

10

"Does he speak English?" Excitement grew at the base of Noah's gut at the idea of Spiro being around for the summer.

"A little." Her eyes narrowed as if studying him.

There was a brief silence between them before she spoke again. "I talked to your father this evening. They can't get up here until sometime next week. He wanted to know if there was anything you wanted him to bring that you forgot."

Noah paused before answering. He packed this morning for the trip in less than ten minutes, throwing into his bag whatever was in his line of sight. There were many things he wouldn't mind having: internet, to start. Missing an entire summer of his favorite television show, *One Tree Hill*, had always sucked. Thank God for the games on his phone.

"Can he bring me two DVDs—season three and four of *One Tree Hill*?" Old reruns were better than nothing.

"I imagine he can. Season three and four?" His grandmother's face showed skepticism over his choice of forgotten items.

"Actually, as many as he can," Noah mumbled.

"Very well." She returned to her dinner.

"Why's he here?" The question freed itself from Noah's mouth, despite any suspicion it would cause.

"What do you mean, *why*?"

"Did you know he was coming?" Noah squirmed in his chair.

"I did..." Grandma Maya gave him one of her frosty looks that conveyed she was questioning the question. "Eros called last month and said the boy's father was sending him." She paused. "He was away at school last year, and something happened. Eros said he wasn't allowed to finish out his studies but promised the boy would be no trouble... Eros could use the help."

"What do you mean, *something* happened?" Noah's heart drummed.

"I didn't ask, and Eros didn't offer."

Noah thought about the possibilities. *What if he's a serial killer or a drug dealer? How do you* not *ask?* "Was he in college?" Noah braced himself for his grandmother to end the twenty questions about something of no importance to her.

"I believe he finished his secondary schooling. I get the feeling he's free spirited—we called them drifters back in the day. He's been here two weeks. Keeps to himself when he's not with Eros."

Secondary studies—Noah knew this was the European equivalent of high school. But more importantly, this guy was a *bad boy*—in some trouble. Noah knew bad boys well. If not for Nathanael when they were in elementary school, he would have spent all his recesses dodging bad boys on the playground. Now, not only was this bad boy sharing his summer with him, but he was also across the driveway in Eros's one-bedroom apartment over the detached garage. Having a bad boy living with them for the entire summer should have freaked him out, yet Spiro did the opposite. Spiro stirred an interest, a keenness.

"I assume he's staying in the apartment with Eros?"

"Yes." Her expression communicated she was over the twenty questions.

Noah's pulse quickened as he diverted his eyes back at his dinner.

After dinner, while his grandmother sat in the living room reading this evening's scripture from her Torah, Noah took to his room. In striped pajama bottoms, he stretched out on his bed hoping to read a couple of chapters of Jean M. Auel's novel, *Clan of the Cave Bear*.

An hour had passed when suddenly voices from outside pulled Noah from his reading. He glanced over at the clock on his nightstand. It was nine o'clock. Curiosity got the better of him, sending him to the window to investigate.

Down below, Eros and his nephew were standing across the yard in front of the barn. Face to face, they stood under the giant floodlight over the barn's double doors. The light gave Noah the means to observe the stranger from afar. From behind the lace sheers, he watched as Eros snapped his fingers in his nephew's face. The young man puffed on a cigarette as he shifted his weight from leg to leg. He was being scolded. What had this bad boy done?

This bad boy was a smoker with long hair. Eros's nephew was the alpha male that Noah did everything possible to avoid in school, just like the Jocks, the Skaters, and the Hipsters. He bet his grandmother had a conniption when she first saw him.

When Eros looked up toward the window, Noah ducked back, aligning his body with the wall. He waited as long as he could before the adrenaline that flooded his body forced him to return to the window.

With broad shoulders and a tapered waist, Spiro wore a tight black tee shirt stretched across his chest like a suit of armor. Noah chewed at his nail, afraid to blink for fear of missing something. His eyes soaked in every ounce of Spiro: the ring curls hanging in front of his face, the way he stood, shoulders slumped as he stayed there taking a tongue lashing from Eros.

Below, the two men separated as Ms. Jimenez exited the house. She exchanged a simple acknowledgment with Eros as she passed by heading to her car. Moments after her taillights disappeared into the forest of trees toward the main road, Eros and Spiro strayed off in separate directions, the nephew disappearing into the barn as Eros walked toward their apartment. Noah's breath hitched as he waited to see if Spiro would re-emerge.

After what seemed like an eternity watching the barn door, Noah gave in and returned to his bed. He sat at the edge of his twin bed, the vision of Spiro now in his room. He imagined what it would be like to touch Spiro. The stretch in his pajamas said it was more than a touch he wanted.

It had been two days since he masturbated, apparently two days too many as his body sprung to life. He lay back on his metal-framed bed as his hand swept across his hairless chest. He closed his eyes as Spiro dominated his thoughts. Spiro was not Noah's first instant crush on a guy. There were plenty of guys at his school that did it for him. None of them were ever a real possibility though because no one knew he liked guys. This last school year, it was Finnian Goldberg, the captain of his school's lacrosse team, who captivated Noah's attention in the halls.

The rhythmic sound of the second hand on the clock between the two twin beds reverberated in his ear. Noah's hand slid down his abdomen and into his pajamas. He stopped before touching himself. Heat rose from his groin, heat caused by Spiro. The old box spring squeaked beneath him. The squeak was a reminder of how much noise the bed made with the simplest shift. Noise traveled through the old house, especially at night.

Noah's hand slipped down another inch, resting beside his heated erection. *No Spiro... my grandma will hear.* He laughed under his breath. His hand resting inches from his groin, Noah's imagination had always been bolder than his actions.

CHAPTER TWO

Spiro stirred, realizing he'd fallen asleep in the barn again. He'd done the same thing two nights ago after he and Eros had gotten into a huge fight. The old queen mattress he'd found lying up against a wall in the barn was far better than squeezing his six-foot frame onto the lumpy couch in the apartment.

The sunlight peeping through the cracks between the wood slats told him it was morning, at least seven o'clock. He rubbed his eyes open some more, thinking about the day ahead. The one thing he knew was that he had to pee.

Still in a sleepy fog, he heard footsteps cross the gravel and stop on the other side of the door. It was seconds before the large barn door slid open about a foot. Spiro jumped to his feet, knowing it was likely Eros.

"What are you doing?" Eros asked as he shuffled past him and to the back wall. At sixty-two, the man walked as if he was a hundred. Years of physical labor gave him bad knees, and a table saw accident years ago severed half his ring finger.

"Nothing." Spiro fought off a yawn that would give him away.

Eros gathered up a bucket and several tools and walked toward Spiro. "Then let's get started." He continued towards the large automobile covered by a tarp in the barn. He stopped and scowled at several wooden frames leaning against the car and an array of paints and brushes. "What are you doing? Is this what you do when you disappear at night?" Eros asked as he picked up a small bottle of paint.

"I'm not doing anything," Spiro lied. Two days ago, amongst the mess in the barn he was tasked to sort, he'd found a bunch of old frames, blank canvases, and dried paint. With a little paint thinner, he salvaged some of the dried oil-based paints. Experimenting with the paints was something to do to pass the time. He'd done some painting back home, but his passion had always been more directed toward drawing. He'd surprised himself with not only how much he enjoyed painting but also that he was also pretty good at it.

"I'm speaking to you! These are not yours."

Spiro rolled his eyes as he roamed a few steps, not really going anywhere. "It's junk. It's not like the old lady would use any of it!" He knew better than to walk away from his *theios*.

Spiro's uncle clenched his fist and shook it in the air. "If you didn't buy it, it's not yours to touch." He stared up at Spiro as if he was ready to take him on.

"Okay!" Spiro wanted to laugh at the whole fist-in-the-air show. His theios was a lot of hot air. He'd never hit anyone a day in his life.

"Have you eaten?" Eros asked as he wobbled past him and out the barn.

Spiro followed him outside. "No. I'm not hungry, but I have to pee."

The morning crisp air carried a light scent of pine mixed with spruce. With the sun rising about an hour ago, it was going to be another beautiful morning on Lake Winnipesaukee.

After running up to the apartment to pee, Spiro jogged out to the dock where Eros was working. Once on the dock, he slowed and walked the remaining twenty feet until he reached Eros.

His theios was on one knee using his hammer to pull up a nail from the wooden dock. "These rotten boards all need to come up."

Still in the same jean cutoffs and black hoodie from yesterday, Spiro stood over Eros's shoulders as Eros pulled up the rotten board from the dock. Speaking Greek, Spiro asked, "Why's the old lady always watching me? She's like Chucky." Spiro turned an eye back at the large three-story white house. His stare moved from the house to the expensive black Mercedes parked on the side of the house.

"Who's Chucky?" Eros asked in Greek.

Spiro laughed that his theios didn't know who Chucky was. "He's a doll that's a serial killer." The beauty of speaking Greek, if ears were to hear, was that they wouldn't know what was being said.

"Don't be disrespectful," Eros grumbled as he struggled to free the next nail.

"Why am I here?" Since arriving in the States two weeks ago, he and his theios had been preparing the house for the arrival of the owners. The old lady showed up a week ago, and the rest of the family was planning to come this weekend. Yesterday, Spiro was relieved when he overheard the old lady telling Eros something about her grandson being the only one coming this weekend.

By Eros's design, Spiro had little to do with the old lady. Eros communicated with her and handed down jobs to him as needed. Spiro had two conversations with her since his arrival. The first conversation was if he was enjoying his vacation to the United States, which he wasn't; nor was it a vacation. The second conversation was when she told him his hair was too long. Since then, he did everything he could to avoid her for fear his tongue would get Eros fired.

Since she rarely left the house and he never went inside, their paths hadn't crossed again. He figured she must have known why he was here, the way she kept track of him through the windows.

"You're here to help me." Eros twisted the hammer around the nail and pulled it free.

Spiro knew that wasn't true. He was being punished. "For how long?"

He'd asked this question at least a hundred times and had yet to receive a proper answer. What he got was a constant *You move too slow, you're lazy, you don't know what hard work is...*

"Until you stop stealing my beer." Eros scooted on one knee and tapped his hammer on the next board.

Spiro smiled, hearing his theios had noticed his beer disappearing. He plodded along behind Eros a few steps before they stopped again. He would let Eros do the work as long as Eros kept going. "Do you like driving the Mercedes?" Spiro asked.

"It's a car." Eros went to work removing the next board.

"Is everyone rich around here?" Spiro scanned across the lake at the surrounding large homes. He'd never been around homes of such grandeur. Everyone on the island of Lemnos shared the same socio-economic status. Spiro had lots of questions. "Does this lake warm up?" Yesterday, while Eros and the old lady were in Concord picking up her grandson, he was going to swim, but after touching the water, it was too cold for his taste.

He was an island boy, born and raised on the tiny island of Lemnos, with its surrounding warm waters. In the middle of the Aegean Sea, the island was a hundred and fifty miles from the mainland of Athens. His small village of Katalako had just over a hundred people. He was a million miles from home, and without his phone, he might as well be on Mars.

16

"It *is* warm." Sounding cantankerous, Eros ripped another nail from the board and tossed it in his bucket.

"Does it snow here?" He'd never seen snow. He sized up the mixed hues of evergreens that made up the bulk of the forest surrounding them. This house, the lake, they struck him as if they were in a hole and he would have to climb the treetops to get out. His eyes darted down to the lake, where six geese skimmed the water's surface as they landed.

"In the winter," Eros mumbled.

A chill ran up the back of Spiro's back. He was used to a dryer temperature. His eyes glanced over the lake looking for the brown and black geese.

"Carry some of this wood back up to the house, and bring the new planks down. You can fill them in behind me."

Eros's voice snapped Spiro out of his daydream. He rolled his eyes as he registered what Eros had instructed him to do. With a sigh, he turned and headed up toward the house.

Near the house, Spiro's gate slowed as he observed a young guy wrapped in a blanket, staring out from the window. *That must be the grandson.* His straw-colored hair was disheveled, and his eyes were a little dark. Yet, he was nice looking.

For a second, their eyes met before the guy moved away from the window. In that second, with little more than a glance, Spiro saw the dull, bleak stare in them. The American with pale skin and tousled hair was little more than an image of a ghost.

He continued past the house and crossed the gravel driveway. The task of hauling lumber between the barn and the dock was now over-shadowed by the guy's sad face that had been etched into his visual memory.

By the time Spiro returned with several planks, Eros had twice the amount of boards pulled up and tossed to the side. "How many are you planning on replacing?" He asked as he lay down the planks he'd carried.

"As many as need replacing." Bent down on one knee, Eros ripped another nail from the decayed wood.

"I saw the old lady's grandson standing in the window. Is he sick?"

Eros hunched his shoulders, adding little more than a grunt.

"He looks sick... or sad." He continued to watch as Eros worked. There was a tinge of guilt, watching the old man down on one knee working. "I can do that, if you want... I mean, if you have something else to do, I can pull up these old boards and replace them."

17

Spiro reached down, asking for the hammer. He'd spent time around Eros when he was a small boy but barely remembered his theios. Eros was the patriarch of the family, and with that came a level of respect.

Eros yanked several more nails from the plank he was working on. Ignoring Spiro's offer, Eros said to him, "You're too smart for this... Why didn't you stay in school? Why did you waste your father's money and get kicked out? You young kids, you think everything is supposed to come to you. You think the whole world is for you to piss on."

"Please, Eros, let me do that." Spiro ignored the old man's rant, took the hammer from Eros's hand, and nudged him out of the way.

Spiro pushed aside his plan to escape by simply trekking up to the main road and hitchhiking into town. Yesterday, he was sure he could find someone heading into New York. He could explore the city on his own, truly see the United States. The plan seemed enticing until he remembered how bad it got in Athens last year when he ventured out on his own. Being thrown in jail was the scariest two days of his life. He wasn't about to repeat that.

CHAPTER THREE

Noah moved away from the window and took to his seat in the sunroom. Barefoot and only wearing his pajama bottoms, he wrapped the afghan blanket from the wicker basket beside the wooden stove tighter around his shoulders. Spiro had caught him staring. In his defense, though, he wasn't staring at him as much as he was trying to wake up. In a stupor, he was simply waiting for his first cup of coffee. It wasn't even eight o'clock yet.

Still in her pastel pink night robe, Grandma Maya entered the sunroom with the steaming cup of coffee he'd been waiting for. "Good morning." She passed him a hot mug. Her hands steadied long enough for Noah to take the cup from her.

He hadn't noticed how twisted her fingers were until now. "Thank you, Grandma." He was barely awake as the smell of the rich brewed coffee floated under his nose.

They sat in the spacious sunroom, its walls covered with green-and-white striped wallpaper. The room's large pane windows facing the lake let in more light than anywhere else in the house, yet the room was still depressing. Years of photographs on the walls dated back several generations. A photo of his mother and aunt when they were kids had been on the end table for as long as Noah was alive. In little dresses, they were in this same room. His mother's scowl in the photograph made it easy to identify which of the two girls she was. On the wall behind the wooden stove was a succession of eight-by-ten school photos of him and Nathanael from kindergarten to eighth grade. After that, there was one of just Noah his freshman year. That was the last picture added to this room.

He held his coffee in one hand and pulled the afghan up and over his mouth to breathe down into it. From his chair, he stared vacantly out the window past the manicured grassy knoll that lay between the house and the sugar-sand beach. For houseguests, this picturesque view of the aqua blue lake and green mountains was breathtaking, but for Noah, it was just water.

"Are you cold?" Her expression said he couldn't be cold.

Noah removed the afghan from over his mouth. "Yeah, a little." He blew the steam across the top of the heavy ceramic coffee mug before taking a sip. His attention was drawn to movement outside. About seventy-five feet from the house, Eros and his nephew were standing on the dock.

She took her seat in the white rattan chair beside him. "It's supposed to warm up later in the week. I imagine the humidity will come with it."

Noah acknowledged her concern for the weather with little more than an "uh-huh" as he eyed what the two men were doing on the dock. His view of Eros's nephew in the daylight revealed that he was cuter than Noah first realized. Even from this distance, Noah's eyes were drawn to the guy's athletic build and thick long black hair. He was wearing cut-off jeans and work boots. He would never wear shorts and boots together, yet this guy made them look hot! He reminded Noah of Bo Duke from the *Dukes of Hazzard.*

"How's school?" Grandma Maya asked as she adjusted the pillow down at the small of her back.

"I don't know." *My grades? My lack of friends? My future plans?* What was she asking? The question was too broad. He'd been attending the same private boarding school since junior high. Nothing had changed in six years. His eyes again glanced over at Eros and his nephew. His heart rate increased as his breath hitched for a second or two.

"'I don't know' isn't an answer. How are your grades?"

"Same as always. An 'A' in everything but PE. I think Mr. Samuel hates me." His PE teacher, Mr. Samuel, who looked like a ferret, barely ever said anything to him. It was like Noah wasn't even worth engaging with.

"And why would he hate you?" Grandma Maya's expression said he was being ridiculous.

Noah shrugged. Ridiculous or not, it was the truth. He hated PE and never tried to hide his misery from Mr. Samuel.

"Are you excited about the fall? When do you have to be on campus?"

"The earliest I can move into the dorm is August thirty-first. School starts on September fifteenth." If Noah had his way, he would be there the first day it was possible to move into the dorms.

As Noah sipped on his coffee, he stared out at the two men on the dock. Yes, Eros's nephew was a stranger, a bad boy, but Noah wanted to meet him. Never in his life had he approached someone he thought was cute. It just wasn't ever going to happen, but Spiro stirred something deep within.

"What did you say Eros's nephew's name was again?" Noah's eyes never left from the two men.

"Spiro," she answered.

Spiro... The name sounded just as funny as it did last night, when he heard it the first time. Noah took a big breath, the first sign that he was finally fully awake. His only real plans for the day were to meet up with his friend Chris at some point this morning. Anything else was more effort than he wanted to put out.

"Another cup?" His grandmother asked as she eased her body from her chair. Not waiting for Noah to answer, she made her way to him.

"Yes, please." He gave her a small closed-mouth smile as he handed off his cup. With her out of the room, his stare became more direct as he studied Spiro slouched over his uncle, watching whatever Eros was doing. Noah's eyes fell to Spiro's long legs and traced them up to his ass. Spiro's stance, arms folded and his butt arched out—he definitely had a nice ass. He and Spiro looked to be close to the same height, but that was all they shared.

Moments later, Grandma Maya returned with his second cup of coffee and a blueberry muffin folded in a paper napkin. "Here you go."

"Thank you." Taking his coffee, he tried to quell the flutter inside him caused by Spiro.

"I suspect it won't be long before Chris is out on the water. Make sure you put some sunscreen on before you go out there today."

Noah rolled his eyes. He didn't need to be told to put on sunscreen.

Grandma Maya looked up. "Did you hear me?"

"Yes, Ma'am." For effect, Noah curled his lip along with a theatrical eye roll this time.

"Not sure what's so fascinating about sitting in a boat doing nothing for hours. You boys should call Rabbi Moshe. This weekend is Shabbat at the Park. You and Chris are old enough to start helping instead of doing nothing all summer."

Being smart, he asked, "Isn't the point of Shabbat *not to* work?" He hated that festival. The music especially irritated him.

He looked out at the dock for his dad's rowboat that he used to float in. There was no sign of it. "Do you know if Eros has put Dad's rowboat out yet?"

She did exactly what Noah just did and looked out the window toward the dock. "I don't see it. It's still hanging in the boathouse, I assume." She released a groan as she sunk down into her chair.

Noah's eyes moved to the end of the dock, past the boathouse where the rowboat usually sat tied up. His eyes gazed back at Eros and Spiro. It was a little weird sitting beside his grandmother while he was having such lascivious fantasies of Eros's nephew. "I think I'll check the temperature outside." In private, Noah could watch him undisturbed from the porch. With his coffee cup in hand, he exited the house onto the side porch.

When Noah stepped on the porch, Spiro glanced up toward the house. Noah looked away and moved toward the front of the porch, out of sight. His pulse raced because he was outside with Spiro. He knew Spiro had spotted him. *Oh, God! He knows I'm out here to look at him. He knows I was looking at him.*

Noah took a seat in the rocking chair on the side porch, where he tried to quell the nervousness that sent him hiding down in the chair.

Lost in a string of thoughts on whether Spiro had a girlfriend or not, and how lucky she must be, he sipped his coffee. Noah went through a list in his head of things he would say to Spiro when they met— something between *Hi, I'm Noah* and *I want you to be my first*. He failed to hear the approaching steps until it was too late.

Spiro was carrying several boards and walking directly toward him. Their eyes met, and in that split second, Noah's breath caught as his brain short circuited. He sprang to his feet and bolted toward the door. His heart was racing as he tripped over the threshold into the house, quietly shutting the door behind him. The reality of meeting this person fled his brain, replaced with an unsettling queasiness as he returned to the sunroom.

His grandmother was still flipping through her magazine. "You weren't out there long. Too cold?"

"Yeah, something like that." Noah cursed himself. How embarrassing. He couldn't believe he'd done what he did. It was probably the stupidest thing he'd ever done. He'd run from Spiro as if Spiro was about to kill him.

Noah took his seat, his eyes returning to the window to watch the stranger from afar. It wasn't because he was shy that drove him into the house with such speed. He didn't think of himself as shy, but more like clumsy around certain people, like anyone not in his calculus or physics classes. Jocks and cute guys weren't on that list because, well, he didn't even exist in their world.

Noah was more of a thinker, a plotter, which also made him a master at chess. He was undefeated in the school's chess club. Chess was a game of calculation and understanding that not everything always goes according to plan. You have to be ready to adjust and problem solve. He'd miscalculated when he stepped on the porch half-naked, with his hair uncombed. He wasn't ready to meet him; he wasn't prepared to have such an impetuous conversation with someone like Spiro.

By the time Noah finished his coffee, his pounding heart slowed and the tightening of his chest had quelled. The porch scene was a debacle. He must have looked like a total dweeb. There was little he could do to fix this kind of impression; he'd simply move on. Not that he didn't care how people saw him; it was quite the contrary. But this morning, he wasn't okay with someone—no, *Spiro*—thinking he was socially inept. He didn't know what, if anything, he could do to fix it, but this had to be rectified.

"I think I'll catch Eros while he's still working on the dock—see if he can help me get the rowboat down." Noah stood up before he could talk himself out of doing something foolish. He knew that, as long as Eros was out there with them, his nephew wouldn't kick his ass just for being a dweeb.

"Okay..." His grandmother stared up at him. The lack of any suspicious expression assured him she was unsuspecting of his motives.

Upstairs and in the bathroom, Noah combed his hair and removed the coffee from his breath. In his bedroom he got dressed, putting on a red polo shirt instead of his normal tee shirt attire. Noah liked how he looked in red. He wanted this cute guy to see him... to really see him. He laughed at his foolishness, as if a red shirt would make that much of a difference, but one could always dream.

His pulse quickened as he made his way down the grassy knoll between the house and the dock. As he grew closer to them, he saw that the old man and Spiro were in a conversation. Although Noah didn't understand Greek, the tone of Eros's voice was harsh. The aggressiveness in Eros's speech caused Noah's steps to shorten, second guessing if he should interrupt them. A plank creaked under his feet, causing both Eros and Spiro to look up at him. It was too late to turn back.

"Good morning, Mr. Rothenberg." Eros put a hand on his knee to steady himself as he stood. Aloof in the shadows, Spiro held his gaze on him. Noah couldn't look away as Spiro's eyes washed over him from head to toe. *Were they brown or green?* Afraid he'd stared too long, he broke eye contact, his eyes sweeping past the visitor's long dark sideburns that cupped his ears.

"Sorry to disturb you." Noah's voice cracked. He cleared his throat and tried to put on a cool and collected face, not wanting to seem like the dork that he was. "I was hoping you could help this morning with the rowboat." His thumb pointed to the boathouse, but his eyes remained on Spiro. Face-to-face, Eros's nephew was... beautiful. A statue of beauty.

Noah tried to look away but couldn't. Yes, Spiro was a hair taller than he. His square jawline, straight nose, and jade eyes rimmed in gold were mesmerizing. Noah's heart sped as he broke eye contact. Excitement swirled in his gut at the proximity of this Adonis.

"Sure." Eros tossed his hammer into his box of tools. Noah's eyes followed Eros as Eros turned and spoke to his nephew.

Noah's eyes drifted to Spiro's bow-shaped lips before moving up to his eyes. Their eyes met, causing Noah's heart to skip a beat. Noah had no idea what he saw in those cat eyes that were staring intensely back at him and caused his heart to flutter. It wasn't disdain, dominance, or dismissal, the usual looks his peers gave him upon meeting him for the first time. It was... *he's really looking at me.*

Everything about Spiro enthralled him. No longer wishing away the next two months before he could escape to Harvard, he was cautiously excited about the summer.

"Hi, I'm Noah." He felt the heat of a blush on his cheeks as he extended his hand. Spiro looked directly at him; his deep stare instantly pinned Noah. His dark locks of hair, jet black, ran the length of his neck and curled at the nape of his neck. Noah tried to release a breath quietly. Adrenaline pumped through his veins like the multiple streams that fed into Lake Winnipesaukee. He'd never acted this boldly when it came to meeting someone. The way Spiro looked at him gave him the boost of confidence that he could actually stand here and talk to him. This was a first, and it surprised him.

Spiro shook Noah's hand. "Um, my English is not so good. My name is Spiro." A deep voice cast from his full lips. Spiro saying his own name sounded more exotic than when Noah's grandmother said it.

Geeze Louise, his teeth are perfect, too. They're so freaking white. Noah stumbled over his own words as he searched for something to say. Spiro's gaze kept Noah from looking for more than a second before lowering his head.

The boathouse smelled of stale air and dust. Unaffected by the bad air, Eros walked over to the wall that held the rowboat. "Let's see. Are you going to want the motor boat anytime soon as well? I haven't gassed her up and checked her out."

Noah glanced over at his grandfather's 1954 Chris Craft Sea Skiff. Suspended over the water, the boat was as clean as the day it was new. "No, just the rowboat today... please." Noah rarely drove the motorboat, except for a few times to the little floating market. Other than that, the beautiful vintage speedboat stayed in the boathouse, hoisted up out of the water on cables.

Eros mumbled something in Greek to his nephew, and then the two unfastened the aluminum rowboat from the wall. Noah's eyes swept up Spiro's slender frame as he stretched up on his toes to do the bulk of the work. A touch of tanned skin and his narrow waist were revealed as his hoodie lifted with the stretch. Spiro was the most gorgeous person he'd ever seen. Noah swallowed, pushing past the lump that had formed in his throat.

Within minutes, Eros and his nephew had the six-foot aluminum boat down and outside on the dock.

"Would you like us to set it in the water for you?" Eros asked.

Spiro trailed Eros outside. Noah's eyes followed Spiro. "Um... yes, please. I'm heading out." Noah attempted to moisten his throat to keep it from drying.

"Anything else?" Eros asked, ready to return to his duties.

Heat rose in Noah's cheeks as he glanced over at Spiro. "No, thank you." As Noah was about to turn away from them, Spiro shot him a wink followed by a playful grin.

What the hell was that? Noah nearly tripped over his own feet trying to walk and decipher what had happened, what the wink and grin meant. He knew what he wanted it to mean, but life was cruel.

****

For the rest of the morning, Noah and his friend Chris hung out on their boats in the middle of the lake. They were far enough out that they could talk in a normal tone yet not be heard by anyone on shore.

Noah's summer lake buddy only got his full attention once Spiro and Eros had stopped working on the dock and couldn't be seen anywhere on the property. The buzz of a chainsaw said they weren't far.

Their boats tied together, he and Chris laid on their backs in their boats as they did every summer since they were ten; the difference these days was the absence of Nathanael. Chris's parents used to call them the Three Amigos.

Under the warming sun, Noah and Chris caught each other up on the school year and big plans that involved college life. This year, Chris also talked of his new girlfriend, whom he wanted Noah to meet.

Noah didn't understand how this would work since all three were going different directions in the fall. He was going to Harvard in Boston, Chris was heading to the Academy for Jewish Religion in California, and Rose, or whatever her name was, was leaving to study in Jerusalem.

Noah listened, even though all he was thinking about was Spiro. In less than twenty-four hours, he'd been sexually awakened by someone he just met—well, sort of met. Spiro hadn't triggered panic within him like most guys did, but the exact opposite, the overwhelming desire to be around him. He'd never touched a guy the way he desired touching Spiro. Noah's new crush trumped his crush on Finnian. Finn was out, and Spiro was in. Yes, Spiro sat Finn on the bench. The vision of Spiro's hoodie rising, his flat belly exposed, caused Noah's groin to come alive.

To cool his erection, he might have to take a swim, but a swim was more energy than he wished to spend. He would take his chances that Chris wouldn't see it. He squinted, looking up at the sun as her heat pressed against him. *Damn!* He forgot to put sunscreen on.

The two talked and floated for hours until Chris's little sister appeared on the shore. She was shouting Chris's name as she waved for him to come in.

"I gotta go. It's my mom's birthday, and we're going into town for dinner."

"Okay." Noah wondered if he'd dozed off as the reality that Chris was heading to shore sunk in.

After securing his boat to the edge of the dock, Noah surveyed the property, house, and barn. He hadn't noticed the absence of the chainsaw's sound until now. He wondered, where they had gone? He made his way along the dock toward the house. With the sun on Noah's bare shoulders and back, the day was warming up like his grandmother promised.

Approaching the grassy knoll, Noah spotted Spiro on the side of the house. A shirtless Spiro bent down on one knee, working up against the house. The mere sight of Spiro's golden-brown back sent a rush of blood to Noah's groin. He'd been in a constant state of arousal all day, thanks to Spiro.

His steps shortened as he studied Spiro's toned build. His breath hitched when Spiro glanced up at him for a second, and without so much as a smile, he returned to whatever he was doing down on the ground.

Noah's steps dragged. Had Spiro dismissed his presence with that look? It was the same look of indifference that the jocks gave him when he walked into the gym or the dismissive glance his father gave him when he entered the room—as if his presence mattered so little that it wasn't even worth acknowledging. Yet, Noah kept walking toward him. The need to be close sustained Noah's momentum, overriding the force of his insecurities.

Five feet away, Spiro stood up and wiped his hands on his shorts. "Hello." Spiro's deep voice stretched out the two syllables as if they were two separate words. The sparkle in his eyes conveyed Noah hadn't interrupted him.

"Hey." Noah's eyes cut to Spiro's bare nipples and back up to his eyes. *Don't look at his chest. Don't look at his chest. Don't look at his chest!* Noah's eyes fell back down to Spiro's bare chest. Spiro's areola, a reddish brown, were bigger than his. The slightly raised nipple made Noah think of a boner. *Damn it, look away!*

"Spiro, right?" He kicked himself, thinking it sounded as if he'd hadn't remembered the guy's name. He pulled his eyes away from Spiro's left nipple. The heat in Noah's cheeks told him that he was going down in flames. He'd be lucky if this guy didn't kick his ass right here for staring at him the way he was. He fidgeted in place before folding his arms across his chest, hoping that would hold him in place.

Spiro's full lips curved into a mischievous smirk. "Yes," he answered. Spiro's beautiful hazel eyes studied Noah with piercing scrutiny.

Noah took a breath. "Cool name. I wish I had a cool name like that. Does it mean anything?" Heat coursed through his veins at Spiro's proximity. As if hypnotized, Noah was entranced by the sultry green and amber light in Spiro's eyes. *Are they green or brown? I wish I had eyes like that.*

The rise in Noah's body temperature had nothing to do with the outside temperature. Spiro's intense stare unnerved him, the way his eyes bore into Noah as if searching for something. If Spiro's eyes were the light and he was the moth, he would be dead. Noah's only escape was to break eye contact and look down. He squirmed for a half a second, the pull to meet Spiro's gaze too strong. He would fly into the light and risk death. His eyes returned to Spiro's as he unconsciously moistened his lips. Spiro excited him in ways he had only dreamt about.

"It's short for Spyridon... I am named after Saint Spyridon." Spiro raked his fingers through his hair, combing it back over his forehead and out of his eyes.

"Aww, cool." Noah grunted, trusting he understood him through his thick accent. "Noah is Hebrew. I hate it."

"I take it you're not religious?" Spiro's smile lessened.

"Um, we're Jewish. Synagogue on Saturday... back in early Christianity, the name Noah was..." He stopped himself, seeing Spiro's brows furrow as he turned his ear toward him. Spiro wasn't understanding him. "Never mind." Noah said. *Nobody cares where the stupid name "Noah" came from.* He was glad he'd shut up before he started rambling.

"I am visiting my theios." Spiro's smiled wavered for a second. "You have a nice home; I like."

Noah's response was delayed because of his concentration on the golden-brown specks within the green that danced in Spiro's eyes. "Um—yeah, no—I don't live here... It's my grandmother's. I come out for the summers."

"For... how long?" Spiro asked.

"Until August. To escape the city... New York." Noah forced himself to take a breath. He had to collect his thoughts before he tripped over his tongue and said something stupid.

"Where the Statue of Liberty is?" The lines in Spiro's forehead creased. "Is that close?"

"No... yeah... kind of. It's like five hours away." Noah's throat dried, causing his words to trail off. It was becoming impossible for Spiro's dark nipples to stay out of his vision. He had to pick something to focus his attention on, choosing Spiro's lips.

The smell of salty perspiration from Spiro's skin was alluring, heightening all his senses and causing his dick to swell in his swim trunks. There was no water that he could dip down under to hide it.

They stood in silence as the amber in Spiro's eyes continued to dance. Their silent stare communicated more than words could have in that moment; their eyes, saying what their mouths weren't ready to speak. Unsuspecting pheromones delivered a chemical message. Noah had never felt like this with anyone in his entire life. He'd never stood in front of someone who he was crushing on and felt they shared the same feelings toward him. He didn't know what to do about the butterflies in his stomach, the warmth spreading throughout his body, the ignition of passion that Spiro caused. He took a deep breath through his nose, trying to calm his breathing.

A voice from the barn called out, forcing both to turn. Eros was calling Spiro as he waved for him to come up to the barn.

"I go." With a cast of his eyes that said differently, Spiro turned, and as he walked away, he looked over his shoulder for a final glance. With a smirk, Spiro winked again.

Noah smiled, knowing Spiro was being playful. His own smile was visible for the world to see. He trailed behind Spiro, staring at his ass and the muscles in his back. With Spiro's back to him, there seemed to be no end to Noah's fascination. It was impossible to absorb all that his eyes were seeing.

With each step, Noah was lured deeper as Spiro's ass moved beneath his shorts. It was a few minutes of uninterrupted lust that he burned into his memory to savor later.

Spiro reached Eros first, and in Greek, the two talked. Noah didn't need to understand Greek to know that it was an argument. Spiro's arms folded around his chest validated Noah's assessment.

Noah was embarrassed for Spiro. This was something private. Spiro didn't need a witness to this verbal beatdown. Noah continued around to the front of the house and stopped before stepping onto the porch. Eros and Spiro were oblivious to their audience.

That night at supper, Noah sat across the table from his grandmother. He welcomed the silence at the table that allowed him to think. This afternoon, he wanted to look up who Saint Spyridon was on the internet. That was, until reality reminded him that their side of the lake didn't have internet and for whatever reason no one could ever explain why.

Spiro's penetrating gaze this afternoon, on top of the wink, had Noah rattled. It was the same stare, minus the stupid giggle that the girls used to give Nathanael when they talked to him. *Could Spiro really be gay? Even if he was, why would he be interested in me? He winked at me twice!* Noah's cheeks burned with heat as he fantasized about Spiro touching him.

"How old do you think Eros's nephew is?" It was a question he'd been asking himself, yet somehow, it had freed itself from his mouth. He avoided his grandmother's eyes, scared she'd see the yearning in his. His breath caught as he waited for her answer.

"Well, I believe Eros said he was, twenty?" Grandma Maya's voice faded as if she wasn't sure.

He had more questions, many more questions about Spiro that he needed answers to, but he had to be careful not to reveal his intentions. If he pushed his grandmother for information too fast, she could become suspicious.

During the meal, the silence allowed Noah to relish the intimacy between him and Spiro. His next question flew from his mouth. "What do you know about him?"

Grandma Maya showed no reaction to the question. "Eros said that his father raised him."

"Where's his mother?" Noah asked before she could finish.

"His mother?" Her tone supported her displeasure at all the questions. She cleared her throat. "I don't know. Eros has never talked about her. Are you concerned about something?"

Concerned? Is that what she thought, that he was concerned? He laughed under his breath. He wasn't concerned; he was crazy in love! Cupid had shot his arrow, and upon hitting its target, the love potion had already taken effect.

CHAPTER FOUR

During the week, Chris had been fulfilling his usual duties of keeping Noah occupied from late morning until sometime in the midafternoon. The two had spent the last several days catching up on the school year as they floated under the hot sun in their rowboats in the middle of the lake.

But this summer, Noah had an additional distraction keeping him occupied. From his boat, Noah kept a watchful eye out for Spiro on shore. Unbeknownst to his new secret crush, while Chris chatted non-stop, Noah watched every day as Spiro worked about the property. For the last several days, Eros had him cutting up several trees on the property that had fallen over winter.

This morning, Noah had been sitting at the end of the dock fishing for about an hour. It was barely ten o'clock, and it was already eighty degrees with high humidity. He watched as his fishing line occasionally swayed in the water. From where he was sitting, he'd seen Eros and Spiro going in and out of the barn several times.

Twenty minutes ago, he'd waved good-bye to Chris from across the lake. Chris and his family, along with their weekend visitors, had all piled into Chris's dad's giant Suburban. Chris had mentioned yesterday that they were going to Shabbat in the Park and had extended an invite. Noah had graciously rejected, jokingly conveying how much he really wanted to go but couldn't.

With houseguests at Chris's place almost every weekend, Saturdays were Noah's least favorite day of the week. Besides the absence of Chris most Saturdays, there were also too many jet skiers and pontoon boats on the lake to get in any relaxation.

Deep in thought about heading off to school in the fall all by himself, Noah had tuned out the roaring engines of the jet skiers. They were all strangers who ripped about the lake as if they owned it. Zoned out in a world of his own, Noah relished the sun as it penetrated and warmed his shoulders and neck through his tee shirt.

The sound of creaking boards behind Noah jolted him from the scenario playing in his head of meeting a guy while at school. Just as he turned, Spiro was about twenty feet away. The initial sight of Spiro in his shorts and his broad shoulders caused Noah's heartbeat to quicken, sending a flood of adrenaline to his brain. He pushed down the standard *Danger! Danger!* alarm that was normally associated with a bad boy heading straight for him. He released a controlled breath and told himself he could do it: *Just don't be a dumbass.* Of course, he could also jump the three feet down into the water and swim away like a frightened mermaid.

Shirtless already, Spiro was wearing board shorts that stopped just below the knees. The faded Hawaiian print shorts hung low around his waist, exposing lighter skin below the waistband. With a soda bottle in one hand, Spiro was munching on a sandwich.

When he reached Noah, there was a twinkle in Spiro's eyes that matched his smirk. "Want some company?"

Noah's insides did a somersault as his eyes crawled up Spiro's hairy legs. His eyes slowed as they passed over his flat stomach and a tiny patch of dark chest hairs between his chest muscles, until he reached his face.

"Sure." One word, and it got caught in Noah's throat.

The ray of the sun was blinding, causing Noah to squint. "Got nothing to do?" Noah asked. The small bulge that stretched the front of Spiro's shorts sent a rush of blood to his own.

"Got plenty to do, but I needed a break." Spiro took another bite of his sandwich before extending it as proof and taking a seat beside Noah. "So, what's there to do around here?"

"Not much." Noah shrugged. With their feet dangling over the dock, Noah racked his brain for something to say. *Say something, you idiot!* The silence loomed between them for a second. "Mostly, I float on the lake and play chess with my friend Chris, across the way there." Noah nodded toward Chris's cabin.

The sound of the plastic soda bottle popped as Spiro took a drink. Noah's eyes were drawn to Spiro's long, narrow neck as he tilted his soda back for a long drink. The throat muscles bobbed in Spiro's neck as they worked to push the liquid and any residual of the sandwich down. *Even his caramel-colored throat is beautiful.*

"Ahh... that was good." Spiro wiped his mouth with the back of his hand as a small burp escaped. "Chess? Maybe you can teach me someday?" He set the soda bottle on the opposite side of him and placed his hands behind him, using his arms to support his body as he reclined.

Spiro's accent replayed in Noah's head as his eyes moved across Spiro's flat stomach, watching as his ab muscles stretched out and flattened. *Sure, I'd be willing to teach you, but what will you teach me?* When Noah glanced up at Spiro, their eyes met. Spiro's right brow raised as his smoldering eyes said that he may have just read Noah's mind.

Son of a bitch! He can read my thoughts! Ordinarily, Noah might have been embarrassed that he was caught, but he was on sensory overload. All his thoughts were short-circuited.

Spiro stared at him, his eyes conveying mischief, his smile enigmatic. Noah told himself to be careful. *What if he's playing with me? Testing me to find out if I'm gay? Would he kick my ass?* Noah's flesh tingled as he noted the quivering deep in his gut. He was blindsided by lust, which could be hazardous to his well-being.

"How come your parents did not come up?" Spiro's voice broke the silence. "Do you always come alone?"

It was as if cold water had been thrown across Noah's face. Spiro's question knocked him from his fairy tale. "Um... no... usually, it's me and Nathanael for the summer. My parents come for the weekends if they can get away."

Spiro sat up. "Who's Nathanael?"

Noah was taken aback for a second. "My brother." No one had ever asked, *Who's Nathanael?*

"How come he didn't come with you?"

Noah's heart twitched, realizing Spiro didn't know. "Um, well... um, he was killed, four years ago. An accident. He was riding his bike in the city... swerved into traffic and was hit."

"Oh, my God. I'm sorry." He sounded rattled.

"Yeah... it's all right." Noah had to squeeze the words from his throat. It was anything but all right.

"I didn't know."

Long ago, Noah had grown tired of people saying they were sorry. If they knew what had actually happened, would they still say they were sorry to him? Noah exhaled a large breath and turned his focus back onto his fishing rod, seeing the tip was bending. He held off picking up his rod, not wanting to scare off whatever was nibbling on his bait. His thoughts jumped from Nathanael to his pole and back to Spiro. From grief to desire, both seemed to paralyze him equally. Instead, he stared at the water below his feet, focusing on the fishing line that disappeared into the water.

The pole stopped moving long enough to say whatever fish was down there had moved on. Noah swallowed and moistened his throat as his eyes shifted onto Spiro's knees. He sensed the heat of a blush on his cheeks as his eyes traveled up Spiro's hairy thigh, sweeping past his crotch to his face, where Spiro's eyes were yet again waiting for him. *He's the one staring at me. He's staring at me!*

Spiro's face softened; the corner of his mouth lifted into a tiny grin. He moved in close to Noah so their shoulders touched. "There's a lot of boats out on the water today."

The warm breath from Spiro's words caused him to turn toward Spiro. The sheer proximity of Spiro's lips from his teased Noah's lips apart. Spiro's long black lashes draped over eyes that held his stare and pulled him in. The greens, yellows, golds, and brown flickered like currents of electricity, holding Noah hostage. Spiro didn't know that he was driving him mad—or did he? Spiro's beautiful stare was capable of stopping Noah's pounding heart. He tried to switch his attention out about a hundred yards to the jet skier rocketing past them as he answered Spiro's question. "Yeah, it's like this for most of the summer on the weekends."

"Where do all of the people come from?" Spiro asked.

Spiro's closeness caused Noah to feel as if everything he did and said was clumsy. Was he talking too much or not enough? He felt the quiver in his gut as he exhaled a held breath.

"Um, on the weekends, most of them are from either New York or Massachusetts. There's only a few on the lake that live here all summer. Got my grandmother, the Alpersteins across the way, the Wolfes down there, and a couple of families around the cove there." Noah pointed to the far end of the big lake. "Everyone else, they'll come and go. The weekends can get pretty busy."

This conversation, whatever they were talking about, did little to suppress the sexual tension running unbridled throughout his body. His throat swelled as a sexual charge ran down his back and into his groin.

In silence, from the corner of his eye, he caught that the tip of his pole bent sharply, and then the entire fishing rod moved. His eye saw it, but his brain wasn't processing that his fish had taken the bait.

"Looks like you caught something!" Spiro's eyes shifted to Noah's fishing rod.

The energy shifted, and Noah grabbed his rod and began reeling in whatever had snagged his line. Interrupted by a damn fish, his brain switched to doing what he knew how to do, reeling in what was most likely a small bass. It took a minute or two to reel the fish up from the water. He confirmed it was a tiny bass before freeing the fish from his hook and tossing it back into the water.

As the fish hit the water and disappeared, movement up by the house caught Noah's eyes. Eros had exited from the steps of the back porch and was shuffling toward the barn.

Spiro turned his attention back to Noah. "Why do you spend your time fishing if you don't keep them?"

Noah shrugged. He never kept them. In fact, he didn't enjoy eating fish. "It's just to pass time."

"To pass time? You should do things you love. You will never get time back." Spiro's eyes drifted over to the water. "My dad's a *fiser-man*."

"What?" Noah didn't understand the word. Spiro's way of speaking English was to slowly enunciate each syllable. The rhythmic tone of his voice was soft, like music playing in Noah's ear, even if it didn't make sense. To ensure Noah was understanding him, his eyes bounced between Spiro's lips and his eyes.

"Um..." Spiro's face tightened as his lips pressed together. "I don't know how you say it in English." He pointed at Noah's fishing pole. "A... *fiser*-man?"

"Oh! A fisherman!" Noah realized that Spiro dropped the -sh- in his pronunciation.

"The island I come from, my dad has a small *fising* boat. He has two guys that work for him. The money is not so good any more. He has a hard time because the bigger boats, the commercial boats, catch five times what he can catch. They make things hard for us."

Noah's ear picked up on the difficulty Spiro had with the *sh* in words. "Grandma says your dad raised you." The fishing industry didn't interest Noah.

"Yes, and my *theia*."

Unsure if he heard the word correctly, Noah asked. "What's a theia?"

"A theia?" Spiro's brows drew together as the corner of his mouth curved. "Um... she... is... Eros's wife."

"Eros is married?" How did he not know that the man had a wife, a family other than his sister in Boston? Eros seemed like a stranger to him. He should know more about the man that had been in his life every summer since he could remember. Noah equated *theia* with *aunt*. "So is Eros your dad's brother?"

"No, Eros is my father's theios."

"Does *theios* mean *uncle*?" Noah asked.

"Uncle?" Spiro's brows narrowed.

"How are Eros and your dad related?"

Spiro's face lit up, saying he got it. "Eros is my dad's father's brother."

Noah pieced the relationships together, putting everyone in their rightful order. Spiro's English wasn't bad. Other than jacking up a word or two, it was Spiro's thick accent that required Noah to focus and listen.

Noah's next question was perhaps too personal, but he couldn't help himself. "Where's your mom?"

"My mom... she's there."

Confusion pressed Noah's lips together. If his mother was there, that meant his mother and father raised him. "Then..." He was cut off by Spiro.

"I think I go. Eros is looking for me." Spiro stood up and adjusted himself.

Noah rose to his feet. Spiro's pinching at the fabric that covered his crotch hadn't gone unnoticed. "What are you guys doing today?" Noah asked.

"Clearing stuff out of the barn. Your family has a lot of stuff."

Noah hadn't been in the barn in years; he could imagine how much old stuff was in there. The last time he was in there, there was his grandfather's car, old furniture, and a lot of gardening stuff... nothing but junk as far as he remembered.

Noah had an idea. It wasn't so much that he was bored as he wanted more time with Spiro. "Need help? Want some company?" He wasn't ready to let Spiro go as easy as the fish he'd tossed back a few minutes ago.

Spiro's brows twisted. "Sure... if you want."

Inside the barn, Eros was stacking several gallon paint cans into a wheelbarrow. A smell of dust and mold hung in the air, causing Noah's nose to twitch.

"Hello, Mr. Rothenberg. What can I get you?" Eros asked.

"Thought I'd give Spiro a hand today." He couldn't breathe in the old musty barn, but he was willing to tolerate it to be with Spiro.

Eros's eyes narrowed as he looked at Spiro.

Spiro shrugged, as if signaling he had no part in this.

In Greek, Eros and Spiro volleyed words for a minute. Noah got the sense that they were talking about him. Noah listened as if he would hear something that said he was right.

Eros shook his head before grabbing the wooden handles to the wheelbarrow. He glanced over at Noah as he steered the wheelbarrow full of junk out of the barn.

Nervously, Noah waited until Eros was out of ear range. "What was that all about? What'd he say?"

The corner of Spiro's mouth curved up. "He said you're too skinny to do any work." Spiro chuckled. "He's giving you five minutes before you quit, and he'll be back to help."

"No... he didn't!" Noah's mouth fell open. "Did he really say that?"

Spiro's grin widened. "No." He picked up a dirty rag and threw it at Noah, hitting him in the face. "Eat my cum stains!"

Noah tore the rag away from his face in a panic. The rag was crusty. His impulse was to throw it to the ground; however, his fingers wouldn't release it. Instead, his fingers caressed the dirty rag. *Is this really his cum?* He held the rag out, between the tips of his fingers. "Is that's what's on this?" *Are you teasing me again?*

"Hey, a man's gotta do what a man's gotta do. It's not like I can whack off with my theios coming in and out of the living room all night. The man never sleeps." Still grinning, he took a step closer to Noah.

Noah understood about a third of what Spiro had just said. Hesitantly, Noah dropped the rag. The thought of Spiro in the barn masturbating sent a charge of excitement through him. He wanted to know more, like when and how. *Who did he think about when he was doing it?* He tried to mask the naughty smile as a visual formed in his head of Spiro pleasing himself.

"Where'd Eros go?" What Noah was really asking was that, if something was to happen between them, were they safe?

"He said he would be back. He's going to pull the trailer around to the front. He wants us to move all these parts out."

Noah spotted the stacks and piles of old auto and boat parts. It appeared they were really going to just work this morning. "All of this?"

He second guessed his offer to help. The price of being with Spiro was heavier than he predicted.

Side by side, Noah did his best to keep up with Spiro, not revealing his lack of strength or energy. He found that, if he talked, Spiro would almost always stop working. "So, why do you say your father raised you if your mom's there?"

Spiro rolled some sort of large engine part onto its side.

Noah questioned whether he should help him as he waited for Spiro to answer.

"My mom... she's not well. She couldn't raise me." The muscles in Spiro's face strained as he lifted the part and carried it over by the door.

There was more to this story. Noah hesitated, questioning if it was his place to press for more, but he wanted to know everything about him, more than he knew about Eros. "You mean, like, she's sick?" He meant *as in mentally ill?* but didn't want to use those exact words.

"Kind of." Again, Spiro stopped short of answering Noah's question.

Spiro's clipped answers and him turning his back on Noah told Noah that he didn't want to discuss his mother. He wouldn't press him for more. He knew avoidance when he saw it. If there was one certain thing about Nathanael's death, it was that nobody in his family wanted to talk about it. It was as if Nathanael simply wasn't there—not that he never existed, but he simply wasn't around.

Eros's return broke their silence, causing them both to act like they'd been working at this speed the whole time.

Noah, Spiro, and Eros worked all day in the barn. They stacked and moved junk into different locations and piles. They had the stuff heading to the dump in one corner, family heirlooms that had no home in another corner, and useless items he wasn't sure why Eros was keeping in the middle.

By late afternoon, with the sun over the metal roof of the barn, the temperature had risen inside. Between sweat and dirt, Spiro's olive bare skin glistened as the sweat rested on his shoulders and back. The dark curls in his hair had fallen, lengthening his hair to his shoulders. No other words suited Spiro other than *gorgeous*.

Spiro's damp skin, his dirty boardshorts, his big, clunky work boots, his thick, wavy hair: Noah tried to commit it all to memory. *Did he mean to brush against me?* His warm, damp skin brushing against Noah's arm meant something. Everything had a meaning.

Noah was finding it increasingly difficult to hide his semi-erection in his swim trunks all afternoon. *Surely, Spiro must have seen it, but he seemed indifferent to it if he did.* Yes, Noah was a virgin, but he was also a young man with testosterone raging through his body, short circuiting normal everyday cognitive functions, tempting him all afternoon.

With both barn doors wide open, the temperature continued to swell in the large barn. Noah was ready to pass out. He hesitated from removing his shirt so his skin could breathe. They would both be a step closer to being naked. Yes, naked, that was what he wanted, to be naked with the *God of Masculinity*. Everything in him urged him to do it. But to reveal his skinny, pale body would put an end to this silly game he was playing in his head.

Spiro was not one of his male peers at Synagogue, the chess club, or his National Honor Society. Noah's lack of muscle tone wouldn't go unnoticed by the God of Masculinity.

He pinched the front of his swim trunks, moving his erection, realizing that he was fully erect now. Yes, like the baboon with a boner at the New York Zoo, there was nowhere for him to hide his erection. Noah's body temperature swelled as panic set in. He wouldn't subject himself to Spiro laughing at him like the crowd of people laughing and pointing at the poor baboon. The God of Masculinity was equal to a crowd of ten thousand.

He had to preserve at least some of his dignity, escape before it was too late. With his back to Spiro, he headed for the door. If it went down before he got to the door, he would stay.

He reached the door with no such luck. "Hey, I think my grandma's calling me." Noah never turned as he exited the barn. Until now, he'd never lost a chess game. If there was one thing bad boys had taught him, it was how to move out of sticky situations and not be put into checkmate... so to speak.

CHAPTER FIVE

Chris's family entertaining visitors all week had turned into a blessing. With his friend absent, Noah's innocent offer to help Spiro—and, of course, Eros—finish cleaning out the old barn was perceived as boredom.

It was anything but easy work for Noah—not the actual labor, but keeping his hormones in check. Being so close to Spiro and having a steady supply of blood pumped to his groin every ten minutes was labor intensive. Several days ago, Noah had to resort to wearing underwear under his swim trunks for extra precaution. Over the last three days of working together, they had freed half of the barn from years of old clutter.

This morning, Spiro had been full of questions about living in New York. "I would love to see the Statue of Liberty one day. Is it as tall as the Empire State Building?"

Noah laughed. He'd come to quickly hear past Spiro's sweet accent, although the sexiness of the low, gruff tone never left him. "It's big, but not that big."

"Do you live far from it?"

"Not really. I can see her from our apartment."

"You guys live in an apartment?" With Spiro's question came a look of confusion.

The question caught Noah off guard until he realized what Spiro might have been thinking of as an apartment. "Yeah, in Manhattan, the Upper East Side." The fact that the apartment was five thousand square feet and on its own floor in the iconic Sherry-Netherland hotel didn't seem important to the conversation. He grew up in the building that held the title of the tallest apartment building in New York when it initially opened. With its stunning views of Central Park, the Hudson River, and Lady Liberty, it was the only place Noah had ever lived.

"Are you close to where the planes crashed into those buildings?" Spiro asked.

Noah's breath stalled at the thought of that day. That day would always live inside of him; it was a part of every New Yorker. "Yeah... The memorial isn't that far. It's down in Lower Manhattan."

Eros had been missing for about twenty minutes when he returned and interrupted their rambling. "I have to run this load downtown and then stop by the hardware store."

He didn't say how long he'd be gone, but Noah knew it would be at least three hours, as slow as Eros was.

With Eros gone, the two slowed in their task, starting on a second pile of stuff that was trash by their standards. As they combed through a stack of bins, it was Noah's turn to grill Spiro with questions. "Can I ask you something?"

"What?" Spiro opened a bin full of *National Geographics*. He held one up to show Noah.

"Toss... my grandma said something happened with you in school?"

Spiro put the entire bin beside the door. "Oh?"

"It's okay if you don't want to talk about it. It's none of my business, anyway."

"No, it's okay. I was at school, in Athens."

"Like college?" Noah interrupted.

Spiro returned to where Noah was standing. "Yeah, the University of Athens, on the mainland." Spiro hesitated before continuing. "It wasn't for me. I hated it."

"What'd you hate about it?" Noah helped Spiro rip open a box that was taped up.

"I don't know, the classes, the teachers..."

"Was it your first year?" Had Spiro been so unlucky that all his professors were like his PE teacher, Mr. Samuels? It never occurred to Noah that he, too, could get to school and have more than one Mr. Samuels. In PE, he was protected. Half his peers didn't dress for PE, either. Other than a sucky grade, it didn't matter in the course of a day.

"Yeah, I didn't make it a year." Spiro laughed.

"What happened?" Noah pulled the last of the tape free and opened the box. It was full of Christmas decorations he'd never seen before. "Toss." He closed the lid back up.

"Really?" Spiro rubbed his forehead. "How about in the giveaway pile?"

"Whatever..." He didn't care what happened to the stuff. He wanted

41

to know what happened with Spiro in school. How much of a bad boy was he in school?

Spiro put the box to the side. "Do you smoke weed?"

Noah shook his head no.

"Oh, well, it was like a party every night. I met this chick, Stefania, who was into me. We hooked up. Her brothers sold weed, so she always had some. The good stuff. By the second semester, I was flunking most of my classes and was on academic probation. So, I said screw it and stopped going. I hated that place."

A chick... Stefania? Jealousy swelled in Noah's chest. *Was she as beautiful as Spiro, a Greek goddess?* "Um..." Rattled by the mention of a girl, he took a deep swallow. "Did you move back home?" Noah asked, wondering if that was the end of this Stefania.

"Not right away. I tried staying in the dorms until they locked me out. After that, I hung out with Stefania and her brothers at their place for about a month."

The mention of a girl—a girlfriend—Spiro's confession to being straight confused matters. *Could he be bi?* There was nothing Spiro could say that would convince him he'd misread their vibe—the way Spiro looked at him, the way he listened to everything Noah said. This latest news complicated things. He didn't know how a girl fit into this, but he wasn't wrong about Spiro.

"One day we got in a fight, and her brothers threw me out."

"Like a *fight* fight?" Noah held up a fist.

Spiro chuckled. "No... it was an argument. I don't remember what it was about. I ended up crashing at another friend's house for a couple of days." Spiro shook his head as if he was reliving it. "Anyway, I ended up getting arrested a week later."

"For what?" Noah stood up. *Shit! He's been to jail! He's like a bad boy 2.0!*

"It was nothing."

Nothing, my ass. What happened? Noah knew that you didn't get arrested for nothing. Noah was dying to know. "For what?"

"Have you heard of 'bite and bolt'?"

"You mean like when you skip out on your bill without paying?" He knew what dine and dash was here in the States, but wanted to make sure he and Spiro were talking about the same thing.

"Exactly. I got busted, and they called the police. My dad had to come and get me out."

"Oh, shit! I bet he was pissed!" Noah tried to think of anything he did to piss off his dad as much as Spiro's dad must've been. The most he could think of was smarting off.

The two kept eye contact as they talked and strode back and forth, moving junk to different piles.

"My dad, he doesn't talk much. But on the ferry back to the island, he wouldn't even look at me." Spiro said.

"Was he mad that you got arrested or kicked out of school?"

Spiro shrugged. "I don't know."

They continued working and chatting, creating another full truckload of junk and two piles of giveaways. "Do you want to take a break?" Noah asked.

"Yeah, let me finish stacking these frames against the wall." Spiro carried several large frames to the other side of the barn. After putting them down, he tore the plastic tarp off the car they had sidestepped around all day. "Get in!" He motioned toward the black convertible Lincoln Continental. "What year is this?" Spiro eyed the massive black car and its whitewall tires. Other than dusty, the car was in immaculate condition.

"Um," Noah's face twisted. "I think it's like a sixty-one." He was taken aback for a second at the reveal of his grandfather's car and Spiro instructing him to get in. Surely Spiro didn't think this thing would start. Skeptical, Noah slid in the passenger side of the old car as Spiro gripped the oversized skinny steering wheel.

"Where do you want to go?" Spiro asked.

Are you serious? Noah's eyes were fixed on Spiro. With Spiro looking straight ahead, he was oblivious to Noah's stare.

"Where to?" Spiro cocked one arm out the window and steered with the other.

Noah's heart fluttered. They were on a play road trip, together, he and Spiro. "Let's pretend we're on your island. Take me somewhere."

As they drove around the island, Spiro pointed out things along the way and explained many things about living on the small island. The rare deer on the hill, the ruins of the castle at the top of the mountain, the Aegean Sea, and the sea gods beneath the water. It all fascinated Noah.

Being in Spiro's company, the dread of summer that once possessed Noah was replaced with excitement and anticipation. He was enjoying every moment with Spiro. This was the best summer he'd ever had. "How long are you here for?" There was a perkiness that Noah couldn't hide.

"Don't know. I guess until the end of summer." Spiro glanced over at Noah.

The end of summer? Noah tensed hearing that all they had was this summer. "And then?" Noah asked.

Spiro shrugged. "I think I'll go home then." He mocked putting the car into park. "Okay, this is my beach. We're here. I love coming here."

Noah stared through the windshield at the pile of junk beside the door as he envisioned a beach. He could smell the ocean, the salty breeze blowing in his face. The goosebumps on his arms said this was a date. Being on the beach with Spiro, just the two of them, Noah's cock swelled in his double layer of protection for the fiftieth time that day! He rested his hand on the seat between them. He pretended they were holding hands. It took a little imagination, but Spiro's hand rested on his, with their fingers clasped.

Today, he was with Spiro on the beach. But what about when summer was over? Spiro's leaving caused his stomach to churn. *Maybe he would return with Eros to Boston? They would be in the same city. They could still see each other.* Being away at school gave Noah a new sense of freedom. He could do whatever he wanted. He could see Spiro as much as he wanted, when he wanted, without his parents interfering.

"We love this beach," Spiro muttered.

We? Who else does he bring here? Is there someone special who goes with him to the beach? Noah was stricken once again with jealousy. "Who do you come here with?"

"Sometimes Nina."

Noah's heart fell deep into his stomach. *Another girl?* He tried to balance his emotions with this new information. As if they'd been pulled apart, Spiro was no longer his. His hand retracted from the seat to his lap, like a glass wall now separated them. He could still see him and talk to him, but something he couldn't see now divided them.

"Who's Nina?" His voice shook.

"She's my cousin, but she's more like a sister," he answered nonchalantly.

Noah could deal with a cousin that was female, but Stefania remained in his thoughts. Had Stefania been here with him? Did they nestle in each other's arms as they lay on the beach? Had they had sex on the beach? Noah wanted to look away, but the gleam in Spiro's eye and his soft grin begged him not to turn from him.

"Did you and Stefania make up?" His reason for asking was purely selfish. He knew nothing about her, but he hated her.

"We haven't talked in months. When I left Athens, I tried calling her twice, but she never picked up."

Noah was satisfied with that answer. They weren't together, he told himself. He wanted to ask if he'd ever been with a guy. This question had to be answered. The line had been blurred. It was also a question too revealing for Noah to ask. It would expose all his cards, uncover who he was. The risk didn't outweigh the gain. Noah had told no one he was gay.

"Do you like the beach?" Spiro's question said he was clueless to the internal battle happening within Noah.

Perhaps all this was one-sided, that he'd been so caught up in the fantasy of having Spiro that he saw what he wanted to see. "I guess."

"I like to come here after the season ends. See, there's no one here. It's only you and me." Spiro's eyes softened as the left corner of his mouth turned up. It was that tiny smile that belonged to Spiro, that said everything was all right, that he still saw Noah, all of him, and there was nothing to reveal that Spiro didn't already know. Noah's heart pounded in his chest, the source of the blood that filled his groin. His entire upper body was moving with every beat. It was painful, almost unbearable, but the alternative wasn't possible, either. He rested his hand back on the red vinyl seat, hoping to feel Spiro's hand again. There was too much room between them. He thought about shifting his body closer to Spiro, but the skin on the back of his legs was stuck to the vinyl. He cursed his grandfather for having such an enormous car.

With this tension between them, if nothing else happened, Noah would be content to sit here with him, like this, for the rest of his life.

"Spiro! Spiro!"

The booming voice caused both of them to jump. Eros entered the barn and stopped in front of the car. Irritation consumed his face. "Get out of there! Gah! I leave, and you two stop working." The old man waddled to the driver's side door and opened it.

They both fled the car at the same time, but Spiro was trapped between the car and Eros.

Eros stuck his finger in Spiro's face. "Why do you not listen to me? We spend our money on your education, and you waste it... And now, you take vacation on it!" Eros shook his finger. "Why do you not work?" Eros asked.

"We were taking a break," Spiro mumbled.

"Do you not think that I want a break, too? That I'm not tired?" Eros grumbled. He took a breath, switched to Greek, and continued yelling at Spiro for several moments. He wiggled his finger and pointed it at the piles they'd created before turning toward Noah. "Mr. Rothenberg, I forget... your grandmother's looking for you."

Noah was embarrassed, as if he'd been scolded too. Eros telling him that his grandmother was looking for him sounded like a dismissal. Had Eros somehow seen what was in his heart? Did Eros see the adoration he had for his nephew?

Noah didn't make eye contact with Spiro, fearing any contact would expose their secret. He took two steps backwards before turning and dashing toward the house. They'd been caught.

****

For the next three days, Noah got the feeling that Eros was ensuring Spiro stayed busy with chores that required no help from anyone. Other than stolen moments throughout the day, where they exchanged little more than a hello, Spiro remained out of reach. In those moments, sometimes words were not spoken, but a cheerless grin that said *I miss you* bridged them together. The lingering stare in Spiro's hazel eyes, coupled with his playful downturned lips, made Noah's heart flutter every time.

Spiro made him laugh, smile, and go to sleep at night with the anticipation of doing it all again the next day. No guy or girl had shown an interest in Noah beyond a casual friendship like Spiro had. There was more than kindness in Spiro's words; his smile said he liked what he was looking at. His questions carried a note of genuine interest. If he couldn't hang out with Spiro, Noah still knew exactly where he was throughout the day. He waited for the moment, even if it was brief, to have his heart charged again.

Noah rarely stepped into the house until nightfall—and that was only after Eros and Spiro took to the apartment for evening supper. Only then did Noah surrender and join his grandmother inside for the evening. After supper, he retired to his own room to stare from his bedroom window out across the yard at the apartment. Noah's memory of the inside of the tiny one-bedroom apartment was sketchy. He was sure he

46

must have been in the apartment, but he couldn't recall when that could have been.

From bits and pieces of information that Spiro had shared, Noah imagined what Spiro and Eros were doing. In the front room, Spiro was laying out across the couch watching TV. Noah smiled, knowing Spiro liked *Wheel of Fortune*. It was a chance to work on his English.

About an hour ago, Noah had picked up his book and was fully engrossed in the story. As his eyelids begin to droop, he searched for a stopping point in the book.

With what seemed like a long blink, he wondered if he had dozed off for a second. Across the yard, the light was out in the apartment. Maybe he *had* fallen asleep. He released a yawn and turned out his light. Surrounded in darkness, he remembered he'd forgotten to brush his teeth. Begrudgingly, he pulled his body from the bed and headed down to the second floor, where the bathroom was located.

Returning to his room, he'd lost that nice relaxed numbness that said he was about to fall into a deep sleep. He was ready to crawl back into his bed when he saw movement outside. His eyes tracked the source of movement at the bottom of the apartment's steps as the shadow moved across the yard. In the dead of night, when the shadow reached the barn, the sensor on the giant floodlight above the doors detected his movement and lit up. The figure's face was concealed beneath a black hoodie, but Noah knew without a doubt that it was Spiro.

This unexpected sight woke Noah completely. Spiro opened the large door and squeezed inside. It was after ten, and Noah remembered what Spiro had said about masturbating in the barn. *Was he joking? Is that what he's doing right now?* A charge of excitement pulsed through his body with the notion that Spiro was in there pleasing himself. Noah's own body responded.

He wanted to go down there; he wanted to see. It would be torture not to. *Could he, without being seen? Perhaps through one of the knot holes in one of the boards.*

He took a knee in front of the window as he waited to see if Spiro would come out. A wild, fierce urgency to go downstairs was met with fear. He wanted to do more than watch. He wanted to be with him, to do the same, if that was what Spiro wanted. But what if he was wrong about everything? His muscles tensed. Could Spiro hurt him? Every look, every smile, that Spiro had given him said no. The adrenaline coursing through his body urged him to get up, yet he couldn't move a single muscle.

He tried several times to push past the fear that kept him paralyzed. What made him think Spiro wanted him sexually? Maybe this flirtation between them was all in fun. Spiro loved teasing him, and Noah loved Spiro teasing him. He self-analyzed every smile, every look, every word—the tone in which Spiro spoke to him.

The drumming in Noah's chest caused his muscles to tremble. It was as if his chest would burst wide open. But what if Spiro was just being nice? What if Spiro said something to Eros? Eros could tell his dad or grandmother. Noah cringed at the thought of his dad finding out that he was gay. Noah was within earshot of his dad plenty of times referring to *them* as queers; but at this moment, none of that was enough to stop him.

He rose to his feet and stopped. He was second-guessing himself. Noah took a half-step toward his door and then stopped again. He took a breath. His feet wouldn't move.

When Spiro smiled at him, it was anything but a normal, friendly smile. He was positive there was a glimmer in Spiro's eyes when he looked at him. A look of promise, perhaps even an invitation. It was the way Gerard Butler smiled at Hilary Swank in the movie *P.S. I Love You.* Noah's favorite movie propelled him forward.

He took another step toward the door, but a creak in the wooden floor stopped him. His heart pounded. He took a breath and then took another step, placing his foot gently on the floor.

Expecting the door to creak, he eased the bedroom door open, ready to stop if it made a sound. The door opened enough for him to slide through. With one foot, he stepped on the first step gingerly, but that didn't stop the wood from creaking. It was as if the creak was magnified a hundred times louder as it pierced his ears. It would have to be like ripping a bandage off. He had to go for it. On his tiptoes, he picked up his steps, every step sending a creak down the stairwell.

He made it to the second landing and stopped across the hall from his grandma's door. He eyed the bottom of her door. Her room was dark. He pushed forward down the remaining steps to the bottom landing.

It took forever before he made it out the front door onto the porch. He took a cool breath, letting the night air fill his lungs.

Noah's anticipation about what he might see sent a flood of hormones streaming throughout his body. His excitement level was beyond any sexual fantasy or sexual experience he'd ever had. In this moment in time, all his insecurities were gone. He was left with a hungry desire for the guy who'd been openly flirting with him for the last two weeks. This desire propelled him forward, closer to the barn, closer to the one who'd ignited excitement within him.

The floodlight over the barn had already shut off, leaving nothing but the light of the moon to guide him. He knew better than to go near the floodlight sensors. He would go to the side of the barn and find a knot hole to peer through, hoping to see inside. He envisioned Spiro's naked body sitting in a chair as he pleased himself.

His heart raced as he stepped closer to the barn. Light illuminating between the planks drew him closer. He inched up to the barn and peered through a slit in the wood. He couldn't see anything. It was quiet. *What's happening in there?*

Noah stood still in the night, waiting for movement inside, his breathing rapid as he tried to be quiet. His eyes bright with excitement, his senses were on fire. He saw a shadow move inside. Yes, he was still in there. Spiro moved across his vision. *He's coming out!*

"Is somebody out there?" Spiro called through the door.

Before Noah could run, the large barn door slid open, sending a stream of light into the night. Heart pounding, Noah braced himself against the wall of the barn.

Spiro stepped out, causing the floodlight to turn on, providing more than enough light to be seen.

Horrified, Noah stepped away from the barn and into the light. "It's me." Sheepishly, Noah took a step toward Spiro.

"What are you doing out here?" Spiro took a half step away from the barn.

Noah didn't have an answer, at least one he was willing to give. "What are you doing in there?" An icy panic crept up Noah's extremities and into his chest.

The corner of Spiro's mouth drew back into a smirk. "I asked you first."

"Um—I saw the light was on inside... from my window," Noah stuttered.

Spiro placed his hand on Noah's shoulder and, with a light squeeze, led him inside, drawing the door closed behind them. "Were you spying on me?"

Spiro's acuteness to what was happening, despite his playful voice, rattled Noah. "No! I didn't know that it was you in here. I told you. I saw the light on and thought..."

49

"What, you thought your grandma was being robbed, and you came out here to save the day?"

Was Spiro insinuating he couldn't protect anything? He studied Spiro's eyes, the muscles in his face; surely, he wasn't serious. "I didn't think we were being robbed. I... I was hoping it was you." The confession escaped on its own. "What are you doing out here?"

Spiro turned and walked toward the back of the barn. "C'mon." Not waiting for him, Spiro moved to the back of the barn and stopped behind the old car.

Noah followed. As he came around toward the back of the car, he saw an old lamp sitting on a dusty dresser, the source of the light. He recognized the old floral hurricane-style table lamp as the one that once sat in the living room. He wondered how long ago it had been banished to the barn. Beside the lamp and dresser was his grandfather's easel covered with a sheet and several smaller frameless canvas paintings propped around it.

Five paintings on various-sized canvases were propped up against the wall. "What were you doing?" Noah stepped closer to the covered easel and peered down at the paintings at his feet.

"I found all the stuff several weeks ago when I first got here. I thought no one would mind." Spiro stepped between Noah and the easel.

Now Noah could smell the oils from the paints. "Did you paint these?" Noah's eyes dropped to the smallest canvas. He reached down and picked the canvas up. He studied the detail in the tiny sailboats in the harbor. "You painted this?" He couldn't hide that he wasn't convinced.

Spiro stepped closer. "Do you like it?"

He positioned the canvas under the light to see it better. A stronger odor of fresh paint floated past Noah's nose. "I can't believe you painted this."

Spiro took the canvas from him and placed it back down. "Be careful. That one's wet." He delicately took the canvas from Noah and put it on the dresser. He picked up another one that was larger and handed it to Noah. "Look at this one."

Taking the painting, Noah was stunned at the detail of the houses, with the barren mountains behind them.

"That's my village," Spiro murmured.

Speechless, Noah put that one down and picked up another one, a picturesque view of a cobblestoned promenade flanked with cafes and restaurants. The use of light from the sun shining through the climbing pink bougainvillea against the old buildings was incredible. "Where'd you learn to do this?"

Spiro moved into the light. "My theia... I come here almost every night. I hope it is okay that I used them. I found it all in some bins. Eros was going to get rid of it all, and I talked him into letting me keep it. Most of the paints were dried up. No good. A couple were new, had never been opened."

Noah looked at Spiro and then back to the canvases. "You're really good."

"Thanks. Let me show you." He moved in closer so their shoulders were now touching.

Spiro's shoulders touching his caused Noah to quiver from the inside out. They were touching! The realization consumed him for a second until the sensation dwindled enough that he could focus on what Spiro was saying.

"This is the market in one of the villages. It's where my family has been for a hundred years. This is fishy-ma market. My dad and others go out every morning and fish. Come back and sell to the market." Spiro picked up the canvas with the boats in the harbor. "My dad's boat is here." He pointed to a small blue-and-white fishing boat docked in a harbor among many brightly colored boats. Again, the same barren mountains sat in the background of the harbor.

Noah's eyes poured over the cluster of tiny colored fishing boats tied up in the harbor. His eyes narrowed on a tiny black cat carrying a mouse in her mouth. He knew it was a female cat, not because of her pink collar, but her sweet eyes said so.

"It's also where all the old men go to gossip, drink, and get away from their wives. They say they are working."

Mesmerized by what Spiro created, he wanted to see all of them and reached for the sheet that covered what was on the easel.

"No!" Spiro grabbed his hand, stopping him.

"What is it? I want to see." He picked up on the panic in Spiro's voice. The grip on his wrist held his hand inches away from exposing what was under the sheet.

"It's unfinished. It's nothing." Spiro muttered.

"So, I want to see." Before Spiro could stop him, Noah yanked his hand away and pulled at the sheet, dropping the sheet to the floor.

Noah stared at the large canvas. His heart had leapt into his throat. He took a deep swallow, trying to dislodge the lump blocking his breathing. "You did this?" His eyes drawn to the painting, he couldn't move.

Spiro stood silent, looking at Noah.

Noah was staring at himself. It was him, behind his bedroom window from the third floor of the house. The detail in his pale face, the blue in his eyes—there was no doubt that he was staring down at Spiro from his bedroom window. Spiro had seen him.

"I see the way you watch me, the way you look at me." Spiro moved a little closer. The sexual tension radiated from Spiro's body onto Noah's.

Noah's heart felt as if it would beat right out of his chest. He heard Spiro, but the words weren't sinking in.

"Say something," Spiro begged.

"Why did you paint this?" Noah pressed. Spiro's answer to this simple question would be the answer to all of Noah's questions about them. An apprehensive look in Spiro's eyes was one Noah had never seen before. Spiro was always cool and relaxed. Did Spiro's answer even rattle him? "Why?" he murmured again, but this time, more to himself.

"I think you're beautiful," Spiro mumbled.

"You do?" *Women are beautiful; men are handsome.* He liked being beautiful in Spiro's eyes. "You think I'm beautiful? Does that mean you like guys, too?"

"In my village, we have a saying. Boys will be boys until they take a wife, and then we must be a man... I have plenty of time before I take a wife."

Noah didn't understand what that meant, but it didn't sound like a denial.

"Am I wrong, the way you look at me?" Standing behind Noah, Spiro's sweet and tender whisper was inches from his ear.

The heat from Spiro's breath as his words called for an admission pressed against Noah's ear. He hadn't realized Spiro had stepped as close as he was. His breathing hitched until he could no longer hold it, releasing air from his lungs at a rate that caused his head to swirl from the depletion.

His breath stopped again as Spiro's lips brushed the back of his neck. The hairs on the back of Noah's neck rose as Spiro's lips pressed firmly against his neck.

"I'm not wrong, am I?" Spiro pulled back from Noah's neck. His words came deep from the back of his throat as his hands clutched Noah's waist. His grip was firm as they took hold of him.

Noah tried to push out the trapped air into his lungs. His body was so light and limber, the gentle press of Spiro's hands turned him around. Standing face to face, they stared at each other.

"Tell me I was wrong." Spiro released Noah and took a half step back. "Was I?"

Noah was afraid to blink, afraid Spiro might vanish, that none of this was real. Dizzy, he was unsure if his legs would support his body as he grappled for an answer.

"You're not wrong." Noah's voice trembled as he murmured the words that Spiro wanted to hear. Noah tried to keep his smile on the inside. He didn't want it to be that obvious how excited he was that his own internal quarrel of whether Spiro liked him, in the same way that he'd fallen for Spiro, had finally ended.

Spiro took a step, positioning one leg between Noah's legs. His hands taking Noah by his waist again, Noah stared into the center of Spiro's eyes. Gold flakes sparkled like fireworks over the lake.

Spiro said something to him, but his brain wasn't processing anything other than he was about to be kissed. The warmth from Spiro's breath said so. His eyes closed as Spiro's lips touched his. Spiro's dry, warm lips pressed harder.

Noah clumsily tried to kiss him back, their teeth bumping against one another as Spiro's tongue attempted to enter Noah's mouth. Spiro pulled back and wiped the saliva from Noah's lips. There was a glimmer in Spiro's eyes; from beneath the beautiful brown hues, there was admiration. Never taking his eye off Spiro, the endorphins in Noah were going off like fireworks. Explosion after explosion, Noah's body quivered. Spiro's eyes said that he was safe. A warmth washed over Noah as a breath left his lungs.

"Relax," Spiro's voice was barely a whisper.

Noah gently nodded, and then slowly Spiro's lips pressed against his again—a simple light kiss to Noah's bottom lip, followed by a soft kiss to his upper lip. "Relax," Spiro whispered as he kissed Noah's bottom lip again, this time taking his lip between his. Spiro landed several delicate butterfly kisses until their dance fell into place.

Air pushed itself from Noah's lungs; his shoulders and mouth relaxed. Spiro's right hand released its hold on his waist and worked its way around the small of Noah's back. Spiro brought him in closer. Chest to chest, Spiro's mouth pressed harder against his. It was enough pressure for Noah's jaw to release, sending Spiro's tongue deep inside his mouth.

Spiro's kiss was hard and fast as Noah fought to breathe. If not for Spiro pressed against him, his legs may have collapsed under him. He couldn't kiss Spiro and breathe at the same time. He gasped for air, causing Spiro to pull back.

"Are you okay?" Spiro's brows narrowed as he stared at him.

Embarrassed, Noah wiped saliva from his swollen lips. "Um, yeah."

Spiro's head tilted into his, their foreheads resting together. "It's okay." Spiro's voice said he knew. His hand brushed the side of Noah's face to the back of his head. "I wanted to kiss you since the first day I met you." His hand caressed the back of Noah's head. "Are you sure you're okay?"

Noah was surprised he was asking him if he was okay. He was more than okay; he was about to faint from the rush of adrenaline and rogue endorphins. "I liked it. I'm sorry."

"For what?"

"For not knowing how to kiss." Noah's voice wavered.

A hint of laughter escaped Spiro. "You did fine." He landed a butterfly kiss to Noah's bottom lip that reinforced his words.

Noah's cock pulsated, causing him to adjust himself in his pants.

"It's late. You should go back to the house before your grandmother sees you're missing. I don't believe she misses much around here."

Spiro was correct; she missed nothing. They had to be careful. The possibility of his grandmother finding them in the barn at this late hour would be horrible, but it paled in comparison to what had taken place in here this evening. He'd received his validation that everything he'd been feeling for Spiro was equally shared.

Spiro's hand brushed the side of Noah's flushed face. "I'll see you in the morning."

Noah was ready to leave until Spiro's hand touched his face. As a surge of emotions coursed through his body, his feet suddenly refused to move. The risk of them getting caught was inconsequential to what was happening right now. His tongue scrolled across his lips as if tasting Spiro on them. "Okay." His answer was directed at himself, more so than to Spiro.

He made his way back toward the house, the sound of his steps across the gravel never reaching his ear. The squeaks from the floor mattered little to him as he stripped himself of his clothes and crawled into bed.

He kissed me! I kissed him! A lifetime of waiting to be kissed was worth every second of what just happened. Noah rubbed his tongue across his lips. The taste of Spiro was still there. The taste of Spiro coiled down into his body, igniting a fire within him that caused his skin to tingle.

In all the crushes he'd had on guys, no one had stirred his desires and stoked this intense fire the way Spiro did. It was unnerving how much Spiro excited him. He was sure he'd never get to sleep.

Tonight, Spiro had kissed him! Excitement rippled through his body, radiating heat. How could he go to sleep after what just occurred? A smile swept across his face, a smile that would stay, even in his sleep.

CHAPTER SIX

Wrapped in a plain white bath towel, Noah exited his bedroom. He'd been awake for an hour, lying in his bed and thinking about last night. Eight hours ago, the impossible happened. It was more than a kiss: It was an awakening.

Aware of his skin tingling, he couldn't contain his joy, which poured from his skin. It was as if he were a race horse, corralled for years, and for the first time he was set free, allowed to run, with no limitations, in a full gallop. He didn't have to hold anything back. There was no self-doubt, no wishing he had a better body, no comparisons to anyone. He was content with being Noah, and that seemed enough for Spiro.

A grin surfaced, wide enough that he couldn't deny its presence. For the first time, perhaps since Nathanael's death, he was happy to be Noah. There was a tiny ping in Noah's heart that he couldn't share it with his brother.

With a little zest in his step, he headed down to the second floor to the only shower in the old house. The squeak of the stairs as he stepped down held a memory of last night, causing a wayward grin and a rush of adrenaline to the brain.

He turned on the hot water and sat on the edge of the tub, waiting for the water to warm. The back of his neck warmed where Spiro's lips had kissed him. The rush of energy flowed through his veins like champagne bubbling over the top of the bottle.

At the desired water temperature, he pulled up the shower diverter knob, sending warm water to the showerhead above him. He'd been in a constant state of arousal all morning and needed to get in the shower to take care of it.

Since puberty, he'd started masturbating during his shower. It was because Nathanael lay in the twin bed next to him. Now, it was habit, and any sticky residue on his hands and body was easily rinsed down the drain.

His long, lanky legs stepped into the tub, and then he pulled the shower curtain closed. His naked body leaned into the hot water as his hands braced his body against the tiled wall. He closed his eyes and allowed Spiro's kisses to bring him into a state of full arousal. Spiro's kiss deepened, penetrating the back of his throat. Noah ran his tongue across his wet lips and swallowed several times, the water tasting of Spiro. He grabbed the bar of soap and lathered the soap between his hands.

After gathering as much lather as he could muster, he slid his soapy hands over his groin. The simple touch of his hand against his cock said that it was prepared to welcome the attention it had been receiving almost every day since puberty.

His mind drifted to Spiro. With a couple of pulls, his hips thrashed as the spasms that ran through his back, pelvis, and legs shook his whole body. He was going to faint. His legs unable to support him, he rested against the wall, his back pressed against the warm, wet tile. The most powerful orgasm he had in a long time... he fought to regain his breath.

It wasn't long before the water temperature fluctuated with a burst of cooler water. With the most important duties out of the way, Noah finished before he was out of hot water.

Once dressed, he made his way into the sunroom. He took his usual seat in his chair and waited for his grandma. Coffee wasn't what he desired this morning as he savored what had taken place between him and Spiro last night. Spiro had kissed him. As if Spiro had been in the shower with him this morning, the two events blended into one. *We kissed!*

He stared out at the blanket of white fog skimming the water's surface. He was a million miles away in his head, experiencing it all over again, when his grandmother entered the room.

"Did I hear the shower this morning already?" Grandma Maya asked as she walked across the room with their coffee.

"Yes." *She knows!* He never took a shower first thing in the morning unless it was to masturbate. His normal morning bath was the lake. Spiro was right. She missed nothing. She knew. Embarrassed, he avoided eye contact with her as she took her seat beside him in the other chair.

His grandmother sat tall in her chair, sipping her coffee as Noah reminisced about last night. The beginning of another erection told him he had to stop, but his brain refused to think of anything other than Spiro touching him. The emotions stirring within him had him all over the place. As if he was high, he fought to sit still.

"I made a coffeecake this morning for breakfast." Grandma Maya said. "Would you like a piece now or later?"

"Um, later, maybe." His eyes cast out over the lake as a lone fisherman in his canoe emerged from the fog. This vision helped to bring his naughty thoughts under control.

"Eros said you've been helping in the barn."

"Yeah." He took a sip of his coffee.

"Did I hear you come down the steps last night?"

Her question ripped through his chest and pulled out his intestines. "No." It was a kneejerk answer to a question that wasn't really a question. *She knew he had.*

"That's strange. Then we have rats." Grandma Maya pulled her multi-colored afghan across her legs and turned toward the large window. "Eros and Spiro went into Concord this morning. They're picking up paint for the barn."

Why was she telling him this? His paranoia was running wild.

"He's also having new tires put on your grandpa's truck since they'll be in town," she added.

What he took in was that Spiro would be gone for most of the morning. Noah had no idea how long it took to buy new tires but calculated in his head that, with the drive, they would be gone at least several hours. The possibility that his grandmother knew his secret was equally as frightening as the reality he wouldn't see Spiro this morning.

After breakfast, Noah made his way down the long wooden dock. Chris was waving to him from his side of the lake. Within minutes, the two were doing what they'd done for the last eight years, floating in the middle of the lake. The fog had lifted about an hour ago, and they were now basking under the warm sun. But this was not where Noah wanted to be. In his head, Noah was a million miles away. He was with Spiro, wherever he was.

This morning, Chris would have to serve as a distraction until Spiro and Eros returned. Chris had always been a distraction for him one way or another. After Nathanael died, Chris filled in some of the void of Noah missing his brother.

It was somewhere around age sixteen, right after Nathanael died, when Noah realized he was crushing on Chris. Nathanael and Chris had always been the two chiefs, and he'd always been the Indian in their tribe. As much as they attempted to make him an equal, he wanted to be the Indian. It made things less complicated.

Noah wasn't sure why, but this morning he felt like a chief in every way, equal to Chris. He wasn't interested in Chris's exploits or how his new girlfriend was creative with her mouth. Usually, Noah enjoyed listening to Chris's stories, but this morning it was chatter that filled the air. He kept his eyes on the house and shore for Eros and Spiro to return.

Noah's mind replayed the night before. It was the only thing he could think about since waking this morning. He was reliving the moment as if it was happening all over again—*and again and again.* He wanted to be with Spiro. Wherever he was, Noah wanted to be there.

"Have you been to Greece?" Noah hadn't realized he'd cut Chris off in mid-sentence until after he'd done it.

"No, why do you ask?" Chris's expression was unreadable.

"Just wondering. There's this guy here helping Eros. His nephew. He paints these paintings of some island in Greece." The painting he wanted to tell him about was the one of him, with his eyes cast down, looking at Spiro.

"My sister saw him! She thinks he's hot. Is he cool?" Chris reached into a small cooler on his boat and took out a soda.

"Um, um... I guess." Jealousy rose in him. He didn't like that Chris's sister had her eyes on Spiro. "She's not his type." He couldn't stop himself. In Noah's mind, he and Spiro were already together. Their kiss, the verbal admission last night, said so.

Chris stared at him, his face contorted, his brows furrowed. "How do you know that? Are you two sucking each other off or something?" Chris let out a cackling laugh.

"What? Don't be a jerk!" Noah snapped back. Chris's comment and laugh sent Noah's thoughts scrambling as bile rose up his throat. This year, there seemed to be a lot about Chris that he didn't like anymore.

Although it went unspoken, for the last couple of years, Noah believed he and Chris were closer than friends. What they were, he couldn't define, though. Chris had never looked at him the way Spiro did.

It was two summers ago, when Chris was rubbing suntan lotion on Noah's back for him that Chris's hand slipped down under Noah's swim trunks. Noah assumed it was an accident until it happened again, several days later. This time, the tips of Chris's fingers stroked the top of Noah's ass. This scenario played out several times over that summer. Each time, his strokes went longer and deeper down into the back of Noah's trunks.

Last summer, their little escapades not only resumed but also went further. The two were laying out, soaking up the sun, back in a secluded cove. Chris's lotioned fingers barely touched Noah's back before slipping under his trunks. His oiled fingers glided across both of Noah's butt cheeks and pressed down between them.

Late into the summer, on the sandy beach cove, Chris once again took their sexual play to the next level. Until that day, his fingers had only lightly explored Noah's rectum. Surprised but willing, that afternoon, Noah allowed Chris to pull Noah's trunks down over his ass cheeks. Under the hot rays of the sun, Noah found himself lying still as Chris finger fucked him. It was enough to bring Noah to a full erection and close to orgasm. He was sure Chris was just as aroused each time it happened throughout the rest of the summer.

But this year, Chris made no attempt to lotion his back. Instead, he talked non-stop about his girlfriend. Yet, with the mere mention of Spiro, Chris sounded jealous.

Noah glanced at the shore for the millionth time. He was done listening to Chris, done with floating in the lake, done with The Life of Chris. He'd never punched anybody in the face, but at this moment he wanted to punch Chris right in the mouth to shut him up.

****

It was well after supper, and Noah had been pacing the well-worn wooden floor in his bedroom for the last hour. *How long does it take to buy paint and have new tires put on?*

This morning, listening to Chris go on and on about nothing, Noah realized that it was he who had grown tired of Chris this year, not the other way around. They shared nothing in common other than Nathanael. The simple presence of Chris Alperstein no longer held his attention the way he had in years past. Noah's heart had weighed in on the relationship; he wanted more than the simple pleasures of someone's fingertips. He wanted Spiro.

It was almost midnight when the dim yellow lights from his grandpa's old truck lit up his window. He leaped from bed to the window. Below, he could only see a little more than Eros's and Spiro's shadows as they exited each side of the truck and headed up the steps to their apartment over the garage. He waited to see if Spiro would reappear and head for the barn. He stood waiting. When the lights went out in the apartment, he watched for another hour before giving up.

CHAPTER SEVEN

The warmth of the golden morning sun woke Noah from a hard sleep. His bedside clock showed it was almost nine. He was surprised he'd slept as long as he had. He sprung from his bed to the window, looking for Spiro. He spotted Spiro across the yard, up about twelve feet on a ladder leaning against the barn.

He washed his face and threw on the same pair of blue-and-lime-striped boardshorts from yesterday. He pulled a fresh folded tee shirt from his drawer and headed downstairs as he pulled it over his head. He took long strides across the yard as he stared at the back side of Spiro on the ladder. Shirtless, his golden-brown shoulders and back glistened. High in the air, Spiro's ass wiggled in his fitted jeans as he struggled to free a plank from the side of the barn.

Spiro turned toward him as he reached the base of the ladder. "Hey! Good morning!" There was a tenderness in Spiro's eyes that matched his voice. He turned back to the barn and pulled the plank free. With the plank in hand, he descended the ladder.

"Whatcha' doing?" Noah's eyes fell to the thin streak of sweaty black hair tapering down Spiro's flat abdomen, trailing into the waistband of his jeans.

"Eros wants a bunch of these rotten boards replaced before we paint this week." He tossed the plank onto a pile of rotten wood. "How're you doing?" There was a gleam in his eye.

"Good... you?" *Are we not going to talk about the kiss?* Noah fidgeted his weight from one leg to the other.

"I missed you yesterday." The light browns in Spiro's chestnut eyes were dazzling with intensity.

"You did?" He had to nudge himself to focus on what Spiro just said and less into his eyes. "Missed you, too."

"Really?" Spiro pulled his cigarettes from his front pocket and lit one. He took his first drag from the lit cigarette and blew out a large cloud of white smoke from the edge of his mouth.

Noah waved the smoke from his air space as he shifted his weight again. "You know, those things will kill you."

"Yeah, so they say."

A nervous energy flowed through Noah's body, a tingle from his toes to his fingers as he searched for something to say next. "Um, I... um, waited for you yesterday... Grandma said you guys went into town."

"Yeah. Eros wanted to drive into Manchester for the new tires. He said the guys at the shop in Concord were trying to take advantage of him and steal his money."

"That's like another hour away." Noah shook his head. "That's stupid! It's not like my grandma can't afford it!"

Spiro shrugged as he took another puff of his cigarette. "You were cute the other night." His mouth formed into a playful grin.

"What do you mean?" *So, they were going to talk about the other night.*

"You gagging. It was cute."

"Oh, that, sorry about that." He wasn't going for cute. It was embarrassing. "You can kiss me again if you want." Noah's surprised himself with his directness. He couldn't believe the words came from his mouth. He was about to step in closer when Spiro's eyes raised toward the house.

Noah's eyes followed Spiro's. Still in her pastel pink housecoat, his grandma was on the front porch, watering her hanging plants. Her presence caused him to take a step back. He looked back at Spiro and then did another doubletake at his grandmother, now staring at them.

"I think my grandma knows."

"Why do you say that?"

"Just a feeling. She knows everything. What if she tells my dad?"

"Tells your dad what? We're standing here talking."

"I know, but we kissed the other night."

"She wasn't there. At least, I don't think she was. How would she know that?"

"I don't know. This morning, she—"

"—I think you're worrying about nothing. You act like you've never been kissed," Spiro teased.

Noah sniffled. "I haven't." The words barely freed themselves from Noah's tongue.

"Really?" Spiro's eyes widened. "But you're gay, right?" he asked. Bewilderment swept across his face.

Noah read the look on Spiro's face. "Yeah, I'm gay, *I think...* But how do you really know?" Not being gay would make things so much easier.

"What do you mean, how do you know? You just know." Spiro's eyes narrowed as his head cocked to one side, as if he wasn't sure what Noah was saying.

"If I've never been with a girl, how do I know which one I'll like better?"

Spiro looked as if he was trying to hold back a smile. "It's not about which one you'll like better. When you jack off, what do you see, a boy or a girl? Close your eyes."

Noah closed his eyes, yet he could still see Spiro; his face, inches from his. The breath from Spiro warmed his cheeks. "I see you," he mumbled. His nostrils detected the rich earthy smell of decomposing leaves and pine needles, causing him to sniffle.

"Does it excite you even more seeing me?" Spiro murmured.

Noah's cheeks burned. He wanted to open his eyes, to really see Spiro, not just a vision. He squeezed his eyes tighter, fighting the will to see. His heart drummed harder; his throat was dry. "Yes."

Noah flinched thinking he felt Spiro touching him. Afraid that his grandma was seeing this, his eyes fluttered as if they wanted to open. Wherever they were, it was just the two of them in a dark space, all alone. She wasn't there. A charge ran up his spine, causing his eyes to burst open. Spiro's face was close to his. He wasn't imagining his breath. It was Spiro's actual breath that he'd felt. He wanted Spiro to kiss him. Their eyes locked onto each other. Before last night, he'd never been this close to another person, a boy.

Spiro cleared his throat. "Did you like me kissing you the other night?"

The words were caught in Noah's throat, so he nodded instead.

"Did you dream of me?"

"Yes." He'd done more than dream of Spiro. "Then, with a boy, how do I know what I'll like?" He very much enjoyed the feeling of Chris's fingers in his ass, but that had been the extent of his sexual experiences with another person.

"You mean like being a top or bottom?"

The question caused Noah a little discomfort. "Yeah."

Spiro laughed. "Okay. Close your eyes again." He waited for Noah to close his eyes. "When you dream about having sex, are you fucking someone or..." He glanced over at Noah's grandmother and then back at Noah. "Or are you getting fucked?"

Noah's discomfort went to mortification. "I don't know?" The sensation of Chris's fingers in his ass, feeling his own fingers probing himself while he masturbated, caused Noah's body to tense. He liked it, but was too embarrassed to say it.

"Really? You don't know?" Spiro slipped him a curious glance.

Noah opened his eyes. "What about you, what do you like? I mean, fucking or getting fucked?" Noah murmured.

"I like fucking."

The words from Spiro's lips caused Noah to quiver. He would let Spiro fuck him.

Spiro again looked over toward the house. "I have to finish this." He took a step back. "Meet me later?" He whispered as if the old lady could hear them a hundred yards away.

Noah nodded. "When?" His eyes cast down at the tiny hairs that circled Spiro's right nipple.

"For lunch," Spiro whispered. "In the boathouse."

Noah glanced over his shoulder at his grandmother. She was no longer watering her plants. From the porch, she stood tall as she watched them. "I don't know if I can wait that long," he whispered. *Noon is a lifetime away.*

****

Noah asked Ms. Jimenez if he could have his lunch wrapped up and for two sandwiches today, one for him and one for Chris. Ms. Jimenez agreed, as this wasn't the first time he'd taken extra food for Chris.

At noon, Noah ran through the kitchen, snatching his lunch from the edge of the counter. He laughed at the notion that she had put it in an actual wicker picnic basket. Before heading out the back door, he grabbed the cheap chess set from the game closet. When he entered the boathouse, Spiro stood with his arms crossed. Seeing Noah, his eyes widened.

"Hey, there." Spiro's eyes dropped to the picnic basket.

"Hi." He felt stupid with the basket. "Ms. Jimenez did this. I didn't tell her to." Self-conscious, he knew he must have looked lame. "Where's your uncle?"

"He went into Concord to exchange the paint. They mixed it wrong. Too light."

"Oh, that's perfect! I brought out my chess set. Since Eros will be gone for a while, I can teach you how to play." He was relieved that they didn't have to rush through their lunch this afternoon and he could finally teach Spiro his favorite game.

"Okay. That'll be fun." Spiro rested a hand on the varnished antique Chris Craft still suspended above the water by a lift. "You guys have a beautiful boat."

Once Noah drew close enough, Spiro took the basket from him and placed it on the ground. He then took Noah by his wrist and brought him in close. Their eyes met before Spiro kissed him.

The first kiss was tender, before Spiro kissed him again. Initially awkward again, the third kiss was stronger, and Noah picked up on the cadence of Spiro's lips much quicker. Their bodies merged closer as Spiro drew him into his chest.

When Noah could no longer breathe, he pulled away before he embarrassed himself by gagging again. He swallowed what he envisioned was a mixture of his and Spiro's saliva before wiping his lips. "It's hot in here. Maybe I should open the garage doors to get the air circulating." He glanced at the large glass garage doors at the end of the building.

Spiro pulled him back. With a harder and more aggressive clash, his tongue made it into Noah's mouth. Noah fought to keep the rhythm of Spiro's commanding kiss. Breathing through his nose, he did a better job at controlling his breath this time. The weight of Spiro's hand at the back of his head prevented him from going anywhere. Their kiss grew hungrier as Spiro slid his hand underneath Noah's tee shirt.

His hand skimmed across Noah's stomach and then dropped into his swim trunks and cupped Noah's aching erection. Spiro's hand around his dick caused him to release a moan as he pushed his pelvis forward.

Their lips separated. "Did you like that?" Spiro asked as he withdrew his hand from Noah's shorts.

"No." Smiling, he used the back of his hand and slowly wiped his mouth. His breathing rapid, he stared into Spiro's eyes. "I guess that means I'm not gay."

Spiro laughed as he grabbed at Noah's cock through his shorts. "My ass, you're not!"

A warm sensation coiled up through Noah's back. This was the first time he'd ever been called "gay" in an affectionate way. It sounded funny, yet endearing. It took a second for him to find his voice. "I brought us lunch."

Spiro snickered as he took a step back. "I brought a baloney sandwich. I bet whatever you brought is better than that."

On the edge of the narrow wood decking that surrounded the two boat slips in the boathouse, they sat with the basket between them as Noah issued the chicken salad sandwiches that Ms. Jimenez had made. "After summer, are you still thinking you'll have to go back to Greece?"

"I guess. They don't tell me anything." Spiro answered. "What about you? When do you go back to New York?"

"We—I normally stay until the end of summer, but I'm going to Harvard in the fall. Initially, I wanted to move into my dorm as soon as I could." The urgency to escape another boring summer seemed ill-judged now. He wanted to stay right here forever.

"Where's Harvard?" Spiro sounded as if he was asking for no particular reason.

"The main campus is in Cambridge, and the medical campus is in Boston."

"Boston?" Spiro repeated. He was silent for a second or two as he separated the bread and examined Ms. Jimenez's concoction before taking his first bite. "When are your parents coming?"

"Who knows? Maybe next week. They were supposed to come up with me on my birthday."

"When's your birthday?"

"It was June tenth... When's yours?" It seemed like the appropriate question to ask, though not the most important.

"February twentieth."

"Why'd you paint me?" Flattered beyond belief, he was sure he knew the answer, but wanted Spiro to say it.

"How could I not? You're beautiful." His head tilted to the side as he stared into Noah's eyes.

Flattery, it was the quickest way to his heart. This was the second time Spiro said he was beautiful. Noah had never been called "beautiful," not even "nice looking" or "cute." He himself didn't believe it. How could Spiro see beauty in his skinny body, flat chest, and pale skin? It was nice to hear, even if it wasn't true.

Not wanting the intimate moment to pass, Noah kissed Spiro. The kiss was only a peck, one that two six graders may have shared on the playground, but with all the confidence in the world, it was impulsive and fun and caused fireworks to ignite within him.

In that moment, Noah had decided he would no longer wait for someone else's fingers to caress his body, to make him feel desired, to bring him such pleasure. He wanted to kiss Spiro again, so he did.

Noah savored what had happened. It was the bravest thing he'd done. His tongue moved over his lips, tasting salt delivered from Spiro's lips. A transfer of something Noah refused to take for granted as he swallowed, feeling a part of Spiro slip down his throat and into the cavity of his chest, warming his entire body. It was now a part of him, forever in him.

Flecks of gold flickered amongst the jade in Spiro's eyes, affixed on Noah, like Spiro was studying him.

"What?" Noah murmured.

Spiro was silent for a second. "Sometimes... sometimes when I look at you, you seem sad. I can see it in your eyes, like it lays somewhere behind your eyes, somewhere deep."

Noah took a big breath. He held it for a second before his cheeks puffed and he blew out the air at once. He thought of the many reasons life sucked. The biggest was that his brother was no longer on this earth with him. "I don't know..." It was easier to brush off Spiro's question.

Spiro stared directly into Noah's eyes. "Eros said you and Nathanael were twins."

"Mmm-hmm." Noah broke the intense eye contact. He hated the usage of past tense. He was still a twin, even if Nathanael wasn't here.

Spiro took a bite of his sandwich. He spoke as he chewed. "I think it would be cool to have a twin."

Noah felt the pull in his chest. He couldn't believe what he was about to say, but he couldn't stop himself. "The day Nathanael was killed, he was actually on his way to the park." Noah paused. "Earlier that day..." He paused again. It felt as if he needed to back the story up a bit. "There was this kid named Kevin who'd been harassing me for a couple of weeks. Earlier that day, I was in the park flying one of Nathanael's kites. Kevin was in the park, too, and came up and pushed me. I accidentally let go of the kite, and it took off. I was about to chase it, and Kevin pushed me into this small lake that's in the park. I landed in the water face first. When I got home, Nathanael saw that I was wet and muddy and asked where his kite was. I told him what had happened between me and Kevin. Nathanael was pissed. He said he was going to kick Kevin's ass and tore out of the apartment... That was the last time I saw Nathanael alive."

Spiro nodded. He remained silent as he picked up his sandwich and took a bite.

Noah took this as a clue that they were done. He followed Spiro's lead and resumed his lunch, but he knew he wasn't done. Spiro had the ability to pull things from him that he shared with no one. He didn't understand why or how, but being an open book with Spiro was freeing, something he wasn't sure he'd ever felt, certainly not since Nathanael was killed.

It was several minutes before Noah spoke again. "Do you want to hear something crazy?" Noah asked in a low, husky whisper. He eyed Spiro with one eye, measuring the risk of sharing something so asinine, something that made him sound a little crazy.

"Sure." Spiro rested on his elbows.

Noah stared down, avoiding eye contact. "About a year after Nathanael died... I thought about trying to change places with him."

"How could you do that?" Sorrow had seized Spiro's face. His brows were wrinkled; his eyes gleaming nothing but compassion.

It was safe to continue. "It was close to our first birthday after Nathanael was gone. My father wasn't looking at me anymore. Even when he was looking, it wasn't at me but past me. If it was me that was dead and Nathanael was still alive, if I were Nathanael standing there in front of him, he would see me. If I died, it wouldn't have been as big of a deal as it being Nathanael."

"Why would you say that?" Spiro sat up. His eyes appeared to be searching for understanding.

"Really. My whole life, before Nathanael dying, I had this feeling I was second to him. Even with him gone, I am still second. Maybe third now, after Nathanael, and then the dead Nathanael." Noah snickered. "Other than family, most people couldn't tell us apart. Some people used to say we sounded the same. It was funny, because if you knew us, Nathanael had a higher voice than me when he was pissed. After he died, I thought, I'll be him. I'll let Noah die. It would be Noah that would go away."

"That doesn't make sense. Everybody knew Nathanael was gone, so how could you be him?"

"Haven't you ever put on a Halloween costume and pretended to be something else? How it takes a life of its own?" He'd never told anyone this, not even his therapist. He knew how psychotic it sounded. "I did it a couple of times with people who didn't know us. I would introduce myself as Nathanael to them. We did it all the time to people before he died. There was this awareness in me that happened, that Nathanael was alive again, like, inside of me."

The expression on Spiro's face transformed from sorrow to bewilderment. "Did you do it around your parents or grandma?"

Noah laughed, "Gosh, no. Standing side by side, if you didn't know us, we looked identical. But if you knew us, it was easy to tell us apart. My face was narrower than his, and he had a birthmark behind his right ear. Also, our cowlicks swirled in opposite directions." Noah touched his hair atop his forehead as he stared at Spiro. He hoped Spiro wasn't thinking he was crazy.

Spiro rubbed Noah's cowlick. "I like your cowlick swirling this way." He pressed his lips against Noah's forehead, delivering a soft butterfly kiss. When Spiro was done, he pulled back and smiled again at Noah. His stare conveyed that Noah was anything but crazy, filled with warmth, desire, and empathy. The mood had gotten somber, too somber for Noah's liking. To escape being pulled back into a dark abyss, Noah drew a breath to reset and then reached down into the basket and retrieved two sodas, handing one to Spiro.

"Thanks." The sound of carbonation fizzled as Spiro popped his soda open. "So, really, you've never had a girlfriend?" He asked before taking a drink.

Noah almost choked on the absurdity of the question. "No!" *Did Spiro think that was possible, or was he being goofy?* Noah had always assumed he wore his sexuality on his sleeve. He'd been called a "fag" and "queer" enough to draw such a conclusion about himself. He didn't think of himself as feminine, but he also wasn't the most masculine in the locker room, either. He'd made no attempts to hide who he was as far as his sexuality was concerned. It was a moot point since he wasn't sexually active.

Noah never had a problem taking teasing from his peers, but the message he was receiving from his father was a different story. He was around age eleven when he heard his father refer to a colleague as "queer." There was little doubt in the tone that "queer" was derogatory. It was repeated remarks like this from his father that told Noah that being queer was something best kept to himself.

"So, how come you've never had a girlfriend or... boyfriend?" A tiny smirk appeared at the corner of Spiro's mouth.

Noah's laugh covered up the awkwardness of the question, which reminded him of his clumsiness around those who threatened his comfort zone. It was a question that would expose him to Spiro.

"Why do you laugh?" Spiro's subtle smile and soft gaze said he wasn't getting it.

Noah's skin tingled. He was being forced to talk about something he'd only ever admitted to himself. He drew a breath and broke eye contact, focusing on the tiny blond hairs on his legs. "I don't know. I'm not really out at school. Plus, I'm kind of busy with other stuff."

"Like what?"

"The Chess Club, the National Honor Society... I belong to several clubs at school. That takes up most of my time." Noah could have named more, but naming all of them sounded kind of lame. Being intellectually challenged excited him; being able to outthink and outplay someone in a game of chess was exhilarating. Confessing to what he knew all along, but never had to admit, being this vulnerable with someone, it all was emotionally draining.

"Oh..." Spiro nodded.

Spiro's simplistic response drove Noah to look at him. His eyes wandered over Spiro's perfectly shaped rose lips, the bridge of his nose, until their eyes met. His heart did a somersault the way the sultry brown and green in Spiro's eyes stared back. *Who was this guy?* The question, coupled with the intensity of Spiro's stare, kept Noah from being able to turn away as he searched for the answers.

Pin-drop silence was suddenly invaded by the roar of a motorboat passing outside. The intrusion of noise, followed by the ripple of the waves as they reached the boathouse and splashed against its pillars, shook Noah out of his head. "Are you ready to learn how to play chess?"

Noah didn't wait for Spiro to respond as he retrieved the small chess set he'd brought with him. He explained the game as he set the pieces up on the board. One of the things Noah loved about the game was it revealed so much about his opponent to him.

Just as he suspected, Spiro was an aggressive player. Unskilled in the game, he moved his pieces fearlessly, attacking Noah. Thinking in the moment, his moves revealed to Noah that he had no long-term strategy. This was likely how he lived life as well.

Noah, too, played like he lived. Methodical and quiet, he was always focused on anticipating what his opponent was thinking and what they likely would do. This deep concentration left no room to dwell on life. He had to concentrate, or he would lose the game.

After losing three times, Spiro had enough. "I hate this game!"

"It's because you play without consequences. You're only thinking about *your* move. You need to be thinking about what I'm going to do. You need to outthink me. A poor plan beats no plan. You can at least improve a poor plan."

"Yeah, whatever! We should take the boat out sometime."

"That would be fun." Noah smirked at Spiro changing the subject. It told him that Spiro didn't like to lose.

Spiro climbed to his feet. "Have you swum in here?"

"No." Noah remained seated as his eyes took in Spiro's body.

"I bet the water feels like a hot spring." Spiro stared down at the water as he toe-kicked off his shoes. "We have some hot springs on the island—where lovers go." His smile suggested he was calling them lovers.

"What are you doing?" Noah asked. The temperature in the boathouse swelled as Spiro pulled his tee shirt over his head and off.

"C'mon. Let's get in. It's freakin' hot in here!" Spiro tore off his socks and stuffed them into his shoes.

Noah's breath quickened, seeing Spiro undoing his belt. *Why would you swim inside a boathouse when you had an entire lake to swim in?* Spiro hobbled out of his jeans one leg at a time, revealing his lack of underwear.

In almost the blink of an eye, Spiro was naked. Noah had seen him in shorts and even shirtless, but seeing Spiro completely naked caused his heart to skitter. His broad shoulders tapered down into a noticeable V-shaped waist. Noah's eyes slowed as they scrolled over Spiro's uncircumcised cock. Was this happening? Noah watched as Spiro cannonballed down into the small body of water under the boat, sending water everywhere.

Energy surged through Noah's body at the spontaneity. With no further hesitation, he jumped to his feet and ripped off his clothes. This was the craziest thing he'd ever done. The overload of adrenaline threatened to rob him of his breath as he dove into the water.

The warm bath water did little to slow Noah's growing erection. He paddled over to Spiro and into Spiro's arms in less than two strokes. Spiro took him up into his chest and kissed him before dunking him underwater.

Noah popped up and grabbed Spiro, sending him below the surface. Like sharks, they thrashed about in the water, wrestling and dunking one another as they tangled their bodies. Spiro's leg slipped between Noah's legs. It was as if two hot iron rods had come together, searing his entire abdomen, bringing the wrestling to a halt.

Spiro pressed his body against Noah's as they kissed. Noah's breath was ragged as he paddled his feet, attempting to keep afloat. Within a minute, Noah lost the ability to do both as his body slipped beneath the water.

Spiro pushed away, and Noah regained his head above water. Gasping, he spit out a mouthful of water and cleared the water from his eyes.

Water glistened off Spiro's olive complexion as he slicked back his wet hair from his face and tucked it behind his ears. The green in Spiro's eyes glowed as he grinned at Noah before taking a single stroke to get to the platform. Spiro lifted his naked body from the water, back onto the platform.

Out of breath and naked, they lay on the platform beside each other inside the boathouse. Isolated from the world, there was something freeing about being naked in his grandfather's boathouse. He closed his eyes as he took in the pounding of his heart.

"I have to go," Spiro muttered. Spiro's voice woke Noah from a slumber. He opened one eye as Spiro's naked body stood over him. Spiro added, "I don't want Eros coming down here looking for me." Spiro grabbed his jeans and pulled them on, followed by his tee shirt. He stared down at Noah's naked body, sprawled on the wooden deck. "Lucky for me, you're gay. I like you."

Spiro's words rang loud in Noah's ears. *He just said he liked me!* Noah's heart skittered at the clarity of the situation. There was no guessing, wishing, or fantasizing. Spiro just said that he knew he was gay and that he liked him!

"Come on. Get up before my theios or someone else comes in." With his hand, Spiro waved for him to sit up.

In the blink of an eye, it felt as if something was being taken away. That tiny taste of spontaneity and freedom was masked with secrecy and judgement. As if being asked to turn off his emotions by getting dressed, he was left with a sense of emptiness. A chill caused Noah's body to shiver as he rose to his feet and located his shorts.

CHAPTER EIGHT

It had been a week since they shared their first kiss, a week of stolen moments during the middle of the day. Some days, intimacy was little more than a passing wink of the eye, a chance meeting with Noah in the yard. It was an understanding, an acknowledgment they shared a secret from the rest of the world. Spiro's attraction for the nervous, pale American beanstalk surprised him. They were opposites, day and night, yet there was something mysterious that lay behind those ghostly eyes of his.

Initially, Noah's wealth intimidated him just a little. There was a sophistication about Noah, the way he talked, his mannerisms, his clothes. Noah's nails were perfectly manicured; his hands, free of any sort of blemish or callous, said he'd never done anything with them. Although Spiro never had expensive clothing, Noah's simple tee shirts and boardshorts had a quality look to them. Yet, Noah never acted superior to him. It was almost the opposite, as if Spiro held all the cards.

Initially, Spiro thought Noah may have been shy, a little nerdy, but there was something about the nerd that excited Spiro. He was realizing that Noah wasn't as timid as those around him assumed he was. The world hadn't seen who the real Noah was. Noah was anything but shy. If given the freedom, there was a mischievous, naughty side that was sexy. He liked Noah, the Noah that wasn't afraid to go outside the box that the world saw him in. He liked him a lot.

Ready to take a break from his morning chores, he had the place all to himself this morning. An hour ago, Eros had taken the old lady and Noah over to the town of Laconia so they could attend services this morning at the synagogue.

Spiro moseyed onto the dock, down past the small boathouse to the end of the dock. He took a seat, dangled his feet over the edge, and lit a cigarette. New Hampshire wasn't like anything he envisioned the United

States to be. The dense forest of pines, white birch, mountain ash trees, and heavy brush was a little claustrophobic initially, but now it was growing on him. He wasn't missing home as much as he was a week ago. Truth be told, this morning, all he could think about was when Noah would return.

Down to the filter of his cigarette, he snubbed it out against the dock and tucked the butt of the cigarette into his shorts. It was hot this morning, hotter than the last couple of days. He surveyed his surroundings, looking for any boats on the lake and then at the few houses on the other side of the lake. He stood up and kicked off his shoes, followed by his shirt, socks, and shorts.

He didn't care if a few neighbors saw him from a distance. It was only a naked body, surely not the first one they'd seen. He wasn't a fan of the cooler temperatures of lake water, but this afternoon it would be refreshing.

From the dock, he dove in headfirst and swam several yards into the clear lake. The initial dive was like diving into an ice bucket, but within several strokes his body acclimated to the temperature. He paddled around for several minutes before making his way back to the dock.

Using the ladder at the end, he climbed back up onto the dock and stretched his naked body onto the warm boards. He released a breath as his heart rate slowed. He shut his eyes to rest until he dried.

The sound of a car door shutting woke him from a light sleep and sent him scrambling for his shorts. By the time he had his shorts on, the car was driving off. He looked toward the house, but from down on the dock the house blocked his view of the driveway. Had they come home and left again?

Spiro slipped on his socks and jammed his feet into his shoes. He was about to put his shirt on when he saw Noah exit the back door of the house and stop at the edge of the porch. Spiro waved so Noah would see him on the dock.

Noah's chin lifted, signaling he saw him as he began to saunter down the knoll and onto the dock. "Hey there," Noah called from about ten yards away. Dressed in a black suit, Noah grinned as he strolled down the dock. He tore a bite from the bright red apple his left hand held. He held another apple in his right hand.

When he was about five feet in front of Spiro, he tossed it to him. "Best apples in the world."

Spiro caught the shiny, red apple with one hand. A smile crept onto his face, seeing Noah dressed in a suit. "Thanks. How was church?"

"It was all right." Noah stopped inches before him.

Spiro's eyes glanced up at the little dome-like black cap on the back of Noah's head. "What's that?" He patted the back of his own head.

"It's called a yarmulke."

Instead of risking looking dumb, he held off asking why they wore it. "Did I hear Eros leave?"

"Yeah, he was dropping me off. My grandma's still there. It was our rabbi's birthday this week, and today a bunch of them are throwing some party for him. I said I wasn't feeling well to get out of there. What are you doing down here?"

"Took a break for a bit. Cooled off in the lake." Spiro glanced across the smooth lake. "I see your friend and his family's gone again." All the cars were gone, and the place had been quiet all morning.

"Yeah, they had a wedding in Connecticut this weekend. Chris's aunt, I think."

With his theios gone, the old lady out of the way, and now Chris gone, Spiro had an idea. "Do you think it would be okay to take your family's boat to check out the lake? Maybe swim?"

Noah's head cocked to one side. "Sure, I guess."

"I know how to drive a boat if you don't. Show me how to lower it into the water."

Noah laughed. "I know how to drive the boat. I've been driving it since I was a kid."

Spiro rolled his eyes as he took a wait-and-see attitude.

"I saw you roll your eyes!" Noah punched him in his shoulder. "We can take it around to the other side of the lake and gas her up, then over to a place I know about. But first, let me change."

While Noah ran inside to change, Spiro headed back to the barn and grabbed three cans of beer from Eros's refrigerator.

Within minutes, they were both back and went to work lowering the vintage boat into the water. Standing behind the wheel, Noah put on a baseball cap and sunglasses that he found wedged in a cubbyhole of the boat. The vintage 1954 Chris Craft Sea Skiff was not the typical blue-and-white fiberglass boat that ran up and down the lake on weekends. She was elegant and assembled with beauty in mind. Built entirely from wood, her bow was a glossy varnished deep mahogany.

The engine roared to life, but immediately started to sputter as if she wanted to die. Noah allowed her to idle for a minute until the plume of white smoke from the engine began to fill the boathouse. With the engine still sputtering, Noah directed Spiro in assisting him in backing the cruiser from the boathouse.

"I'm not sure why it's smoking so bad!" Noah glanced back at the massive plume of smoke left in the boathouse. He spun the wheel a little to the right and back to the left, steering the boat beside the dock.

Spiro waited until the boat was close enough before leaping from the dock onto the boat. "It could be several things. Maybe a low compression ratio, your injectors, or timing, but I think it might be old fuel."

Between the loud engine and Spiro's accent, Noah didn't understand any of what Spiro had just said. "It's almost on empty!" Noah yelled over the engine. "We'll have to get gas. Hold on!"

Spiro braced himself in the front seat beside Noah and cracked open a can of beer. With the wind whipping across his face, the boat sputtered across the water as if the engine would fail at any moment. He watched the trail of smoke to see if it was lessening.

Spiro was in awe at the mountain of trees that surrounded the house as they distanced themselves from the shore. Seeing the forest of bright green trees that covered the mountain range from the middle of the lake was a much grander view than from the shore.

With the engine now purring, Noah looked behind him and saw that the white smoke had stopped. "I think we'll be all right now!" He shouted over the roar of the hundred-fifty-horsepower Mercury engine.

"Yeah!" Spiro wished he had his sunglasses, with the wind whipping across his eyes. "Do you want a beer?" He hollered to Noah.

"Sure!" Noah held out his hand and took the can that Spiro opened for him.

He was about to turn away when Noah pulled the back of his swimming trunks down over his pale ass and arched his ass out toward him. "Thanks!" His devilish grin said he'd learned nothing this morning in Synagogue.

"I like that!" Spiro reached across the seat to touch the beautiful, pale ass, but Noah was too quick and pulled his trunks back up. "I have to drive!" He shouted as he thrust forward on the throttle, knocking Spiro back into his seat. With the added speed, the beautiful Chris Craft ripped across the smooth lake, leaving in her wake a spray of mist that glistened through the sun.

Within a few minutes, they had crossed the lake and entered a narrow section that led to the Lake Winnipesaukee floating gas station. With a full tank of fresh gas that resolved their smoke problem and a paper bag full of snacks charged to the house account, they were back on their way.

It was about ten minutes before Noah had them around the backside of a small cove, where he slowed the boat to a crawl. "The water's low here. There're too many rocks. I don't want to chance it. There's another place we can go, if you want to check out some trails."

"What's back there?" Spiro pointed to the shore as he cracked open the last of the three beers. He took a gulp and held it out for Noah.

"There's a cool trail that goes back about three miles. It's not too steep. At the top, you can see the lake and everything. I haven't been back there in years." Noah took a gulp and handed the can back to Spiro.

"Can we swim over?" Spiro stood up to gain a better look at the sandy shoreline.

"Yeah. I guess."

"Let's do it." Spiro toe-kicked off his tennis shoes.

"Okay." Noah removed the anchor from a side cargo pocket. He tossed the anchor over the side, and then he, too, toe-kicked off his shoes and removed his shirt.

"I'll race you!" Not waiting for Noah to respond, he propelled his body off the boat, arms out, headfirst into the water. Underwater, he kicked twice before rising to the surface. Noah was behind him, splashing and kicking. They had another forty feet to go, so he slowed, letting Noah pass him.

Once Noah passed him, Spiro grabbed his ankle, bringing them both to a dead stop as their bodies sank underwater. Wrestling, the two fought to get on top of the other, splashing and kicking to exhaustion. The wrestling turned into kissing as they both kicked their feet to stay afloat. Their wet kiss deepened as Spiro's tongue found Noah's.

Just as Spiro was about to reach underwater for the drawstring to Noah's trunks, Noah's entire body jerked. Noah jerked again as he began choking and seconds later vomiting chunks of apple and beer into the water.

"Are you okay?" Spiro asked as the vomit broke into pieces and dissipated into the lake.

"I swallowed water!" His choking decreased into sniffles as he used the water to clear snot and vomit from his face.

Spiro swam in closer and wrapped his arm around Noah's waist. Paddling his legs, he supported him above the surface of the water. "Are you going to be all right?"

"Yeah." Noah sunk his mouth below the waterline and took in a mouthful of water. He rinsed his mouth and spit the water out.

"Are you sure?" Although the color reappeared in Noah's face, Spiro wasn't convinced.

"Really, I'm fine. Let's check out the trail." Noah's body dipped a little below the water as he kicked out and swam toward the shore.

The two paddled until they could stand in the waist-deep water, twenty feet from the shore. Standing on the small sandy beach, Spiro looked around. There was a rock firepit, with several logs as makeshift chairs. A little up the way was a narrow path that led into the thick brush.

Barefooted, the two took to the trail leading into the forest. "The last time I was up in here was the year before Nathanael died." Noah had taken the lead. "Watch for poison ivy." He pointed to a green plant as he passed it.

A few feet behind Noah, Spiro approached the plant, committing it to memory. He'd never heard of poison ivy, but it sounded deadly. "Is it really poisonous?" Spiro's stride shortened as he moved around the plant.

"Yeah, don't touch it." Noah took the bend in the trail and headed deeper into the woods. "If you see a bear, don't run."

A bear? Spiro stopped in his tracks. He detected eyes behind the trees on him, ready to jump him. "Are you kidding?"

"Don't worry; there's never been a bear attack—yet." Noah waved his arm for Spiro to catch up. "C'mon, you big scaredy cat."

Spiro paid close attention to every plant he passed as they began their hike into the wooded forest of birch, maple, and pine trees. "This is pretty cool in here."

They'd walked into the forest about fifty yards when Spiro decided to ask a question that had been burning in his brain for the last few days. "Can I ask you something?" His eyes rose from the small dogwoods scattered along the trail. "What's up with your mom and dad?"

Noah kept walking. "What do you mean?"

"I mean, why aren't they here, with you? Or why aren't you in New York, with them? Seems weird." Noah's silence made him wonder if Noah was ignoring the question.

Noah was silent for several more steps before he spoke. "After Nathanael was killed, things weren't the same anymore... I'm pretty sure they hate me."

"Why would they hate you?"

Noah took several steps. "If I wasn't such a wimp, if I learned to fight, if I just hadn't said anything to Nathanael the day he was killed, he'd still be alive."

Spiro didn't like that Noah referred to himself as a wimp, but he wasn't going to interrupt him to tell him.

"He was on Fifth Avenue that day because of me. The bus driver who hit him was on his cell phone at the time. He claimed Nathanael swerved out in front of him, and it happened in a split second." Noah stepped over a rock in the middle of the trail.

He took several steps before speaking again. "I hadn't said anything to my parents about what had happened at the park until the morning of the funeral. We were in the limo that morning heading to the service. I don't know why, but I felt like I had to tell them the truth. It was killing me that it was my fault. After I told them, they didn't say anything. That night, it was late when I walked into the kitchen. My dad was in there making a peanut butter and jelly sandwich. I could tell he wasn't talking to me. He wouldn't even look at me when I walked in."

Noah glanced over at Spiro as if making sure he was listening. Spiro looked at him and nodded, showing that he was.

Noah continued, "I asked him if he hated me. I remember him not saying anything for a long time. Then, the only thing he said was that I needed to learn how to stick up for myself, that Nathanael wasn't here to protect me anymore. He told me to stop being a wimp, and then he just walked out."

Spiro heard the word again. He now knew where Noah gained his identity as a wimp: his father.

"Even today, they can't look at me without grieving for him... So, they don't." Noah added, "It's like I'm invisible to them."

"Who do you think took it harder, your mom or dad?"

"I don't know." Noah was quiet for several steps. "I guess, really, maybe my mom... I knew my dad was angry. He wouldn't even talk to me for a long time. But my mom, it was harder to tell. She seemed normal, but was working more. I think she shut me and my dad out, though. And then he started doing his own thing. We did the whole family counseling thing for a couple of sessions, and then my dad refused to go anymore. It was easier not to talk about it. Now, we don't talk about Nathanael at all, as if he was never here."

Spiro watched as Noah ducked, dodging a low-hanging branch in their path. Spiro asked, "Is it true that twins' brains are connected?" He grabbed the branch from Noah and squeezed by it.

"If you mean, did we think alike, yeah, most of the time. We could finish each other's sentences and read each other like a book."

Free from the branch, Spiro fired another question at Noah. "What do you do when they're working?"

"During the week, I basically live alone. I have school. My games. I don't know, watch TV, I guess. My dad does a lot of lecturing all over the world, so he's gone a lot. My mom has her practice, so she's there or at the hospital."

"That sucks." Spiro would give anything to have a normal conversation with his mother.

"Yeah... no, not really. I get to do what I want. Next year, I'll be away at school, so I'm looking forward to that."

Although Noah tried to sound like it didn't matter, Spiro picked up on his tone that said otherwise. His and Noah's families were different in every way possible. Before getting to know Noah, he was jealous of Noah's life, but now he wasn't so sure. There was a sadness to Noah's life. Spiro knew something about how life could suck. He'd disappointed many people in his life already just with screwing around and getting kicked out of school. It made him sick to think how much of his family's money, money they didn't have, was wasted on him.

The two started up a steeper climb dotted with large rocks. They used their hands to brace themselves against the rocks. After about ten minutes of this, the trail ironed out again into a dirt path.

Noah stopped when they came to an old wooden bridge. "This is Beaver Creek." He peered over the side of the bridge.

Spiro stopped beside him and looked down over the bridge's rail. Below was a small creek that meandered down the mountain. Here, some of the tall, narrow trees were covered with light moss. His nose crinkled at the pungent odor of wet, decaying earth.

"What are you going to school for?" Spiro asked.

"Pre-med. I think I want to be a maxillofacial surgeon."

"A what?" Spiro didn't have a clue what Noah had said.

"A maxillofacial surgeon. It's someone who works on facial bones and the neck. Like a real bad car accident and the face is all busted up, or like someone that has a deformity in their face. Do you know what a cleft palate is?"

"Yeah."

"Okay. I think it would be cool to go to other countries and fix people who couldn't afford to have their faces fixed—to really change someone's life by giving them a sense of normalcy. I'll have to get a dental degree on top of my medical degree."

Spiro couldn't even imagine how smart Noah was to pull off something like that. He tried for a simple art degree and couldn't do it. For the first time, he truly did feel inferior to Noah. He prayed Noah didn't ask about his schooling.

In silence, they wandered up the trail another quarter mile before Noah came to a stop. "Shh. Listen."

"What's that noise?" The wind rustled through the leaves, mixed with a buzzing hum. He took in a big breath of air into his lungs. The earthy decomposing leaves and rotting wood was a scent unfamiliar to him.

"That's a cicada." Noah grinned.

"What's a cicada?" Spiro's brows crinkled.

"It's an ugly-ass bug that lives in the ground for, like, fifteen years. Then they come up to mate. Don't worry, they don't bite or sting. The only thing they're interested in is screwing and laying eggs. They're so horny, they won't even stop to eat."

"Are you bullshitting?" Spiro looked down around his feet.

"No, I'm serious."

Spiro moved closer to Noah and stood beside him. "How much further?" He looked up the trail, seeing that, at about fifty feet, the trail took a bend.

"I think we're almost there." Noah looked around and then up into the trees.

Spiro listened to the rustling of the leaves and the cicadas.

"Are you okay?" Noah asked.

Sweat beaded across Spiro's forehead from the humidity in the forest. His shoulders and back glistened from perspiration. "Yeah. It's hot back in here."

They continued, and within a matter of minutes they reached the summit. Facing the lake, Noah took a seat on a large boulder.

Spiro tried to catch his breath as he sat beside Noah. The bottoms of Spiro's feet were raw from hiking barefoot. "This is cool." His eyes surveyed the breathtaking views of the clear blue lake below them and surrounding luscious green hills and mountain range. Overlooking the valley below, the dense green forest stretched in every direction over the horizon whichever way he looked. "Wow! We don't have trees like this on the island."

"Really? What's it like?"

"We have mountains like this, but they are mostly bare. We say, *faraklo*... How do you say it in English... bald?"

"Like, nothing on them?" Noah asked.

"Yes, yes! Lava from many, many years ago. It is all over, but we have trees, too."

"Are the volcanoes still active?"

"No, not for thousands of years."

"Do you like to hike?"

"Very much. My dad and I used to hike. There's a castle, well, not so much a castle anymore, but it used to be a castle on top of the mountain. Very old. We would hike up there when I was little. You can see the entire island from up there... like this." He looked out at the mountain range. "We could also see the big boats that bring people to our island."

"Like ferryboats?" Noah asked.

"Yes."

"What about your mom? You said your mom was sick. What's wrong with her?"

Spiro didn't mind talking about his mother, but he was surprised that Noah asked about her. "When I was born, she suffered a brain bleed and was in a coma for several months. When she woke, she wasn't the same. She couldn't talk or anything."

"Wow, is she okay now?"

Spiro rolled his shoulders. "My theia takes care of her. Eros's wife."

"Oh. so your mom lives with you guys?"

"Yeah." With the amount of work and dedication his theia devoted to caring for his mom, he didn't know what they would do without his theia. "My dad's getting old. He still goes out every morning on the boat, but most times he sleeps in his chair beside her."

Spiro knew that his family only had money for the necessities in life. His family was so poor that Eros had to pay for his ticket to America. His family didn't have that kind of money. Between Eros and his sister in Boston, they'd spent a fortune flying him to the States so Eros could do something with him, something his own father couldn't do. The money spent on sending him to school, that he pissed away like it was nothing, was forever gone. He was seeing that he'd screwed it all up. Unlike Noah, there was no safety net for a second chance for him.

He looked out across the lake. No longer was this a place of claustrophobia. It was absolutely breathtaking, possibly the most beautiful thing he'd ever seen. Everything was stunning. He leaned over and kissed Noah.

Noah's lips gently pressed back as the kiss deepened a little. When Spiro placed his hand behind Noah's neck to deepen it even more, Noah pulled back.

"C'mon. We should head back down." Noah stood up and dusted off his ass. He didn't wait for Spiro as he began his descent down the trail toward the boat.

The trip back to the boat was a lot faster and a whole lot quieter. When they arrived back at the sandy beach, Spiro was about five steps behind Noah. "Is everything okay?" Spiro asked.

Noah looked up at him. "Yeah. Why?"

"You just got quiet up there." Spiro wondered if it had anything to do with the kiss.

"No, I'm fine."

"Okay." Spiro wrestled with whether he believed him as he dove into the water to rid the itchy sweat that covered his body. The two paddled side by side back to the boat.

Noah climbed into the rear of the boat first and then extended his hand to Spiro to help him out of the water and into the boat. Seeing Noah's wet, glistening body on board the boat was too much. He had to touch him, feel him. On purpose, but intended to seem like an accident, Spiro stumbled as the boat rocked to one side. He fell into Noah's body, knocking him off balance, and the two fell onto the long, cushioned seat at the rear of the boat.

Spiro went in for a kiss and felt Noah's mouth fall into sync with his kiss. Noah's mouth tasted of fresh lake water. Noah's hand wrapped behind his head, and his pelvis pushed up into Spiro. A moan escaped from the corner of Noah's mouth as their kiss deepened. As their bare chests slid against each other, Noah's breathing was feverish. Within minutes, Noah worked to loosen the drawstring on his bathing suit and slid his wet suit down.

Spiro liked his aggression, the side he showed no one but him. Following Noah, he, too, stripped off his shorts. When their naked bodies pressed together, Noah's skin was damp and cool. He'd been with other guys before, but never with the intense feelings he had for Noah. The splash of the water against the boat as it bobbed and rocked in the water played in Spiro's ear.

Until now, they'd done little more than enjoy long make-out sessions. The urgency to have sex with Noah hadn't been as strong as the need to be with him. This afternoon, Noah's moans and aggression were intensified. He savored the sweetness of Noah's breath as it pushed out of his lungs.

Every time Spiro began to ease up, Noah refused him, pressing their mouths tighter. They moved at a feverish pace, their hands roaming each other's naked bodies, committing every curve to memory. Spiro could feel every goosebump on Noah's skin. His lips skimmed across Noah's slender neck and bony collarbone. Noah's slender body under his felt more like Stefania's than a guy's.

Noah begun to thrust his body with more force as he moaned louder through their kisses. He wanted to slow Noah down, but there was something arousing about Noah's recklessness that stoked his fire even more. Within minutes, Noah cried out into Spiro's ear. His incoherent mews took Spiro over the edge soon after.

After regaining their breath, Spiro used the only thing within sight to clean Noah's belly.

"Hey, that's my tee shirt." Noah muttered.

He stared into Noah's blue eyes as he wiped the last of their mess up before cleaning himself. He was sure he'd never felt what he was feeling for Noah with anyone, including Stefania.

The sadness in Noah's eyes had been replaced with a softness. The white flecks within his blue eyes made Spiro think of how the sunlight sparkled through the clear waters around his island. He knew that if he looked deep enough into Noah's eyes, he could see below the surface. Just like the ocean bottom, it was something that few people got to see.

With everything Noah had shared with him during their hike this afternoon, Spiro was sure the sadness was still in there, but in this moment he didn't see it. Noah was beautiful, but wounded—hurt by the people on this earth that were supposed to protect him.

Spiro had no concept of how this could even be possible. As much as he'd screwed up this last year, his family had never turned their back on him. Family just didn't do that. Gratitude washed over Spiro, followed by an awareness that he was actually happy, and he hadn't even realized it until just now.

He was happy, happy to be here in the States, happy to be hanging out with Noah, happy not to be in freaking jail or wandering the streets. His theios had taken him in because that's what family did. Maybe he could stay with Eros even after summer? He could ask Eros, convince his theios that he was worth keeping around? Because of his theia's and Eros's age, he could be of use to them if he stayed with them in Boston. His relationship with Noah wouldn't have to be limited to a single summer. How did he make it happen? Spiro had no idea.

CHAPTER NINE

Noah stood in the driveway as his parents drove away. Two days ago, he was surprised by their arrival, and he waited for his dad to say something about the boat being out.

He'd had maybe three whole conversations with his dad during their short weekend visit. Neither the boat nor his long hair ever came up. Noah didn't understand the purpose of driving five hours for a two-day visit. They'd come and gone in less than thirty-six hours. During that time, his mother spent her hours combing over files, and his dad paced the property with nothing to do but identify everything that Eros needed to fix.

Their visit was nothing more than a disruption to the peace and quiet of the lake house, and more so to his and Spiro's summer. Neither his mom nor dad had asked how he was doing. Neither saw he'd fallen in love since the last time they'd seen him; neither saw he was happy.

But Noah saw them—two souls that appeared already dead. Deep crow's feet etched the corners of his mother's eyes. Her lifeless grey hair was pulled back into a bun so she didn't have to style it. Her forehead had been carved with wrinkles from years of scowling. His father was just as bad. At six-five, two hundred and seventy-five pounds, his dad's knees were beginning to exhibit signs that his massive body had destroyed them. His thick, out-of-control grey eyebrows framed eyes sunken into a pale face that long ago stopped showing happiness or contentment.

For Noah, their visit served as a reminder of a life he vowed never to have. Going away this fall to college was a new life waiting for him. He hadn't realized just how much he wanted it until last week, when he and Spiro were on their hike. He'd bared his soul to Spiro about his parents and his relationship with them. Second to the loss of his brother, being invisible to them hurt more than anything in the world. When Spiro kissed him on the mountain, all he could think about was what if someone saw them kissing. The irony was, that was exactly what he wanted from his parents—for them to see him.

With his parents gone, Noah followed the shriek of the chainsaw into the woods where he knew he'd find Spiro working. Through the white birch trees, standing in a small clearing, Spiro ripped the beast of a saw through a fallen pine tree, turning it into firewood. They had about another hour before the sun would set for the day.

"You know, you're standing in the middle of poison ivy!" Noah shouted in Spiro's ear. He wasn't sure Spiro jumped because he startled him or because he believed he was standing in poison ivy. "I'm kidding!" Noah laughed as he stepped back, ensuring he was out of the way of the jagged wielding blade.

"You scared the shit out of me!" Spiro cut the chainsaw off and put it down on a stump. "You're lucky I didn't wheel around and cut you in half with that damn thing."

He was probably right; it wasn't the safest thing he could have done. "Sorry." The smell of freshly cut pine hung in the air.

"How was your visit with your mom and dad?" Spiro pulled up the end of his tee shirt and wiped the sweat and dirt from his face.

"It was all right." The sight of Spiro's exposed stomach and his tight abdominal muscles dominated Noah's attention. Spiro's super-hot body must've resulted from physical labor. His eyes lingered for an additional second or two. Even if he joined the gym, Noah couldn't conceive of ever having a body like that. A tiny pool of saliva pressed against his tongue, causing him to swallow. "I've missed you." Noah took a step closer, into Spiro's personal space.

Spiro looked around as if ensuring they were alone. "Eros says he's taking you and your grandmother into Concord tomorrow for some sort of dinner or something?" Spiro murmured.

Noah glanced toward the house and nodded for Spiro to follow him deeper into the woods. "Yeah, she wants me to have a new suit for school, and then we're going out to dinner. Kind of like a celebration before I leave for school."

Holding hands, the two strolled through the forest of white paper birch trees and ferns, leading them toward the main road. Twigs and dry leaves crunched under their feet as the trees shielded their secret love affair.

"I don't want to go." What Noah was really saying was that he wanted to stay here, with him.

"Why not?" Spiro asked.

"I don't know..." Noah didn't want to risk sounding too needy. "Can I see you tonight? Are you going to the barn tonight?"

"I'm out of paint."

"I can buy you more. I'll be in town. Tell me what to get." Noah sensed something in Spiro's voice, a reluctance. There were other reasons to go to the barn; they'd proved that already. The last time they met was three nights ago, before his parents' arrival.

"You don't have to do that. I was just messing around with the stuff I found. It's not a big deal." Spiro told him.

"Is something wrong?" Noah didn't want to talk about paint. There was a somberness in Spiro's voice that concerned him. Did it have to do with why Spiro didn't want to see him tonight?

"Eros and I played chess last night. I beat him twice. All he's been talking about today is a rematch tonight. I don't think I can break free."

Chess? Spiro was opting for a game of chess instead of being with him. He suddenly regretted teaching Spiro to play. They hadn't been together in days. Had something happened while his parents were here that he didn't know about? "How about tomorrow?" Noah murmured.

Noah hadn't said anything to Spiro, but he'd been fantasizing about taking things further with him. He wanted Spiro to have him. He wanted to give this to Spiro. He wanted to give this to himself.

"When? What time are you guys leaving?" Spiro let go of Noah's hand as he stopped and turned inward to him. With the sound of the passing cars on the roadway, the trees kept them in hiding from unsuspecting vacationers.

"Not until after lunch. Grandma and Ms. Jimenez are making Challot before we go, for some bake sale. Meet me in the boathouse in the morning, before we leave."

"Okay... I'll tell Eros that I'm working in there, that your father wanted me to wax the boat or something." Spiro's voice sounded as if he was thinking as he added to their scheme.

"After breakfast. We can hang out in there before I go." Energized, he gave Spiro a kiss. If he fell in love any more with Spiro, his heart would explode. This summer, there was never a minute in the day he wasn't thinking about the next time they would be together... and tomorrow, they would be.

Noah pulled Spiro into his chest as he stared into his eyes. He sensed that something was still wrong. When he kissed Spiro, he'd gotten little more than a peck back. Was Spiro already growing tired of him and didn't know how to tell him?

"What did you mean when you said that boys will be boys until they get married or something like that?" Noah asked. From the day he heard Spiro say it, he never understood it, but it always had an ominous tone to it. Maybe, whatever it meant had something to do with Spiro's gloomy mood.

Spiro moaned, as if thinking. "It's just something we say." He reached up and brushed a strand of hair from Noah's face. "It's like, it's okay to mess around with other guys until you get married. Then you have to be faithful to her."

"Are you planning on getting married someday?"

"I don't know. Aren't you?" Spiro murmured.

"No..." This conversation was weird, as if they'd shared nothing the last four weeks. He didn't want to entertain the thought of Spiro getting married one day. "What do you think will happen when summer's over?" Noah nervously asked.

"I don't know. I was wondering the same thing."

"So, you've thought about it?" Noah asked.

"All the time, every day."

Surprised by Spiro's answer, he pushed further. "Do you want to see me again? You know, Harvard is right there, close to your theia."

"I thought about that. I was thinking about asking my theios if I could live with him and his sister in Boston."

"Maybe I could get an apartment in the city." Noah couldn't hide his excitement at the prospect that they would be together.

"That would be so cool!" Spiro's entire face brightened as well.

"I love you." He kissed Spiro again.

This time, Spiro took his shoulders and brought him in closer. "I love you, too." Embracing each other in the woods, Spiro kissed him again as he pulled him tighter against him. Locked in a kiss, Spiro took his breath away as his legs grew weak. He loved Spiro more than anything.

****

The next morning, an eager Noah woke early. Unable to keep his excitement tamped down, Grandma Maya picked up on his cheerful mood. He played it off as being eager to go into town. After breakfast, Noah ran back up to his room and grabbed a few last-minute things he might need for his plan.

When he entered the boathouse, a shirtless Spiro was sitting in the rear of the boat. He had already found the bottle of champagne Noah had stolen and stashed in the boat. "Congratulations!" He shouted as he stood and held up a glass of champagne for Noah.

"Congratulations for what?" Noah asked as he hurried to him and climbed into the boat.

"I don't know. Isn't that why people drink this stuff, because they're celebrating something?" They touched glasses; Spiro said, "*Yasoo!*" with a big grin.

Noah took a sip of the warm champagne before remembering he didn't like the stuff. His other option in the house was a bitter wine that tasted like sour grape juice.

He put his glass down and wrapped his arms around Spiro's neck. He didn't want to waste another minute of their time with talk of champagne. Their lips brushed as their foreheads came together. The spark in Spiro's eyes agreed with him.

Their kiss, effortless now as their lips fell into the dance they'd created together. Spiro's body pressed against his, a whimper escaped Noah. The outside world slipped away as Spiro's hands took his waist and drew him closer.

With tempestuous kisses to Noah's neck, each kiss from Spiro's lips caused Noah's breath to hitch. Overwhelmed by emotions, his shoulders relaxed as his neck gave way to Spiro's touch.

"You're sexy as hell," Spiro murmured as his lips moved back up to Noah's lips.

The challenge of keeping on his feet as the boat rocked in its tiny slip was proving too difficult for Noah the more he surrendered to Spiro's touch. Unable to stand a second more, their bodies dropped to the floor of the boat.

The boat rocked and crashed against its slip as they came out of their clothes. Naked, Spiro pulled him into a fiery, passionate kiss. His hands worked their way around Noah's body, caressing the skin of a body that was once too skinny, too pale, that lacked any physical strength.

Spiro had spent the entire summer stripping all the shame and embarrassment Noah had over his body image, one kiss, one conversation, one day at a time.

Noah wasn't sure he could hang on long enough for what he wanted. "Do you want to fuck me?" Noah murmured through their kiss.

"Are you sure?" Spiro asked. "I don't have any condoms."

Noah was never surer of anything in his entire life. "I have some." He stretched and lifted the seat cushion up and pulled out a small paper bag he left stashed in the boat. He flipped the bag upside down, tossing out a tube of KY and the box of condoms.

Spiro grinned as he picked up the box of condoms. "Magnums? *Really?*"

"I didn't read the box; I just grabbed them!" Two days ago, when he decided that he wanted to go all the way with Spiro, he took the boat over to the floating market at the main boat launch under the pretense of picking up gum.

As if the words *"I'm going to get fucked"* were stamped across his forehead, Noah was positive the old lady who rang him up knew why he was buying the condoms.

Noah hastily squeezed a little KY onto the tip of his finger and pushed it up inside himself. He thought about it for a second—more was better—so he pushed another gob inside of him. "Okay." His eyes conveyed his nervousness.

"That's not enough. Here, let me do it." Spiro took the tube of KY from Noah's hand. He started with one finger and gently lubed Noah, increasing the number of fingers with more lube.

"Okay, now breathe," Spiro instructed.

Noah uttered a gasp when Spiro began to push inside him. It hurt far more than when Chris finger fucked him or when he did it to himself. His entire body was on fire as pain ripped through his stomach. He squeezed his eyes shut. *Was it supposed to hurt this much?*

"Stop! Stop... Stop!" Noah couldn't take a second more. His eyes flooded with tears as pain shot up his spine.

"I didn't even put it in yet." Spiro pulled back.

"Yes, you did!"

"Barely... you gotta breathe." Spiro tried not to laugh. He knew it wasn't funny, but it was, kind of.

"I can't! I can't!" Noah held Spiro's body at bay, stopping him from bearing down any further. Frozen, he worked to get a hold of his breathing, anything to stop the pain. There was no way he could do this!

Within a minute, the pain subsided slightly, enough for the will to try again to return. Drenched in sweat, he blamed it on the temperature in the boathouse. He exhaled a big breath. "Okay... I'm ready." He braced himself for another round.

"You gotta breathe!"

"Okay! But don't yell at me. That doesn't help." Noah's eyes expressed how focused he was. He drew a deep breath as Spiro pushed slowly inside him. "Slow!"

Noah's breath quickened. He tried to focus on his breathing as Spiro entered him and came to a stop. Noah pushed air down into his lungs as he closed his eyes. The weight of Spiro's body on him, in him, brought a tear to the corner of his eye. He wasn't sure if he could continue; the exchange of pain over pleasure was nowhere equal.

"I love you," Spiro whispered. He remained still as he looked down at Noah. The light in his bright hazel eyes, staring softly at Noah, demanded his attention.

The tenderness in which Spiro looked at him said he would be okay, to focus on him, to trust him. As Noah did this, he lost focus on the pain. He'd fallen in love with Spiro the day they met; he was sure of it. No one had ever made him feel alive like Spiro had. He was never invisible in Spiro's presence. It was the opposite; Spiro made him feel like he was the only thing that mattered. Spiro had just said that he loved him. *Spiro loves me!*

Noah's body gave way to Spiro. He knew it wasn't possible, but it was as if Spiro's entire body was engulfing his from within. Spiro was in his arms, the tips of his fingers, his neck, in his head. Spiro was a part of him, consuming him.

Lost in his own euphoria, time vanished for Noah. The entire world disappeared from his existence. Yes, Spiro's body was on top of him, but it was weightless. As Spiro's body moved in and out of his, waves of euphoria washed over Noah. He was engulfed in emotions when he suddenly climaxed. The muscles in his legs, ass, and back trembled as he gasped for air.

But Spiro wasn't done with him yet; he continued to thrust into him. Fighting to breathe, Noah heard the change in Spiro's grunts as they became throatier. There were three more big thrusts, and then Spiro cried out as his body went rigid and froze in ecstasy.

After a second or two, Spiro rolled off Noah. "Jesus! I think the whole lake heard you," Spiro huffed. His breath was croaky as he slid the condom off and tossed it to the side.

"Really?" Noah didn't care. He was too focused on his breathing to care about anything else.

They lay breathless, wrapped in sweat on the floor of the boat as it stilled. Spiro's body pressed against the back of Noah's; his arms wrapped around Noah like a cocoon. The heat in the boathouse was almost unbearable, but Noah refused to move, not wanting to change anything in this moment.

Noah's butt muscles pulsated like a heart pumping blood. He wasn't sure if it hurt or if it was amatory: Good or bad, it was a reminder of what had just occurred. Every so often, a surge of energy jolted Noah, causing his entire body to quiver and shake. With his head resting on Spiro's arm, he closed his eyes. Spiro's breathing was light; the warmth of his breath, caressing the back of Noah's ear.

Noah nuzzled his butt up tighter against Spiro, feeling Spiro's manhood pressed on his ass. His body jerked as another jolt surged up through his body. He wanted to close his eyes and go to sleep. How nice would it be to snuggle up in Spiro's arms and fall asleep? He knew his grandmother would be looking for him for their trip into Concord. She would send Eros out looking for him.

Against his will, he pulled away from Spiro. "C'mon, we should get dressed before Eros comes looking for us." As he rose to his feet, the muscles in his ass contracted, allowing Noah to appreciate for another second what just occurred. The two scurried to get dressed and left the boathouse before Eros came for them.

That afternoon, the car made its way down the mountain toward Concord. Noah sat in the backseat. He tuned out the conversation between his grandmother and Eros. He was a little nauseated and focused on the cramping in his stomach.

He ran down a checklist of everything he'd eaten last night and this morning. He wanted to attribute his cramping and pain to something he ate, but it could have been complications from what he and Spiro had done this morning.

He had no idea that sex would hurt as badly as it did. What else didn't he know about having sex? It had been hours ago, and his ass still throbbed. It was good, but now he was worried. Could something be wrong? His mind went to the worst-case scenario. Had they ruptured something? Was he was bleeding internally? If he was dying, there was no way he could ask his grandmother for help—*he couldn't.*

The first half of the trip at the tailor's was a blur as Noah tried to hide his discomfort. He tried to control his breathing and push past the cramps as they shopped for new clothes. What had occurred between him and Spiro this morning? Maybe he was seriously hurt.

There was no way of hiding this from his dad if he had to go to the hospital. The doctors would know how the injury occurred. His body broke out in a sweat as the worst-case scenario played out in his head. His secret was unraveling, and he couldn't stop it.

By the time they made it to the restaurant, Noah was sure he would vomit. He'd been fighting the metallic taste in his mouth for the last ten minutes. His stomach pains drove him into the restroom before they could be seated. He made it to the first stall as his stomach muscles heaved bile all over the floor in the stall. Positioned over the toilet, another wave of vomit drove Noah's face into the bowl. He tried to breathe as rancid bile spewed from his mouth.

His lips and stomach quivered as a third attack on his body nearly sent him into convulsions. His eyes filled with tears; he waited to ensure nothing else was coming up before lifting his head from the toilet bowl. He cleaned himself up the best he could at the sink and waited a few minutes until his uneven breathing subsided a little more. Noah made his way into the dining room to find his grandmother. His sunken eyes and sallow skin gave him away.

"Are you okay?" She asked.

He must have looked far worse than he imagined. "No." Noah swallowed the taste of bile. "I think I need to go back to the house." He didn't take his seat, questioning the hour-long drive and if he should wait a few minutes before attempting to get in the car. Every muscle in his body ached.

Ashen-faced, Noah tried to relax. However, even the most expensive and luxurious seats in the world weren't enough to deliver him any comfort for the ride home. His stomach roiled as the colossal sedan sped down the highway. Maybe Spiro would have an idea of what was wrong; he always did. He needed to be with him.

Arriving home, Noah went straight to the bathroom, where the contents of his bowels decided they also wanted out. When he was sure he could risk going up to his bedroom, he crawled up the next flight of stairs and collapsed on his bed. He prayed he'd wake up in the morning.

CHAPTER TEN

It had been a week since their rendezvous in the boathouse and brutal gastrointestinal issues that plagued Noah for several days afterwards. The two young men walked along the edge of the lake, talking. They'd been walking for about a half hour. Noah knew they didn't have much time. Eros wouldn't be gone for more than an hour, two at the most. Plus, Noah's stomach was rumbling. They both looked out to the lake as a speedboat towing a skier zipped past them. Noah smiled, seeing the little girl skiing behind the boat.

"Do you guys only come for the summer?" Spiro asked as he picked up a rock and flung it across the surface of the water.

Noah watched as the rock skipped three times before disappearing under the surface. "For the most part. Once we shut up the house, it's a lot of work to reopen it for just a weekend or two. Years ago, we came up for a Thanksgiving. My dad's sister and her family came up. In the fall, it's really pretty up here. For a few weeks, all the leaves on the trees turn this beautiful mix of reds, yellows, a real pretty purplish red, oranges, and browns. It's like looking in a box of crayons."

"Eros said it snows here."

"Yeah. In the winter, it's freezing cold." Noah's stomach rumbled again.

"I bet it's pretty. I've never seen snow."

"How's that possible?"

"Lemnos gets cold but no snow. They say it snowed there once about twenty-five years ago."

The rumble in Noah's stomach caused him to grimace, missing the last part of what Spiro said. Last week, when he let Spiro fuck him, he really thought some internal damage had been done. Only after a couple of days, when his stomach settled, was he sure he wasn't going to die. He'd reverted to his ongoing assessment that his stomach issues had more to do with something he'd eaten. He was positive it had to be something he'd eaten, not the sex. Troubled, he retraced everything he'd eaten over the last couple of days.

In the last two years, his stomach issues had been increasing more frequently, which contributed to his recent weight loss. This all started long before Spiro took his virginity last week. He wanted last week's bout with the severe cramping, vomiting, and diarrhea not to be about what he and Spiro had done, but something he'd eaten. To prove it to himself, he let Spiro fuck him again two days ago. Within hours of them having sex, he again was sent racing to the bathroom for hours that evening.

"Feel that?" Spiro asked.

"What?"

"The raindrop? I think it's about to rain."

Noah looked up at the dark grey clouds, surprised to see them. Deep in his head, he'd been oblivious to the storm clouds that had rolled in over them. He hadn't felt the drop, but yes, those were definitely storm clouds. They should turn back. He stopped, ready to turn back. "Can I ask you something?"

Spiro's brows came together. "Yeah, what?"

"It's kind of embarrassing."

Spiro hunched his shoulders. "Okay, what?"

Noah didn't know how to ask his question without sounding gross. Maybe it wasn't food, but maybe they were doing something wrong that was causing his stomach issues.

"Just say it," Spiro said.

"Okay... When you fuck me, afterwards, I have trouble... stomach issues."

"Like what?" A look of worry rose in Spiro's eyes.

"You know... like..." Noah rubbed his stomach as he grimaced. "And then I have to go to the bathroom a lot... I mean, *a lot*." Noah couldn't look at Spiro.

"I know; that's happened to me a couple of times, too."

"Really?" An overwhelming sense of relief washed over Noah. As bad as the cramping was, it was normal. "You've been fucked before?" He wasn't sure why this surprised him.

"Yeah, of course. Your body just has to get used to it."

Noah tried to imagine getting used to it. Did Spiro mean he had to get used to the stomach pain afterwards or get used to being fucked and the pain would stop? It didn't feel like it was something someone should get used to. Noah didn't want to say it, but he hoped Spiro was wrong. He desperately wanted it to be something he was eating. He didn't know much about lactose intolerance, but maybe he was. He hardly drank any milk, but ice cream and cheese would be nearly impossible to go without. Maybe he could just eat less of them.

They were almost back to the property when the grey skies lit with lightning bolts, closely followed by several sharp cracks of thunder. Within seconds, a heavy, warm rain pelted them like bullets in a wild, wild west shootout. They ran as fast as they could along the shoreline until they reached the property.

"In the boathouse!" Spiro pointed toward the dock. They ducked into the boathouse to escape the torrential downpour.

"Damn! Where'd that come from?" Spiro's heart was beating rapidly.

Soaked from head to toe, Noah fought to catch his breath. "My grandmother calls it hunch weather!" Noah snickered.

"Hunch weather?" Spiro asked.

"Yeah! When it comes down hard like that, it makes you hunch." Noah only meant to glance at Spiro, but Spiro's shiny, wet face caught his attention. The curls in Spiro's hair were flattened and pressed to his face. The brown hues in Spiro's eyes danced and glittered as he stared back at Noah. Spiro's innocent smile said he was completely oblivious to how beautiful he was.

"Get in the boat." Noah panted as he climbed in. The Chris Craft had become their bedroom over the last two months.

Spiro kneeled and quickly tore off his boots before jumping in. Watching Spiro, Noah peeled off his wet shirt. He grabbed a beach towel from one of the cabinets and gave Spiro one end as he dried his face with the other. When he was done with his end, he released it, moved in, and brushed the towel from Spiro's face.

They both leaned in until their lips met. Noah felt Spiro breathing as Spiro wrapped his arms around Noah's waist and pressed his hands against Noah's ass, bringing them together. "You're wet!" Noah mumbled through their kiss.

"Okay, then, let's get undressed," Spiro panted. He didn't wait for Noah as he started on his belt.

Within seconds, the two were naked and lying on the floor of the boat, their bed. Spiro lay on top of Noah, his body hovering over Noah's as his tongue slowly probed until Noah let him fully in. Spiro's weight pressed against Noah's body. Passionately, the two kissed as their bodies glided over each other. The friction between their bodies quickly heated as sensation continued to build. Chest to chest, their arousal matched their moans.

Noah reached out to retrieve the K-Y Jelly from its usual spot under the cushion of the seat above their head.

Spiro grabbed his arm, stopping him. "Noah... maybe we shouldn't."

"But I want to," Noah begged.

Spiro rolled off Noah and onto his side. "If your stomach's not..." Spiro paused as if searching for the right word. "...good? This would not be good to do."

"It will be all right." Noah wasn't convinced, but he wanted to make love. He knew Spiro loved to fuck, and this was something he could give to him.

"Can we not?" Spiro sat up.

"Yeah. I guess." It felt like a rejection, as if Spiro didn't want him.

"C'mon." Spiro pulled Noah's naked body beside his as he reclined. "I just want to be beside you." His hand caressed Noah's thigh and came to rest on his butt. With a light squeeze, Spiro cupped Noah's ass.

Noah released a moan. Spiro had doused their lovemaking as quickly as the rain had come, but Noah still had a little hunger in him. He wasn't ready to concede as he climbed on top of Spiro. The two started kissing again. Slower this time, they moaned and shifted their bodies against each other. Within minutes, they both climaxed, just seconds apart.

Spiro held Noah as they both slowly came down from their orgasmic high.

"How's your stomach?" Spiro asked as he brushed his fingers lightly over Noah's arm and up his shoulders.

"Um." Noah took a second to assess his body. "It's a little upset." He hated to admit it.

"See. Now aren't you glad we didn't fuck?" Spiro gently kissed Noah on the bridge of his nose. Through the large garage door windows, they watched as lightning lit the skies in brilliant streaks over the lake.

Noah tried to ignore the rumbling deep in his stomach, not wanting it to dominate what was happening. This was one of the best days of his life. He was snuggled in the arms of the most amazing person he'd ever met. He was in love. Although he couldn't share his secret with anyone, he knew Nathanael would've been okay with it, even happy for him. It would have been awesome to have shared it with him.

Noah had been listening to Spiro's breathing when he drifted into a light sleep. The sound of the door creaking open stirred him awake. His brain still cloudy and without thinking, Noah sat up. The ray of light behind the figure prevented him from seeing who it was. Noah squinted to make out the shadow as Spiro raised up. The shadow disappeared, and the door slammed closed.

A tendril of panic coiled within Noah as air stalled in his lungs. He had to know who it was; was it his grandmother, Eros, or...? The list didn't end. It could have been anyone.

Noah pulled on his shorts and leapt onto the platform. His heart in his throat, he cracked the door open and looked first toward the house. The rain had stopped. His ear caught the sound of stomping feet on the dock.

He winced, seeing Chris running down the dock toward his rowboat, tied beside Noah's at the end of the dock. He wanted to run after Chris, but his feet refused to leave the ground. With every passing second, Chris rowed farther from the house. Noah's heart raced, knowing his best friend had seen them.

"What happened?" Spiro came up behind him as he pulled his tee shirt over his head. "Who was it?"

"Chris. He must have come looking for me. He saw us!" He went through the lies he could say to Chris to make him believe he hadn't seen what he'd seen. He had to convince Chris it wasn't what he thought... *What else could it have been? They were naked. They'd been discovered.*

Maybe he could tell him the truth, and Chris would understand. Of all people, Chris would understand. Noah looked toward the house. Eros was back and walking between the house and the barn.

"Shit, your theios is back." Noah muttered as he watched Eros.

Noah's brain went into overdrive. He had to talk to Chris, find out what he saw. He and Chris played around plenty of times. How was this any different? If anything, Chris was gayer than he. It was Chris who started everything between them. Could Chris even see if they were naked in the boat? He wasn't sure what Chris saw. He tried to tell himself they were sitting in the boat, so what was the big deal? He was panicking. He would give Chris some time. He would go to him tomorrow. He had no idea what he'd say...

****

The next morning, Noah made his way downstairs. He didn't know whom he should talk to first, Spiro or Chris. When he reached the lower landing, he paused to eavesdrop on his grandmother, who was talking in the kitchen. The tone of her voice was cause to pause and listen. She was apologetic, adding that she was humiliated.

Noah deciphered that she must have been on the phone. The caller had her apologizing profusely. He'd never heard her yield to anyone. Before she hung up the phone, he overheard her say, "I'm calling his father when I hang up with you."

There was no mistaking they were discussing him, but who was the caller? Was it about him being sick the last couple of days? Was she worried? This would have been unusual. All his life, he and Nathanael had to be near death to get medical attention from any of the three brilliant doctors in their life. Noah took his place in his chair in the sunroom and waited for her to come to him.

It wasn't long before Grandma Maya entered the room. She sat a cup of tea on the end table beside him. "I don't think you should have any caffeine this morning," she said. "This should help your stomach."

So she is *worried about me.* "Thank you." He tried to read her. Her mysterious conversation still had him apprehensive. Her body language said she was concealing something.

"I need to start breakfast." Grandma Maya never made eye contact as she moved toward the door.

"Who were you talking to?" He couldn't stop himself from asking. He had to know.

She stopped in the doorway but never turned. "Mrs. Alperstein."

Noah's breath hitched. Chris *had* snitched him out.

"I'm sending Eros and his nephew into Concord for groceries. Do you need anything?"

Noah stared at her back. Her tone said more than her words. She didn't say Spiro's name. She'd reduced him to *his nephew*. And Eros didn't grocery shop for them by himself. Ever. He didn't know the difference between a challah and a regular loaf of bread.

For the rest of the day, Noah remained in his room. He needed to talk to Chris but was too embarrassed to talk to him right now. Nor could he face his grandmother a minute more. His room was his only option. He didn't have any solid proof that Chris had said anything or that his grandmother knew, but he was ninety-nine percent sure he was right. He couldn't understand why Chris would snitch him out; it made no sense. In his anger, Noah thought to tell on Chris. With the things Chris had done to him, he was just as gay.

From his room, he listened as the phone rang several times throughout the day. The house phone never rang, and today, it rang several times in ten minutes. By five o'clock, when Eros and Spiro failed to return, he knew it was more than shopping. Nothing about the day was right.

He must have dozed off when the sound of voices woke him. Excited at the possibility it was Spiro and Eros, he leapt from the bed and went to the window. Instead of seeing the truck, his father's silver Volvo was out front.

Noah opened his door and heard his mother and father's voices. *When did they arrive?*

His stomach quivered as he made his way downstairs. When he reached the bottom of the stairs, his father, exiting from the living room, stopped Noah from taking another step. The look in his eyes told Noah that he was in trouble. Over his father's shoulder, he saw Mr. and Mrs. Alperstein in the room with his mother. His father's stern look stopped him from entering the room as everyone stared at him.

"I need you to go back upstairs to your room," his father ordered.

"But Dad..."

"Now!" His father's authoritative voice shut down any argument. "I'll be up in a minute!"

Noah didn't turn his back on his father as he retreated backwards toward the stairs. When it was safe, he turned his back and took the steps two at a time to escape. *They knew!*

In his room, he considered marching back down there and telling his parents it was his life and they had to stay out of it. He wanted to tell Mr. and Mrs. Alperstein to go to hell and take their snitch of a son with them. Anger boiled his blood the longer he stewed over what was happening downstairs. They had no right to treat him like a child. They were discussing his life as if he had no say in the matter.

How could he have been so careless and gotten caught? How much trouble would Spiro be in? He should go to the top of the stairwell and eavesdrop on the conversation. At least he would be in a better position to fight when his parents approached him about it.

He eased the door open and stopped as soon as it creaked. His parents' voices echoed all the way up the staircase. They were in the midst of one of their great shouting matches where nobody won. He listened for a few minutes, listening to see if the argument was about him. Once he confirmed it was, he closed the door and stepped lightly to the window.

The lights in the apartment above the garage were out. *Where are they?* It wasn't normal for them to be gone all day. Something wasn't right; he could feel it. Noah returned to his bed and collapsed. Sick to his stomach again, he rolled onto his side and curled into a ball.

By morning, between nothing in his stomach and a lack of sleep, Noah struggled to rise from the bed. He had to find Spiro.

If his dad wanted to fight, he would give him one. Spiro was worth it. It didn't matter that in a few weeks he would be in school and Spiro would be on the other side of the world, but his dad would not be the one who took this away from him.

He threw on his swim trunks and a tee shirt and headed downstairs. In the dining room, he found his parents sitting at the table with his grandmother. In silence, they sat as if someone had died.

His mother looked up from her bagel topped with cream cheese and a paper-thin slice of briny lox, red onion, and a slice of tomato. "Good morning." There was no emotion to her face.

Noah took the corner seat between his mother and his dad. "And what's good about it?" Noah aloofly replied.

His father never looked up as he sipped his coffee, keeping his face behind his newspaper. Noah was okay with him not making eye contact. He wasn't ready to talk to him, either. He poured himself a cup of coffee, picked out a cinnamon raisin bagel, and coated it with cream cheese.

"That's too much cream cheese. It will upset your stomach." His mother's tone was harsh.

Giving her the stink eye, Noah picked up his bagel and held it in front of his mouth. "I'm an adult. I know how much cream cheese to put on a bagel, but thank you."

"Tone... watch your tone, young man!" A stern voice came over the top of the newspaper.

That's fine. There were other ways he could convey his mood. He heaped two big spoonsful of diced fruit on his plate, making sure he slammed the spoon hard enough on his plate to communicate his fury.

They sat in silence as the tension in the air loomed over the table. He ate half his breakfast before giving up. Tired of the bullshit tension, Noah couldn't take sitting in their presence a minute longer. "I'm going for a walk!" He pushed away from the table and was about to exit the room when his father spoke.

"Pack your stuff. You'll be returning to the city this evening with your mother. I'll stay behind for a few days and close up the house." The tone of his voice was firm and left no room for a debate. Noah was very familiar with this tone, and it scared him.

Noah stomped out as his father's words replayed repeatedly in his head. *Why would his father stay behind? Close up the house... that's a month earlier than usual.*

Noah jumped from the porch to the ground and sprinted toward the apartment above the barn. He took the stairs three at a time as he bolted up the steps. "Spiro! Spiro!" He called, the panic revealing itself as he climbed the steps.

The door was unlocked. He knocked but didn't wait for an invitation as he swung the door open. "*Spiro! Spiro!*" He was in panic mode; real time was playing out on fast forward. "*Spiro?*" Noah realized that the tiny apartment was empty.

On the opposite side of the room was an open closet, empty hangers on the wooden rod. He rushed into the sparsely furnished bedroom and stared at the old twin bed in the corner. The bed was made. The room was immaculate, like no one had been there, at least not in the last decade. Where had they gone? Had his father sent them somewhere?

Noah ran from the apartment down to the barn. He crashed through the doors, hoping they were there. The barn was dark inside, but he didn't need any light to know they weren't there.

He scurried back to the corner where Spiro had set up his art supplies. Paint cans, easels, and paintings sat undisturbed. Noah fell to his knees in front of the paintings. Spiro was gone, and there was nothing he could do. Had he lost Spiro?

In a fit of anger that exploded inside of him, he grabbed the large painting on the easel that was covered by a sheet. He was about to slam it to the ground, but something forced him to stop and remove the sheet from it.

He studied the painting that he hadn't seen before. His eyes filled with tears, seeing the painting of the fishing boats docked along the long pier. Spiro had painted many of them, all from different viewpoints. How had he not seen this one?

They had spent the summer talking about his village, the town square, and this dock he fished from. Noah knew it well, as if he'd been there. He stared at the old wooden dock. This was where Spiro learned to clean fish and pack them in ice to be delivered to vendors. Behind him, the door creaked open, followed by footsteps. He rose to his feet. Whoever it was, they couldn't see the paintings. They were all he had left of Spiro, and it wasn't enough.

He moved away from the paintings and to the other side of the car as his father appeared. "What are you doing in here?" His father's gruff voice exemplified his mood.

"Nothing!" Suppressed rage began to boil at the very sight of his father. He knew his dad was responsible for Spiro being gone. He was a hundred percent sure of it. Just like he was a thousand percent sure that his father would never forgive him in this lifetime for the death of Nathanael.

Noah attempted to storm by his father, trying to lead him further from the paintings.

His father grabbed him by his arm, stopping him. "I will not have a queer for a son!"

"That's fine!" Noah stared into the fiery eyes of his father. With all his strength, Noah ripped his arm loose from his father's grip and stood his ground for the first time in his life.

The rage in his father's eyes, as if taunting Noah, was telling Noah to come for him: *Come on! Do it!* The thunder in his father's eyes said he was going to do what he'd been wanting to do to Noah for four years— if Noah dared.

Noah looked down at his own clenched fists. He wouldn't survive his father. It would be over in less than a second. His father would only be doing what was supposed to have happened to him, not Nathanael.

Anger consumed Noah as the two stood there, looking at the other. *Queer. Fag. Homo. Killer. Sissy. Wimp.* His father was right about it all. He was all those things; he was even too weak to kill himself. His hands unclenched and dropped to his side.

His father hissed, seeing he wouldn't get his way. No, not because

Noah was too weak, but because he'd rather jump in front of a bus and go out like his brother than to give his Goddamned father anything.

Noah knew they'd crossed a line they could never come back from. Each of their deepest, darkest secrets had come to light. He turned his back on his father and drew a breath. He was done. With his head lowered, he watched his feet step one after the other as he walked from the barn. He was still alive, yet his life was over.

CHAPTER ELEVEN
Present Day

Preparing to land, Noah pushed the tiny serving tray on the small twin-engine plane against the back of the seat in front of him. A nervousness grew in his stomach, knowing this was it.

Nightfall covered the one-hour flight over the Aegean Sea. Noah was on the last flight out of Athens to the island of Lemnos. He had arrived in Athens early this morning from New York via London, but because of a holdup in customs, he'd missed the earlier flight that would have gotten him onto the island by late morning.

Twelve years in the making, this trip was his best friend and roommate Rodney's impulsive idea. Rodney once told him that not even a pregnant nun who miscarried the second coming of Christ could grieve as long as Noah had over a summer love affair.

But Spiro wasn't just a summer's love affair. Noah was sure he hadn't concocted their feelings into something bigger than what it was. Spiro had said that he loved him. There was no doubt in Noah's mind that he loved Spiro. A bond was created that summer, left intact because of the lack of closure. Without permission, Spiro had taken so much of his heart when he left that day. He'd left Noah incapable of loving another man as deeply as he'd loved that summer. It was a love impossible to get over or to move on from.

It was after Noah's most recent breakup with his latest boyfriend, Mark, the serial cheater, that plunged Noah deep into his latest round of *what ifs* regarding Spiro.

Over the years, Noah had spent countless hours researching Greek islands and searching social media sites hoping to find the vanished man who stole his heart so many years ago. What he was searching for, Noah wasn't sure, other than validation it was real.

Two nights ago, after two bottles of wine, Rodney had enough and convinced Noah to go do it, and within an hour Noah used a credit card to book a flight leaving J.F.K. airport in six hours. And now he was here, *doing it*. Looking for a lost love embedded in his heart so intensely, it was as if it happened yesterday.

When the plane touched down on the tarmac, he was jolted back into reality as the aircraft swayed and thrust against its own propulsion to slow down and stop. Seemingly to slow down, the plane vibrated as the sound of air rushing by roared through the cabin. Noah pushed back in his seat as he gripped the armrests. He tried to push the thought from his head that it would suck to come all this way just to crash and die on the runway.

At thirty years old, Noah made his living designing and maintaining websites. Thanks to his grandmother, his single greatest asset was his two-bedroom apartment in Greenwich Village that he purchased with his inheritance. Although he'd used the bulk of the money to buy his apartment, he held on to some of it just in case of a rainy day. Over the years, he never touched the account, not even the interest it was drawing. He didn't need it. He was doing just fine living pay check to pay check like everyone else. With an eccentric drag queen as a roommate, Noah's day-to-day excitement and entertainment was living through the adventures of Rodney.

With the propellers on the small plane stopped, the co-pilot pulled back the curtain and crawled out from the tiny cockpit. "Welcome to Lemnos!" He affirmed in English, "We need to wait for the ground crew to free us, and I'll have you on your way."

In the dimly lit cabin, the modern-day Adonis who doubled as their co-pilot switched to Greek, presumingly repeating what he had said in English to the nine passengers on board.

As if understanding Greek, Noah nodded as he examined the beautiful bone structure in the co-pilot's jawline. The thick five o'clock shadow and lustrous dark eyebrows made his mesmerizing brown eyes sparkle as they moved from passenger to passenger as he spoke.

Noah could bed men that gorgeous, but he hadn't been successful at getting them to stay. A walking skeleton, Noah struggled to keep his weight up to his current hundred and forty pounds. At five eleven, he weighed the same as when he was eighteen years old.

Plagued with digestive issues for years, it was right before his college finals at the end of his first semester at Harvard that he suffered one of the worst episodes in his life. He'd been enjoying his freedom away from home, eating an endless array of pizza, French fries, potato chips, and soda, which sent his stomach issues into overdrive. Rushed to the hospital via ambulance, he was near death.

It took months to get the inflammation and sores in his intestines and rectum to heal. After months of testing, he was diagnosed with IBS— *Irritable Bowel Syndrome.* Controlled now by a clean diet and medication, there was little he could do about adding weight.

When the door of the aircraft opened, the oppressively muggy cabin air was replaced with a mixture of jet fuel fumes and warm air. Glad to be free of the plane, inside the small, virtually deserted airport terminal, he was met again with a stale, stifling lack of air.

Noah saw what he was looking for, the sign in English that read *Luggage;* under it were several Greek letters. He was thankful that the tiny island, population sixteen thousand, was English friendly. He moved closer toward the small luggage conveyor belt and waited for his luggage. While waiting, he removed his phone to text Rodney. He glanced at the time on his phone, seeing that it was almost ten o'clock. He calculated the time difference between New York and Greece. New Yorkers were seven hours behind, so it was still early back in the States.

I made it. Just landed on Lemnos— He hit send.

Within seconds, Rodney replied. *Super. Have fun, find Mr. Right, or at least get laid!*

Noah shook his head at his roommate's reply. Rodney, born in Dubai but raised in upper Manhattan, was a cross between the eccentric Phyllis Diller and Andrew Dice Clay. An Emirati drag queen of super wealth and equal energy, Rodney was also his best friend.

With the conveyor belt at a standstill, Noah pulled up the photos on his phone he'd taken of Spiro's paintings before he left. It was Christmas break during his first year of college that he drove back up to the lake house to retrieve the paintings. He hadn't been to the house since he lost Spiro earlier that summer. They were still in the barn, tucked behind a dresser, just as he hid them. He took them to a storage facility and rented a small storage unit to hide them.

Noah stared at the row of boats docked in their wooden slips in the pictures. He wondered if it was the same dock they had flown over right before touching down onto the airstrip.

Would it be that easy? To walk to the dock and find Spiro working?

Perhaps cleaning fish from the morning catch? Would Spiro's elation at seeing him show on his face? Like in the movies, would Spiro drop whatever he was doing and run to him from the far end of the dock? Would they fly into each other's arms as onlookers smiled and clapped? Noah smiled at the image of the two of them reuniting with fireworks in the sky.

A bell rang, and the conveyor belt began moving. Sure that his one piece of luggage would be the last to pop up, Noah was surprised to see his pricy Italian bag among the first pieces to surface. The bag was a birthday present from his latest ex, Mark—an expensive gift that he later discovered was charged to his own Visa card.

After retrieving his bag, Noah exited the airport. Outside, he looked around for a cab to take him to the coastal village of Myrina, where the main shipping port was located. In everything he had studied on the internet about the village, he was sure Myrina was the same village that was in so many of Spiro's paintings.

The village of Myrina was the only village on the island that had a pier inside a large cove. It was where most of the large fishing boats docked and where the large ferries from the mainland arrived. It was the center of the village where everything was happening, like Spiro talked about. Pictures on the internet even showed that this island had the ruins of a castle. Spiro had talked about the ruins and hiking to them. They flew over the lit-up ruins of the Byzantine castle atop the mountain during their descent.

Noah was confident he was in the right place. Everything Spiro had once said about the island was here, on Lemnos. In all his internet searching, the one thing he couldn't find was Spiro. How could someone today not have any kind of an internet footprint? Of course, there were a million people with the name Spiro in Greece. How they talked so much about the island and Noah never got the name of the actual village that Spiro lived in or his last name was baffling. Maybe he had and at the time had no idea how important that information would be later.

Leaned against a beat-up little cab, a tiny, elderly Greek man stood scrolling on his phone. There was no breeze, causing the warm night air to press against Noah's skin.

"Excuse me... English?" Noah asked as he approached the car.

"Yes! Yes." The cab driver tucked his phone into his pocket as he opened the back door for him. "Get in. I take you where you want to go."

Noah was about to step into the cab when the young Adonis co-pilot, rolling his black flight crew bag behind him, caught his eye. A tiny grin brushed across the co-pilot's face as his brows raised. Noah's gaydar sounded; he knew that smile.

No longer the geeky nerd that he was as a teenager, other than being underweight, he thought of himself as a solid seven. Noah returned the smile before stepping into the cab. It felt good that he could attract someone as good looking as the Greek co-pilot. Perhaps, six months ago, another place, he might have taken the Adonis up on his offer to engage, but not anymore.

Noah stared out the window into the dark landscape as the cab drove down toward the coastal village of Myrina. Absent of any plant life, the terrain was stark and barren. He closed the air conditioning vents dispensing warm air and lowered the window to get comfortable.

"Are you from the States?" The cabbie shouted over the roar of the engine.

"Yes, New York," Noah answered. The cabbie's voice made him think of Eros. He suddenly pictured him and Spiro sitting on the dock eating lunch. He could hear Eros calling for Spiro. It was the same voice as the cabbie's. A low, pleasant hum warmed Noah's blood.

"I was once there in seventy-four. Nevada. I loved your country, but no work for me. I had to return to feed my family. I was born here. Right here. This is the most beautiful place on earth. A gift from the gods. How long are you staying?"

Due to the cabbie's broken English, Noah only made out bits and pieces of what he was saying, but pieced together enough to understand most of it. "Not sure," he mumbled. He had booked his room for three weeks, but if he found Spiro, who knew? He could always get a cheaper room and stretch his savings a little longer. The beauty of being a web designer was that he could continue working from the island.

"Ahh, not long enough, four, five weeks, and then you will be a changed man. Relaxed—new again." As they neared the coast, the moon lit up the sapphire blue ocean on the horizon. Half listening, Noah nodded in agreement as he stared out to sea.

They rounded a bend in the road and then dropped down the hill into the tiny, touristy village of Myrina. Noah took in a breath and exhaled as he looked around the dark and narrow streets. He booked his hotel because of its proximity to the pier. On the internet, the hotel was about a mile away, on the opposite end of the cove that the village wrapped around.

Noah paid his cab fare and grabbed his luggage from the seat of the car. "Thank you."

Exhausted from two days of traveling, Noah trudged into the small lobby of the two-story hotel. It seemed much larger on the internet. Behind the front desk was an older, olive-skinned woman with beautiful gray hair. "Good evening. Welcome to the Blue Oceania Seaside Resort."

"Hi, I'm Noah Rothenberg. I booked my reservations online." Without waiting for her to ask, Noah placed his passport and the credit card he used to book the reservation on the counter.

"Thank you." She took his passport and returned to her monitor. After several minutes of clicking and murmuring, he was booked into the hotel. She placed a map of the hotel on the counter in front of him. "Our bungalows are located on the back side of the resort, facing the ocean." She pointed to the doors behind him. "Through the doors, follow the pathway." She signaled a young boy standing at the back doors to come to her. "He will take you."

In Greek, she spoke to the young boy, who took Noah's bag from him. The young boy motioned for Noah to follow him. The boy escorted him through the lobby and out to the back of the property.

"Americano?" The boy asked as he weaved down the lit wooden planks toward a row of bungalows about one hundred yards off the main hotel.

"Yes, from New York."

"Ahh, New York." His smile suggested he knew of New York.

They passed several bungalows, softly lit and discreetly tucked amongst the vegetation. Quiet and tranquil, the entire hotel appeared to have retired for the evening. The sound of the ocean breaking as it swept up the beach caused Noah's shoulders to relax for the first time all day. He inhaled a breath of the cool, salty ocean breeze brushing across his face.

The young boy opened his room, then entered and turned on a light before gesturing for Noah to enter. Noah stepped in, immediately feeling the hot air trapped in the room.

He and the boy worked together, turning on lights and opening windows, bringing the minimalist two-room bungalow to life. The quaint bungalow was done in white, island-style furnishings with blue accents.

The young boy slid the glass door open to a small veranda with views of the ocean. "With the door open, you'll get a breeze. It will cool down fast. You can sleep with the door open. It's safe." Fresh air flowed into the room as the boy moved into the other room. "Sir, your bedroom and bathroom are in here."

Noah followed the boy into the bedroom. It was half the size of the front room, with one double bed in the middle of the room. On one wall was a door he presumed led to the bathroom.

The boy stood, smiling at Noah.

Oh, he's waiting for a tip. Noah opened his wallet and saw that he had given the cabbie what few euros he had. All he had was American dollars. He handed the boy a twenty, which made the boy grin.

"Thank you, Sir." He looked around as if he should have done more to deserve such a tip. "Can I get you anything else?"

"No, but thank you." Noah excused the boy and then shut the sliding glass door. *New Yorkers don't sleep with their doors open.*

After brushing his teeth, Noah crawled into bed and closed his eyes, bringing Spiro in close to him. He said good night to Spiro aloud, something he started doing a month ago.

****

A knock on the door jolted Noah awake. Baffled about who could be knocking in the middle of the night, what with two days of traveling, the time change, and extreme jet lag, he thought he was dreaming. A second knock at the door rattled him fully awake, confirming that not only was it a real knock, but it also was morning. "Yes! Hold on!"

Naked on top of the thin white sheets, Noah scrambled into the other room to get to the door before whoever it was came in. He used the top sheet as a robe as he took several giant steps across both rooms, reaching the door as it opened.

"Housekeeping, Sir." A young Greek woman cracked the door and peeked inside.

"Can you come back? In about an hour?" Noah stopped the door from opening fully and used it as a shield to hide behind.

"Yes. I come back. So sorry," the lady apologized.

After closing the door, Noah dragged his feet back into his bedroom. It was as if he'd been drugged. He could barely hold his eyes open. He

115

grabbed his phone off the nightstand and saw it was eight a.m. Being naked in front of a young woman was not how he envisioned this day starting.

After a shower, Noah dressed and stepped from his bungalow, where the cool morning island air hit him. Sometime during the middle of the night, he'd realized that the tiny wall AC unit in the front room of the bungalow wasn't strong enough for the cool air to reach the back bedroom. Maybe he should reconsider having at least one window open for air flow at night.

The entire coastline was virtually empty, with less than a handful of people strolling about. It was by far the cleanest and most tranquil seashore he'd ever seen. He stopped to snap a picture of the charcoal-colored sand and bright blue coral water with his phone. Maybe it was too early for beachgoers.

He was sure Rodney had experienced places this enchanting, but he wanted to share it with his best friend anyway. With a few swipes on his phone, the picture was sent to Rodney with a one-word text—*Paradise.*

Continuing up the path, the luscious, wide range of greenery and flowers that flanked the wooden pathway to the main lobby was like something from the New York Botanical Garden. Last night, the grandeur of the property had been lost on how tired he was. From everything he had read in his traveler's atlas, the tourist season had ended several weeks ago, but there was still another month of dry eighty-degree weather in store for the island.

Noah made his way out to the narrow cobblestone street in front of the hotel. He was eager to start the hunt for Spiro. A quiver ran up his spine; he couldn't believe he was here, halfway around the world, doing the thing he'd dreamt about doing for years.

Since the hotel was on the edge of town, there were two ways to walk to the pier: the straight path along the beach or through town, following the narrow streets. He eliminated the beach route. If Spiro was still painting, there was a chance he would see his work hanging in a shop somewhere.

At a brisk pace, he headed up the street toward the labyrinth of narrow streets that, according to the internet, weaved through the village and out to the fishing pier.

The sun warmed the back of his neck as he made his way closer to the main section of town. The streets had a mixture of small stores and what he assumed were apartments on the second story. It was a little surreal seeing all this in person. With the aid of the internet, he'd taken this exact walk more than a dozen times on his computer, and now he was here, in Greece—to find Spiro.

The village was quieter than he imagined. A few people were out strolling and shopping, and several shopkeepers were busy sweeping their shopfronts. Some appeared to be opening for the day as displays and picture boards were still being set out. *Where was everyone?* Although he knew the season was over, Noah hadn't expected to find the island so deserted.

He turned off the main street and entered an alley of clustered buildings connected to one another. What he assumed to be street names were painted in blue on the buildings that occupied a corner. He stopped and took several pictures for Rodney. *Rodney would love this place.*

The alleyways twisted between white-walled buildings: little boutiques, jewelry stores, bars, restaurants, art galleries, and every other shop he could imagine. It didn't take long to realize that most of the souvenir shops shared the same merchandise and repeated themselves every couple of blocks.

Scooters were parked every few feet, which he'd read was the locals' main mode of transportation. There was no way of getting a car down these narrow alleys. Small churches were scattered among the shops. When he poked his head inside one of the little chapels, he was surprised to see it was no bigger than a bedroom and had no seating. His eyes wandered beyond the windows into the shops, hoping to find Spiro. Would it be that easy?

Lost, he had to stop several times and inquire with a shopkeeper if he was still going the right way toward the port. The younger the shopkeeper, the more likely he spoke English back to him. Otherwise, they pointed.

Just before reaching the conclusion he would never find his way out of the complex maze, he came to the port. Freed from the maze, the view opened up to a cement pier and the breathtaking Aegean Sea. A salty breeze rushed into his nose, sending a blend of briny sea air, fish, and cigarette smoke to his brain. Everybody around here seemed to smoke.

The swish of the surf drew his eye to the hundreds of boats tied up along the dock. The brightly painted array of boats harmoniously moved up and down with each swell as the waves knocked their hulls around.

Here and there, Noah saw a few portly old men sitting around drinking their coffee, smoking cigarettes, and playing checkers.

He crossed to the other side of the cement pier, stopping at the edge. Tiny fish darted below the oil-soaked surface of the water. Most of the boats were empty, except for a couple. The men on those boats paid him no mind as he considered each of them, eliminating the possibility they were Spiro.

The painting he had that Spiro had created years ago was nothing like this pier. His was an old wooden dock with a mixture of canoes, sailboats, and fishing boats with a backdrop of the sun setting on the water. He'd read that the current pier had been built five years ago to accommodate the larger, faster ferries that shuttled people between the islands and the mainland.

With the old wooden dock gone, Noah was still sure he was in the right place. From almost anywhere on the island, he could see the ruins of the Byzantine castle high on the mountain, the highest point on the island. He remembered he and Spiro talking about a castle up on a hill. His pulse raced, feeling how close he was to being reunited with his lost love.

In the distance, one of the large ferries headed to sea. He again pulled his phone out and took more pictures, capturing the boat in the morning light. The tranquility of the island during this early morning reminded him of the lake house.

He crossed back to the other side of the pier and moseyed along the souvenir shops that lined the waterfront. Stores filled with tee shirts and postcards, mixed with sidewalk cafes and bakeries, the pier was exactly like the photos on the internet. The smell of coffee and chocolate, neither of which was on his diet, wafted in the air as he strolled along the pier.

In and out of the stores that were open, he checked out the few young males that were working, hoping one would be Spiro. Would he recognize Spiro? Would he look the same as once upon a time? *Would Spiro's eyes see me as they once did?*

When Noah arrived at the end of the port, the realization set in how small this village was. He turned to reinvestigate the sequence of shops in reverse order. There was a gift shop he wanted to revisit. Although he wasn't looking for gifts, he'd seen a tee shirt in the window that made him laugh. He wanted to get it for Rodney.

The bell above the door rang, broadcasting his entrance into the shop. *Who was it alerting?* he wondered, as the shop was empty.

Expecting someone to emerge from the back any second, Noah browsed through the first rack of tee shirts, amused at the funny comments on them. Most of the tee shirts he'd seen before, but there were a couple that made him laugh out loud. At least five minutes had passed before the bell above the door sounded again. A young kid hurried in and brushed past him.

"Hel-lo." The skinny kid laid his phone on the counter as he positioned himself behind the register. Dark, thick hair tousled down in front of the kid's eyes. His tight jawline and narrow neck was that of a twenty-year-old. It was the kid's accent, delivered in a strong, husky voice, that resembled his Spiro.

"Hello." Noah's gaze slowed over the boy, seizing the opportunity in the greeting to take him in. He was no older than he and Spiro were once upon a time.

"May I help you with something?" The kid gave little pause before turning his attention to his phone on the counter.

"No... I'm just looking." Noah's eyes swept over the unsuspecting soul whose only concern was what was on his phone screen. Of course, it wasn't Spiro: He knew this as a rush of adrenaline swept through his body, causing his throat to thicken and dry.

He returned to the tee shirts, flipping through several, all of whose words were now a blur. The similarities in the kid's voice and Spiro's had unnerved him. "Thank you." Without waiting for a response, Noah rushed from the shop.

Outside, Noah relished the fresh air as it filled his lungs. His breathing slowing to normal as he scanned up the street, recognizing how real all of this was. He and Spiro: They were inevitable. Finding Spiro dominated his attention more than any of the shops as he walked the block back to where he began.

From where he was standing, far in the distance, his bungalow was visible on the other side of the cove. He could walk to it and be there in half the time it took to go back through the village. But he wasn't ready to head back to his room. He hadn't come seven thousand miles to sit in a room by himself.

He would take the narrow village streets again, choosing different streets and alleys to explore more of the old village. Back inside the complicated cobblestone maze of streets, the area he'd wandered into appeared more upscale than the other streets and shops on the pier. A mixture of ivy and bright pink bougainvillea dressed the walls and trellises above his head every so many stores. There was an air of lavishness and pretentiousness that didn't exist on the other streets. Diamond shops replaced picture frames and snow globes, and high-end women's apparel draped the mannequins instead of tee shirts and hoodies.

He stopped in front of a small shop that seemed to be a restaurant. Three small wrought-iron bistro tables sat in front of a large-paned window. The name *Daphne's* was painted in big, white letters on the window. The black and white awnings over the door and the window made him think it was likely French, as opposed to Greek.

More curious than hungry, he read the specials written on the chalkboard placed near the entrance. The entrees sounded intriguing enough to draw him in. Inside, the cafe was empty, which was no surprise.

"Hello. Welcome to Daphne's. Have a seat anywhere." A woman slightly older than him smiled at him as she emptied a tray of pastries into the glass display counter.

He settled on the table beside the window.

Within minutes, the woman arrived at his table. "Good morning," she said as she handed him an oversized laminated menu.

"Good morning." Noah smiled up at her. Dark brown hair pulled straight back and into a single ponytail, the woman's full apron covered her skirt and blouse. He hadn't seen someone wearing a full apron since his grandmother. *Was she Daphne?*

"Just you?"

"Yes."

"Breakfast or lunch?"

Noah looked at the time on his phone. It was just a little after ten o'clock. "Oh, I can get lunch this early?"

She shrugged. "It's not so early."

"I think lunch." He appreciated the option between breakfast and lunch. This gave him more possibilities, since he was unsure exactly what would be on the menu that he could eat.

The woman said something over her shoulder in another language to an old man sitting on a stool behind the counter.

"Do you know what you'll like or need a minute to decide?"

"A minute, please." Noah glanced down at the menu as she walked away. The entrees on the menu were printed in Greek, followed by English. One side had an array of breakfast choices, and the other side had soups, salads, and sandwiches. He skimmed each item long enough to eliminate it as a choice for one reason or another.

Noah looked up just as the little old man approached his table with a small basket of bread. He never made eye contact with Noah and retreated.

Noah and his doctor had argued for years whether his food choices aggravated his IBS and contributed to his stomach issues. At home, he had his dietary selections down to a science. He wasn't a breakfast eater, so his first meal was generally a sandwich on gluten-free white bread or lunch meat and gluten-free crackers for lunch. For dinner, he could get away with being a little more diverse if he stayed away from dairy, fatty, or fried foods.

Noah hadn't considered food choices when Rodney had talked him into this trip. This menu was his first challenge. By the time she returned, he'd settled on the *avgolemono*, a chicken soup with egg and lemon juice mixed with broth.

"I think I'll have the av-gole-mono?"

"The avgolemono, yes, my favorite. And to drink?"

"Water."

"Bottled or tap?"

"Bottled." Ordinally, he wouldn't pay for bottled water, but if he didn't know the source of the water, to avoid further stomach issues, he chose bottled.

While he waited for his lunch, he pulled out his phone and snapped several pictures of the inside of the café. He attached them and several of the port and texted them to Rodney—*No luck yet but about to have my first Greek lunch.*

Rodney replied. *Ain't no people in the pics???*

Right? Noah laughed that Rodney had also picked up on the lack of people. He tucked his phone away when he saw the woman returning with a large bowl.

She sat the bowl of soup in front of him. "I'll be right back with your water." She returned in less than a minute with a glass liter bottle of Pellegrino. She poured half the water into a glass and sat the bottle on the table.

"Where's everyone?" Noah's eyes fell to the iceless glass of water.

"Who?" Her brows narrowed.

"Everyone. People. There's no one around this morning."

Her face brightened. "Ah... The season is over. They're all gone."

"But, like, the people who live here, on the island. Where are they?"

She shrugged as she gave him a warm smile. "Perhaps work or maybe school."

"Oh." *Everyone?* The island was a stark contrast from New York. He'd read that, during the off season, Myrina, the island's capital city, had a population that fell to a mere six thousand. All the other villages were smaller, some with only a few hundred.

"Are you visiting?" She asked.

"Kind of. I'm sort of looking for someone."

"Someone is missing?" She asked.

"Well, not missing." Noah blushed. "I guess he could be missing. I met him years ago in New York. I think this is the island he said he was from. His name is Spiro." Noah threw the name out, hoping he would see a reaction. *She might know him. Wouldn't that be funny if he worked for her and was in the back room?* He laughed under his breath.

Her face contorted as if thinking. "Spiro... Dr. Spiro Fotopoulos from Thanos?" Her head cocked to one side.

"Who?" Noah tried to repeat to himself what she said to commit it to memory.

"He and his wife moved to the mainland last year."

He was certain she wasn't talking about his Spiro. *It was possible that he could be married... but a doctor?* It didn't seem likely, but it was a reminder of how little he knew about this person. "He had an uncle that lived in America. His uncle's name was Eros."

"Pappas?" She repeated.

He didn't understand what she'd just said. Her accent made the name sound different. "I don't know." He nodded from embarrassment.

"In the village of Kalliopi, there is a Spiro Pappas. He's an old man."

Noah's head shook. "No. he would be around our age. Tall, nicely built, black hair, greenish brown eyes." He stopped, realizing that not only was he describing half the men on the island, but he was also describing what Spiro looked like years ago.

"I'm afraid that there are many Spiros." She shrugged. "Have you been on the pier? Many men work the boats. Perhaps he's there."

Noah pointed to the direction of the pier. "The pier where the ferry comes in?"

"Ah, yes." She smiled. "In the morning, there's lots of fish and shellfish you can see as well. The pier is busy in the morning."

He didn't see Spiro as a fisherman, either, but it had been years. He remembered he said his dad had a small fishing boat. *Maybe he followed in his dad's footsteps. Anything is possible.* Another question came to him. "Do many locals live here in Myrina, or do they live somewhere else, like one of the other towns around?" He'd already planned on checking out the other villages, checking them off until he found him, but perhaps she could help narrow his search faster.

"You might want to visit Kalliopi, Panagia, or maybe Kavirio. Many locals live there."

"Okay, I will. Thank you." He repeated the villages in his head, hoping to remember their names.

After the server left him to his lunch, Noah checked his phone one last time to ensure Rodney hadn't sent another text. He hadn't realized he was hungry until he swallowed his first bite. The tart, lemony broth tickled his taste buds. From the backroom, the old man emerged and began sweeping the floor in the dining room. The old guy swept around the chairs without moving any of them.

The woman re-emerged from the kitchen and, after a brief dialogue between her and the old man, he shuffled into the back room. With his entertainment now gone, Noah sipped his soup. His entertainment now relied on the few people strolling up and down the narrow street.

Within a couple of minutes, the old man and a much younger guy emerged from the back, carrying out a large wooden credenza. *Father and son?* Noah watched as they shuffled across the floor with the large piece of furniture. When they made it to the far corner of the dining room, they pushed the credenza against the wall.

"Je viens litteralement de le realizer ici par moi-meme!" Agitation in the young man's face revealed more than whatever he said. The old guy dismissively waved him off before wobbling away.

Using his one year of French from the tenth grade, Noah identified a couple of the words in their banter as French, which surprised him.

The young man scoffed as he turned toward Noah, their eyes meeting. His face softened as he made his way over to the table. "Hel-lo." He took the bottle of water and poured the remaining water into Noah's glass. "Can I get you more wa-ter?"

"No, I'm good." Noah broke eye contact. The waiter's cinnamon eyes, matched with his sexy accent, intimidated Noah. "I'll take the check, though." *Was everybody on this damn island molded from a Greek god?*

"Is everything okay?" The waiter asked. Dressed in tight black jeans and a white dress shirt, the waiter's sleeves were folded back, exposing his wrists. As he cleared the empty bowl from the table, Noah eyed his black tattoo of a sinister poison bottle labeled with a skull and crossbones on the back of his wrist.

"Yes, it was delicious." Hesitantly, Noah peered up at him. Yes, he was gorgeous. Around the same age as Noah, his dark thick brows narrowed almost into one against his olive complexion. *Okay, saying he was simply gorgeous was a discredit to him.*

Noah was attracted to darker-skinned men, but he preferred them thicker than this guy. Skinny or lean rarely attracted him. It was like he was having sex with himself.

The muscles around the waiter's mouth loosened; his alluring stare lingered a second or two before he excused himself and retreated to the kitchen.

A few minutes later, the woman returned and placed his bill on the edge of the table. "Thank you."

"Thank you." Noah inspected the bill: ten euros and sixty-four cents. "Do you take American money?"

"Yes." The woman pulled up the bill and stared at it. "That would be twelve American dollars." She placed the bill back on the table.

"Thank you." If he remembered that ten euros was twelve dollars, it would make future calculations easier. He liked that, for twelve bucks, he had a phenomenal lunch.

Back on the cobblestone streets, his plan was to find Spiro as he strode through the narrow alleys toward his hotel. As he curved around several streets, the shops seemed familiar. When he saw that he was approaching Daphne's again, he realized that he had walked in a large circle. He'd had years to devise a plan, and here he was, going in circles. How had Rodney talked him into such a stupid idea?

Arriving at the hotel, Noah again took in the beauty of the small boutique hotel as he crossed through the lobby and made his way out back to his ocean-front bungalow. The soothing swish of the surf caused him to take in a big breath of air and exhale slowly. No, this wasn't a stupid idea at all. He was here for love, and this place was about as romantic as you could get. The thought of sharing it with Spiro sent a rush of adrenaline throughout his body. Providing Spiro didn't have some swanky villa with grander views of the ocean, his cute little bungalow might just be perfect.

CHAPTER TWELVE

Full throttle, down the last stretch of the narrow two-lane highway on the island of Lemnos, Spiro steered his old, ratty motorbike with one hand as he used his other to push his Ray-Bans closer to his eyes. This morning, Spiro rode shirtless and without his helmet. The joy in riding without a shirt and helmet was exhilarating and something he rarely did during the high season with all the tourists gawking at him.

His tee shirt waved in the wind from his back pocket. There was nothing like the wind hitting his face and the sun on his back as he zipped around the last section of the curvy mountain road that lay between the village of Myrina and his village, Katalako. With a view of the vibrant blue Aegean Sea in front of him, the small coastal village of Myrina lay at the base of the mountain.

He'd gotten out of the house late this morning and had pushed the bike as hard as it would go, covering the eleven kilometers in record time. Spiro and his motorbike had traveled the main highway that stretched from one side of the island to the other since he was a little boy. He slowed his bike as he entered the outskirts of Myrina. He had one stop at the pharmacy before going to work.

A year ago, the only pharmacy in the village of Katalako had closed its doors forever. The Myrina pharmacy was now the closest drugstore to their home. In his lifetime, he'd seen a sizable number of stores close in Katalako as the village of Myrina continued to grow due to its modest tourism.

The village of Katalako, which meant in Greek, 'something put in a pit', was surrounded by hills and was untouched by tourism due to its being so far inland. With a population of a hundred people, his village still followed a traditional way of life. The island of Lemnos offered tourists something different from the more popular islands like Santorini, Crete, or Mykonos. The island of Lemnos was like going through a time warp machine, undisturbed for centuries. A well-preserved culture was still alive, but dwindling with each passing year.

Lemnos offered pristine beaches that were quieter, hotels that were cheaper, and a sense of tradition in every meal, all for a fraction of what it cost to visit the other islands.

Spiro beeped his horn, seeing his friend Mateo, standing outside the new Blue Oceania Seaside Resort. Mateo was wearing his black-and-white houndstooth pattern pants and white double-breasted chef's jacket, obviously heading in to work. He was perhaps one of the best chefs on the island, having learned everything he knew from his mother and grandmother. The dolmades he made last week for movie night were out of this world.

In the center of town, Spiro pulled up in front of the pharmacy. He parked his motorbike on the sidewalk and debated if he should put his shirt on before going inside. *Nah, it's too nice of a day, and it's only Dominic inside, anyway.*

Inside the tiny pharmacy, he snagged the Greek version of a Kit Kat bar off the shelf as he headed toward the back counter.

"Hey, Spiro." Dominic waved from behind the counter.

"What's up, Doc?" He and Dominic had been friends as long as either could walk. Dominic was one of those pharmacists who took their Doctor of Pharmacy degree in the literal sense. Strait-laced-looking, leaning more toward the nerd side, Dominic was part of his and Mateo's Saturday night movie group.

"I have your mother's prescription ready. It came in last night on the last ferry."

Spiro leaned on the counter, dismissing Dominic's lingering stare at his bare chest. "Just in time. She has some of the Baclofen left, but it doesn't control her spasms as well as the Valium."

Spiro picked the bottle up from the counter and read the label, ensuring it contained the right meds. He handed the bottle back to Dominic.

"Are you going to Pride this weekend?" Dominic asked as he rang up just the prescription.

"Nah, I can't. The owners of the gallery are coming, and I have to help Nina get the place cleaned up." As much as Spiro wanted to go and knew he could share a hotel room with Dominic, he didn't like blowing that kind of money for a weekend anymore. The ferry to Athens and two days of drinking and eating out would put a huge dent in what little savings he had.

He'd done well this season, selling more of his paintings than he'd ever sold in a season. But that money had to last his family throughout the low season. His hourly wage for working at the gallery helped, but the bulk of his money came from his paintings. Without the vacationers, money over the next several months would be tight.

Dominic frowned. "What, are they coming to collect and count their cash?"

Spiro rolled his eyes. It wasn't that he didn't like the owners of the gallery as much as he didn't respect what they were doing. They stocked cheap mass-produced replicas of real art. It was a slap in the face to every real artist on the island.

"Is Nina still seeing that guy?" A light flickered in Dominic's eyes.

"George? Yeah." Spiro knew Dominic knew the guy's name and why Dominic was asking. Dominic and Nina dated when they were younger, but then he dropped her when Aella became pregnant with the first of their three kids.

From Spiro's own experiences with Dominic many years ago and Nina's sexual prowess, George was a far better catch than Dominic. On such a small island, between Mateo, Dominic, and some of their other friends, they'd all been a little more than friends at one time or another.

Although Dominic and Aella had been married for seven years and had three children, Dominic still enjoyed the company of men for one weekend out of the year, and that was Athens's Pride in September.

"Well, tell Nina I said hi." Dominic handed over the bag of medication. "If you change your mind about this weekend, let me know. We're catching the one-thirty on Friday."

That last ferry for the day heading to Athens would put them in the city as the bars were beginning to pick up. There was also no doubt the party would start on the twelve-hour ferry over there, but that wasn't enough to persuade Spiro to change his mind.

Back outside, Spiro lit a cigarette and paced around his motorbike as he smoked. There was a part in him that regretted not saying yes to the weekend, but the last two years he'd gone, the heavy drinking and wild random hookups weren't working for him anymore.

The downside to island living was that he'd dated or had sex with every known gay man on the island, and didn't care to revisit any of them.

Sure, there was the occasional hookup with a vacationer, but that was just sex.

He took another puff of his cigarette before stepping on it and smudging it out with his shoe. He secured his tee shirt deeper into his back pocket before jumping on the motorbike and riding the short distance to the gallery. It was his day to open the gallery, and he was already thirty minutes late. The plus side to island living was that nobody cared.

CHAPTER THIRTEEN

Noah had been laying in bed for the last hour, drifting in and out of a light sleep. The thought that he wouldn't find Spiro was becoming a reality. Coming to Lemnos may have been all for not.

Over the last three days, he'd visited several other villages on the island. He'd walked more miles in the last several days and talked to more people than he cared to. Without outing himself to perfect strangers, he'd become good at telling his story to total strangers about how he knew Spiro.

Everyone knew a Spiro. The name was as common as Steve. If they said Spiro worked at the market, he went to that market. If he hung out at a bar after eight o'clock, Noah went to the bar after eight o'clock. None of them were his Spiro.

His Spiro was probably married with kids. He probably wasn't even as shockingly good looking as he was when he was twenty. Fat, bald, and no teeth could be a game changer. Noah hated to think he could be that shallow. He hated shallow. He knew how it felt to be judged solely on his looks. Being a seven at best on the hunk meter made it easy to detect shallow people.

He thought back to the men he'd dated over the years. None was especially handsome, although they were always higher on the hunk meter than Noah. The one common denominator they shared was their skin was darker than his. Without question, he was physically attracted to men with darker skin. He often wondered if this was an imprint left from Spiro.

Minus the one-night stands that said they would call and didn't and random internet hookups, there were four men Noah considered a relationship: Nabeeh, Jesus, Clive, and Mark.

Nabeeh was a tall, dark, and handsome gift from India. They lived together for a hot minute. The sex wasn't that good, but Nabeeh was sweet. After four months of living with the guy, Noah was a little surprised when that ended. Who knew they still did arranged marriages these days? That was something Nabeeh probably should have told him before they moved in together.

Then there was Jesus, the playboy who was unreachable for days at a time. He was highest on the hunk meter out of everyone. Noah should have known he wouldn't be a keeper, but you can't hate a guy for hoping. Six months of Noah trying to keep that relationship afloat, wondering if they were together or not was about as much as Noah could endure before sending Jesus out the door.

Clive was the one he would have married, had things turned out differently. A Lenny Kravitz lookalike, Clive was kind, loved animals, and was a saxophone player in a band. It was like the Fourth of July every time they had sex. Noah would never look at another saxophone player's lips or fingers the same again. That lasted almost a year, until the band moved to London and he wasn't invited.

His last relationship was with Mark, the guy who was perfect, except he didn't have a job. Mark was the out-of-work actor that refused to work between jobs. His excuse was that work took him out of his creative space.

Noah wasn't sure which night it was that Mark stayed over and remained for four months, or when Mark started using one of Noah's credit cards for his daily living expenses. Mark's secret addiction to coke also had something to do with the relationship ending within four months.

Then there was Rodney. In theory, Rodney counted as a one night stand, but in Noah's defense, they were both drunk and had just met that evening in the bar. Noah rolled onto his left side as he winced, remembering the specifics of that night with Rodney. With two drunk bottoms, that night was almost a disaster from the beginning, but out of that came a great friendship. Rodney was like the perfect boyfriend in many ways. He made Noah laugh, he never asked to borrow money, and he did all the cooking and cleaning.

Why hadn't he made Rodney come with him on this trip? If Rodney was here, he wouldn't be lying in bed, sulking. He would be laughing until his side hurt at something Rodney said that only he could get away with saying.

He wondered if there came a point in every gay man's life that they actually hated men. He didn't actually believe he did since he was here looking for a man. The men in his past all said his IBS wasn't an issue, but it always seemed to be, at least for them.

Over the years, Noah discovered that, for many men, sex was the actual act of penetration. For them, everything else was just foreplay. He enjoyed being a bottom, and he loved sex. It just took more preparation and awareness for him than the average bottom. He always had to be aware of how his body was feeling or would respond to being penetrated. If he thought that he might be having sex that night, he literally starved himself that day to ensure he wouldn't have any embarrassing mishaps that night.

With IBS, he was not always completely available to meet his partner's needs when his body was cramping, bloated, or constipated. He tried to mask much of the disease from them, having sex when he wasn't feeling it. He feared that, if he said no, they would walk from the relationship. During an actual flareup, the last thing he felt like was having sex. At the end of his relationship with Mark, his ex blamed the lack of sex as an excuse for cheating on him.

The soothing rumble of the ocean waves sweeping the beach outside his window caught his attention. He needed to stop being Negative Noah and get up and start the day. He rolled over in bed and faced the window as he mapped out his day of the villages he would search.

****

With no Uber on the island, Noah had the hotel call him a cab. While he waited, he purchased a bottled water from the hotel gift shop for his trip. His first stop this morning was the small rural community of *Plaka*, a beautiful village on the farthest east end of the island, population three hundred.

If Spiro was there, somebody would know him. Mostly residential housing sparsely scattered in desert terrain, Plaka was mentioned by several people during yesterday's search.

Unsuccessful in Plaka, Noah worked his way back to Myrina, stopping in several small villages along the way. He'd learned that, the smaller the village, the harder it was to communicate to shop owners and locals. Greek was spoken fast, and none of it sounded like English.

Back in Myrina, it was a little after three o'clock, and as usual, most of the businesses were closed for the afternoon. Noah had learned from the hotel staff that the island still observed the old tradition of *mesimeri*, which meant midday quiet time, the Greek form of the siesta. During mesimeri, which was from two to five, businesses closed, and roadwork and construction stopped. Employees used this time to lunch with their family and to nap. During mesimeri, the village of Myrina was like a ghost town.

On the pier, Noah found a small market that was still open. Inside, the scents of fresh bread, smoked meats, and spices stirred Noah's senses, sending his stomach into a flurry. He was suddenly hungry. Looking around, he saw that the store was more of a deli with just three aisles. He wandered down the middle aisle examining the unfamiliar products on the shelves. Along the back wall was an expansive glass case filled with cured meats. On the counter were several baskets of various types of baguettes and smaller display cases that contained pastries. Behind the counter stood a short, round man.

"Good afternoon." The man wiped his hands with the apron tied around his large waist.

After staring at the selection of choices, Noah settled on a croissant and bottled water. Back on the main pier, he found a bench across from the boats. With his first bite of the croissant, he realized the warm, flaky pastry was filled with ham and some sort of white cheese. As much as he loved cheese, he knew it didn't always love him. He cautiously nibbled on almost half of the sandwich before deciding it was a bad idea to eat the whole thing.

At home, it was easy to avoid his trigger foods. But away, it was safer to avoid food altogether if he could. It wasn't worth the pain and suffering. Over the years, he'd conditioned his brain not to think about food; he could go all day without eating. Food wasn't important to him anymore. He ate enough to get through a day, and that was it. With the warm sun casting down on him, Noah's shoulders relaxed as his breathing slowed.

Everything around him—the brightly painted boats, their unusual shapes, the sound of their hulls banging in their slips—it was all perfect. The cabbie he met on his first night was right: This was the most beautiful place on earth.

As a New Yorker, the lack of people around was a little unnerving, as if there'd been an apocalypse. There wasn't anywhere he could go in New York where a ton of people hadn't gotten there before him. Central

Park, filled with thousands of people, was about as tranquil as the city got.

He exhaled a large breath, and on a whim, he decided he was done looking for the day. His feet hurt, and he wanted to be still a little longer. He'd never been much of a sunbather, but he had an urge to do nothing but lay on the beach and read a book. He'd paid the gorgeous beach almost no attention since arriving. It would be a shame to spend the money he was spending on an ocean-front room and not use it to its fullest.

Back at the room, it didn't take Noah long to change into his boardshorts, grab his Kindle, a blanket, and the sun umbrella from the room and head out.

He strolled onto the beach about a hundred yards from his bungalow and stopped. This was as good as a spot as any. He had no intentions of getting in the water, but that didn't mean he still couldn't enjoy the sun and surf. He'd paid for it.

With his blanket spread out, he kicked off his flipflops and stretched onto his back. He leaned back, rested his head on his backpack, and shut his eyes. It took a minute to fall back into the relaxed state he had back in town. With the calming sounds of the waves breaking out beyond the cove and the sun on his face, his breathing slowed as he exhaled a long, cleansing breath.

It took a minute, but he released another big breath as his pulse slowed. He came here with hope in his heart and gave it a good try. He tried, and it didn't work out. It was ludicrous to think he could fly halfway around the world and find this great love—as if Spiro was sitting around, waiting for him to arrive years later.

Noah pondered if he should call the airlines to see if he could change his flight and head home earlier... He rejected that idea. Leaving the island without finding Spiro wasn't an option yet. He exhaled another large breath, feeling the muscles in his neck, shoulders, and chest release their tension.

Noah was engrossed in the novel of one of his favorite authors, Patricia Nell Warren. This book was about a college runner sleeping with his coach. It was one of the many male/male romance books he'd downloaded before leaving New York. He was fully absorbed in the book and failed to hear someone walking up behind him.

"*Excussez*, me, Sir."

Startled, Noah arched his neck to see behind him. A short young man in shorts and a polo shirt stood over him. The hotel logo on the left breast pocket of his shirt was Noah's first clue he worked for the hotel.

"May I bring you something from the bar?" He asked.

Surprised the bartender had trekked all the way out here for him, the warm sun and leisureliness made him contemplate ordering a vodka cranberry. The cheese croissant for lunch earlier said that he better not stray off his diet that much. He grabbed the water bottle he purchased earlier and saw that it was about empty. "Can I get some more water? Water would be great." The sun caused him to squint as he stared up at the man.

"Absolutely. Do you have a preference?"

"No, as long as it's bottled, whatever you have. Surprise me."

"Very well, Sir. My name is George. I'll be right back."

As the bartender walked away, Noah smiled at the fact that every other person he met was named George. Apparently, the name George was as common as Spiro. Noah hesitated a second before returning to his book. There was a man and woman about two hundred feet away playing with a small child. The child and woman were running back and forth from the waves coming in. On the far side of them was another sunbather in a black Speedo lying out. From a distance, he had the potential of being cute.

The sunbather was the incentive Noah needed to reposition himself, exposing the other side of his body to the sun. He watched the guy for a while. The sunbather hadn't moved and was perhaps sleeping.

Fighting the urge to close his eyes for his own quick power nap, Noah opened his eyes after a long blink. The sunbather was now standing. After brushing sand from his ass and legs, the guy made his way into the water.

From afar, Noah saw how thin the guy was. He was too thin for Noah's liking, but it didn't hurt to look. The sunbather was waist deep, brushing water onto his shoulders and face when George returned.

"Hello, Sir." George had a tiny table in one hand and the bottled water in the other. He placed the table beside Noah and then removed a cloth napkin and a glass from the front pockets of his apron. He lay the napkin on the table and then set the glass and water on it. "I brought you a menu if you would like to order something. I can get that for you as well." Before leaving, he handed Noah a small binder that contained drinks and appetizers.

His thirst now quenched, Noah was about to return to his book when he realized the sunbather was walking in his direction. Pretending to read his book, Noah focused on the words on the screen as he waited for him to pass from the corner of his eye.

"Salut. Vous étiez de Daphné hier" The man stopped in front of him. His accent was thick.

"Um... I only speak English." Noah was sure the man was speaking French. One year of high school French proved that it wasn't a total waste of time. He was also sure he'd asked him a question, but had no idea what he said.

Heat rose in Noah's cheeks as the man blocked the strong ray of sun with his body. The front of his tiny black Speedo revealed everything God had given him, and it appeared the good Lord had been generous. A trail of ebony hair rose from the top of his Speedo up his flat, sun- kissed abdomen to his chest.

"Oh... English? Excuse me, I am sorry... I was wondering, weren't you in Daphne's the other day?" the man asked.

It clicked... He was the waiter. Almost naked, he was a hell of a lot cuter than in his waiter outfit. "Oh, yeah! You work there, right?" Noah pulled his eyes away from the thin piece of fabric that covered the man's crotch.

"It's my sister's place. Daphne. I come over after the season ends for a holiday with her and our dad until Christmas." The man brushed back his wet hair from his face. "I am Nico. May I sit?" With long bangs that dropped in front of his face, Nico's black hair was clipped short on the sides and back.

"Sure." Self-conscious of his pale white skin and lack of muscle tone, Noah sat up to shield some of his body. "Where are you from?" Noah asked, assuming the guy was going to say France.

Nico squatted. "I live in Tel Aviv." The uncertainty of his ability to speak English was evident in his slow, melodious speech.

It took everything Noah had not to look between Nico's open legs. "Are you Israeli?"

"No, French. My work takes me to Tel Aviv. And you... Americano?"

"Yes. From New York."

"Someday, I hope to visit your country."

"What do you do?" Noah's eyes darted between Nico's open legs. Nico's creamy, tanned thighs in the crouching position weren't so skinny anymore. *Nico was beautiful.*

A smile crossed Nico's face, exposing beautiful white teeth. The smile also suggested Nico had caught him staring at his crotch. "I don't want to talk about me. I'd like to know about you. You're from New York... They call it the Big Apple, no?"

"Yes." It was less than a glance, but Noah was sure Nico caught him a second time looking at his crotch. He had to stop looking.

"Where in New York?" Nico's stare was intense.

"New York... in the city." The fact that he lived in Greenwich Village seemed insignificant to someone who'd never been to the States.

"You are... how do you say, *sexy*." Nico's eyes moved down Noah's legs and back up. A smug grin reappeared.

Noah's skin flushed. This never happened. No one with the looks of Nico said he was sexy. Nico's flirting and forwardness was relentless. Was it for real? Noah pulled his knees up into his chest and wrapped his arms around his knees.

"Have dinner with me." Nico's expressive brows said he wasn't shy.

Is this some kind of a cruel joke? It took a second before Noah could commit to looking at him. His eyes traveled up Nico's long neck, past his extended Adam's apple, to his brown eyes. They stared back at each other for an awkward second before Noah found his voice. "Why?"

Nico snickered. "Why do you ask *why*?" Between Nico's expressive eyes and mischievous grin, there was definitely a *why*.

If there was any doubt about what was happening here, the tattoo of the bottle of poison on Nico's wrist was shouting the truth. "I can't. I'm here with someone... Well, not with someone, but I'm here to be with someone." As tantalizing and mouthwatering as Nico may have been, Noah wasn't looking for a hookup.

"Where is *he*?" Nico ran his hand through his wet hair, slicking it back. "Why are you out here alone? You sit here by yourself. Who would do this?" Dejection swept across Nico's face.

Noah's breath hung onto Nico's words. "Well..." The story he had recited to perfect strangers for the last five days had him tongue tied. "Well, I met *him* back in the States. I'm looking for him."

"Ah. So, then, it's only dinner for me and you. What's the harm?"

Noah looked out toward the ocean to get away from Nico's stare. Nico was the lion, and he was the antelope, destined to be devoured by this beautiful creature. "... Okay, just dinner." His heart leapt from his chest at his commitment.

"To prove it's only dinner, you can meet me at my sister's place." The corners of Nico's large brown eyes crinkled at his grin.

"Daphne's... okay. What time?" Was he committing to this?

"Nine o'clock." Nico rose to his feet. "I see you then." He took a step away and then placed two fingers over his lips. *"Au revoir."*

As giddy as a thirteen-year-old girl meeting her teen idol, his eyes remained on Nico as he made his way up toward the hotel. Nico's clipped hair revealing his long neck, his back, skin the color of honey, and that ass... There was no way this antelope would make it out alive.

****

Throughout the evening, Noah had been attempting to talk himself out of his not-a-date with Nico. The whole thing was silly. He wasn't interested in a hookup. Why would Nico be so forward? Maybe he should at least text Rodney.

Hell, no, that was a bad idea. The last thing he would do is take advice from Rodney about dating... *This isn't a date!*

Was Nico a hustler that prayed on unsuspecting tourists, hustling them out of their last penny? Did Nico think Noah was a rich American? Was it about sex? Was he a serial killer? Would his family find his body? Noah wondered what Nico did with the bodies to hide them! He kept throwing random ideas out there, hoping something would stick and make him change his mind about going this evening.

He removed the nicest shirt he'd brought from the tiny closet and held it up, assessing if it was doable. This was the shirt he would wear on his first date with Spiro. He started with the bottom button and worked his way up to the second-to-the-top button. *Too high? Maybe if it was Spiro, but not for Nico.*

It was almost nine o'clock. The last thing he wanted was to show up before Nico and be that guy who sat there for hours, waiting on a date who wouldn't show up... *Damn it! This isn't a date!*

Even if it wasn't a date, the solution was to be a tad bit late, fashionably late. This was the only advice he would ever use from Rodney. He laughed at how insane he was being. It was his sister's place; of course, Nico would show—maybe.

After a brisk walk via the beach, he arrived at Daphne's a couple of minutes after nine. He took a deep breath as he asked himself what the hell he was doing. As if the gods knew he was about to run away, the front door opened, and a couple came out. The man held the door open for Noah, forcing him to step inside.

The low lighting made the space appear different, more intimate. Intimate didn't work in Noah's favor. Almost empty, three of the ten tables were occupied with patrons. His eyes scanned the table he sat at when he was here for lunch. Beyond that was Nico, tucked away in the far corner of the restaurant.

Daphne appeared from the back with a plate in each hand. "Hello." Her smile said she knew he was there to see her brother. She nodded toward Nico.

Nico stood as Noah approached the table. *"Bonsoir."*

"Hey, there." He was proud of himself. His one year of French paid off again.

Nico leaned in and lightly kissed both his cheeks.

Simultaneously, they both sat down. "You are very handsome." Nico winked.

Noah took another deep breath, hoping it would stop his leg from bouncing under the table. "Thank you."

Noah's eyes shot to the flickering candle set in a blue viola glass in the middle of the table. Visions of the full front of Nico's tiny black Speedo rushed him. He pushed the vivid image away; he only wanted to think of Spiro.

Nico reached out and took his wine glass. "Can I get you something from the bar? I'm drinking a pino noir. Daphne's good at picking out wines." He swirled the wine in his glass before taking a sip.

"No, thank you. I'm good." Noah wanted to say yes to the liquid courage, but he also needed to stay on his toes with Nico.

"Oh," Nico's head bobbed. "Water, then?"

"Yeah, that would be great." Noah rubbed his palms against his pants to remove the dampness.

"Okay, I'll be right back." Nico took another sip of his wine before leaving.

Noah's inner voice reminded him once again that he shouldn't be here. He drew a breath as he contemplated leaving. This was not right to do to Nico... or Spiro. His body jerked as if attempting to get up, but his legs stayed firmly on the floor.

It wasn't long before Nico returned with a chilled bottle of water, a small plate of various olives, and a bread basket. "I hope you like olives. Our *tante* does these especially for Daphne."

"They look good." Noah took a piece of bread instead, knowing the olives contained a fair amount of fiber and were on his trigger list.

Nico took a sip of his wine and held his glass below his chin. "How long does the island get to host such a beautiful man?"

"Well, I've been here for five days already. I'd planned for three weeks. If it takes longer to find him, then I guess I have to wait and see."

"How do you know this man is here, on the island?" Nico's tone said it was a possibility, as if he held a secret. "Lovers so long ago. It's romantic, but maybe it is not so doable anymore." The tiny candle sparkled in Nico's eyes as he held them on Noah.

"I guess I would never know if I didn't try." Noah hesitated at what he was about to say. "I love him. I've never stopped loving him. I'm not sure I will. He has my heart." His words were calculated, and by the expression on Nico's face, they were a direct hit. If this was a game of chess, he just put Nico in checkmate.

It was a safe assumption to think Nico always got what Nico wanted. Charismatic and beautiful, he had the whole French accent, the alluring brown eyes, and to some, a killer body. But Noah was no more interested in him than the first day he saw him. Perhaps in a different life he would be, but not this one.

"Well, maybe... you gave your heart away too soon?" Nico held up his glass. *"Amour!"*

"I didn't come here to fall in love; I came here because I *am* in love." Noah picked up his water glass and tapped it against Nico's wine glass. "To love."

"Then we eat, no?" A wistful smile arose on Nico's face as he put his glass down. "Daphne has prepared something exquisite for us tonight. You wait here, and I'll be back!" He rose to his feet again. His face was somber, as if he had suffered defeat.

He was gone long enough for Noah to wish he had never come out this evening. This was a mistake, and now he was trapped.

Nico returned with two large bowls set on plates. "Boeuf Bourguignon!" He placed the first plate in front of Noah. The aromatic bouquet of aromas rising from the bowl was orgasmic.

Noah peered down into his bowl at the big chunks of beautiful beef, potatoes, and carrots nestled in a stew-like gravy. He was unsure what was in the stew, but he had to try it. There was no way he could pass on a dish that smelled this delicious.

Nico sat in his seat and took another sip of wine. "To food. She is *my* lover this evening." He didn't wait for Noah this time but saluted into the air before taking a sip. Nico then tore a nice chunk of bread from the loaf and put it on Noah's plate before tearing a piece for himself.

After two bites of his stew, Nico sat his spoon down. "Have you had the chance to visit the castle yet?" He asked.

"No, not yet. I'm not sure I'll get up there." He had been staring at the ruins up on the hill above the village since he'd been here. At night, it lit the entire sky. It was on his list of to dos; he was hoping it would be with Spiro.

"Well, that's too bad. You've come from far away; you should see it. Perhaps if this mystery man appears, he will take you. If not, then I will take you!" His words commanded nothing less than agreement.

"Okay." He waited a second, ensuring Nico would not ask him another question before putting a nice piece of beef into his mouth. The dish was unlike anything he had ever tasted.

Throughout dinner, Nico and Noah traded stories of their childhoods, parents, and their life back home. During the middle of dinner, Nico opened another bottle of wine.

"Tomorrow afternoon, I will pick you up, and we shall find this mystery man of yours. The island is only so big." Nico's speech was slurring.

"Oh, no. You don't have to." Noah responded without considering the offer.

"But I want to. How do you do it alone? You don't speak the language. I know the island. I can be of use."

"Do you speak Greek?" Noah raised a brow.

"I do." Nico smiled as if he'd found his way in the door.

Noah wasn't sure why he was surprised that Nico spoke Greek. He could have used Nico several times over the last few days to translate for him. "No. It's okay." Noah semi-contemplated Nico's offer.

"But I must! The sooner I show you that this man... what is his name?" Nico asked.

"Spiro."

"The sooner I show you that this Spiro is not here, I can have you to myself." Nico pressed his hand against his heart. "I wait for love."

Noah pushed aside the thought of them sleeping together. As tempting as it may be, he hadn't traveled half way around the world just to have casual sex with someone. "Thanks, but I can do it by myself."

Nico held up his glass and toasted into the air. "I see you at noon tomorrow!"

"Okay! Okay." Noah conceded, hoping Nico was drunk and wouldn't remember any of this in the morning.

CHAPTER FOURTEEEN

Up early this morning, Noah finished checking all his accounts and shot off a handful of emails to his clients. He had to advise several of them of changes they needed to make to keep their sites either secure or current. He needed to work on getting his billing statements out next, but that was his least favorite part of running a web design business.

Not having the mental focus to add up billing hours, Noah closed his laptop. The evening with Nico played out in his head. Nico was a charmer. He hoped that Nico was too drunk last night to remember that he'd offered to help him today.

As he came from the shower, his phone chimed. He couldn't imagine who was texting him. It was from Rodney: *Whatsup??*

A quick calculation told Noah it was four a.m. back home. *What's up? What are you doing up this early?*

Girl, I aint went to bed yet. Me and Miss Anita-Man had a show. We're trying to raise money for the Angel Babies, Rodney replied.

Noah tried not to laugh, knowing they both sucked at lip syncing and neither one could sing. *Angel Babies?* Noah typed out and had barely hit send when his phone rang. It was Rodney calling him. Noah swiped, answering his phone.

"Girl, Anita-Man tried to steal my solo! You know the bitch is a rotten nasty thief!" Rodney launched into last night's events. "Oh, I need to lower my voice before she hears me. You know, the bitch got big elephant ears to go along with that stomach she thinks nobody can see!"

"Is she there?" Noah smiled at how right Rodney was about Anita-Man.

"Yeah, we had a little after-hours party last night. Just us girls."

"I know you didn't let her sleep in my room!"

"Girl, I wouldn't let that thief up in your room. She's in my room, and I'm watching her ass on my cameras. I'm in yours."

Noah scratched his forehead as he sighed. He didn't know what was worse, the reminder that Rodney liked to record his sex or that Rodney had most likely snooped through everything in his room.

"What's going on there?" Rodney asked.

He didn't know what to lead with: Nico or Spiro? "I'm thinking about seeing if I can change my flight. Come home early. I've looked everywhere. He's probably not living on this island anymore... Anyway, I met this guy on the beach yesterday. Actually, I met him two days ago, but ran into him yesterday. We met last night for dinner. His name is Nico."

"Nico... as in Nikodemos?" Rodney asked.

"No, he's not Greek. He's French. His sister owns a little restaurant on the island, and he's here helping her out."

"Is he cute?"

"He's French. What do you think?"

"Well, look at you! So how was the date?"

"It wasn't a date; we're just friends."

"You just met; he can't be your friend. Friends are what come from a bad date."

"He's not my type. Way too aggressive, all hands, and I'm not here for that." Noah let out a harsh breath. "Anyway, he was supposed to help me comb the island today, but—"

"—why do you always do that?" Rodney asked.

"Do what?" Feeling an argument coming on, Noah rolled his eyes.

"Push people away."

"I'm not pushing anyone away! I'm not interested in him, and he's clearly looking for sex." Maybe he was pushing this guy away, but it was only because he wasn't who Noah wanted. He knew who and what he wanted.

"I doubt that!" Rodney's tone was sarcastic and clipped.

Noah's shoulders tensed. "What does that mean?" He knew it was a slam, that Rodney was being bitchy.

Rodney was silent for a second. "I mean..." His voice slowed. "You've been there for a week. You haven't found the missing Spyridon. Have some fun. You're on the other side of the world. Let loose. Be spontaneous!"

"Are you kidding me? This whole trip you've talked me into has been spontaneous!" His mind rolled back to Rodney saying he was pushing people away. Noah reflected on a conversation with his therapist. She said he was yearning for intimacy because he lacked it with his parents and that, with men, he was looking to replace his father. That idea had always creeped Noah out a bit, but he couldn't deny the obvious and what he'd learned over the years about himself. He was seriously done with seeking unobtainable love from guys.

"Now you're lying to yourself. Girl, you've been planning this trip for twelve years! There ain't nothin' spontaneous about it."

Noah wanted to push back, but as always, Rodney was right.

Rodney didn't let up. "What happens in Greece stays in Greece. If you're coming home early, you can at least get laid before you come back. Get something for your money. You can screw this guy while you're still looking for your boo. You ain't married to neither one of them... *yet*." Rodney snickered.

"I shouldn't have come. This is stupid." Noah took a chair out on the terrace and stared out at the ocean. It was spectacular, the color of the ocean, an intense blue, different from what he was used to looking at back home.

"Girl, you're avoiding my advice!"

"What... to get laid?" Noah rolled his eyes as he took his attention away from the sea.

"Yeah! You need to get you some. So, when you board that plane, your ass ain't got no choice but to stand for the whole seventeen-hour flight. How much has this trip cost you?"

"Rodney!" The last thing Noah wanted to do was think about how much money he was spending.

"If you get laid, I'll pay for this entire trip! When are you supposed to meet this Nico again?"

"At noon. In front of the hotel." He refused to entertain Rodney's advice on having sex with Nico. But what would be the harm in letting him help search for Spiro?

He'd been nothing but honest with Nico. If Nico still wanted to help, why shouldn't he let him?

"It's noon now. You need to go out there and see if he's there! Don't leave that man out there looking for you!"

"Okay..." Once again, Rodney was right. "I have to go, then."

****

Standing out in front of his hotel, Noah fidgeted with his phone. Nico said noon; it was now quarter after. It was another ten minutes before the silly horn of a scooter caused him to look up. Approaching on the scooter was a man wearing a black racing helmet.

The scooter skid to a stop in front of him. Nico raised the tinted glass visor. *"Bonne après-midi!"*

"Good afternoon to you, too." Noah had to admit, Nico was kind of sexy on the bright-red Italian Vespa.

Nico reached behind him and unstrapped the extra helmet from the side of the scooter. "Here you go. Safety first."

"I'm not getting on that!" Noah took a step back. Hell no, there was no way he was getting on that scooter. He'd seen how crazy people zipped around, squeezing into places they shouldn't and narrowly avoiding being taken out by buses and trucks.

Nico laughed. "I'll drive like a grandma. Come on. We have many places to go, and I'm not walking a hundred miles to find you a lover."

A hundred miles? Noah didn't want to get on the back of the bike. "Do you promise?"

"Yessss." Nico held out the helmet. "Come."

Strapping the helmet on made Noah's head feel like a bowling ball. "Where to first?" He stalled, not wanting to climb on.

"You said you already searched Myrina; I know a gallery in Moudros, on the other side of the island. It's an upscale gallery. If he is as you say he is, then he is there. You said he said his village had a pier. There's a fishing pier there as well... And then we can check out a village called Kaminia. There's a good tavern there. We'll stop, have a drink and something to eat. Kaminia has wonderful beaches. It's a nice trip."

Noah got the feeling that Nico wasn't at all trying to help him find Spiro, that this was a ruse. Nico was slick; he had to give him that much. However, since he hadn't had any luck yet on his own, he would play along. What harm could come from spending the afternoon with Nico combing the island?

Be spontaneous, he told himself. "Okay." With his arms around Nico's waist, they were off. Noah had to admit, having his arms around Nico's waist and his chest against Nico's back felt nice.

They zipped around the island. Nico pointed out sights along the way and made several unexpected stops in villages that weren't on the map. Two hours into their journey, Noah's thighs were killing him. He had to get off the bike.

"How close are we to Moudros?" he yelled through his helmet.

Taking one hand from the handgrip, Nico pointed up ahead. "Very close."

Noah saw the red-tiled roofs ahead. After an hour there, combing stores and galleries and inquiring about a missing man named Spiro, they were off to their next stop, Kaminia, which included a stop at the tavern. Noah made Nico promise he'd only have one glass of wine, and if he broke his promise, he was calling a cab to come get him.

Inside the tavern, it was obvious the bartender knew Nico. They exchanged kisses on the cheeks and conversed in French. Noah nursed a glass of warm water and munched on old pretzels on the bar, while Nico and the bartender laughed and carried on in French.

When Noah announced it was time to leave, Nico suggested one more glass of wine. When that didn't work, he suggested they see the beach.

"I'd rather not. We should go to the next town. We need to keep looking."

"It's on the way. It will be fine. You'll like it; I promise. It's more beautiful than the beaches in Myrina."

Nico was right. The coastline was spectacular, but this wasn't why he was here. With zero luck finding Spiro and no leads, Noah concluded that, when they got back to his hotel, he was calling the airlines to see about heading home tomorrow.

It was almost seven o'clock when they arrived back in Myrina. Nico asked to make one stop to pick up new menus for Daphne. "She texted me, asking if I could pick them up for her."

When they arrived at the printing shop, Nico parked the scooter in front of the store's front window. Noah hopped off the scooter to stretch his legs. Had his thighs not been killing him, he would have hobbled to his hotel from there.

He removed his helmet to get air while he waited for Nico on the sidewalk. Some of the businesses were still closed for mesimeri. When Nico emerged, he handed Noah a stack of papers wrapped in plastic. "Can you hold these?"

Noah was about to climb on the back of the scooter when another motorbike sped past them and stopped about twenty-five feet up the street. In an instant, Noah knew the helmetless driver was Spiro. His hair was shorter, his face fuller, but the shape of his chin, his jawline—it was

Spiro. Noah let out a gasp as panic swelled within him. His stomach tightened. He couldn't peel his stare away from Spiro. He studied him with piercing scrutiny, afraid that it wasn't so.

Nico must have seen the color drain from Noah's face. "Is that him?" Nico asked.

"Yes! Yes! That's him." Noah's eyes then took in the whole picture, including the female who got off the back of Spiro's motorbike. Tall and thin, she removed her helmet and tossed her long, black hair into place. She was beautiful.

"Well, aren't you going to go to him?" Nico's eyes went back and forth between Noah and Spiro several times.

Noah swallowed the sudden lump in his throat. "I can't. What if that's his girlfriend or wife? No, I can't." Noah shook his head. He couldn't do it.

CHAPTER FIFTEEN

"What are you doing?" Nico's eyes shot back and forth between Noah and Spiro. "You go to him... no? This is what you wanted!"

"But... he's got a—*girlfriend...* See? Or his wife. I can't."

"You can't? But you've come from far away to find him. There he is. Go!"

"No!" Noah pushed back.

"Then I will... Spiro! Spiro!" He shouted across the street.

When Spiro turned his head their direction, Nico bumped the back of Noah's shoulder and pushed him forward. "Go to him!"

Noah wanted to melt into the sidewalk, but first he needed to kill Nico. Frozen, he stared at Spiro. Spiro, still sitting on his scooter, was looking at them as if he and Nico were dancing clowns doing the tango. It took a second before Spiro's eyes widened and the muscles in his jaw slacked, freeing his mouth to open. His feet planted on the ground, Spiro raised off his seat.

Nico pushed Noah, forcing him to take another step, as natural gravity propelled him to take the next step. This reunion wasn't the running-on-the-dock scene that Noah imagined. It was as if it was all in slow motion. With each step, Noah moved a little closer. It couldn't have been more than twenty steps, but it seemed like a thousand. He was trying to read Spiro's expression—*surprised, confused, pleasantly surprised*—he couldn't tell. No running toward each other, embracing in a massive bearhug as they twirled in a circle: Spiro simply stared at him.

"Hey, there." Noah closed the gap between them to about three feet and stopped. His eyes shifted to the female, then back to Spiro.

"Noah? What are you doing here?" Spiro stepped off his motorbike. In two steps, he had taken Noah into his arms, wrapping his arms around Noah as he patted his upper back. He pulled back. "I can't believe it's you!" His beautiful hazel eyes sparkled with recognition.

149

Noah fought to dislodge the trapped air in his throat that was preventing him from speaking. "Yep, it's me. How are you?" Nervous laughter carried Noah's words as he stared at the flawless olive skin, and manicured black stubble around Spiro's jawline that replaced the once-boyish face. His strong brows and thick black hair gave him the look of an Arabian prince. Spiro was still a hair taller than him, and his body had filled out into a man's. His physique was not that of a gym rat's, but well-toned. Noah was suddenly ultra-awake, rejuvenated by adrenaline.

Spiro took a step back, his eyes looking at Noah from head to toe. "My God, look at you!" There was a giddiness in Spiro's voice as his eyes swept up and down Noah.

Noah was positive he saw Spiro glance down at his hand. Instinctively, he did the same to Spiro's hand. There was no ring on Spiro's finger. He remembered something Spiro had said one day as he lay nestled in his arms so many years ago. *Boys will be boys until they take a wife, and then they must be a man.* Noah looked at the woman, who was staring him down. Expressionless, her eyes were less hospitable than Spiro's.

Behind them, in the store's window, Noah spotted paintings. The words above the door read *Art Gallery*. He laughed inwardly. Whoever concocted the name Art Gallery was a genius.

Spiro looked over his shoulder back at the building. "We work here. Nina manages the gallery. I do... how do you say, the labor?"

Warmth spread within Noah's chest. Although Spiro's English had noticeably improved, there was comfort in hearing that he still enunciated in English each syllable. Noah tried to smile at the woman; instead, his eyes shot past her at the gallery. The labor? *Is that a modest way of saying you're the artist?*

Spiro turned his head toward the woman and back to Noah. "Nina is my cousin." He held out his hand and waved for her to come closer.

Nina tucked her helmet under her arm and extended her hand to greet him. "Hello." Her face softened; her "hello" was delicate and angelic.

Noah released a pinned-up breath of air from his lungs as he internally did a happy dance that she was only a cousin and not a wife or girlfriend. "Oh... it's nice to meet you." Noah shook her small hand.

"Nina, this is the guy I told you about in America. But I see he's not a boy anymore." Spiro's brows raised. "What are you doing here?" Spiro asked again.

"My therapist says I have abandonment issues." Noah was trying to be funny, but after saying it, he realized it was more truth than he needed to share so soon. "Your English, it's much better."

Spiro grinned, "Yes! Yes! I speak English to all the travelers. Everyday!" He proclaimed his confession as if it was a badge of honor.

As if wanting to be polite before she interrupted, Nina softly cleared her throat. "I'll leave you two. It's nice to meet you." She smiled and nodded at Noah before walking away.

Noah let the real answer to Spiro's question hang as Nina unlocked the double glass doors to the gallery and slid both back out of the way. As he turned back to Spiro, the sound of a motor bike's engine reverberated in Noah's ear. "I can't... believe..." Noah disregarded the sound of the engine. Spiro was as beautiful as he was years ago. He had grown into a man, a handsome man.

"But what are you doing here?" Spiro stared.

"I'm here... I came to find you." Noah hesitated. "I..." He wanted to say that he loved him, that he never stopped, but his voice faltered.

Spiro reached out and touched Noah's arm. "I heard someone calling me. I thought—"

Noah cut him off. "That was..." He turned, looking for Nico, but Nico had driven off. Noah scanned the street. Nico had disappeared.

"I'm shocked to see you! It's good, I mean." Spiro rubbed his hand up and down Noah's arm. "How long have you been here—on the island?"

"Almost a week." He stopped short of saying he'd been interrogating the entire island for the last five days, looking for him.

"We go somewhere, to talk. We must catch up." Without warning, Spiro grabbed him again and gave him another hug. This time, it was a little slower and tighter.

He'd dreamt about being in Spiro's arms for so long that, when it happened, it was a little surreal. "Okay." Noah's ability to think had been wiped away.

"Come inside. With me. I tell Nina that I'll be back. Come! Come!" The excitement in his voice bubbled with each word.

Noah stepped into the art gallery behind Spiro. Nina had disappeared behind a curtain, to wherever that led. The walls were covered with paintings. Not a single space of wall was left empty. It wasn't exactly an art gallery, but more of a store that sold paintings, and by the looks of it, an assortment of other novelties, from postcards and greeting cards to calendars and picture books.

Spiro moved toward the back of the store. "Nina and I just got back from Athens. We have to go to the mainland about once a month. We ship all over the world. Paintings, see!" Spiro waved his arm as if he was the host on the *Price Is Right.*

"Are these yours?" Noah wasn't positive he'd been in *this* store. Had he somehow missed this street? The streets and stores had all blurred together days ago.

Spiro laughed, "Ah, no, no... Nina! Nina!" Spiro called for his cousin behind a curtain. He flipped the curtain and disappeared into the back.

Noah listened as Spiro and Nina conversed in Greek. He couldn't stop smiling. A knot twisted his stomach as he meandered around the small store. There was a long glass counter separating him from the back room. On the counter was a cash register and a small spin rack of Greek CDs for sale.

Spiro emerged from the back, smiling. "Come, come. We go. Let's find someplace and talk. We need to catch up!" His voice left little doubt he was pleased to see Noah.

Back outside, Spiro stopped beside the motorbike he'd parked outside the store. "We walk!" A smile stretched his stubble-covered cheeks.

Noah's gaze dropped to the motorbike. Rusty and old, it was definitely an antique.

Choosing to walk, they made their way to the pier. Within minutes, they were sitting on the edge of the pier with their feet dangling over the side, just like old times at the lake. The excitement fluttering in Noah's stomach began to slow, allowing memory to take over as the sound of the boat hulls banging in their slips recalled memories of their time spent in the boathouse. A tiny grin was unavoidable.

"Tell me, why are you here?" Spiro's voice returned to a normal pitch as he pulled out a pack of cigarettes and plucked one from the pack. He paused, looking at Noah for a second before lighting it.

Conflicted about where and what he wanted to start with, Noah drew a breath for one more second as his brain processed that Spiro was still a smoker. He'd imagined this day a thousand times, and none of them equaled how he was feeling.

With excitement, conflict, and anxiety ripping through him, his body trembled as if cold. He knew so little about this person, the person he was in love with. The tiny negative devil on his left shoulder screamed in his ear. *Because he doesn't have a ring on his finger doesn't mean he's not married or involved with someone.*

But Spiro's enthusiasm said differently. "I don't know; I guess I wanted to see you." Noah's voice quaked.

"It's been..." Spiro's brows arched. "Twelve years. No?"

"Yes." Noah nodded. "It has been."

"A long time." Spiro grinned as his penetrating stare revealed his own disbelief that this was real.

In a single look, Spiro managed to melt the absent years away. Noah found himself suddenly that nervous kid again: eighteen years old and full of questions and doubts that this could be for real. His breath caught, trapping his question in his throat. He'd never forgotten that conversation they had in the woods, the day Spiro asked him if he planned on getting married. It was a bizarre conversation where Spiro talked about boys being boys until they got married.

He had to know. "Um, so... are you married or *anything* like that?" Instead of looking at Spiro, he stared up at a flock of seagulls flying low toward them. A flock of seagulls possibly shitting all over him was a better option than looking at Spiro if he said yes.

If Spiro said yes, Noah decided he would throw himself off the pier and plunge into the ocean, never to be seen again.

"Huh, me? Nooo!" Spiro waved the notion off. He hung his head for a second before looking at Noah. "And you?"

"Nooo!" *Okay, this is good. I'm on first base.* This was viable.

"How is this not possible?" Spiro smiled into Noah's eyes.

Noah's lips unconsciously parted, seeing that Spiro still possessed that beautiful smile, that sexy grin that rose more on the left side. "What do you mean?" Noah's heart drummed out of control. He was madly in love with this man.

"You're handsome. Girls should love you. No?"

"Well, I'm gay, I mean, still gay." Nervous laughter escaped him as he said the word, as if he was coming out. "I haven't dated anyone for a while." Noah counted the months in his head.

Spiro shrugged. "Okay, then... men should love you." A fragile smile crept across Spiro's face before he looked down at the water.

The sudden silence was almost awkward, if not for a chance for Noah to breathe. The sound of his breathing, the squawk of the seagulls flying overhead, filled the space as Noah reminisced about their summer.

Spiro looked up and ended the silence. "Where are you staying?"

"At the Blue Oceania Seaside Resort," he murmured.

"Oh. This is the best hotel on the island. Very nice! My good friend is the chef in the restaurant."

"My bungalow has this great ocean view." Noah held back that he had to dip into his savings to afford this trip, and had picked the room, knowing how romantic it would be once he found him.

"Do you live here? I mean, in Myrina?" Noah asked.

"No. We live in Katalako, about eighteen kilometers from here."

Noah caught the *we* in his sentence. "What... that's about eleven miles away?" He'd spent the last eight hours on the back of a moped, combing the entire island with a crazy Frenchman, and Spiro lived eleven freaking miles from here.

Spiro nodded. "I don't know your miles."

"Well, I'm still in New York."

"Ahh, New York. I still think about that summer." Spiro smiled.

"You do?" *Was this an unexpected steal to second base?*

"Oh, yeah. When Eros sent me away, it was the saddest day of my life."

"It was?" *So it was Eros that sent him away?* "Oh, wow. I always thought it was my dad that kicked you and Eros out that summer. I didn't know it was Eros that made you leave."

"No, no. Your father wasn't there. Eros and I were getting ready to go out that morning to work. Your grandmother knocked on the door. Eros stepped outside to talk with her. I knew something was wrong because she'd never come up to the apartment the whole time I was there. I could hear her and Eros talking, but I couldn't make out what she was saying. After a couple of minutes, my theios came in and told me to pack my things, that we were leaving. It was your grandmother that sent us away."

A floodgate of memories rushed Noah at once. He remembered coming down the steps when his grandmother was talking to the Alpersteins on the phone that morning. "She told me that she was sending you guys to the store. You guys never came back that day. Then my parents showed up that night. It wasn't until the next morning that I realized you guys had actually left and weren't coming back."

"Yeah, that morning, at first, I thought something had happened to my mom when your grandmother showed up at the door. I tried to ask what happened, but Eros refused to talk. He wouldn't even look at me."

"So, what happened to you guys?" Noah was getting answers to questions he asked himself for years.

"A cab came and picked us up down at the end of the driveway. While we were waiting was when I finally caught on that he was mad at me, that somehow I caused whatever was happening. We took the bus into Boston that night. My Theia Melenna, who lived in Boston, picked us up. I was there for two or three days before I flew back home."

"Did you know that my parents found out about us?" Noah asked.

"The only thing that was said about any of it was that your grandmother wanted me gone, that I messed up everything that Eros had worked for. I got the feeling by the way Eros and Theia Melenna were acting toward me that they knew something, but nothing was said."

"Yeah. I finally put the pieces together that night when my parents showed up. The Alpersteins were there, and they were all downstairs, having this big powwow. My dad was so pissed off that night. The next day, I was down in the barn, and my dad was screaming and cursing at me, calling me all kinds of names. Even though your name never came up, he told me that he wasn't going to have a fag for a son."

Spiro shook his head. "I'm sorry."

"No, it's not your fault that my dad's a fucking homophobe."

"Well, I still feel bad. How are they now... I mean, with you being gay?"

Noah thought about how much he wanted to reveal. His parents were the last people on earth that he wanted to talk about. He had so many questions for Spiro, that he figured Spiro had just as much right to ask his questions as well. "They hate it. It's one of those things we just don't discuss. My dad and I, we barely talk, but it's not just about me being gay. He has his own issues. My mom and I talk, but we're not close." Noah recalled his and his father's fight in the barn that day. They could never salvage any part of their relationship after that fight. It was strained before that weekend, but afterwards they didn't speak to one another. Days turned into weeks, and then Noah left for Harvard.

Noah cleared his throat. "I was devastated when you left... There's so much I wanted to tell you."

"Tell me. Tell me now. I want to know everything. How was Harvard? Are you a doctor now?"

155

Noah laughed. "No, I'm not a doctor. I got sick my first year at school. I had to leave."

"What happened?"

"Do you remember my stomach problems? How I was sick a lot?"

"Yeah."

"Well, it turned out I have what's called Irritable Bowel Syndrome. It's an intestinal disorder that causes the pain in my gut and constipation and—" He didn't want to go into the nasty part of the disease, the stuff that no one wants to hear. "Anyway, they think, at least some people do, that it's caused by stress and what you eat. I have to take medication and watch what I eat, and that seems to help manage it."

"Are you okay?"

"Yeah, I am. When it got bad, I swore I'd die. That was my first year in college. I was in pain for months." Although Spiro's simple question asking if he was okay could have come from anyone. The authenticity in his voice caused warmth to spread within Noah's chest. Spiro still possessed the ability to make his heart swoon with the raw genuineness of his words.

"So, they cured you?"

A snicker slipped from Noah. "You can't cure it, only manage it." He blushed at Spiro's attentiveness. "This trip has been somewhat of a challenge, though."

"I'm sorry."

"No, don't be sorry. It's not your fault. It's not like I'm going to die or anything." There was so much that he wanted to talk about, none of it being his IBS. Like when they were kids, during their walks in the woods or lying in the boat, they were full of questions for the other. "I finished my schooling at New York University—online. Got a degree in Information Technology. I have my own company now. I create and manage websites."

"Your own company? That doesn't surprise me. You're smart."

"Thank you. What about you? Did you ever go back to school?"

"Me? Noooo. I told you many years ago, it wasn't my thing."

"Do you still paint?"

"Yes. I still paint. But like I say, I help Nina in the gallery. Hanging the pictures, packaging the ones we sell. We have to take them to the mainland for shipping. It's too expensive to ship from here. This is a lot of work."

"That's good, you're still painting. So is your work for sale in there?" There was a part of Noah that suggested he should let him know that he had all the paintings Spiro had left behind. After all, they were his paintings. For so many years, that was all he had of Spiro.

"No, the owners of the gallery pick the stuff that we sell." Spiro's left eyebrow rose. "Hey, do you still throw up when you drink water?" Spiro laughed.

Noah laughed as well, remembering heaving in the lake. "That's not funny. You cheated and nearly killed me!"

"This is not true." Spiro chuckled as he leaned his shoulder into Noah's. "There is much to talk about." Spiro's chin rose. "I take you to dinner tonight." His face softened. The greens in his eyes penetrated deep into Noah's.

The green and brown sparkles in Spiro's eyes hadn't changed. He still had the most beautiful eyes Noah had ever looked into. Noah released a breath as his lungs expanded with another full breath. "Okay, but I'll pay."

Neither looked away from the other.

Spiro smiled. "No, I pay. This is not a date, yes?"

It took a few minutes for Noah to put the verbs and adjectives in the right order. "So, you're saying this is a date?"

"Yes!" Excitement rose in Spiro's voice. "It is very much a date. You come this far, far away to find me, then I pay. Meet me at Simonetta's tonight. You will like it."

"What time?"

"In two hours. I must go back to the gallery. Make sure Nina is okay. We have much to talk about. Perhaps all night."

Noah tried everything to hold back the creeping smile that curved the corners of his mouth. If it would be an all nighter, he hoped for more than talking. "Okay. I'll see you in a bit. I'll find it." His head nodded as it sunk into his shoulders. *I'm going on a date tonight with him!*

Spiro stood. "I can't believe you're here. I'll see you tonight." The gleam in his eyes, the curve in his smile, said more than his words.

Noah tried to hold his excitement from bursting out. A smile, a glance, an expression, they still communicated so much to the other without having to speak a word. He was so in love with this man. He wondered if that, too, had already been communicated to Spiro. He tried to tamp it down, saying it was only dinner. There was much to talk about, years of catching up. He'd done the impossible. He'd found the love of his life, not once, but twice.

****

Noah looked at the tiny sign above the frosted glass door, ensuring he was at the right place. He'd passed this restaurant at least a dozen times over the last week. Since leaving Spiro this afternoon, Noah had been analyzing every word Spiro had said to him.

Earlier this evening, while he was getting ready for his date, his brain had hit overload capacity. He was overthinking it all. He was one hundred percent sure Spiro was not only happy to see him, but that he was interested. The way the green gleamed in his eyes, that soft, beautiful smile, they both said how much he liked looking at what was in front of him. Would they sleep together tonight? If he slept with Spiro so soon, would that send the wrong message? Hell, he didn't even ask Spiro if he was seeing anyone. This could still all be for naught. He needed to hear the voice of reason.

Rodney was no help and made things worse. His advice was: Sleep with him tonight. If it's still good and if he calls the next day, you're good.

Noah stepped into Simonetta's and was surprised. There was no restaurant, just a long hallway that led diners past the kitchen to the back of the building into a large courtyard. Several customers were seated at tables around the yard. Medium-sized olive trees in giant clay pots separated the tables. Dim white lights were strung from tree to tree, providing an ambiance that was intimate and discreet.

A young girl that couldn't have been a day over fifteen greeted him. "Good evening." With the girl's hair pulled into a single ponytail, her smile revealed a mouthful of braces.

"Good evening." Noah's eyes passed over the girl, his eyes scanning the room for Spiro. "I'm meeting someone. Spiro..." *Damn it!* How was it he could be in love with someone, travel halfway around the world to find him, and still not know his last name? The hostess turned toward the yard, and they both scanned the yard. Noah had spotted Spiro in the back corner of the yard when Spiro stood and waved. "Oh, there he is." Not waiting for the girl, Noah headed straight for his date.

They greeted each other with a simple hug, one that Noah would have given to his grandmother. Noah caught a hint of a light, citrusy scent from Spiro's hair. He waited for Noah to sit before taking his seat. He couldn't believe just how handsome Spiro was. When they were young, Spiro was a thing of beauty, and now with years on him, Spiro was one of those men that was divinely gorgeous, in a league of his own.

"Okay, before we go any further, what the hell is your last name?" Noah joked. "I can't believe I've traveled halfway around the world to find someone, and I don't know their last name."

"It's Papadopoulos." The bewilderment on Spiro's face suggested he wasn't catching the humor.

"Had I known your last name, it might not have taken me years to find you. There's so much I should have asked you back then. We were living so much in the moment."

Spiro bobbed his head. "That's not so bad, to live in the moment. The only thing certain in this life is that we did not die yesterday. We know nothing of tomorrow."

Noah smiled. "You're still that cloud moving in the wind, aren't you? It's one of the things I admired about you." *I love you.* "You never had a plan, rules, or an agenda." Noah's eyes fixed on the beautiful man sitting across from him. He wanted to kiss him, to touch his face, to rub his cheeks against the tiny black stubble that covered Spiro's lower jaw and neck.

"I can't believe this afternoon. When you called my name, I couldn't believe it was you."

"Yeah, I know. Your eyes bulging out of their sockets was priceless. That was my friend who shouted at you, not me." He still couldn't believe Nico had done it.

"I thought you were standing with a guy, but then he disappeared."

"That was Nico. He was helping me find you."

"Then I must thank this Nico someday."

The young girl came over and spoke to them in Greek. Spiro and the girl volleyed words for a minute before she excused herself. Noah understood none of it, but he gathered they were discussing the menu. The robust spices that filled the courtyard were warm and hearty.

Upon her returning to the kitchen, Spiro returned his attention to Noah. "Tonight, they have cooked a lamb stew and a bluefish. I told her to bring both. You choose and eat what you like."

She returned and sat two shot glasses and a bottle of ouzo on the table. Spiro unscrewed the cap from the bottle. "Ouzo?" he asked before pouring.

"No, thanks." Noah stared at the clear liquid in the bottle. He'd read that the licorice-flavored drink was the equivalent to a tequila shot for the Greeks. He could use a shot of tequila right now, but was concerned about his stomach. Not only was he a nervous wreck, but he also had no idea about the meal Spiro had ordered for them. He wasn't above putting out on a first date, especially tonight, so he had to be careful. He'd had more than one disastrous date to learn not to eat or drink if you're planning on having sex. As a bottom, during sex, digestive issues could be disastrous.

"No? You don't like?" Spiro's expression said it couldn't be possible.

"No, I probably would, but it's because of my stomach." Without thinking, Noah leaned into the table, shielding his stomach.

Spiro filled one glass and took a shot. He grimaced as if it was burning his throat. He recapped the bottle and pushed it aside. "Do you still play chess?"

Noah smiled, seeing Spiro's face twist up like a baby eating creamed peas for the first time. Spiro was beautiful. "Yeah, I do. Haven't in a while. My roommate hates to play."

"Well, maybe we can play again while you're here. I challenge you to a rematch!"

Noah laughed under his breath, hearing little had changed with Spiro. He was ready and willing to take on the master with little fear.

"You know, you are as handsome as you were years ago." Spiro held up a finger. "I saw this before I drank the ouzo!" The corner of Spiro's mouth curved into a slight smile as the gold flakes in his eyes danced in the light.

Noah winced at the thought of how gangly he was growing up. Perhaps Spiro only thought he was cute back then because he was drinking that ouzo stuff. Spiro was still as sweet and adorable as he was when they were kids... but now, that adorable and sweet Spiro was eye fucking him. He saw the same look in Spiro's eyes earlier, when they were sitting on the pier. That same smile now, the deep stare: he was a hundred percent sure he was being eye fucked right now.

Noah's arousing thoughts caused his cheeks to blush as a flutter ran from his chest to his head. The rush of oxygen caused him to feel lightheaded for a second. Without shame, Noah knew he would give himself to Spiro tonight without hesitation if that was what Spiro wanted. Perhaps one should always have a hesitation, but this was not the case.

Noah wanted nothing more than to be possessed by the person in front of him. He wanted to be naked, lying beside this man, on the beach, in the boathouse, in the barn, right here, if that was what Spiro wanted. *Are there no limits tonight? Have I gone mad?*

That hot summer day in the boathouse, the moment Spiro pushed deep inside him, their souls had connected forever. Noah knew little about the grown man in front of him, yet it was as if they'd been together forever. If Spiro asked, he would sleep with him tonight. All he had to do was ask.

Over the years, Noah had never been opposed to just having sex with someone if he was into them. He wasn't a slut, and it was never ideal. But sometimes, a person needed to satisfy an itch. It was one of the perks of being a gay man... Anonymous, cheap sex was somehow acceptable.

But this wasn't what he was feeling tonight. What was going through his heart was something deeper, a longing to be consumed by Spiro. It was the same as years ago, and again this afternoon when Spiro recognized him—and now. Years of therapy told him to *slow down. Be careful. Don't be stupid.*

When their dinner was served, they continued talking as they ate. Noah was a master at appearing that he was eating, nibbling on bits of food. Keeping it light, he shared a little about his job, his friend Rodney, and the passing of his grandmother that led to the selling of the lake house. He held back his depressing track record with men.

It was approaching midnight when the two left the restaurant and emerged onto the dark narrow street. All the stores were closed for the night, and the street had been abandoned hours ago. It was only the two of them. Goosebumps rose on Noah's arms as the chilled air attacked his skin through his shirt.

"Are you cold?" Spiro asked. Illuminated by a thin slice of the moon, his eyes revealed his concern for Noah's comfort.

Noah tried to play it off. "I'm okay."

"With the breeze coming off the ocean at night, the nights are cooler. We've been waiting all summer for this breeze. I'm sorry it's not warmer for you."

"Is it always like this, this time of year?"

"Yes." Spiro stepped in a little closer. "The best time to be here if you like warm weather is around your birthday."

Noah's brows rose. "How do you know my birthday?" The warmth of Spiro's breath caused him to inhale.

"It's June tenth, right?"

"Yeah! How do you know that?"

"Really? I'll never forget your birthday. It was the day you arrived at the house." Spiro's hand lightly touched Noah's arm.

His touch made Noah draw a breath. "Oh! That's right! Trust me, I remember." Noah smiled at the thought of that day. It was the beginning of the best summer of his life.

There was a moment of silence as the two stood on the narrow sidewalk. Noah looked at the moon, trying to fill the space with something. As he looked down, Spiro came in and kissed him. Startled, it took a half a second for it to register and their mouths to sync.

Their kiss deepened as Spiro backed him against the building. Savagely, they kissed for several minutes before Spiro pulled back. "You are handsome. I've wanted to kiss you since this afternoon." Spiro's penetrating stare kept Noah pinned to the wall.

The cool nighttime temperature had vanished. Noah's body was on fire, heat rising from his chest, extending all the way to the tips of his fingers and toes. He could feel heat on his cheeks as well. There were no words to come close to how Noah was feeling. Instead, he leaned in as their heads closed the gap between them.

Spiro gripped the back of Noah's head and pulled him in, deepening their kiss again. The taste of ouzo engaged Noah's taste buds as he recalled how magnificent Spiro was at kissing. This kiss was anything but gentle as Spiro's warm tongue invaded Noah's mouth.

Occasionally, Spiro's light facial hair scraped against Noah's cheeks, serving as a reminder that his once young lover was now this man. It was the only difference. Whatever else he didn't know about Spiro was of little importance right now.

Noah's pulse quickened as his body temperature escalated to an inferno. Spiro dominated him, pressing him up against the building. Spiro's rough hands clasped Noah's face. They were the hands of a man. Paint, solvents, chemicals were likely the culprits.

Noah's legs wanted to give out under him, but he was being held between the building and Spiro's body, pressed against his. Locked in a fiery kiss, the world disappeared around him. When Spiro pulled back and released him, Noah slid down off the wall as his heels returned to the sidewalk.

Noah's breath had been stolen. He wiped the moisture from his swollen lips as he stared into the hunger in Spiro's eyes. "Come back to my hotel." Embarrassed by his bold offer, it was either that, or they would have sex right there in the alley. Noah held what little breath he had as he waited for an answer.

"Ah, I would love to." The back of Spiro's hand brushed Noah's cheek. "But it's late. I must go home this evening. Tomorrow, I will see you again."

"Um, o—okay." Noah couldn't deny that he was more than disappointed that Spiro had said no, but he loved Spiro's assertiveness in saying they would be together tomorrow. Like a child on Christmas Eve, he wanted his present now. He was rock hard, with the heaviest balls he'd had in years. They were almost painful. "Okay," Noah muttered again, this time more to himself as he processed that the night was over.

"Do you want a ride back to your hotel?"

"No. It's just down the street." He needed to walk off his erection and absorb some of the cool air. It really was for the best that they said goodnight here and now. Another minute in this man's presence and Noah would climax in his pants without ever touching himself.

"Have you been to the castle?" Spiro asked.

"No... not yet." He'd regained his breath.

"Then meet me on the pier at nine, at the base of the mountain. You'll see a trail. Wait for me there."

"Okay."

Spiro leaned in and gave him a light, soft kiss, tugging on Noah's bottom lip playfully. "*Kalinýchta*," he whispered from his lips into Noah's own breath.

Noah had no idea what Spiro had said—something perhaps as crazy as *I love you* or *I want to marry you*.

As Noah fantasized over the words, Spiro hopped on his motorbike, and with a push of the button the tiny engine rumbled. He straddled the motorbike and hobbled it from the sidewalk onto the street. Within seconds, he was gone.

CHAPTER SIXTEEN

Spiro arrived in Myrina early so he could pick up a few things at the market for the picnic he'd planned for Noah. He'd used his phone to research foods that people with IBS could eat. With lunch and a blanket in his backpack, he headed to where he promised to meet the man who appeared yesterday from nowhere and returned to his life. They were boys so many years ago. It seemed like another life.

At thirty-two years old, Spiro had never forgotten that summer. It was such a brief moment in his life, so out of the norm of everything before and after it. He was an island boy, born and raised on the island like his father, grandfather, and great-grandfather. It was as if that summer belonged to someone else or in a movie he'd seen.

That summer, he met the rich American whose parents were doctors, with an expensive house on the lake. Their life was about fancy boats and prestigious schools. None of that had been a part of Spiro's life, so how could that summer belong to him? Being in the United States that summer was like a different world, a world he hadn't seen since.

Yesterday, his life was simple. And now, his heart fluttered for the guy he hadn't seen in years. A smile swept across his face. Noah was here, here for him, and he was as cute and innocent as he remembered.

Spiro rounded the corner and walked onto the cement pier. The port was busy with fishermen tying up their boats and securing their equipment for the remainder of the day. Being a fisherman was tough. They had to go out to sea in the middle of the night to be back by early morning. It was his father's life, a life Spiro never wanted.

He saw a girl patrolling the pier, attempting to make eye contact with the few tourists that remained. Tourists were easy to spot. He had plenty of experience doing exactly what she was doing. She was holding a stack of flyers in one hand as she held up one in her other hand. She was drumming up business for someone, handing leaflets to anyone who would take one.

He, too, once sold his paintings here. He would lay them out on the pier for the passing tourists who strolled by, attempting to make eye contact and stop them for a few minutes. Few gave him a glance, but he knew if he could get them to stop, maybe he could charm them into buying one of his paintings.

Back then, he did small eight-by-ten paintings on cheap canvas. For years, he was mass producing what it was they would buy. He could paint several pictures of a Santorini cliff line in a night. He sold them to remind tourists for years how special their trip was. He'd laugh, knowing the moment he had them hooked, usually before they even knew it, that they wouldn't walk away without one. That, too, seemed a lifetime ago, but it definitely belonged to him.

Noah wasn't at the base of the mountain when Spiro arrived. He saw the trail that led to the ruins of the medieval castle. He chewed on his cuticle as he paced, waiting for Noah to arrive. It wasn't long before he spotted Noah on the opposite end of the pier, walking toward him. Noah's head was down as he strolled along the edge of the wharf. Noah was as beautiful as he was yesterday.

About twenty-five yards away, Noah finally saw him. An adorable smile swept across Noah's face as he raised his arm to wave. Noah was as endearing as when they were just kids. *Am I the only one that can see this? How does the world not see this?* Spiro's desire flickered to life. Was this something that perhaps Noah only revealed to him, not for the rest of the world to see?

The tall, skinny American made him grin, but he waited until Noah was in earshot before speaking. "Good morning."

They'd lost so much to the world already, and with a few tourists roaming, Spiro wasn't willing to share a simple greeting to him with them. It was for Noah and Noah alone.

In brown cutoffs rolled below the knee and a tight black tee shirt that hung off Noah's thin torso, he was about as sexy as any one person could be. The skin on his pale cheeks was as flawless as the skin of a baby. The morning light showed off the rust highlights in his sandy blonde hair. Yes, Noah stole his breath and made his heart race like no one ever had.

"Good morning." Noah's smile enlarged, causing the dark circles under his blue eyes to fade a little.

"Did you get your work done this morning?" Spiro reflected on what Noah said during dinner last night about working in the mornings in his room.

"Well, not everything. But there are no fires I had to put out. You look nice." Noah's eyes glanced down at Spiro's body.

"Fires?" Spiro's head cocked to one side. Noah's compliment fell to the side as he tried to figure out the *fires* phrase.

"Not real fires. Emergencies." Noah grinned as he laughed under his breath.

Side by side on the narrow dirt trail leading up the hill, the two meandered as they chatted. They shared moments of silence as they both seemingly took in the surrounding barren hillside and the beauty in it.

"Whatever happened to Eros? I never saw him after you guys left that summer. Did he fly back with you?" Noah asked.

Without missing a step, Spiro bent down and picked up a twig laying in their path. "No, he stayed in Boston. That summer was the last time I saw him, too. He died the next year." Memories of his theios that summer caused him to take a deep breath. He was a cantankerous but cute old man. Spiro wished he knew him better, but time and distance never allowed that.

"I'm sorry. He was a nice guy. It's kind of weird, but that was the last summer I spent up at the lake house, too. Before they sold the place, I took a drive up there. I wanted your paintings. I hid them in the barn for a while. I still have them."

Spiro stopped and turned toward Noah. "You did! Really?"

"Yeah. I was hoping you'd be famous by now, that your paintings would be worth millions. I could sell them and never have to work again!"

What Spiro wouldn't do to be rich! "That would be good." He wondered how wealthy Noah was. He couldn't imagine being able to drop everything and fly to America for a couple of weeks. It would cost thousands of euros. Long ago, he'd stopped thinking his paintings would make him rich. It was just a way to make money and survive. Spiro lovingly poked Noah in his side before continuing up the hill.

"Ouch!" Noah reacted to the poke. His mouth curved into a warm, confident smile that lit his face. "Finders keepers. They're mine now."

Spiro knew that he'd left several paintings behind, but the one he specifically remembered was the one he'd painted of Noah. About ten years ago, he tried to recreate it from memory. When he'd completed it, he remembered thinking his memory of Noah was already failing him. Although he had no idea what was off, it wasn't quite Noah.

Halfway up the trail, Spiro pointed to several small deer grazing in the field ahead.

Noah's brows raised, seeing the deer. "Oh, my gosh, those are the deer you told me about!"

"When?" When had he spoken of the deer to Noah?

Noah lowered his voice to a whisper. "Do you remember that day? I think we were cleaning out the barn or something. We were sitting in my granddad's old car, and you were talking about them."

"That's right." He hadn't thought about that day in years.

"Tell me again. How did deer get up here?"

They both stopped as deer heads and ears popped up and watched them. "I imagine they walked."

Noah laughed. "No, I mean on the island?"

"They're called European Fallow. Back in the seventies, a bunch of females, three males, and a couple of babies were brought here from the island of Rhodes. A group of people were trying to preserve their original genetic diversity by moving some of the deer here so they could repopulate the island. They've been here ever since."

The deer began moving away from them. Their intrusion had interrupted the animals' morning meal. The ground was bare, with patches of grass and weeds worn by their grazing.

The trek uphill took less than twenty minutes before they arrived at the castle ruins.

"This is cool." Noah stared at the large formation of boulders that outlined what remained of the castle. "The night I flew in, I remember seeing it. It lit the entire mountain. I read that it was first constructed back in 1186 AD by some king or emperor."

"Then you know more about it than me." Spiro had studied it in elementary school, but most of his knowledge came from conversations with others.

There was almost nothing left of the castle but enough to give visitors a sense of what it must have been like hundreds of years ago. Built of stone, some walls still stood. Positioned on the highest point above Myrina, the castle sloped into the hillside. They had a stunning view of the entire island and the Aegean Sea.

"I read that the island had been occupied at one time by the Romans, the Venetians, and then the Turkish." Noah's cheeks had turned a burnt red from the sun. The strong winds blowing across the top of the mountain revealed his hardened nipples through his tee shirt.

"Yes, but it's ours now. Can you imagine seeing war ships approaching the island from up here?" Seeing Noah's hardened nipples pressing through his shirt, Spiro felt bad he'd forgotten to tell him to dress warm because of the winds. They also stirred sexually arousing thoughts of what he wanted to do to them.

They were the only two visitors at the castle, and they had the entire landmark to themselves. Spiro clasped Noah's hand as they strolled over the hilltop.

"It's beautiful up here." Noah stopped long enough to deliver a light kiss.

Hand in hand, they climbed over the rocks and the ruins. Being silly, they mapped out what they envisioned were rooms. With much of the ruin unrestricted, they carried on as if it was a thousand years ago.

Whenever they encountered one of the many informational boards in Greek, Spiro read it aloud, translating it to English the best he could.

"I can't believe this all isn't fenced off or something." Noah took a seat on a large boulder, hanging his feet over the edge. "If this was in America, we'd have either torn it down to build apartments or roped it off and sold fifty-dollar tickets to see it."

Spiro took a seat beside Noah, leaving no room between them. "But this belongs to us. You don't buy a ticket to see something that's yours."

The warmth of the slab of rock they were sitting on, combined with the sun beaming down on them, helped to combat the chill of the wind. It had been years since he'd been up here. Spiro closed his eyes, took in a breath of clean air, and exhaled. "Are you hungry? I picked up some snacks. I hope you can eat them." Spiro reached for his backpack he'd set down behind them.

"What do you have?" Noah glanced at Spiro's backpack before looking back at the gorgeous views of the Aegean Sea in front of them. "The view is breathtaking."

Spiro dug into his pack and handed a bag of pretzels over. He then took out a bottled water and squeezed it between them.

"I can't believe I found you. I swear, I searched this whole island." Noah rested the bag of pretzels on his lap.

"Our house is not far from here. It's me and my mom and dad, my cousin Nina, and my Theia Kyra. I have a small studio out back. Years ago, my dad built it, intending for it to be a garage. When it was done, I moved back from Athens and moved in there instead. It's big enough for my bed with room for me to paint."

"The aunt you live with now, is this the same aunt that lived in Boston?"

"No, that was Eros's sister, Theia Melenna, who was in Boston. She died years ago. My Theia Kyra is Eros's wife."

"How's your mom and dad doing?" Noah asked.

"My dad's getting old. He still goes out every morning on the boat, but most times he's sleepy and crabby. My mom's fine." A heaviness invaded his heart. He drew a breath to prevent it from taking over the mood. "Do you have any plans for today?" Spiro asked.

"Nope. You're it."

"Do you like the beach?"

"Yeah, I guess. Never been a big fan of swimming in the ocean, though."

"Okay, then I'll take you to a place that I like to go on the other side of the island. It's much warmer there. Like here, it's empty."

****

After tinkering with the engine, Spiro started the motorbike, and they were on their way. Noah held tightly to Spiro's waist as they weaved along the one-lane country highway to the other side of the island. Surrounded by large expanses of dried grass and rolling hills, the temperature had climbed about ten degrees higher than it was in Myrina.

It was late afternoon when Spiro and Noah reached the turnoff to their next destination. Spiro drove the motorbike off the road and onto a narrow dirt road that snaked down toward the ocean. At the end of the road, they parked the motorbike and hiked the remaining hundred yards to the beach.

Spiro removed a small blanket and the bottled water from his backpack. He unscrewed the cap and waited for Noah to finish taking a picture before handing Noah the bottle of water.

"What all do you have in that thing?" Noah stared at Spiro's backpack as he took a large gulp of water. He waited a second or two before taking another swig and giving it back to Spiro.

"Everything." Spiro answered before taking a sip. He screwed the cap back on and lay it down on the blanket. "I love this beach. When the tourists are all over the place, I can come down here, and there's nobody here.

Noah sat on the blanket and brought his feet to his chest. "Do you remember that time we were sitting in my granddad's car in the barn? We were playing like you had taken me to the beach. Is this the beach?"

Spiro stripped the knot from his shoelace and removed his shoes. "Yep, that's this beach. See, you've been here before." He pulled off his socks and stuffed them into his shoes.

Noah followed his lead and removed his shoes and socks. "It's a lot warmer down here." He stretched his legs in front of him and buried his feet into the warm sand. When he looked at Spiro, their eyes met. "What?" Noah asked.

"Nothing." Many things were going through Spiro's mind, all of which had to do with Noah.

"No, tell me what you were smiling at." Noah pled.

"I can't believe how handsome you are. That you came all this way to find me." This still made little sense to Spiro that someone would travel so far to find him.

"Me? Handsome?" Noah laughed and shook his head.

"Why do you laugh at me?" Spiro was confused. "What is it that I say that is so funny?"

"It's not funny. It's sweet." Noah answered. "Especially coming from you. I bet you drive the men and women on this island crazy trying to date you."

"Why do you say that?"

Noah cocked his head. "Come on! Do you know how gorgeous you are?"

Spiro brushed off Noah's compliment with a frown and a wave of his hands. "Beauty, it's like a painting. It depends on who's looking at it. Anyways, who could I date on the island? The island is small. There is no one else to date for me."

"So, you've gone through them all already!" Noah teased. "Whatever happened to that girl you were seeing that summer you visited, that you were so in love with?"

It took Spiro a minute to figure out what girl Noah was talking about. "Stefania?"

"Yes. That's her!"

"Stefania is not someone I see anymore. When I came back, she wanted no more to do with me. She had fallen in love and was no more in love with me. She loved someone else. What about you? You are here for me, so this means you are not seeing anyone, no?"

"No."

Spiro grinned. "This is good for me."

"Did you have other girlfriends?" Noah asked.

"Over the years, I've had many girlfriends." Spiro wondered why Noah was asking.

"How about boyfriends?" Noah's expression sobered.

Spiro shrugged. "Not as many."

"Any you loved?" Noah asked.

"There was one... that I questioned if I loved in the beginning of the relationship. Peter... We were together for two years. We lived in Athens. And you?" Spiro was intrigued how it wasn't possible that this sweet man wasn't taken.

"I've never had a girlfriend." Noah asserted. "But over the years I've dated a couple of guys that I would say I loved." Noah brushed his hands together, clearing the sand off them. "I'm not sure that the feeling was always mutual though. What happened with Peter?" Noah asked.

"Peter had a thirst for men that I couldn't satisfy."

"Oh." Noah raised a brow. "So, he didn't love you as much as you loved him?"

The word "love" reverberated in Spiro's ear as he hesitated a moment. "No... Actually, I think I was in love with the life he offered me." Spiro nodded. Relationships were the sort of thing that hadn't worked out for him. "How about you? Have you been in love?"

Noah smirked. "When I was eighteen. There was this boy I met. At the time, I was crazy about him!"

Spiro grinned at Noah. "What do you mean, *at the time*?" He rolled his weight into Noah's body, sending them both backwards onto the tiny blanket. He used the tips of his fingers, tickling Noah's side and stomach, sending him into a fit of laughter. Spiro couldn't resist laughing as well, as Noah screamed and squirmed. "Did you say 'was'? What do you mean, *was*!"

"Okay! Okay! I am! I'm still crazy about you!" Noah proclaimed as he laughed.

Spiro stopped his giggling torture. Noah saying that he was crazy about him scattered everything else Spiro had been thinking. Noah's body under him sent a surge to his groin and throughout his entire body. Bringing their mouths within the same breathing space, Spiro kissed him.

It was only a brief kiss before Spiro drew back. He was unable to peel his gaze away from the beautiful blue eyes staring back at him. How could one person so quickly get into his heart? He stared into Noah's eyes for the answer.

Love... the word played in his head. It was a word that people used too easily. Love was easy to define when Spiro thought about his mom, dad, or family members. It had never been as clear to him when it came to other people. How long did it take to fall in love was the million-dollar question he could never answer. It was way too soon to be talking about love, anyway.

With their bodies still pressed together, Noah's erection rubbed Spiro's. His own body responded. He tamped down the idea of having sex right there on the beach. He was sure Noah hadn't come all this way just for sex. He needed to create a little separation. He pulled back and rolled to the side. "Do you remember the first time we had sex?"

"Of course, it was in the boat." Their eyes were glued to one another's; Noah's rosy cheekbones blushed a little more.

How does one have such perfect skin? "Yeah... it was also the day you barfed in the lake." Spiro gave Noah a playful smirk right before they both erupted into laughter. "That was so gross." Still laughing, Spiro could barely talk. "I felt bad for you. I thought you were going to die on me."

"You made me swallow so much water, I thought I was dying." Noah answered through his own laughter.

"If I remember, you swallowed more than water that summer." Spiro barely got it out before laughing.

"Yeah... you totally corrupted me. It's your fault entirely." Noah laughed.

"Are you ready for another snack?" Spiro adjusted his erection in his pants before pulling his backpack up from their feet. "I didn't know if you were lactose intolerant as well, so I stayed away from cheese and stuff."

"It depends on what it is and how much. I can do a little, depending on what it is. It's kind of like gluten. I can eat bread; I just have to watch how much. If I can, I buy gluten-free stuff."

Spiro pulled food from his backpack and arranged it before them. "Let's see. I got you a boiled egg, a banana, a bag of almonds, and a chicken breast... I asked, and they said they broiled it, so no oil."

Noah reached for the banana. "This was sweet of you. No one has ever thrown me an IBS picnic before."

"I can't believe that." Spiro took the bag of almonds and tore them open.

They finished lunch by washing it down with the remaining water in the water bottle. "Do you want to go in the water? It's still warm." Spiro stood and stepped off the blanket.

"No, I'll pass." Noah's eyes steadfast on Spiro, Noah brought his knees to his chest and wrapped his arms around his legs.

"Okay. I'll be right back." Facing Noah, Spiro pulled off his shirt and tossed it on the blanket. He saw Noah's eyebrows raise as he took in the tattoos that covered his upper right arm, as well as his right shoulder and chest.

"Oh, wow, I guess... you like tattoos." Noah pointed to Spiro's tattoos.

Did he not like tattoos? Spiro thought that Noah's tone and his wrinkled brows spoke louder than his words. "It was something I got into years ago." Spiro guardedly answered as he unsnapped his jeans and allowed them to fall to his feet. Naked, he was about to explain the significance of the art that covered a large portion of his upper body, but the gleam in Noah's eyes on his cock stopped him. Noah appeared pleased, which sent a flow of blood back to Spiro's groin. "Here I go. Are you sure?"

Noah's face was inches from his cock. The flirtatious grin on his face caused Spiro to hesitate. Spiro's rising erection pulsated as he scanned their surroundings up the cliff, ensuring they were alone. Yes, they were alone. The sexual tension between them caused the hairs on his arms to rise. He needed to get in the water to douse the flame that was rising with each tempting thought of taking Noah right here on the beach.

Spiro made it out past where the waves break before turning to watch Noah on shore, taking more pictures. He couldn't believe Noah was here. Their summer, so many years ago played out in his head. Memories flooded his brain.

It was a tumultuous time in his life. He was a twenty-year-old trying to figure out the world and his place in it. So much went on that he'd never had the chance to deal with his feelings about losing Noah that summer. It was one punch after another for years after that. The biggest of them all was Peter. Spiro shook his head, refusing to go there.

With the sun rays burning down on Spiro's stomach, the buoyancy of the water allowed his naked body to float above the water. He'd spent hardly any time at the beach the last couple of summers—something he didn't realize he missed until now. He worked all day, every day.

The quietness allowed his mind to drift. Noah showing up here was beyond anything he could have expected for his life. It was beyond believable.

His body rising and falling with the waves relaxed Spiro, but he wanted to be close to Noah. He wanted to be beside him, talk to him, quiz him on everything he missed out on over the years. He tried to slow his brain as he made his way back to shore.

When he could stand, he rose from the water. A wave hit him from behind and threw him face down into the water. Back on his feet, he heard Noah's laugh, carried by the wind.

As he made his way up to Noah, Spiro grinned seeing Noah taking pictures of him as he walked towards him. Out of breath from fighting the waves, Spiro waited until he was closer to Noah to speak. "Yes, you would not have enjoyed that. The water is much colder than expected." Spiro ran his hands through his hair, clearing the excess water from his hair and ears before grabbing his cigarettes from his pants pocket.

Noah stared up at the naked, toned body standing before him as Spiro lit his cigarette. His wet, golden-brown skin glistened in the sunlight. "I can't believe you live here. This place is beautiful." Noah snapped another picture of Spiro's naked body.

"You better not put those on the internet!" Spiro held his cigarette at bay as he exhaled.

Noah smirked as he put his phone down beside him. "Why? It's not like you're even on the internet. What's Facebook?" Noah challenged.

"I know what Facebook is." He'd had this same argument with Nina and all his friends. The internet wasn't his thing. Why would he want to talk to people he would never see or meet? Everyone he knew that he wanted to talk to lived right here on the island.

"You should at least have a website."

"Why do I need a website? For what?" Now Noah was making no sense at all.

"For your paintings. You have no idea how good you are, do you? You could sell paintings all around the world."

"To who?" Spiro pushed down his embarrassment that he was selling his paintings from the back room of the gallery. He wasn't good enough to convince the owners of the gallery to let him hang some of his work in there.

Noah sighed, exasperated. "To all kinds of people. What if someone who bought one of your paintings had a friend who loved it and wanted one? They'd have to come all the way here to buy it. But what if they could order it on the web and have it shipped?"

"I don't want to do that." It seemed like more trouble than it was worth. All he wanted to do was paint, but he also knew that he had to sell paintings to make a living.

"I could design a site for you," Noah offered.

Spiro extinguished his cigarette between his fingers and tucked the butt into the pocket of his jeans. "No, no, no." He waved off Noah's offer. "I'm freezing now." He dropped to his knees on the blanket and threw his cold, wet body on top of Noah. He again wrestled Noah onto his back. Noah's squeal was more than his resistance. Before Noah could free himself, Spiro rolled the blanket over both of them, wrapping them in a cocoon.

A single kiss. He wanted more. Their lips met again, and their kiss deepened as Spiro clasped his hand behind Noah's head and held him. Although they were alone on the beach, Spiro had to stop himself. He pulled away and stared down into Noah's eyes. "You excite me very much."

Noah chuckled. "I know. I can feel it."

Embracing each other and wrapped in the blanket, they dozed lightly. Spiro wasn't sure how long he'd napped when the sound of the waves creeping closer alarmed him. He lightly kissed Noah, who appeared to be sleeping. "Hey, are you asleep?"

Noah moistened his lips. "No, just lying here, listening to the ocean and your breathing."

Spiro kissed him. "What would you like to do tonight?" Spiro asked.

Noah opened his eyes. "Really—I would like for you to come back to my place."

It was what Spiro wanted to hear. He needed to know that was what Noah wanted as well. "I would like that very much. Shall we go?"

Noah nodded yes.

CHAPTER SEVENTEEN

With Spiro behind him, Noah couldn't open the door to his bungalow fast enough. The entire ride back from the beach, with the sun setting on their backs, all he did was fantasize of the two of them making love. The rush of excitement racing through him was as if he was eighteen all over again. It was the same feeling he had the first day he met Spiro, standing on the dock when he was just a young boy. Spiro made his heart leap, made him giddy... made his body beg to be touched.

Inside the bungalow Noah flipped the light switch beside the door. "Sorry I have nothing to offer you to drink other than water." He wasn't sure if they would do the whole Song and Dance of ten minutes of polite chit chat, or head straight to the bedroom. Either way, he needed a couple of minutes to prepare. "Would you like some water?" Noah offered.

"No thanks." With a sheepish grin, Spiro moved past Noah stepping into the middle of the room. "No bed?"

Noah nodded toward the bedroom. The sexual tension between them made it clear they would skip the song and dance. "Make yourself comfortable. I'm going to take a quick shower and I'll be right out." He needed to wash the day's sweat from his body, and make sure he was clean where it counted.

After his shower, Noah removed a strip of condoms and lubricant from the side pouch of his suitcase. He put them on the nightstand so Spiro could see them. He then stood in front of the small mirror over the sink as he wrapped a towel around his waist. He hesitated whether to put a tee shirt back on to cover himself. How he wished he had Spiro's well-defined physique, and not one of a Swizzle-stick.

He exhaled, expelling some of his nervous energy before making his return to the living room without a tee shirt.

Spiro was sitting on the edge of the couch. He looked up from the magazine but then smirked at the towel around Noah's waist. He tossed

176

the magazine onto the coffee table without removing his eyes from Noah.

A million butterflies took flight inside Noah's belly as he stepped closer to the small couch and stood over Spiro.

"Well look at you." Spiro took Noah by the waist. "As beautiful as I remember." Spiro tugged on the towel, freeing it from Noah's waist and dropping it to the floor. "Now that's better."

Spiro stood as he ran his hand from Noah's waist up to his neck, stopping when they were face to face.

Their eyes locked onto each other; Spiro's warm breath brushed under Noah's nose. He placed one hand on Noah's lower back above his ass and pushed lightly until Noah's bare skin pressed against Spiro's clothes. Heat radiated from Spiro's body as their lips touched.

In a deep kiss, Spiro's hand moved up and cupped the back of Noah's neck and cocked his head, and like a puppet Noah relinquished his mouth to him.

Had Noah known they would make love in the living room, he would've pulled the curtains and turned off the light in the room. They were on full display to anyone walking by on their way to the hotel's beach. He could hope it wasn't the case, but that wasn't enough to end what was about to happen.

Spiro stopped. His gazed swept past Noah's eyes before moving down to Noah's abdomen. Without a word, he took Noah by the hand and led him into the bedroom.

They stood beside the bed as Spiro kissed him again. Deep in the kiss, Spiro stopped, and with one hand, lay Noah on his back on the bed.

Crossways on the bed, Noah's feet hung inches from the floor. With a glazed love-struck eye, he watched as Spiro undressed, dropping his clothes in a pile where he stood.

In the light's glow from the front room, Noah remembered his breath being taken away earlier on the beach, when he'd seen the golden tan that swept across Spiro's ass in the sunlight. No trace of a single tan line. His ass matched the sun kissed skin on the rest of his glorious body. He wanted to touch his butt right then, sure it was as soft as years ago. An ass that was once soft to the initial touch, yet hard as a rock when gripped. How was it possible that one man could be so beautiful for so many years?

Spiro moved to the edge of the bed and straddled his body over

Noah's head resting on the mattress. Noah knew what he was asking and took Spiro into his mouth.

Face up, laying on his back, Noah tilted his head back to work more of Spiro into his mouth as he slid deeper in. A hint of ocean salt from Spiro's swim earlier tingled against his taste buds. Noah struggled to breathe but refused to stop. He fought the need to touch himself, he knew better.

Relief came to his tightening jaw when Spiro stopped long enough to straddle Noah's stomach. He kissed his chest and neck, working his way to his lips. Each soft kiss caused Noah's breath to catch. Spiro's body nestled down beside his as they explored each other's bodies with their eyes, hands, and mouths.

Spiro's mouth pressed hard against his as they kissed, his tongue making love to Noah's mouth. After a while, Spiro's mouth worked its way down Noah's body to his cock. The heat from Spiro's mouth on his cock would take all control away that Noah might maintain. It wasn't long before Noah was close, and Spiro may have sensed it and slowed down.

The ripples of pleasure stopped as Spiro rose to his feet. He picked up a condom from the nightstand and showed it to Noah. "Is this okay? I mean, you can, right?"

Noah knew what Spiro was asking. "Yes. I'm good."

He rolled Noah onto his belly. With one finger, Spiro lubricated Noah's ass. He stretched him, increasing the number of fingers until he was ready. From the corner of his eye, Noah saw Spiro slip the condom over his cock. His cock pressed against Noah's hole for a second before it pushed past the first set of nerves. Spiro pushed further until his body was pressed against Noah's back.

Noah wished he had a second to adjust but Spiro didn't afford it. Slow and gentle, Spiro moved in and out of him. His strokes were deep, occasionally stopping before driving back into him.

Spiro lifted Noah onto all fours. Positioned behind Noah, Spiro's strokes deepened as he slid a hand around to Noah's throat and pulled his head back. The air lessened in Noah's lungs.

With one hand pressed against Noah's ass and the other around his throat, Spiro pushed deeper and faster into him. Fireworks were exploding in Noah's head, one after another, as Spiro drove into him. Noah tried to turn to see Spiro, but Spiro pushed his head forward.

Noah's body couldn't take much more as he collapsed onto the bed. Spiro's body followed, his strokes not letting up. He continued to pound into Noah, the sound of his balls as they smacked against his ass sounded as if he was being slapped.

Deep inside him, Spiro rolled Noah onto his side and thrust into him as he lay on his side. Lifting one leg, Spiro held Noah's leg in the air as his drive deepened, hitting nerves that had never been hit.

In complete euphoria, Noah couldn't stop himself. He took ahold of his cock and stroked himself as Spiro continued to pound his balls against him. The sound of Spiro's breathing deepening as his strokes became more forceful told him Spiro was getting close. Noah tried to time it, he wanted them to climax together.

Spiro stopped as he let out a cry. Noah tried to push Spiro's body from his as Spiro emptied himself. He wanted to see it.

He pulled out of Noah and rolled him onto his back before taking Noah's cock in his hand. With a little lube, and a couple of strokes he finished Noah off, causing Noah to explode onto his chest and neck.

Spiro fell onto the bed beside him. Breathless, Noah's entire body pulsated. He wasn't sure if he was having a heart attack as his heart pounded against his chest. With his eyes closed, his entire body was on fire.

"That was incredible!" Spiro uttered through his heavy panting.

I love you, Noah said to himself.

Wrapped in each other's arms, Noah had never been as close to and safe with anyone as he was with Spiro in this moment.

With the sound of the ocean passing through the open window, nestled against Spiro's warm frame, Noah's depleted body gave way to sleep.

****

The next morning, Noah woke from the best sleep of his life. His ass still pulsated as if Spiro had drilled a hole in him the size of a VW Bus. Yes, it was a reminder of last night, a reminder that made him smile.

With Spiro still nestled under his arm, there was no way he would move and leave Spiro's arms. Being in this bed, beside the man he'd dreamed about for years seemed like the end of a marathon puzzle session, the puzzle that had been spread out across the kitchen table for months. The puzzle was finally done.

Spiro's beautiful thick dark hair, and smooth olive skin was breathtaking to stare at. Last night, during what could be described as mind-blowing wild monkey sex, he was on sensory overload. Now with Spiro asleep, in his arms, Noah took it all in. His heart could burst at this very moment it was so full of love. He knew the boy; he knew the boy well. But he knew nothing about the man, yet he was in love with the man. A love that had never left him, but smoldered when there was someone else in his life. He tapped it down enough to allow him to believe it was only a fond memory and not his future.

Spiro was that model that graced the covers of fashion magazines. The model that everyone stared at and wondered how one person could be so outrageously beautiful. His eyes travelled over Spiro's tattoos. Initially, Noah was surprised to see them, but knowing Spiro had always been a nonconformist, they weren't that shocking.

His eyes traced the black and grey massive tattoo that covered the entire side of Spiro's right upper chest and shoulder. It was some sort of Greek Mythology mural. Although he'd never been a fan of tattoos, the monster looking grey octopus rising from the ocean was cool. The octopus's tentacles were reaching out and wrapped around a Centaur who was rearing up. Surely, that meant something.

He studied the intricate details that were embedded in Spiro's tattoos. There was a woman's face, stormy waters, and tentacles that changed into chains the closer they got to the Centaur.

Noah shifted his weight in the bed to get a better look at the ink that covered his lover's upper arm, the two soldiers dressed in armor. Wrapping around his entire upper arm, one soldier was kneeling over the other soldier, who appeared to be dying. Noah wanted to know the meaning of his art, there was a story here.

He nuzzled the side of his face into Spiro's arm as he wrapped his arm around his body. Yesterday couldn't have been a more perfect date. Their hike up to the castle, just the two of them, sitting, staring out at the ocean as the rays of the sun warmed their backs. The wind brushing against his face was exhilarating as he held tightly to Spiro's waist as they drove through the countryside. The salty mist in the air as they lay peacefully on the beach was serene and perfect. *Yes, yesterday was a fairy tale date.* Noah exhaled a breath as the warmth from Spiro's body radiated against his face.

Of all the sex he'd had, no one had ever made love to him like Spiro had last night. He could still feel Spiro inside of him. Sex in the past with Clive was pretty good, but now, this morning, it was *Clive... Clive who?*

He lay there another hour listening to Spiro's breathing as he fantasized about a life with him. He had found him two days ago yet he was ready to spend the rest of his life with him. He knew he was moving quickly, but no one needed to know his thoughts, they were his and he would run with them.

Spiro was slow in waking up. His breathing was light with an occasional gentle sigh. He rolled from his side onto his back as if trying to find a more comfortable position. He stirred on his back every couple of minutes until his eyes opened.

Noah said nothing as Spiro's sleepy eyes stared at him. It took a second before the glazed look in his eyes turned to recognition, followed by a smile. Spiro brushed his long wavy hair back from his face. A second or two later, Spiro released a roaring yawn and moaned as his shoulders pulled back as his chest puffed out. The lion was awake. On Noah's hunk meter, where no man had been a ten, Spiro rang off the charts.

Noah didn't know if he should greet him with a *good morning*, a kiss, or straddle him and pick up where they left off last night. His body rejected the idea of straddling him, so instead, he leaned down and gave him a light kiss. "Good morning."

"Good Morning. What time is it?" Spiro's beautiful sleepy eyes stared at him.

Noah stretched his naked body over Spiro to reach his phone. "It's almost seven." He was about to check his messages since his phone was in his hand when Spiro clenched his waist.

Spiro brought him down beside him and pressed their bodies together. "How are you feeling this morning?"

It took a second for it to register what Spiro was really asking. "Oh, good. I'm okay. Sore as hell, but that has nothing to do with my IBS. That's all your doing."

"Okay, just checking." He teased Noah's lips, touching them with his lips, baiting him with every touch.

"Mmm." Noah moaned at the touch of Spiro's lips as he dropped his phone on the mattress and closed his eyes and took what Spiro was offering, and what he wanted.

In ecstasy, he savored the tangy taste of Spiro's mouth. Their kiss deepened as their naked bodies pressed together, their erections sliding against each other's bodies. From the first day they met, it was Spiro's assertiveness, that confident way in which he did what he wanted that lit Noah's fire. He was doing it still. He took what he wanted.

Low incoherent moans came from both of them. Last night's extraordinary reunion and sensual foreplay was in contrast with this morning's raw sex. Hot and straightforward, this morning they each climaxed in a matter of minutes.

When Noah had caught his breath, he asked the question that had been in the forefront of his brain since his eyes opened this morning. "How come you never tried looking for me?" Yes, he was moving too fast and the question, and or answer, could be a major buzz kill. But he trusted whatever Spiro's reason was, that it would satisfy him.

Spiro lay on his back staring up at the ceiling. He brushed long strands of his hair back from his face before speaking. "I don't know. I guess..." Spiro went silent.

Noah sat up in the bed, ready to hear whatever Spiro was about to offer him.

Spiro sat up. "I guess... I was scared. I didn't know what happened. I was sent away so fast. Yeah, eventually I came up with my own reason that it was because of us. My theios and theia sent me back so fast that I was worried the police were looking for me, you know, for what we did."

"The police?" Noah didn't understand.

"I was scared that maybe your dad, or the police, were looking for me for years. I didn't know if I broke some kind of law in your country. Your parents scared me when they were around. Your mom seemed meaner than your dad."

"Mean?" Noah would have called her detached, ridged, cold, maybe even snooty, but certainly not mean. He wanted to laugh but knew Spiro was being serious. "No, they never called the police or anything like that. I looked for you. For years I searched Facebook, Instagram, Snap Chat, Grindr, Tinder, you name it, I was there looking for anyone named Spiro who lived anywhere in Greece. Without your last name, it was impossible, but I never stopped looking."

"So why did you come here?" Worry flashed across Spiro's face.

Noah smirked, "A bottle of wine."

"Excuse me?" The corner of Spiro's mouth curved into a tiny smile.

"I had just broken up with this guy that I was seeing. My roommate talked me into sharing a bottle of wine with him trying to cheer me up.

I'm not a big drinker and after two glasses of wine I was buzzing pretty good. I guess I started crying over you like I had been doing for years. Rodney had had enough. He talked me into buying a ticket, and before I knew it, I was flying out of New York. I've never done anything like that in my life."

"You mean like being spontaneous?" Spiro's hand rubbed Noah's shoulders, and then down his arm before clasping their fingers together. "I'm glad you did."

"Yeah, me too." Noah pressed his nose against Spiro's skin, committing his scent to memory. It didn't matter that it wasn't as spontaneous as Spiro believed.

"So how did they find out about us?"

"Do you remember my friend Chris, the guy that lived on the other side of the lake, the one that walked in on us in the boathouse? I never was told for certain, but I'm pretty sure that he told his parents, who called my grandma. The day I found this out, grandma said that you and Eros had gone into town for something. You guys never came back, and then my parents showed up that night. We never talked about you. They were more freaked out because their son was a homo."

Spiro's brows said he was thinking, contemplating. "Why would someone do that?"

Noah had never really figured out Chris's motive; self-preservation, shame, jealousy, Noah didn't have the answer. "I don't know. A couple of years ago I was on the computer and his name and picture popped up as someone that I might know. I went to his page and sure enough it was him. I saw that he had just announced that he was getting married to some girl who he'd been dating for about eight months. I sent him a message congratulating him. He never replied back." It wasn't that Noah wanted to rekindle their friendship. Far from it, it was calculated, he was attempting to open the door of communication so he could probe for an answer to a question that wouldn't change anything.

Noah surmised, based on the absence of a reply, as well as some of Chris's other posts, that he likely leaned toward the far right. He wondered if that also included his fingers.

"Okay. So, I told you about Peter. What about you? How many hearts have you broken?" Spiro asked as he lightly moved the tips of his fingers across Noah's abdomen.

Noah snickered. "Not many. After you left, I went away to school.

I met a couple of guys, but it wasn't anything serious. Then I got sick and had to go home. When I was really sick, the last thing on my mind was a relationship. I was just trying not to die. Once I started feeling better, I started talking to guys online." Annoyance swelled in Noah's chest thinking about all the lies and bullshit people posted in their profiles. "After kissing a lot of frogs, I met this guy and moved in with him." Noah hesitated with what he was about to say but continued. "I look back at that now and I was just trying to get away from my parents. That relationship only lasted a couple of months, and then we broke up. That guy ended up getting married."

"To a guy or girl." Spiro rolled over and grabbed his cigarettes off the nightstand. He gave Noah a nod asking if he minded.

"Yeah, it's okay." At one time or another, Noah was sure he'd told himself he could never kiss a smoker. He chuckled to himself. Obviously, this wasn't the case. His bad boy with tattoos was a smoker. "A girl. It was an arranged marriage."

"An arranged marriage. Now that's old fashioned."

"Yeah, the whole thing was weird." Noah tried to remember Nabeeh's fiancé's name. They had the nerve to send him a wedding invitation a year later. "When I moved out of his place, I didn't want to move back home, so I got my own place. My grandma died a couple of months prior. I inherited money from her estate."

Spiro smiled as he leaned against the headboard. "Well thank God for arranged marriages."

"Yeah right." Noah playfully hit him on his nipple. Spiro's chest muscle barely moved. "Tell me about you. What happened after you came back here, besides *Peee-ter*." Noah purposely made fun of Peter's name.

"Well, when I got back home, I had no money. So even if I found you, what could I do? I wasn't sure you wanted to see me. I was pissed off and the furthest I could get was Athens. I attempted to find Stefania and found out she and a good friend of mine were together. He was a much better friend to Stefania than to me. So, I drank pretty heavy and smoked a ton of pot. I liked being numb, not feeling anything, or worrying about all the mistakes I had made that had cost me everything. I ended up living in a friend's van for a couple of weeks before he kicked me out. Crashed wherever I could for about six months. Then one day, Nina showed up. She had come to find me. My mom was sick in the hospital with pneumonia. We were told there was a chance she could die. I sobered up fast. Because of my dad's bad back, my Theia Kyra needed help with my mom. They needed help lifting her in and out of the tub, turning her in bed. My dad couldn't do it anymore. It was an easy decision that I had to come home."

"When did you meet Peter?" Noah couldn't avoid the jealous tone as Peter's name rolled off his tongue.

"That was several years later. I would go to Athens for the weekends. Sometimes I needed to get away from the island. I met him one night in a bar on the mainland. He was older, very wealthy. For a couple of months, he would buy me a ticket to fly over every two weeks to visit him. One day, at his request, I stayed. My family was pissed. It turned out he wasn't exactly the person he said he was. He was into kinky stuff."

"Like what?"

Spiro rolled his eyes, disgusted at the mere thought of it. "Well, like threesomes that always ended with him just watching me with whoever he brought home. One day I was in the kitchen doing dishes and I heard him come in. I yelled that I was in the kitchen. When I turned, Peter was standing with this guy who was completely naked. I didn't even know who this guy was, but I knew what Peter wanted. I went from washing dishes in the sink to fucking a complete stranger over it. Peter was another dumb mistake in my life. I knew he wasn't right for me. I was not right for him. We stayed together longer than we should have because I was too embarrassed to come home. He was a way for me to get off the island." Spiro stopped and scratched at his nose before threading his fingers through his hair, pulling it out of his face. "This last time, I came back... I went to work with Nina at the gallery and never left again."

If Noah had any worries about Peter, Spiro had laid them to rest. He had no reason to believe Spiro was holding anything back. He'd never questioned Spiro's integrity about anything. Peter was no more of a threat to them than any of Noah's past boyfriends were to Spiro.

Spiro pulled his naked body from the bed, stretching onto the balls of his feet as his arms almost touched the ceiling. The cheeks of his ass dimpled as he came down. Spiro was only a few inches taller than him, but wow, their bodies were as different as night and day. Noah's resembled one that belonged to a schoolyard kid beside Spiro's.

Spiro moved around the bed and into the bathroom. Relieving himself, Spiro's pee hitting the water in the bowl sounded like a horse relieving himself. The thought of Spiro's cock sent blood rushing to Noah's groin.

Noah lay and listened to the sounds coming from the bathroom. Now water was running. Was he washing up? The sound of him spitting sounded more like he was brushing his teeth.

"What are your plans for today?" Spiro appeared at the door and leaned his naked body against the frame.

"Nothing. I was originally going to go home early, that was until I found you." Noah sat up in the bed. He was intrigued by where Spiro was going with the question before his eyes settled on the V that tapered down to Spiro's waist. A thin layer of body hair did little to conceal his chest tattoos. He was the epitome of macho; tall, muscular, and inked. Noah's ass twitched at the sight of Spiro's uncut cock. It was divine.

"Really. You were heading home? Why?"

"I was thinking I wasn't going to find you. I hadn't made the decision, but I had been thinking about it."

"So how long are you here for?"

That was the million-dollar question. "I had planned for three weeks. Today is the end of my first week." He couldn't stop staring at Spiro's naked body propped against the door frame. The wild and bushy hairstyle when Spiro was twenty had now been tamed.

Spiro pushed off the door frame. He nodded as if he was pondering something.

"What are you thinking?" Noah asked.

"I was thinking... I have to go home to check on Mom, make sure that everything is okay. And I have to open the gallery this morning. Nina texted me, reminding me that the owners of the gallery will be here this Friday." He paused again as his brows narrowed.

"Well, I can find things to do for the day. I don't want to keep you from your family or work." He had to check in on his clients and ensure their sites were running like they should. He picked up his phone, still on the bed. "What's your number? I'll text you mine, and you can text when you're done. Maybe we could have dinner this evening or something." He already knew what the *or something* was.

"I have something better. Why don't you come with me? You can meet my family and then go to work with me."

Spiro's proposal surprised him. Meet his family, *already*? It seemed a little soon for an introduction, even though Noah was almost done planning their wedding! "Are you sure?" Noah wasn't sure he was ready to meet the parents. Noah never introduced anybody he was seeing to his own parents; nor had he met anyone's parents that he dated.

He remembered years ago, when he was talking a lot about Rodney, right after they met. His mother once asked... what was it?... she said, "your friend," with the emphasis on the word *friend.* He immediately knew what she was implying and, in a panic, corrected her. Noah rolled his eyes at how stupid the whole thing was.

Both his parents had long ago stopped asking about girlfriends or whether he would be interested in going out with the newest girl at the Synagogue. There were two things they didn't talk about, his sexuality and Nathanael.

"Yes, I want them to meet you." Spiro leaned in and kissed him. A hint of toothpaste permeated Noah's taste buds. "Did you use my toothbrush?" Noah jokingly asked.

Spiro frowned. "No!" He held out a finger. "I used my finger. Want to smell?"

Noah's nose crinkled. "No... it's the same finger that was in my ass last night."

"One of them." Spiro laughed.

Embarrassed and speechless, color rose in Noah's cheeks.

"I've washed it since then—" Spiro winked at him "—which I would like to do to the rest of my body, if you don't mind me using your shower?"

"Go ahead." Noah wished the tiny shower was big enough for two. "I'll take one after you." His heart thrummed at the idea of meeting Spiro's parents. "I'd love to meet your family."

"Ex-cel-lent! Do you want to take your shower first? And then I can."

"No, it's okay. You can go first."

"No. I insist."

"Why, am I funky or something?" Noah's nose wrinkled as he sniffed his armpits.

Spiro's face lit up. "No! That's not what I meant at all. It's your place. The hot water, I want to be sure there's enough."

Noah's heart melted a little more. Spiro must have known how small the hot water tank was in the bungalow. "Give me two minutes." Noah sprang from the bed and into the bathroom.

****

In less than a half hour, the two were out the door. The morning temperature was the coolest it had been since Noah's arrival. He second-guessed whether to go back in for a sweater. They made their way toward the main building without his sweater.

"Are you hungry?" Noah asked. "The hotel is still serving breakfast."

"Nope. Not a breakfast eater... you?"

"Nope, me either. I'm good for now."

Past the hotel and out on the street, Spiro propelled the motorbike through the streets out to the countryside. Noah nestled down behind Spiro, trying to block the cool air from hitting him. In no time, they had reached Spiro's village.

They pulled up to a small, yellow stucco home with a red tile roof. The houses were sparse, each sitting on about a half-acre. With no lawn or shrubs, the neighborhood was old and run down. They hopped off the motorbike and parked it beside an old beat-up pickup truck in front of the house.

Noah looked around the neighborhood. Adjacent to Spiro's house was the concrete framework of another small house. "Are you getting new neighbors?"

"No. That's the house Eros was building for him and Theia Kyra for when he came back. No money to finish it."

"Do you guys own it?" Noah stared at the grey, concrete-walled structure. It was missing the windows, doors, and roof.

"Uh-huh. Come."

Noah picked up on the excitement in Spiro's voice. There was not an ounce of reservation in his voice about bringing someone home. He followed Spiro through the screen door, stepping right into a small living room with a low ceiling.

Noah's eyes went straight to the large hospital bed pushed against the wall. There was a petite, frail woman in the bed. Above her head on the wall was a gold tone crucifix. Not wanting to stare, he overcompensated and turned away from her. Against the other wall sat two brown recliners, positioned in front of a small, flat-screen TV on the wall. A small table between them held a lamp and water glass. There was an old man sitting in the chair closest to the hospital bed.

In Greek, Spiro spoke to the old man, who appeared to have been sleeping in the chair. He raised his head and mumbled something back. Deep wrinkles on the man's dark olive face bore into his mottled skin. "This is my dad." Spiro told Noah.

Spiro signaled for Noah to step closer. In Greek, Spiro spoke to his father again. The man put down a small string of ruby red beads he'd been rubbing between his fingers and held his hand out to shake Noah's. His expression was beyond fatigue.

"He doesn't speak or understand any English," Spiro said. "And this is my mom." Spiro took his mother's hand and rubbed it. In Greek, he spoke to her.

Her hand ripped from Spiro's as her arms twisted. She moaned, as if speaking. A lump formed in Noah's throat as he looked down at her. She was tiny, no taller than five feet. Her hair was long and grey. Her arms continued to twist about, close to her body, as she moaned.

When she stopped, Spiro took a washcloth that hung from the side rail and dipped an end of the cloth in the water glass on the small table. He dabbed the washcloth across his mother's chapped lips. She released a soft moan.

"She said it's nice to meet you." He dipped the cloth in the water again and wiped the saliva that had run down her cheek.

Noah wondered whether those had been real words. How was it possible to have understood what she'd said? He wanted to tell her it was nice to meet her, but he didn't know if he was supposed to tell her or talk to her through Spiro. "It's nice to meet you, too." His heart ached for the woman. He thought about what she may have looked like in her youth. Was she once as pretty as Nina? Noah noticed the delicate lace doilies on two small tables. So beautifully done, he wondered if they were handmade by someone, perhaps family.

Another woman appeared from what could have been the kitchen. Stout, she didn't look much taller than Spiro's mother. She dried her hands on an apron tied around her waist. Her eyes studied Noah.

Spiro went to her, kissed her, and then said something in Greek to her. She nodded and then spoke to Noah as if he was Greek. When she stopped, Spiro grinned. "This is Theia Kyra. She wants to feed you."

"Oh..." Surprised, he was tongue tied for a second. "Did you tell her who I was?" Unsure that she didn't understand English, he kept his question cryptic.

"Yeah, yeah!" Spiro answered before turning back to the old woman and speaking to her. The only thing Noah understood in their dialogue was the word "Americano."

Spiro and his aunt conversed for several minutes before she shrugged and then retreated into the kitchen. "I told her we're going to the gallery, that we'll eat out. I have to take care of Mom, and then we can go."

Noah nodded okay as he stepped aside and let Spiro pass him as he moved back over to his mother. He spoke to her, causing her to moan again. Spiro removed the light sheet over his mother, her hospital-type gown, and socks. His body shielded most of his mother as he tossed her gown in a basket.

Noah turned his head to give her privacy. His eyes took in the paintings on the wall. The room was filled with what was no doubt Spiro's work. Studying every piece, his eyes moved from painting to painting. It was mind-boggling that he knew the artist. Spiro's work was some of the best paintings he'd ever seen.

After several minutes, Spiro called to him, "Can you hand me those sheets on the chair?"

Noah grabbed the sheets in the chair and handed them to Spiro. Seeing that his mother was dressed, Spiro was rolling his mother to one side of the bed. He peeled the sheets from the mattress, rolled her to the other side, and slipped the sheet from the bed.

He used a clean sheet and repeated what he did in reverse order. The entire time, his mother moaned.

From the corner of his eye, Noah kept Spiro's dad in sight. He never moved; the old guy just sat there, staring at the TV as if he was the only one in the room. In minutes, Spiro had changed the sheets on the bed and tucked his mother in, smoothing the sheets over her. He said something to her before kissing her forehead. Her brows furrowed.

"Let me say goodbye to my theia and change. Do you mind if I stay with you again tonight?"

Noah nodded. There was so much to process, far more than he dreamed. Outside of the possibility that Spiro could have been married, Noah hadn't envisioned any sort of a life connected to Spiro. Sadness filled his chest.

"Great. Give me a second." Spiro's face lit with excitement as he gathered the wet cloth and bowl of water he used to bathe his mother.

Spiro hurried into the kitchen. He heard Spiro and his theia speaking before hearing the back door open and close. Noah again studied the old man in the chair who was paying him no attention. This time, he held his stare just a little longer before switching over to Spiro's mother. She appeared to be resting comfortably or asleep. He monitored the sheets for a second or two, ensuring he could see that she was breathing.

He cleared his throat, trying to push out the air lodged in his windpipe. The noise caused the old man to glance over at Noah. Not knowing what to do, Noah just smiled at him. Politely, the old man smiled back as he fingered his beads.

"Um... you know, your son laid my ass out last night," Noah muttered, mostly trying to rid himself of the overwhelming sadness that had taken over.

The old man looked up and smiled again as he nodded, clearly not understanding a word that was said. Noah chuckled under his breath, but it did little to change his sadness.

When Spiro emerged, he was wearing a pair of burgundy jeans and a white button-down, long-sleeved shirt: simple, but stunning. The mere sight of Spiro lifted his mood. This evening couldn't come fast enough for Noah.

CHAPTER EIGHTEEN

It was a little before ten a.m. when Spiro and Noah arrived at the gallery. He loved having Noah's arms wrapped around his waist the entire way over. The empty, narrow streets made of stone were starting to come alive. There was an old man sweeping in front of the ice cream shop adjoined to their store. In Greek, Spiro told his neighbor good morning and that he would be over in a bit.

Inside, Spiro turned on the lights in the showroom and then proceeded to the backroom. "Do you drink coffee?" He asked Noah, who was right behind him.

"No, I try to stay away from anything that has a lot of caffeine in it."

"Oh, that's right." Spiro committed the connection to memory. "It must be hard."

"Not anymore. At first, it was. I wanted to eat and drink what I wanted. After enough times of feeling like you're dying because of a freaking slice of pizza, you learn."

Spiro filled a mug with water from a tiny sink. After heating the water in the microwave, he added three teaspoons of instant coffee and two sugar cubes to complete his morning coffee.

Noah kneeled in front of a stack of paintings laying against the wall. "Wow, these are nice." He flipped through them as if studying each one.

"I'm glad you think so. Those are mine."

"No way! They're beautiful. Why aren't these out there, too?" Noah slowed down flipping through the paintings, now taking longer to study each piece.

Spiro winced. "The owners pick what they want to sell. That's why they're coming tomorrow. They're arriving with new paintings."

"Do they have a problem with your stuff?" Noah rose to his feet with one of Spiro's larger pieces. It was an ocean scene, with an elderly couple sitting on a bench at the edge of a cliff looking out toward the ocean. Spiro had captured the light reflecting off the ocean. "This is beautiful! This should be out front."

Spiro glanced at the piece Noah was holding. "The crap they sell is mass produced, to sell to the tourists. It's what they all want." He could go the rest of his life without seeing another painting of Mykonos, Santorini, or a white church with a blue roof.

"Sometimes, tourists are looking for one of Lemnos, something specific to their trip here. This is what I paint, and I sell them my paintings, real paintings. The owners don't know this." Spiro's head tilted as he studied Noah, watching for a reaction to his deliberate deception. A nervousness fluttered in his gut as he watched Noah examine his art.

Spiro knew he was good, way better than any other artist on the island; that wasn't what made him tense. It was revealing the truth about who he was. He wasn't rich like Noah. He didn't have a career that allowed him to fly all over the world. He peddled art from a back room in secrecy. He lived with his parents in the same house he was born in. He'd spent a week's worth of wages on dinner the other night at Simonetta, hoping to impress Noah.

"So, this is on the island?" Noah asked.

"Yes, the cliffs are near Fanaraki. I'll take you there." The drive out to Fanaraki beach wouldn't cost him much.

Noah studied the piece a little longer before putting it down. "What do you do with all your art when they're here?"

Embarrassed about the truth, Spiro revealed a little more of the reality of who he was. "We move them next door." To avoid eye contact with Noah, he put his cup on a small table. He picked up two pieces of his art and walked to the back door. "Can you get the door for me?"

Noah rushed to get ahead of him. "You want me to take some?"

"No. I'll do it. Watch the gallery. Let me know if anyone comes in."

Over the next thirty minutes, Spiro made several trips between the two shops until all his paintings had been removed. Noah sat on a stool behind the counter where he could watch the gallery—and Spiro. Spiro finished as his cousin Nina arrived.

"Good morning," Nina greeted them in English as she put her purse on the counter and removed her coat.

"Good morning. I've moved all my stuff already." Spiro switched to Greek. "What are you doing here? I thought you weren't coming in until later."

She laughed and responded in Greek. "Yeah, I know, but I wanted to make sure we got everything done that needed to be done before tomorrow." Nina waved the conversation off as not important.

"Is it still okay that I take tonight off?" He felt bad for asking, knowing that meant she would be here all day. He followed her into the back room.

"Of course. I won't stay this morning. I wanted to get a few pieces rehung with you here, and then I'll go back to the house and check on everyone."

"I changed the sheets on Mom's bed this morning and put her in a clean gown. Noah and I can hang the pictures. You should've texted me."

Nina glanced over at Noah. "I was up the street. I slept at George's last night. I was already right here." She pushed the message button on the phone, and messages began to play. She scribbled names and phone numbers as they talked. "I see you and the American are hitting it off."

Spiro tried not to laugh. "Yeah, I slept at his place last night."

Nina's eyes grew big as she looked at Noah again and then back at Spiro. "No!" She waved for him to follow her back out front where they'd left Noah.

Conversing in Greek, Nina and Spiro talked about Noah as if he wasn't in the room. "I can't believe you guys already did it. Gay men move so fast," Nina said as she pointed at a picture on the wall she wanted taken down.

"Don't judge me." Spiro removed the framed painting and replaced it with one that was against the wall below it. "Besides, it's not like we just met." Spiro moved his hands away from the picture and stepped back. "Is it straight?"

Nina cocked her head to the left, staring at the picture. "Move the left side up a touch." She crossed her arms as she examined the picture. "In my next life, I want to come back as a gay man. It's not fair you guys aren't judged for being hoes."

Spiro pushed up the left side of the frame a half inch. From the corner of his eye, Noah moved into his peripheral vision as he meandered around the studio.

"How was it?" Nina asked.

"As good as I remembered. He's a sweet guy."

Nina took a few steps over to the next switch she wanted to make. "You haven't talked about him in years. What made him show up? I think it's a little stalkerish."

Spiro knew this was coming. She didn't withhold advice about anything. "He said he hadn't stopped thinking about that summer back when I went to the States." Spiro glanced at Noah, who was staring at them. He continued, knowing Noah didn't understand Greek. "I didn't think I would see him again."

"What were you guys, like, fifteen back then? Do you think he's in love with you?" She motioned for him to exchange the picture on the floor for the one hanging above it.

Spiro shrugged. Noah was *crazy* about him, as he put it yesterday. He didn't use the word love. It was flattering that someone thought about him all these years and would fly halfway around the world to find him. He hesitated with what he was about to say. It seemed a bit whiny, but Nina had always been his trusting soundboard to lean on.

"I'm a little embarrassed. Here I am, working in a gallery and haven't done anything with my life, compared to him."

"What does he do?" she asked.

"He does that stuff on the internet, makes websites or something like that. He has his own company."

"And—you're an artist, one of the most brilliant painters I've seen. Anything he's done doesn't compare to your talent."

It was nice for her to say that, but he wasn't convinced it was true. "Thank you."

"Wasn't his family super wealthy?" Nina asked. "I remember Eros coming home to visit one time, and I would listen to stories about them."

"Yeah. Both his parents are doctors." Spiro answered. "His grandmother was a doctor, too. He got some kind of big inheritance when she died."

Spiro shot a glance at Noah, ensuring he wasn't understanding anything they were saying in front of him. He hated that he questioned why Noah was into him. He wasn't naïve about his own good looks, but he believed no one's looks simply made them attractive. Other than his looks, what else was attractive about him? Spiro could never answer that question.

Nina's eyes followed his, giving Noah a glance. "This trip has got to be costing a pretty penny. How long is he here?"

"Another two weeks. He's staying at the Blue Oceania, in one of the bungalows." Spiro glanced over at Noah and then back at Nina. It had been years since he'd had such a strong attraction to someone like what he was feeling with Noah. It seemed ridiculously fast, but now he couldn't stop thinking about him.

"Is he still living in New York?" Nina asked.

Spiro saw Noah look at her. He realized that, without a Greek translation, she said, "New York."

"Are you two talking about me?" Noah's arms were folded across his chest as he looked at Spiro and Nina.

Spiro cringed. Sheepishly, he moved across the room, leaned over the counter, and kissed Noah's cheek. "We are. I was telling her you're here for another two weeks. That two weeks was not long enough for me." Spiro leaned over and kissed him again. Afterward, Spiro pulled away and wiped his lips with his tongue.

Noah's eyes followed Nina across the room as she moved to the next picture. Dressed in a short skirt and jacket, her three-inch heels clicked against the tiled floor as she sauntered around the room. She, too, was the picture of beauty, with long black hair that fell to the middle of her back. She could have easily been a model.

It was a second or two before Noah's eyes reverted to Spiro. Without words, his sweet blue eyes begged for another kiss. He was easy to read. His authenticity was one of the things Spiro found endearing about him. But they only had two weeks, and then Noah would be leaving.

There was zero chance he would have the money to fly to the United States... It wasn't a ferry ride across to the mainland; it was on the other side of the world. *Was this all for nothing?* He pushed the question away. "Hey, at two, when we close for the afternoon, what do you say we grab some lunch and hang out at the hotel's beach?" Spiro asked Noah.

Noah nodded. "I'd like that, but let me pick up lunch. That way, you don't have to try to figure out what I can and can't eat."

"No. I can figure it out." Spiro declared.

Noah shook his head. "I insist, or it's a no."

"Well, okay. I guess lunch is on you." Spiro hand palmed Noah's face and shook it.

"When you two can stop ogling and playing with each other, can you help me rehang these pictures so I can get out of here? When I'm gone, you two can act like rabbits in heat if you want." Nina's voice grabbed their attention, causing them to separate.

In response to her instruction, they rushed to her side. Spiro removed the painting on the wall in front of them and handed it to Noah.

The three of them worked together for the next hour, changing out numerous pictures on the walls. They moved all the ones that were taken down into the back room to be stored with the rest of the inventory. It was a little before ten when Nina announced she was finished, leaving the cleanup to them.

With only the two of them in the gallery, Spiro went to work on the front windows after he sent Noah to clean the bathroom. Deep in thought, Spiro sprayed the cleaner on the window for the third time. The streaks were refusing to come out. But more so, he couldn't rid himself of the question that plagued him: *What would happen in two weeks when Noah had to leave?*

In no way was Spiro ready to see Noah leave. His arrival on the island was as much of a surprise as when he first met Noah. Having Noah in his life just seemed to make everything better. Before Noah showed up, Spiro was content—or at least, he thought he was. He got up, painted in the morning, went to work, came home, painted some more, and went to bed. On his one day off, he gathered with his friends for a night of movies, good food, and laughter. He was fine with all of that, until now. Noah was offering him love... At least, Spiro thought he was. Why else would someone fly from so far away if it wasn't for love? But if he loved Noah back, how would that work out? He told himself to relax and enjoy today, but that brought him little comfort.

Spiro was a thousand miles away in his head when Noah emerged from the back. "Okay, that's done, but you're out of this stuff." Noah's booming voice startled Spiro. His sleeves were rolled up, and he held up a bottle of disinfectant, shaking it, proving it was empty.

Shaking himself from his trance, Spiro forced himself to smile. "Put it on the counter, and I'll text Nina to let her know."

Nina's question rose again inside Spiro to a level of legitimacy. "So, what happens in two weeks... with us?" He stared into Noah's eyes as if he would see the answer before hearing it.

"Well, I was thinking the same thing. I can stay longer if you want."

"How long?"

"I don't know, maybe another two weeks. Maybe come back for Christmas or something."

"That would be nice." Nina's voice wouldn't shut up in his head... *Do you think he's in love with you?*

"I don't want to be in the way or anything." Noah moved over to where Spiro was standing beside the window.

Spiro took him by the hands, interlocking their fingers. "You wouldn't be in the way—in the way of what?" Noah said that he was crazy about him. What was the difference in being crazy about someone and being in love? Love seemed so much bigger than crazy. Was crazy another way of saying that Noah was in love with him still?

Noah held his stare. "I don't know—work, your painting, a boyfriend you still haven't told me about."

The last part of Noah's statement caught Spiro off guard. "A boyfriend? I swear, there is no boyfriend. If there were, I'd tell you." Butterflies fluttered in his gut. He'd never felt this way about anybody. In the past, there'd been several guys he liked, but he didn't think about any of them like he did Noah.

It had only been a few days, but with Noah, there was no pretending and posturing like in a new relationship, when they're trying to impress each other. He didn't have to pretend that he didn't smoke. He didn't have to pretend to be an artist. He was someone who sold his paintings from the back room of a gallery. As much as he wanted to hide some things about himself, he found it was easier to be honest with Noah.

With Noah, he was doing and saying things he'd hadn't done in years, like this morning, taking someone to meet his mother, which he had never done before. The risk taker that he once was, so many years ago, was not him anymore. He'd learned to avoid risky behaviors because they led to trouble. He laughed at Noah's notion that he was seeing someone. If so, that person wouldn't have a chance the moment Noah arrived.

"I'm not ready for you to go."

"Okay," Noah murmured.

Was that doubt in Noah's voice? *Was he hesitant?* He wanted Noah to stay. He brought Noah into his chest and folded his arms around him, hoping that it would reinforce his invitation. The warmth of Noah's body pressed against his. The beat of their hearts fell into sync, each thumping at the same rate. He ran his hand through Noah's hair, which was soft as a baby's.

Everything about Noah was familiar, down to the smell of his skin. In no way could Spiro articulate what Noah's skin smelled like, but he knew it like his own name. He took another gentle whiff of Noah as he hugged a little tighter. Yes, Noah did all of that to him.

Spiro's insides twisted. He forced himself to release Noah. "Why don't you go to the store and pick up lunch? I'll meet you at your place at two." He took a step back, separating them a little.

"Are you trying to get rid of me?" Noah laughed.

"No, but I know you have work, too." The endorphins firing within Spiro were as strong as any drug. The sooner Noah left, the sooner he could sort out and understand what the hell was happening with him.

"Is there anything special you want for lunch or a place I should go for it?" Noah asked.

"Surprise me. I'll eat anything, whatever you get." Spiro placed a soft kiss on Noah's forehead, knowing Noah was clueless to the turmoil within him. There was a split second where he'd almost said, "I love you." The words caught in his throat, where they stayed. He placed another soft kiss against Noah's forehead and held his head between his hands. His heart thumped as if he'd had one too many coffees this morning, but it wasn't coffee at all, and he knew it.

CHAPTER NINETEEN

Noah saw Spiro as he came around the narrow pathway that led down to his bungalow. The mere sight of Spiro caused his heart to skip a beat. He had everything ready for a lunch set out on the hotel's private beach.

Spiro knocked twice before opening the door. "Hey, babe. I think I have some good news." Spiro covered the three steps it took to reach him in the tiny kitchenette. He gave Noah a kiss. "The owners of the gallery texted Nina. They won't be here tomorrow after all. They're not coming for another week or a week and a half. I'm so relieved. The last thing I wanted was to be at the gallery without you for two days while they were here."

"Me, too... Wait... You mean I scrubbed that bathroom this morning for nothing?" Noah joked as he handed Spiro one of the two bags on the counter. "Here, take this."

"Living room or terrace?" Spiro asked.

"Neither. We're heading out to the beach. Oh, I found us a chess game, so I accept your challenge this afternoon."

Spiro's face twisted. "I see your memory is still good."

"Yes, it is. Prepare to be beaten!" Noah looked around before seeing his flip flops and sliding into them. "Why aren't the owners coming?"

"I don't know, but I talked to Nina on my way over. I worked out a deal with her for the next week. Since we're slow and the season's over, you and I can open the gallery in the morning. You can work from the gallery, and she'll handle the gallery in the afternoon." Noah gathered the rest of the stuff off the counter for their picnic as Spiro kept talking. "That way, I can show you the island. While you're here, there's no reason both Nina and I have to be there at the same time."

"Wow, that was nice of her." Noah tucked the extra blanket he'd found in one of the closets under his armpit and ushered Spiro out the door.

On the beach, Noah lay the blanket on the sand and kicked off his flip flops. "Are you hungry?" He asked as he stared out at the handful of people up and down the cove. It was a sight he couldn't get over, an empty beach—unheard of, back home.

"I'm starving." Spiro toe kicked off his shoes and took a seat on the blanket. "How was your day?" he asked.

"Great! I got a little work done, talked to my roommate back home, and went shopping for us." Noah pulled their lunch from one bag.

Spiro removed his lunch from the wax paper. "Pitas? What kind?"

Noah leaned over to look at which one he had. "That's mine, chicken. I got you lamb."

"Are you not a fan of lamb?" Spiro asked as they traded sandwiches.

"Not really. Plus, mine has none of that sauce or onions on it."

"The sauce makes it good." Spiro inspected his pita. "They left the onions off mine, too."

"No onions for you today, my friend." Noah shot him a seductive smile that explained why he wasn't getting onions.

Spiro held his stare before a grin took over his entire mouth. Noah was the first to break eye contact, placing a large container filled with a chopped Greek salad between them. "I figured we could share the salad." He stuck two forks into the salad. "I have to admit, this trip, the stress, the food, it's been a little harder on my stomach than I imagined."

"Oh, have you been having trouble?"

Noah grimaced. "A little."

"Is there anything I could do?"

"No. I just have to watch a little better what I'm eating. Stress also causes it to flare up." He leaned in and delivered a soft gentle kiss to Spiro. "But my stress is gone now." He raised a brow and smirked. "At home, my diet is easy. I don't get a lot of enjoyment from food anymore."

"What do you miss most?"

"Nothing, at this point. The tradeoff isn't worth the pain. But if I know I'll be eating out somewhere and I'm unsure about it, I'll take my medication thirty minutes before eating. It helps." Noah pinched a piece of chicken from his pita and ate it. The dry chicken was bland.

"Your dad, other than his bad back, is he okay?" Noah asked after two more bites of his pita.

"What do you mean?"

"I mean, he seemed a little out of it this morning. Was he tired?"

"He'd just gotten in. But that's pretty much how he always is, up every morning by one to be down on the dock by two. They come back in around eight. When he's home, he never leaves his chair. He's been sleeping out there in his chair for years now. He hardly leaves her side anymore."

"Wow, I feel so sorry for him. I couldn't imagine."

"She's been like that since I was born—thirty-two years, now. He's stayed faithfully by her."

Noah could never remember that kind of love or passion between his own parents. "I can't say for sure, but I think my dad cheated on my mom years ago. For a long time, I think there was something going on between him and a nurse that worked in his office. You know, when you get a vibe between two people when they're in the same room. It's obvious to everyone around them."

"Do you think your mom knew?"

"Not sure she cared." Noah thought about it. "When Nathanael died, that's when things changed. They both buried themselves in their work. The year following Nathanael's death was one of the loneliest periods in my life. I remember this deep hollowness in me and a sense of nonexistence when I was around my parents."

"Yeah, when I was there, I never got the feeling that any of you were happy. You were so quiet."

Noah nodded. "I miss Nathanael, a lot. Things were so different before he died."

"In what way?"

"I don't know. After he died, we all stopped talking to each other. We never talked about him. Celebrating my birthday was too painful for them because it was like we weren't supposed to be happy on his birthday."

"But it was your birthday, too."

"Yeah, but you can't compete with a dead person. They always win."

Spiro leaned over and gave Noah a delicate kiss. "My family has told so many stories about my mom, before she had me, and it's like I knew her, though I hadn't been born yet. You know, you hear the stories over and over, and then they're real to you. I know so much about her that I miss her. Is that weird?"

"No, I get what you're saying."

Spiro laid down his pita and picked up the salad. "When I was young, I tried to make what had happened to her my fault. You know—the way she is now. That I was the reason she's like she is. There was nothing anyone could say that would make me change my mind, that it wasn't my fault because of me being born. If it wasn't for me, she would have had a normal life."

Noah wondered how accurate Spiro's statement was. Did he no longer feel it was his fault anymore? What exactly was a normal life? "I think it's cool how your whole family's there for her—Nina, your theia, your dad." Noah paused for a second to collect his words, ensuring they emerged as he intended. "Seeing you this morning, talking to her, taking care of her, the love you all have for each other: It's special."

He watched as Spiro stared down into the salad as he ate from the bowl. Spiro and his family were an amazing family, and Noah was a little envious. "Is your family cool with you being gay?" Noah asked.

Spiro put the salad down and took off his shirt. He then stretched out on his side. "I guess. We've never talked about it. It just is. It's not like I ever had to come out to them. It just seemed to evolve. I can't remember the last time somebody asked me about a girlfriend."

"You're lucky." Noah's expression dulled. "It was one reason I moved to the Village. I had to create some distance between me and my parents. It was a constant effort being around them, not living up to their expectations, not being married, not being the obedient son that did whatever he was told. It was easier to avoid them. I have to force myself to go into the city to see them. They're both busy doing their own thing."

"I thought you lived in the same city." Spiro repositioned himself.

"I live in a neighborhood called Greenwich Village, so we call Manhattan the city." Noah's breath hitched, seeing Spiro's large bicep flex as it held up his head. Noah glanced at Spiro's tattoo that covered his shoulder.

"How far is that from your parents?"

"Twenty or thirty minutes, depending on traffic. I love living in the Village. It's a younger crowd. The university's there, with a ton of coffee houses, breweries, and gay bars, way more relaxed than in the city. Could you see yourself living anywhere else?" Although he didn't say it, Noah meant could Spiro see himself living in New York... *with him*?

Spiro's nose wrinkled. "Nah, not any more. I enjoyed Athens for a bit. There was always something to do, but I got tired of being around so many people all the time."

It was not the answer Noah was hoping to hear. "Then you wouldn't like New York." Maybe he meant between Athens and here, he would choose here. "If you could go anywhere, where would you go?" He would try it a different way.

"You mean, to live?"

"Yeah, or to visit."

"I enjoy being close to my family. But I wouldn't mind seeing Dubai. I can't believe how rich they are."

So, he would leave... Noah tried to pinch back his smile. "My roommate's from Dubai. And yes, his family is super freakin' rich."

"That's cool. What's the deal between you and him?" Spiro held his eye contact.

Noah knew what Spiro was asking. "We're just friends. Yeah, when we first met years ago, we tried to hook up, and that was bad." Noah shook his head.

"What was bad about it?"

"It just was. We were drunk, and it didn't work." Noah left it at that. Spiro didn't need the messy details. "But Rodney's a nice guy. Even though he comes from a lot of money, you would never know it. It's funny to hear the shit that comes from his mouth. He's this gay, overweight, flamboyant Middle Easterner, who talks like he's from the Bronx. Lord knows, he has every reason in the world to lack self-esteem. Instead, he grabs the world by its balls and makes it scream uncle ten times a day."

Noah paused, thinking how much Rodney and Spiro would like each other. "Tell me about your tattoos." There was a story behind all that ink, a blueprint of who Spiro was, and Noah wanted to know all about it.

Spiro shrugged. "I kind of got the impression you didn't care for them."

Were his thoughts that transparent? Noah's cheeks turned a burnt rose. "I think they surprised me... But now, I can't imagine you without them. They're who you are, and I like them."

"This is Achilles and Patroclus." Spiro's finger traced the Greek soldier on his arm, carrying the naked body of Patroclus. He read the Greek inscription that wrapped around his bicep. "It is the cause, not the death, that makes the martyr." His finger moved to the black and grey breastplate that covered the right side of his chest. "This is the battle for life. The octopus is spewing its poisonous ink in a storm. Its tentacles are wrapping around Centaur, entrapping him into slavery. The octopus symbolizes evil." His finger moved to the woman's face who covered his shoulder. "This is Athena, the goddess of war. Kind of like my mom, she signifies strength."

Noah knew the story of Achilles and Patroclus, and he understood the significance of Athena. He was unsure, though, how a centaur fit in. "What's the centaur's significance?"

"They were a little wild and had a likeness and proclivity for trouble. This is Chiron. He was a little more civilized than his brothers and was Achilles's tutor when he was young."

"Who in your life is a centaur?" Noah asked.

"My dad. When he was younger, he was known for being a fighter. People were scared of him. Nobody wanted my mom to marry him. They had run off and got married, and I guess, for years, her parents had disowned her."

Noah studied the tattoo of Athena that hovered over the octopus and centaur. She was much larger than both of them, covering his entire shoulder blade. The whole portrait was making sense now. It was his life told in ink. Noah wondered who in Spiro's life was Patroclus.

Noah wasn't big on making out in public, but he pushed it aside. There was nothing more important than fulfilling his need to be close to Spiro. It was another first, another moment where the rest of the world just wasn't important.

Noah slid his body down beside Spiro, and the two stared for a moment into each other's eyes. Spiro's hands stroked Noah's hair and came to a rest at the back of his neck. Spiro pulled Noah's head gently until their lips touched, followed by several light butterfly kisses.

Spiro was stealing Noah's breath. Spiro wrapped his arms around him and brought him in closer, where their kiss deepened. A rush of endorphins swelled up in Noah's brain, causing him to release a sigh of joy. There was never any doubt that he loved Spiro back then, and now, being in his arms again, there was no doubt he was in love with him now.

From the moment he found him, he wanted to say, "I love you" to Spiro. Noah had been in love with him for twelve years and never stopped loving him. Now they were together, and he was holding it back, too afraid that it was too soon.

The three words hung at the tip of Noah's tongue. When was the right time to say it? Was there a certain amount of time that had to pass before it was okay to say it? By whose standards was he not allowed to confess his love? In every relationship he'd ever had with another guy, he'd been the one to use the word first. Just once, it would be nice to hear it from someone before he said it to them.

The word "love" was not spoken often in his house when he was growing up. He couldn't find a single memory where either of his parents said the word to him. If he had to go by feelings, it was his grandmother who showed the most concern and compassion, but he wasn't sure she'd said the words to him, either.

Nathanael was the only one who'd said the words to him. They told each other all the time they loved each other. Phone calls, text messages, in a hug, they said it all the time. Maybe they told each other constantly because nobody else said it to them. The muscles in Noah's face tightened.

When the words didn't come from Spiro, Noah slipped out from under Spiro's hold and sat up. He prayed Spiro wouldn't sense anything and tried to act as normal as he could. He gathered their trash and stuffed it into the plastic bag.

"I got us dessert." He pulled out a container that held gluten-free blueberry muffins. "I saw these, and they looked good."

Noah handed a muffin to Spiro and then picked up his. Noah was hoping it would be a decent muffin. He took a bite... *Damn It! Gluten is the apple from the Garden of Eden.*

The muffin was dry and tasteless, forcing Noah to wash it down with his water. The fresh water cleansed his throat as it rehydrated his body.

Spiro flipped over and positioned himself onto his stomach. The dip in Spiro's lower back made his ass all that more visible and impossible not to stare at. The mischievous wink and devilish grin from Spiro said that he caught him looking. It was the same beautiful grin from many years ago. That grin that said, *I see you, all of you.*

To pull his mind out of the gutter, Noah grabbed the cardboard box containing the chess set. "Do you remember how to play?"

"Of course." Confidence rang in Spiro's voice. "I taught my dad how to play years ago. He and I play all the time."

Noah was a little surprised and relieved that he didn't have to explain the game again. In a couple of moves, Noah saw that Spiro had become skilled in the game. No longer attacking Noah's pieces, Spiro seemed to be thinking out his moves now.

Spiro lost the first game and, without asking, reset the board for a rematch. Even if Spiro stood little chance at winning, he did make Noah think. Spiro was no longer an easy win.

"You've gotten good," Noah told him.

Glancing up only for a second, Spiro grinned as he continued to set up the next game. "Yes. I've learned that, sometimes, losing teaches you more than winning. There's nothing to learn in winning."

Noah laughed. "Aren't you the philosopher?"

Since Nina had agreed to run the gallery this evening by herself, they sat and talked and played chess for hours on the beach. They shared and traded stories of the years they'd missed out on each other's life. It was the stories about Spiro as a kid, running around the island, his family, and old history that held Noah's interest for hours.

There was a moment of silence as the sun dipped below the surface of the water. Noah couldn't think of a time he'd been happier in his entire life. Yes, he was in love. Every ounce of him was in love.

CHAPTER TWENTY

Like the previous three afternoons, after closing the gallery for mesimeri, Noah and Spiro's first stop was Spiro's house. They checked in on Spiro's mother before they set out for their afternoon adventures.

By the second day, Noah was helping Spiro with his mother and even joked with her a few times about how bad her son was. With Noah at his side, he tended to his mother, ensuring she was in a clean nightgown and had clean linens.

"I love how comfortable you are here at the house." Spiro had changed his mother and put the full bag of dirty laundry at the back door for Nina.

"I enjoy being here. I like seeing you with your family." Noah glanced over at Spiro's father, who was fingering the set of beads that always seemed to be in his hand. "Is that a rosary that your dad has?"

Spiro looked over at his father. "No, they're called *kompoloi...* Worry beads. They're like, um... something that helps when we want to relax. You just hold them and they help with anxiety. Some people say they help to guard against bad luck too, but that has never worked for me."

Noah sat in the empty chair beside Spiro's dad just as Kyra came in from the kitchen. She spoke to Spiro and then shuffled back into the kitchen.

Spiro turned to Noah. "Theia Kyra said lunch is ready. After we eat, we can get on the road."

In the kitchen, Noah took what had become his chair at the kitchen table while Theia Kyra served up rooster with handmade pasta. Spiro took his seat at the table, and Kyra served him first. Telling her "thank you" in Greek, he waited for Noah to be served. Then he waited for Noah to take a bite, hoping he would love it as much as the fish stew she had cooked for them yesterday.

"Oh, my God! I've never tasted chicken this good!" Noah devoured his meal as if he was starving.

"I'm glad you like it. She said she wanted to fatten you up." Spiro watched as the Noah that usually picked at his food ate with great enthusiasm. "She said you're too skinny. I tried to tell her." He tossed his hand in the air as if surrendering.

"Leave her alone, and let her try! I've never eaten this well in my life."

"Yeah, I'm scared that you might get sick or something. I try to tell her what you can and can't have."

It was sweet how Spiro tried to look after him. "Did Eros live here, too, before he moved to the States?" Noah asked.

Spiro thought for a second. It wasn't that he didn't know the answer; he needed to put things in sequential order. "No... he and Theia Kyra had a house in Kornos, about thirty minutes from here. After he moved to the States, Theia Kyra stayed there for a long time. The plan was that Eros wanted to finish next door. He was going to come back, and he and Theia Kyra would move next door to us. She doesn't drive, so my dad had to go over there all the time to take her shopping, appointments, and all that stuff. After I left the second time to go live with Peter, she started looking after Mom. After Eros died, she couldn't afford to keep their house in Kornos and moved in with us."

"Why did you guys never finish the house?"

"When Eros lost his job, there was no more money." Spiro stopped as Nina entered the kitchen through the back door. She gave Theia Kyra a kiss before fixing herself a plate.

"Can I join you guys?" She asked in English.

"Sure." Spiro took another bite of his lunch.

Hearing that the house was never finished because Eros had lost his job with Noah's family was a kick in the gut. "How's George?" Noah murmured. The color in his face had drained.

"He's fine. He's hoping to meet you before you leave." Nina made eye contact with Spiro. "How was the gallery this morning?"

"Slow. No sales at all this morning. We had two people come in." Spiro left out the part that, because they were so slow, he and Noah had sex in the back room an hour before they left.

"Oh, God, maybe I'll talk George into coming over tonight and hanging out with me. If it's as slow as it was last night, I'm going to close at eight."

"Does it usually die down this fast at the end of the season?" Noah asked.

"Sometimes. You never know." Spiro shook his head as he spooned in another mouthful of pasta.

"So, what's on your guys' agenda for this afternoon?" Nina asked.

"We're heading out to Aliki Lake." Each day, Spiro had picked out an adventure that would cost little to no money but was more spectacular than anything else on other islands.

After lunch, Spiro and Noah drove to the coastal salt marsh of Aliki Lake, on the eastern part of the island. Driving through the middle section of the island, Noah had seen enough pictures of the Sahara Desert to appreciate the beauty in the stretch of sand dunes before him. When they reached Aliki Lake, Noah oohed when he spotted a colony of wild flamingos as they fed in a grassy marsh. He stared at the massive colony like a cat watching a mouse.

"I can't believe they're white. Ours are pink."

"They're pink because of the brine shrimp they eat. Some zoos give them a special food that causes them to turn pink." Spiro nodded toward the flamingos. "These guys aren't that lucky."

****

The following day, they visited Kontias, one of the oldest villages on the island. The old, rustic village was like traveling back in time at least a hundred years. As they wandered through the village, Spiro shared his knowledge on the history of the traditional houses and windmills that made the village famous. They stopped in a small shop no bigger than his family's kitchen, where they enjoyed a traditional lunch of meatloaf stuffed with boiled eggs.

Yesterday, on their visit to the thermal hot springs after seeing the flamingos, Noah shocked him when he agreed to go nude in the public ancient baths. He loved seeing Noah move out of his comfort zone. Spiro knew that every time Noah did it, he was doing it because Spiro had asked. He'd never seen someone smile as much as Noah did. There was a sparkle in Noah's blue eyes that radiated and said he was game for anything.

On Sunday afternoon, when they left Spiro's house, Spiro talked Noah into going helmetless. He promised Noah that it was for a good reason, well worth it if he trusted him.

While whisking through the countryside, out in the middle of nowhere, Spiro slowed the motorbike to a crawl. A robust aroma wafted under their noses. "Do you smell that?"

Noah lifted his head from the middle of Spiro's shoulder blades. "Yeah! What is it?"

"It's wild thyme! Isn't it wonderful!" Before Noah could answer, Spiro rotated the throttle, accelerating the motorbike to top speed. They sailed through the vibrant purple, aromatic countryside with the wind in their faces.

That afternoon, they hung out on Cape Plaka, where they enjoyed watching the kite surfers below. Spiro and Noah talked for hours while the surfers did their tricks, defying gravity as they sailed into the air over the water.

That evening, wrapped in a blanket, they sat on the edge of the cliff under the lighthouse, where they had the perfect seats to watch the sun set across the water. Minutes before the sun touched the water, a school of bottlenose dolphins swam close to the shore below them. Spiro pointed them out as the dolphins' dorsal fins moved across the surface of the water.

"Oh, wow. I've never seen real wild dolphins!" Noah raised up to see them better as they passed. "That's so cool!"

"I know. I love seeing them." A light chuckle seeped from Spiro at how cute Noah was. *What was a "real" wild dolphin?* Seeing Noah's excitement with everything he saw this week reminded Spiro how beautiful the island was. All week, Noah had been bubbling with excitement as if Spiro had created it all by himself.

"Are the owners still coming tomorrow?" Noah asked as he nuzzled up under Spiro's arm.

"Yeah... I'm not looking forward to the next couple of days. I'll miss you not being at the gallery with me."

"You said they will be here for two days?" Noah rested his chin on Spiro's shoulder.

Spiro stared down into his eyes. They were as blue as the ocean before the sun set. "Yeah, until Tuesday. They'll fly out in the afternoon." The cold winds blowing up the cliff put a chill in the air, causing him to draw Noah in tighter and pull the blanket over his shoulders.

"Will I see you at all?" Noah asked.

"Sure. I'll come by for my lunch break and after we close..." He stared out to sea.

"Not sure if you remembered, but my flight back to the States was supposed to be this Friday."

"Already? No!" This time, it was Spiro who raised his head.

"We talked about me staying longer. Is it still okay? I mean... I just need to know to change my ticket. If it's not, I understand, I can still come back for—"

"No, I want you to stay," Spiro said. "Change it!"

"Okay." Noah kissed Spiro's upper arm, resting his lips against his skin for a second or two. "Do you know what else is tomorrow?" he asked.

"What?" Spiro was still grappling the fact they had almost run out of time.

"Our anniversary, two weeks."

"Are you kidding, tomorrow? Of all days, tomorrow... okay, so when I come home for lunch, don't plan anything. We'll go do something. I'll plan something special."

"You don't have to. I was joking. It's not a big deal."

"Yes, it is!" Spiro had an idea, but he needed to check with his friend to see if he could pull it off.

****

The next day, with almost no time to prepare and the owners in the gallery, Spiro and his friend Mateo texted all morning, planning the perfect surprise. On Spiro's lunch break, he drove Noah to the other side of the island to a small cove on Agios Ioannis Beach. They maneuvered the motorbike down the gravel road toward the beach. At the end of the road, they parked the motorbike.

"No offense, but I can't believe this damn thing runs." Noah swung his leg over the seat and stretched his legs before handing his helmet to Spiro. Spiro secured their helmets to the side of the motorbike.

"Are you kidding me? She's a champ. I've had her since I was, like, ten years old."

"It looks like it." Noah joked as he switched his attention to the beautiful heart-shaped cove surrounded by huge volcanic rocks. "This is cool; it's shaped like a heart. The water is so clear." He took a breath of air and exhaled as he raised his arms.

"The tourists call it Lover's Beach." Spiro took Noah's hand and clasped his fingers. They hiked the rest of the way down to the beach. Once on the sand, they walked the beach about a hundred yards to the end. They stood in front of an unusual, but intriguing, rock formation at least twenty feet tall. The formation marked the end of that side of the cove. The bizarre-shaped boulder wasn't actually rock, but a volcanic formation made of petrified lava left from three thousand years ago. Music from the bar and restaurant on the cliff drifted down to them. A set of rock steps formed a trail up to the tavern where the music was playing.

Instead of up the steps, Spiro led him into a large cavern illuminated by candlelight. Twenty feet inside the empty cavern was a small table, covered with white linen, a chair placed on each side. "I hope you're hungry."

"You told me not to eat, so yes, I'm starving. What is this place?"

"They're caves that formed thousands of years ago after the volcano erupted and the ocean pounded into the rocks. Have a seat." Spiro held out a chair for Noah and waited for him to sit before he did.

As soon as Spiro sat down he held up the bread basket and offered Noah a piece of bread.

"Thank you." Noah took the basket of bread and tore a piece from the crusty country loaf.

A booming voice entered the cavern. "Hello." The man then switched to Greek and rattled something off that made Spiro laugh.

Spiro stood. "Noah, this is my good friend Mateo. Mateo, this is Noah."

Mateo extended his hand, and the two shook. "It will be my honor to cook for you this afternoon."

"Mateo is the head chef at the Blue Oceania restaurant."

Mateo cut in. "My good friend owns the Aqua Blue Bar and Grill, above us, and he was nice enough to offer his kitchen this afternoon. Please, sit, so I can get started!"

"May I start you both off with a ginger cocktail, made with fresh ginger? It's non-alcoholic, with no added sugar." Mateo asked them.

Noah's expression said he was skeptical of the drink, but he took a tiny sip of the cocktail. "Oh, that's good."

It made Spiro proud that he could show Noah that he had friends of such importance. Once Mateo left the cave, Spiro picked up his glass and held it in the air. "Happy anniversary."

"Happy anniversary." Noah picked up his glass and tapped it against Spiro's.

"I know you said you didn't need one, but I have something for you—sort of an anniversary gift, I guess." Noah pushed an app on his phone. "Now you don't have to do anything with it. It's a website where people can find you."

"Who's looking for me?" Spiro leaned over the table to view his screen. The first thing he saw was a picture of himself and then one of his paintings.

"Well, me, for one! Twelve years, did you forget?"

"What is this?" Spiro took the phone and scrolled through the website.

"What you're looking at is the mobile website. It looks different on a computer." The excitement in Noah's voice jumped several octaves.

Spiro was flattered that he would do something like this, but he still didn't understand the need for a website. "This is nice." He tapped a button marked "gallery," and a picture inventory of his work popped up. He scrolled through several of the photos on the site. "When did you do all of this?" Seeing his photos on the phone was a little weird.

"I have my ways. Do you like it?"

"I love it! It's the nicest gift I've ever received. Thank you." He wondered how much something like this cost to do. "So, how will people know it's there? Besides my stalker?" Spiro's head nodded, making it clear he was referring to him.

"I'm not a stalker!" Noah laughed. "Just a boy in love."

A boy in love... The words exploded in Spiro's ears. *Noah said he was in love... with me?* He suspected as much, but hearing it, the actual words *in love*, it suddenly felt like there was a responsibility on his end to say it in return.

Spiro forced down a nervous, hard swallow. His focus shifted from Noah spending money on him to hearing he was in love with him. Was he supposed to say it back to Noah? Saying it back didn't seem genuine if he didn't love him. *Do I love him?* He didn't know the answer.

He reanalyzed what Noah had said: *a boy in love.* There was no other meaning he could conclude. At a loss for how to respond to Noah's admission, he saw the nervousness in Noah's eyes.

"Okay, guys, for our first course this afternoon, we have grilled octopus salad, dressed with a little olive oil and lemon." Mateo's booming voice against the walls of the cave broke the tension between them as he entered. Mateo sat the small plates of the gorgeous salad down in front of each of them. He took the pitcher filled with his ginger concoction and topped off each of their glasses. "Enjoy." He smiled and bowed before disappearing again.

Spiro returned to his salad. He wavered. Should he address what Noah had said or just eat? Noah's expression, his eyes, pleaded for him to address it. "I hope you can eat it. I told him no fried or fatty foods, or anything in a creamy sauce." Spiro picked up his fork and started eating.

Noah picked through his salad. "Yeah, it looks great. It smells delicious." His tone was anything but excited.

Although the conversation halted as the two ate their first course, it hadn't stopped in Spiro's head. He appreciated Noah's gift, his declaration of love, him flying all the way from America to find him, but he had a hard time wrapping his brain around why Noah loved him. He had nothing to offer Noah. They were from two different worlds. Spiro was a poor islander. It was Mateo who invented the idea of this elaborate lunch in the cave. Spiro's plan was for Mateo to put together a simple picnic to take to the beach. In silence, the two ate their salads.

Still not knowing what to do about Noah's declaration, Spiro felt that too much time had passed to bring it up now. He knew he was taking the easy road, but bringing it up again scared him. Hearing that Noah loved him didn't frighten him, but saying it back and not being sure about it didn't seem right. The temperature rose inside the cave.

Everything about Noah was sweet and endearing: his soft, blue eyes, the flawless, pale skin that graced his cheeks, the fact that when he was nervous, he rambled... Spiro's body heat continued to rise as a metallic taste formed in his mouth.

Mateo soon returned with their main course, fresh sea bass and roasted Brussels sprouts.

Halfway through the course, Noah put down his fork. "I know we've talked a little about it, but... I've wanted to ask... would you consider coming to New York?" Noah's voice shook.

Spiro heard the pleading in Noah's question. "To visit?"

"No... to live."

"To live?" Spiro's lips remained apart. A flush of hot adrenaline shot up the back of his neck. How could he answer that question truthfully without breaking Noah's heart? He couldn't leave his family, his mother, his aging theia. He'd left them too many times before for his own selfish reasons, and every time, it was a disaster. Now his parents, his theia, they needed him here. There was no way.

Noah chuckled. "I'm not asking you to marry me. You don't have to be freaked out. Your face is paler than mine right now."

"No, I'm not freaked out," he lied. "It surprised me." He lied again. "You mean, like, move in together?" He used his cloth napkin as if he was wiping his mouth, but it was hiding the lie that was less painful than the truth.

"I'm not saying like next week or anything, but maybe at some point. New York is a great place to showcase your art. There are so many studios and art galleries that would love to have someone like you. I know you don't know how good you are." Noah's words were quick, his pitch elevated. "I could help you. There's plenty of room in my apartment, or we could find something bigger, with a place where you could paint."

Spiro had to stop him. He couldn't leave his family. Plus, he had no money for an apartment in New York. Even if they used Noah's existing apartment, he couldn't afford the ticket to America.

"Noah..." There was so much being said at once, and he was still stuck back on Noah telling him he loved him. And now, they were talking about moving in together. He cleared his throat for another second of delay. "I can't say I haven't thought about it. This last week has been incredible... It has..." He reached across the table and took Noah's hand. "Can I be honest?" He knew he shouldn't say it, but he owed it to Noah to be honest. He never wanted to lie to him, but he also never wanted to hurt him, either. "Sometimes... There've been times this past week I felt... like you... well, maybe, you're way ahead of me. Like maybe you might be in love with who I was years ago. It feels so fast." He stopped, seeing the hurt on Noah's face. He didn't want to hurt him; he couldn't.

"No... no..." Noah tried to wave him off. "It's not a big deal." He paused again. "It was just conversation. New York is a great place for an artist!" The hurt on his face said it was a big deal.

Silence filled the air for several long minutes before Noah spoke again. "Should I... not change my flight this Friday? It's okay if I don't."

Spiro was ready to reject the idea of him still leaving this week, that was, until Noah added, *It's okay if I don't.* What did that mean? He had to ignore whatever it was supposed to mean. "Change your flight. I want you to stay." His voice wavered. Noah's eyes said that he had been crushed. He knew Noah was hurting, but what was he supposed to have said? It was all so fast.

Weeks ago, if someone had told him he would have these strong feelings for someone in the next two weeks, he would have believed the message was being sent from the heavens, from Momus, the god of satire and mockery. Until Noah, he was content with being single—happy, even. And now Noah was all he could think about.

Noah was offering him something, but it came with a price. He could never leave his family, his mother; it wasn't an option.

Noah retracted his hand from under Spiro's. There was a tightness in his face that revealed his hurt. Spiro searched for words to make it better, but none came to him. He didn't have the money or the freedom to be as impulsive as Noah. He had a responsibility here, and that was his family. He wanted to say yes, yes to all of it. Yes, if it made Noah happy, yes to wipe the hurt from his face, yes, to give Noah everything he wanted. But there was a price for doing that, and that was his family.

Noah broke the silence. "How are the owners?"

The question was benign. He appreciated Noah's attempt to lighten the mood. Noah's confession of love and wanting him to move to New York was not possible to dismiss. Neither of those conversations could be pushed to the side with a simple, unimportant, benign question.

"It's weird. They didn't bring any new inventory to restock the gallery. I'm not sure why they're here." Spiro looked at his watch.

Their time was ending, and this lunch wasn't at all what he wanted for Noah. With thirty minutes left to drop Noah back at the hotel and return to the gallery for the evening, talking about it would have to wait until later this evening, after he closed the gallery.

That night, when Spiro returned to the bungalow from the gallery, his plan was to talk about their earlier conversation. But once he and Noah were together, bringing it up would be painful, like ripping a fresh scab off a new wound. He got it; he did. He hurt Noah this afternoon. Noah had poured out his heart and confessed his love for him. He didn't like the way things were left, but it was all happening so fast.

Tonight, Noah had crawled into bed. After giving Spiro a grandma kiss, he turned his back to Spiro and turned out the light. He knew Noah was still hurt as he wrapped an arm around Noah's body and brought his naked body close to his. Noah's back and shoulder muscles released as he let out a long, slow exhalation.

Even with Noah mad at him, he needed Noah close to him. Spiro had one question on his mind; everything else was not important. *Am I in love with Noah?*

Could it be as simple as a yes or no? It didn't seem like something that should be answered with a simple yes or no, that it was that simple.

CHAPTER TWENTY-ONE

Noah felt bad about giving Spiro the cold shoulder this morning. They'd hardly said two words to each other before Spiro left for work. Yesterday's lunch was an epic failure. Noah wanted to place the blame on Spiro, but he knew he owned some of it. How could he have actually brought up moving to New York so soon? *I talked about everything but the color of the wedding dress I already bought for a spring wedding. I told him I loved him and got nothing back. I asked him to move to New York and was rejected.*

Once again, he poured out his heart to someone who didn't want it. How was it he kept getting into relationships with unattainable guys? How could he have been wrong about Spiro? He wouldn't have poured his heart into this had he not believed Spiro felt the same.

His heart said to send Spiro a text saying he was sorry. *But sorry for what?* Sorry that he reacted to being rejected? Sorry that he wanted more from the person he was in love with? An "I'm sorry" text didn't feel like it should come from him. Was he being overdramatic, overthinking? They hadn't gotten into a fight. It wasn't a breakup, but the excruciating pain of rejection was evidence he'd been stabbed in the chest.

He lay in bed and stared at the jeans and shirt Spiro wore yesterday that was still laying over the chair. It was as if Spiro himself was sitting in the chair. "So, you don't love me?" Noah asked. *Am I really talking to a pair of jeans and a shirt?* He had to get up and get out of this room. He needed fresh air.

The fresh air did little to cheer him. After going through several stores, he made his way toward the pier. *Maybe it's time to go home. Maybe I should go right now.*

The sun warmed the back of Noah's neck as he made his way past the cluster of stores on the pier. He tried to fight off the avalanche of emotions that was suffocating him. Was he nuts to think he would actually be more important to Spiro than Spiro's own family? With any guy he'd ever dated, he was never the priority; hell, he wasn't even a priority for his parents when he was growing up. He'd struggled his entire life asking for what he wanted from people. Instead, like a baby bird being handfed, he just accepted what little pieces of affection people rationed out to him. What was it about him that made him so unlovable?

His eyes fell to his shadow in front of him. As he stared at the shadow, a woman walked past him, stepping on the shadow's head. It was his head that she just stepped on and never missed a step as she kept walking. *Wow!* He held out his hand and watched as the shadow did the same. He raised his hand above his head and watched as the shadow copied him. The shadow was there. He and anyone on this earth could see it, yet it went unnoticed almost always. Was he any more in this life than a shadow?

Other than Rodney, he thought Spiro had been the only person who understood him and actually saw him. From the first day he met Spiro, he had the magical ability to make him feel safe, sexy, smart... and more than just a shadow.

Okay, so Spiro didn't say he loved him, but he must have some feelings for him. He wasn't convinced that it was only about sex. He'd seen it in Spiro's eyes, the way he looked at him. Noah knew this was a slippery slope. He didn't want to be that guy that said Spiro needed more time to fall in love, when no amount of time would change it.

He looked up and focused on a man coming toward him. The man's head was down as he peeled back the skin of the banana he was eating. It was Nico. His impulse was to turn and head the other way before Nico saw him, but then Nico spotted him.

"Hey, Nico." Noah muttered once he was closer.

Nico grabbed him and kissed his right and left cheek. "You're still here?"

"Yeah." He forced a smile, attempting to hide his grief.

"That's good! Everything worked out for you two lovebirds?" Nico's smile grew larger, his pearly white teeth reminding Noah how nice looking Nico was.

It had until yesterday. He was embarrassed about how to answer Nico. It was easier to avoid the question altogether. "I never got the chance to thank you."

Nico waved off the thank you. "It was nothing. It was fun hanging out with you. For my own selfish reasons, I wished things would have turned out differently, though."

Nico's compliment and the prospect of them getting together sent heat to Noah's cheeks. "We need to stay in touch. You have my number, right?" Noah fidgeted, shifting his weight to his other foot.

"Yeah, I have it." Nico paused as if he wanted to say something. His hands dropped to his side. "Bring lover boy by the restaurant sometime. I'll treat you two to dinner."

"Okay. Thanks. I will." His answer was a bit of a lie. The whole conversation was based on a big fat omission.

"Don't leave the island without saying goodbye. I mean it, you two come for dinner." Nico's smile showed its disingenuousness. Perhaps they were both covering up a lie.

They walked off in different directions, Noah continuing toward the docks. He continued past the fishing boats along the wharf until he arrived at the ferry terminal at the end. With the absence of the ferry in the port, the chain-link gate was locked shut.

Noah read the informational board posted outside the fence. He located information on the ferry that went to Athens. It departed on Sundays, Tuesdays, and Thursdays, at one-thirty in the afternoon and again at eleven-thirty in the evening. He pulled up his flight itinerary on his phone to see which ferry would help him leave the island as soon as he could. He glanced away from his phone down at his shadow. He stared down at the shadow as he raised his hand again and watched as the shadow did the same. He knew he probably looked a little crazy manipulating his shadow like a puppet on a string. The realization that he was essential to the shadow's existence said he was more than it. He controlled it. A sense of power tugged at him.

To hell with it, I'm staying... He wasn't ready to give up on them. If he left, what chance did they have if he wasn't in the same country? Manipulating or controlling the situation, call it what you want, but he had to stay for things to work out in his favor for once.

Back at his bungalow, Noah placed the salad and sandwiches he'd picked up for lunch in the tiny kitchenette. He was about to log in on his laptop to push his flights back when he saw Spiro coming up the walkway. He tried to shake off his tension and breathe as Spiro came in. He wanted all the tension behind them, to start anew.

"Hey, there." Noah stood in the middle of the room. "I was about to check into pushing my flight back."

The subdued expression on Spiro's face converted to an obvious fake smile. "So, you're not mad at me anymore?" His voice wavered.

There was no part of him that was mad at Spiro. He loved him. Dark circles under Spiro's eyes emphasized his anguish. In two steps, they were in each other's arms. A single kiss followed a tight hug as Spiro caressed the back of Noah's head.

"I'm sorry," Noah murmured into Spiro's chest. His head rested between Spiro's pecs serenely.

Spiro's hand dropped and rubbed up and down Noah's back. Locked in an embrace, a transfer of energy flowed from Spiro's chest, deep into Noah's body. Makeup sex would work for him right about now. The closeness after making love, wrapped in Spiro's arms, was what he needed. Blood flowed to his groin.

When Spiro released him, he did so with a step backwards. "I'm glad you're not mad at me." He stopped, but looked as if he wanted to say something else.

Noah waited through the unsettling silence until he couldn't take it a second longer. "Are you ready to eat?" Noah mumbled. It certainly felt as if they just made up, yet, nothing was actually resolved. He stared into Spiro's commanding gaze, the gaze that never allowed Noah the freedom to simply look away. He wanted to make love, for all the anguish to be removed from his body. "I picked up sandwiches and a salad again." He attempted to push away his alluring thoughts of Spiro fucking him.

"I'm not that hungry... We got bad news this morning," Spiro said.

Noah's heart sunk with the prospect of more bad news.

"This morning, the owners of the gallery told us they're closing it."

"What? For how long?" Noah spun on his heels, looking back at Spiro.

"For good." Spiro was right behind him. He took both Styrofoam containers that held their lunch off the counter.

"Why do you think they're closing it?" Noah grabbed two bottled waters from the tiny refrigerator and nodded toward the terrace.

"They said they couldn't afford to keep it running, which I get. Nina does the bookkeeping and after paying us and the bills, there isn't that much left. If we don't make enough during the high season, it's nearly impossible to last out the winter."

"Was this all by surprise? Had they talked about closing?"

"I'm sure they've known all summer. They could have told us so we could've at least prepared, maybe found another job."

"I'm sure that's why they said nothing. They didn't want you guys quitting on them in the middle of the season."

"You think?" Spiro took a seat at the small bistro table on the terrace.

"What will happen with you and Nina? Did they say when they're closing?"

"At the end of the month."

"The end of the month! That's in two weeks." Noah saw the distress on Spiro's face. "What do you think you'll do?"

"I don't know." Spiro picked at his salad.

"Do you think one of the other galleries would hire you guys?"

"No. Not going into the low season. No one's hiring this time of year. If anything, they're letting people go." Spiro plucked a piece of meat out of his pita. "I owe you an apology for yesterday." Spiro laid his pita down. "Yesterday, our conversation caught me a little off guard."

"Which part?" Noah held his breath as he waited for the possibility that Spiro would say that he loved him, that this was why Spiro looked so nervous.

"The website, my paintings, moving to New York. All of it. This morning, I was thinking about it... I remember you talking years ago about going away to school, becoming a doctor and everything. And though you didn't, you still made something of your life. We're so different." Spiro paused as he rubbed his forehead. "I don't have big dreams. I don't live in a world where I'm dreaming of being a big artist. The other day, you said it for yourself, you thought I would be this rich, big-time artist by now."

"I was joking with you," Noah interrupted.

"I believe you think you were joking, but you come from a world where people do big things. Look at your parents—hell, even your grandparents. We're not like that. There isn't anything big that we're reaching for or waiting to happen. We work, doing what is needed to put food in our mouths and keep the roof over our heads. If those two things are met, then hell, life is damn good for us. We expect little from this life. I'm not trying to be an artist; I paint because people buy it. I'm good with that."

Confusion swept across Noah's face. "Do you not want to paint?"

"No, I love to! I just don't desire the same thing from it I think you do."

This was not at all the conversation Noah envisioned. It didn't sound like there would be an admission of love. It sounded ominous. Was this the breakup?

Spiro closed the lid on the rest of his lunch and pushed it aside. He took a deep breath and exhaled as he leaned back in his chair. "It's a lot..."

"What's a lot?" Noah murmured.

Spiro took his cigarettes from his breast pocket and popped one from the pack. He lit it, took a long drag from it, and exhaled. "It's all so fast."

And there it was, the *let's see how it goes*, the classic breakup. The muscles in Noah's stomach twisted. He swallowed, hoping to keep what little food down there from coming up. "Okay, then, we just take it slow... if that's what you want." He knew Spiro was right, it was fast. But even if he agreed with Spiro, it didn't change the fact that he was love with Spiro.

Spiro exhaled smoke into the air. "I don't know. I don't know what I want."

"I'm not asking you for anything." That was a lie.

"I know you're not... Look, after work tonight, I have to go by the house. I'll stay there. I'll text you."

Noah knew what a breakup felt like, and this exhibited all the emotions of a breakup. "Okay..."

That evening, Noah tried not to focus on the time. It was almost nine o'clock, and the gallery would be closing. Would Spiro text him before leaving the gallery or after he did whatever he had to do at home?

By eleven o'clock and no text, Noah decided that it was a breakup. He crawled into bed, trying to ignore how empty the bed was with just him. The stresses of the entire day had physically made him sick.

When Noah opened his eyes the following morning, alone in the bed, something that once was the norm, an empty bed, was terribly amiss now. He reached for his phone, already knowing that Spiro hadn't left a text while he'd been sleeping.

Had a text come in, even in his sleep, his brain would have signaled an alert like a piercing tsunami warning. He lay in bed for several minutes, debating whether to send the first text, a harmless good morning.

Maybe Spiro's mother wasn't doing well, and that was the reason for the absence of a goodnight text from him. His emotions were a runaway train. He tried to switch his thinking to the best-case scenario instead of the worst-case, but anything he came up with didn't seem plausible. The line between being positive and being foolish was blurred by the ping in his heart.

He pulled up the thread of texts between him and Spiro over the last week. *Good morning*, he texted and pushed "send."

He held the phone and stared at his screen as if an instant reply would happen. Had he actually been dumped yesterday? The absence of a text from Spiro solidified it. With the weight of the phone in his hand, it felt like it was the weight of twelve years of his life. When nothing came after a minute or two, he fought back a tear as he put the phone on his nightstand and went for his shower.

He exhaled a big breath, trying to hold off crying as water cascaded down his neck and back. In one conversation, he sabotaged everything. Why did he bring up New York?

The *I love you* part was a slip, but he owned the rest, talking about New York, his apartment, the stuff about the great art galleries and him being able to paint. He was begging Spiro to move to New York. It was pathetic.

Spiro said he was way ahead of him. If this was true, where was Spiro? He had to have been at least past the *Let's-get-to-know-each-other* phase.

Noah rinsed the soap off his body and grabbed the towel off the hook on the wall. He towel dried his hair as he walked around the bed to retrieve his phone. He checked his phone for a text from Spiro.

His heart leapt as he saw he had one new message. He opened his messages and saw it was from Rodney: *Hey, what time is your flight coming in?*

In three days, he was flying home. He hadn't changed his flight yet. Now, he was uncertain about pushing the date back. Spiro told him to push it back, that he wanted him to stay. So why did it feel as if he should bump up his flight instead of pushing it back?

Was Spiro too much of a chicken shit to tell him the truth? Was he being ghosted now? If so, it was bullshit! How hard was it to tell someone the truth? He hated every guy he'd gone out with, because every relationship had a lie in it.

It was almost nine. He made his way down to the gallery to talk with Spiro. *He could at least tell me to my face.*

The walk was filled with what if's and explanations for Spiro ghosting him. He tried to convince himself that it would be better knowing the truth as opposed to being ghosted. Ghosting was a messed-up thing to do to someone. He didn't see it coming with Spiro.

The sound of the bells above the door signaled his entry. Perhaps Nina and Spiro were in the back with the owners. He regretted coming as a nervousness swelled in his gut. He would not make a scene. But he had a right to know that it was over if that was the case.

A small, young woman emerged from the back. "Good morning." Her warm welcome said she had no idea who he was.

"Good morning... is Spiro in yet?" He asked.

She clasped her hands. "No. He won't be in today. May I help you with something?"

She must be the owner. He wouldn't tip his hand on who he was. "No, thank you." He wanted to retreat, but she stopped him.

"How can I help you? What are you looking for?"

Lady, I'm not buying anything. I'm here to get what's mine already. He was stuck. "Oh, um... no. I just wanted to say hi."

The woman's smile faded at the loss of a sale.

Noah tore from the gallery before she could quiz him further. He moved down the street and around the corner before stopping to catch his breath. If Spiro wasn't at work, then he had to be at home. He hesitated with his idea of going to his house... but he needed answers.

The short cab ride to the house was more nerve wracking than the walk to the gallery. The pit of his stomach twisted as saliva increased in his mouth. Spiro's dad's truck was missing, but Spiro's motorbike was parked against the house.

It brought him a little comfort to know that his dad wasn't here. He paid his fare and thanked the man.

Noah knocked on the door, hoping Spiro would answer and they could talk outside. He waited but didn't hear any noise inside. He knocked again. It took a minute, and then clicking from the other side said someone was at the door.

The door opened, and Spiro's theia appeared. Dressed in a seafoam housecoat, her expression said she was surprised to see him.

"Is Spiro here?" He tried to look past the old woman into the house, but it was dark.

Her brows narrowed. "Spyridon?" She repeated before launching into Greek. She spoke as if he was understanding what she was saying.

Understanding none of what she was trying to tell him, he held out his hand, signaling for her to stop. "I'm sorry, but I don't understand." He tried to see inside the house past her.

She shook her head as she continued talking. The inflection in her voice climbed the more she talked, and then she stopped. It was clear she was waiting for him.

"I'm sorry, but I don't understand." He shook his head and gestured, trying to somehow communicate that he didn't understand her.

She stepped away from the door as she opened it wider. She waddled away, leaving the door open for him.

The drapes in the front room were still closed. The house was quiet and cold. Spiro's father wasn't in his chair, and the hospital bed was empty.

He stepped over to the unmade bed and touched it. He hoped the old woman would understand why he was here. "Where is she?" Noah asked. He was ready to search each room.

The few times he'd been back with Spiro, they stayed in the front room, the kitchen, and Spiro's room, but he'd been there enough to know that the small house was empty.

The woman kept talking as she picked up a medicine bottle. She held the bottle up for him to see that it was Spiro's mother's medication. "Yes, yes. That is hers." He pointed to the empty bed.

The woman nodded and said one or two words before returning the bottle to the end table.

"Spiro?" he asked her again.

She shook her head no and picked up the medicine bottle again to show him.

"The pharmacy... doctors?" he asked.

Her face was blank. She wasn't understanding.

"Are they at the doctors?" He asked again.

This time, the woman walked from the room into the kitchen. She was gone for a minute before returning. She held up her hand. She had a hospital wristband and offered it to him.

Noah took the band, knowing what it was. "Hos-pit-al?" He asked.

The woman's face brightened as she nodded yes.

"They're at the hospital?" He was unsure if she was understanding or guessing, just as he was doing. "Thank you." He tried to give her the band back, but using her hands, she gestured no.

He stuffed the wristband in his pocket as he tore from the house. Outside, he realized he'd sent his cab driver away. He pulled out his phone and wasted several minutes searching for a cab on the island. He wasn't finding any websites for cabs.

He saw Spiro's motorbike and knew it was his only option. He raced to the motorbike, and saw that the key was in the ignition switch. He'd seen Spiro start it enough to know what to do. Driving it couldn't be that much harder than riding a bicycle. He hoped the damn thing would start.

He fired up the engine, straddled the motorbike, and guided it onto the street. Once there, he eased the throttle forward as the motorbike increased its speed. Confident that he wouldn't fall over, he picked up his feet as the motorbike picked up a little more power. He was a little wobbly, but it didn't take him long to gain confidence as he steered the motorbike toward the small hospital on the side of the mountain around Myrina. He'd seen the hospital several times as he and Spiro sped past it on their adventures.

His heart was racing; he couldn't get to the hospital soon enough. Anxiety swirled around him as he tried to focus on his driving. In the little side mirror, Noah saw a big truck coming up behind him. His eye caught the helmet still hooked to the rear of the motorbike. He'd forgotten to put his helmet on. He slowed the motorbike as he moved over to let the truck pass him. The wind from the truck shook the bike as it passed.

Why hadn't Spiro texted him to let him know? A simple text and he would have been there to support him. Was it that he didn't want his support? Did it mean he wasn't being ghosted? The anger he harbored for Spiro seemed narcissistic. This was about Spiro, not him. Even if they weren't together, he still wanted him to be okay.

The entire drive was a blur as he turned off the main road and drove up the hill toward the small hospital. It'd taken forever, but he was here.

He raced into the hospital and rushed to the first person he saw with a badge, a young man in a white lab coat talking on his phone as he strolled down the empty hall. "Excuse me, Sir!" Noah grabbed the man's sleeve. "Can you help me?"

Startled, the man's expression softened as his eyes focused on who was grabbing him. "Yes?" He pulled his arm back. "How can I help you?"

"I'm looking for someone. I think she's here, with her husband and son. Her name is Adelpha, Adelpha Papadopoulos." Her name rolled off his tongue as if he'd known her for years. "She might have come in yesterday." He showed the man her old hospital wristband.

"Are you family?"

Noah knew why he was asking. "Yes, she's my theia!"

The man escorted him down the hall to an office the size of a closet. Inside was a small desk and a computer. There wasn't enough room for both of them inside, so Noah stood in the doorway. His eyes scanned the tiny room, wondering if this was the man's office.

The man bent over the computer on the desk staring at the monitor as his fingers typed at the keyboard. "I don't see an admission for her. We have records for her, but I don't see a recent admission for her. I checked to see if she might still be in the ER, but I didn't see her there. Perhaps she's gone home already."

"No. No, she hasn't!"

The man frowned as he went back to his computer and typed on the keyboard again. The sound of keys echoed throughout the small room.

"No. She's not here." The man straightened up. "I'm sorry."

CHAPTER TWENTY-TWO

Noah didn't have the strength to get out of bed. Unable to sleep most of the night, he'd been lying there for hours with the sheet over his head. Yesterday played over and over in his head. After leaving the hospital, he'd returned to the gallery first, hoping Spiro would be there. Through the window, he waited, hoping that either Nina or Spiro would appear from the back. When that didn't happen, he drove back to Spiro's house. With no sign of Spiro or his father's truck in front of the house, he gave up and returned to his hotel. He had no idea where they could be.

Noah pulled the sheet off his head and checked his phone for the one hundredth time. He'd sent Spiro a dozen texts yesterday and this morning, none of which he replied to. Spiro was ghosting him. He didn't want to believe this, but what else could it be? He'd walked out of here two days ago and didn't have the guts to at least break it off. This hurt far worse than twelve years ago. No one was sending him away this time or trying to keep them apart. He left and was too cowardly to say goodbye. If he didn't want to move to New York, Noah could understand. That didn't need to be a deal breaker. If he didn't love him, but at least was into him, he was willing to settle for that, too. But to ghost him, that meant Spiro felt nothing for him. Every guy Noah had confessed his love to flashed before him. Was Spiro just like them?

How could he have been played for such a fool? The way Spiro looked at him, his soft caress, everything he said to him, they weren't from someone who didn't care. Noah refused to accept that he could have been that stupid, that Spiro was like the rest of them. So, then, *what happened?*

In his sweats, he sat on the terrace and caught up on all the accounts he'd neglected over the last several weeks. Normally, at home, work was a great filler of time. It was a job that drove him to think as well as something he could do with little interaction from other people. But this morning the technical aspect of IT did little to keep his mind from drifting.

By late afternoon, when he had enough of work, he took his shower and walked up to the hotel restaurant for a late lunch. He hoped to see Mateo. Maybe Mateo would have answers.

He sat at a corner table and ate his salad in the nearly empty dining room. Like a slow poison to his soul, loneliness had disguised itself in the comforts of being an introvert by choice. He debated calling his mother all day. It wasn't often that he wanted... needed his mother, even if she'd failed him time after time. The last time they talked was a week before he left. He wouldn't have called her then, had he not been leaving the country.

During that call, when Noah told her he was going to Greece, her initial reaction was jovial, stating he deserved a vacation. Her response cooled when he added that he was going to visit Eros's nephew: *You know, the one that was at the lake house years ago.* Her silence told him she remembered.

Before he could talk himself out of it, he pushed the call icon on his phone to his mother's office. The phone rang several times before his mother picked up.

"Hey, there." The stoniness in her tone said she was multitasking. "Are you home?"

He could picture her, sitting at her desk, combing through a stack of charts on her desk. "No, I'm still here. I'm flying out tomorrow."

"Oh... okay..." Her voice trailed off back into the familiar silence.

Anger swelled up in him at her aloofness. It spoke volumes. He kicked himself for not listening to his instincts. This call was a mistake. "How're you doing?" He asked to fill the silence.

"Busy here. Your father's in Sweden until Sunday. I'm heading out to California for a conference in the morning."

He knew she wouldn't ask how he was doing, how the trip was, or anything about Spiro. There was the familiar avoidance in her voice. It was just as well she didn't. "Mom..." He interrupted her.

"Yes?" Her tone was clipped.

"Nothing." He shook his head. "I wanted to let you know that I'll be back tomorrow; that's all."

"Okay, Noah. Well, when I get back from California and you get yourself rested, you need to come for dinner. It's been too long. You need to see your father."

"Okay, Mom. I'll call you next week. We'll plan something." He could be as polite and insincere as she. He drew a breath. His brain said not to do it, but his heart pushed him. "I love you." Although the silence on the other end was expected, it hurt.

"All right. I'll tell your father you said hi when I talk to him." She hung up the phone first.

Setting his phone on the table, he told himself the call was a mistake. It only made him feel worse. Her inability to say she loved him, he questioned why it was so hard to do? He told Spiro he loved him and was rejected... *Rejected?* Was this the reason people didn't say it? He'd been rejected his entire life, by his mother, his father, countless men, and now again by the one person he thought for sure he was safe with. Love was more than a word for him. Love was a feeling, an emotion that he couldn't just turn on and off. Years of therapy and none of it was doing him any good at this moment.

Back in his room, he packed his bags, leaving out the clothes he would travel in. On the couch, he curled up with his phone and opened his Facebook account. In his feed, Rodney had posted several photos of his show last night at the Voodoo Room. Noah had never missed one of Rodney's shows. In fact, he cheered the loudest for him.

Although he would never tell Rodney, most drag queens intimidated Noah. Brassy, their tongues could cut you to death as they smiled at you. He never knew if they were serious. As he scrolled through Rodney's pictures, for the first time since he arrived, he was missing home. He missed the comforts of his apartment, the traffic, the people, the noise!

He stared at his phone, debating whether to call Rodney. He wanted away from the silence that trapped him in this room. He needed to hear someone's voice, someone he trusted. He dialed Rodney's number, expecting his voicemail.

Rodney picked up the phone on the second ring. "What's wrong?"

He hadn't said a word, yet Rodney knew. Maybe the fact he was calling instead of texting was the clue. Rodney always knew when something was wrong.

"Noah, what's wrong?" Rodney asked again.

"I think it's over." Noah's words were barely audible.

"What do you mean? What happened?" Rodney shrieked.

Overwhelmed, Noah couldn't breathe. A tear fell from his eye. He hadn't cried until now. Uttering the words, admitting it aloud, it was too much. He wiped away another tear. Not wanting Rodney to hear him crying, he fought to breathe as he silently cried. He was alone, and the quicksand that was his life was about to overtake him. He was choking on his own breath.

"Noah! Are you there? What happened?" Rodney pleaded.

"I don't know..." Noah wiped his eyes and cleared his throat, trying to pull it together enough to at least talk like a grown man. He spilled everything he could think to tell his friend, at times, rambling. Rodney just listened. His tears had dried by the time he'd finished.

"That's bullshit! Don't sit there and wait for him. You need to get on that plane and bring your ass home. I don't know what he's doin', but he's trippin'."

"Is it me? Am I somehow this screwed-up person no one wants to be with, and I don't know it?" He was in love with a man who broke his heart not once, but twice. He wished he wasn't in love, that he could hate Spiro for what he'd done.

"Baby, it's not you. You're an incredible person. You're smart, kind, honest... thrifty—"

"—Rodney!" It was always only a matter of time before Rodney could force a smile out of him. *Thrifty*? "Then why is it that every guy I've dated has screwed me over in some way?"

"Honey, that's what guys do! God gave them a dick and a brain, but not enough blood supply to use them at the same time!"

Noah tried not to laugh at Rodney's witticism, but it was funny. "Okay, then, what's my mom's excuse?"

"Oh, girl, Mommy Dearest has the biggest dick of them all."

Noah exhaled a large breath as he tried not to laugh at Rodney calling his mother Mommy Dearest.

Rodney continued, "I've told you about the ice princess. You'll die of frostbite waiting for her to warm up."

He knew Rodney was right. His mother had never been a nurturer. Having Nathanael in the world was his comfort; they nurtured each other. They shared a womb. Best friends. Emotionally connected—telepathically. He hadn't known loneliness until after Nathanael's death. It was as if a part of Noah himself had died. It wasn't until the summer he and Spiro met that he felt alive again. No one since could make him feel alive like Spiro. How could he have been so wrong about Spiro? He'd wasted so many years, elevating him up on this pedestal as this great love, and it wasn't even real. The pain in his heart was excruciating, the loss, the loneliness, the pain was crushing the little bit of life he had within him.

****

The alarm on Noah's phone chimed, letting him know that it was five a.m., time to get up. Last night, after talking with Rodney, Noah had avoided the empty queen-sized bed and instead had fallen asleep on the small couch.

Through the window, the sky was still dark. This had been the first time since arriving three weeks ago that he'd awakened to an alarm before the sun had risen. The emptiness of the room compounded the hollowness inside him. He tried not to think about Spiro. Instead, he tried to be excited about going home, back to the city, having dinner with Rodney, but his thoughts came back to Spiro every time. He needed to leave this place.

An hour later, when Noah arrived at the airport, it seemed much smaller than when he passed through it three weeks ago. So much had happened since then. He and Spiro passed the tiny airport a dozen times on the motorbike as they zipped back and forth between the two sides of the island. In those moments, it was just an airport. Now, it seemed like so much more. It was the passageway to the end of a dream.

Three weeks ago, when he first walked through the airport, he was high on the possibility of finding Spiro, elated with the possibility of finding love. Now, this morning, he was at a crushing low, lower than he'd been at the end of any of his failed relationships. He wanted to isolate himself, and what better place to do it than on a seventeen-hour flight surrounded by five hundred total strangers?

Noah walked through the glass doors into the small lobby of the airport and approached the ticket counter, where two employees stood.

"Good morning." Noah placed his passport on the counter for the agent.

"Good morning." The agent smiled as she slid his passport off the counter. "How are you this morning?" she asked. Her question was meant to be kind; it felt anything but.

After checking in and surrendering his one piece of luggage, the agent pointed him to the other end of the small terminal, to gate 3B, where his flight to Athens would be boarding in about twenty minutes. He found a spot facing the window, overlooking the small aircraft on the tarmac. He unslung his backpack off his shoulders and sunk into the uncomfortable padded bench. He'd been fighting a dull ache behind his brows since last night, and now it was a full-on headache that felt as if someone was squeezing his head. He knew it was from not eating, but there was no way he could put anything in his system and risk his IBS flaring up before getting on an airplane. He would rather deal with a headache then his IBS.

He scrolled through his Facebook account on his phone, although none of it permeated his brain. It was almost midnight in New York. He took the chance that Rodney was still awake and shot him a message.

About to board my flight. See you soon.

Cool. Can't wait to c u, Rodney responded.

Noah's assumption that Rodney was still up was correct. Knowing each other so well made him smile. *What are u up to?*

Getting ready to leave the club. This place is a bore. Rodney added three sad face emojis.

By yourself?

Nope.

Do I know him? He knew Rodney's type: white, clean cut, and beefy.

Yep.

Who? Out of curiosity, Noah had to ask.

About thirty seconds went by this time before Rodney responded. *My right hand... lol.*

Noah chuckled under his breath as he typed his response. *Have fun.* He added a heart emoji.

Rodney replied with an emoji of a pair of ruby-red lips.

The announcement over the PA system, first in Greek, followed by English, broadcasted that Noah's flight was boarding. He tucked his phone away and dug into the side of his backpack for the boarding pass the agent had handed him when he checked in.

He slung his backpack over his shoulder and dropped behind the six people already in line, waiting for the gate door to open. Within a few minutes, the line was moving. This was it; he was leaving. When it was his turn, he handed his boarding pass to the agent. She scanned it, smiled, and gave it back to him. He tucked it into the side pocket of his backpack and passed through the doors onto the tarmac. The whir of the propellers as they spun on each side of the small twin-engine plane vibrated the air surrounding the plane.

He was about to climb the steps into the plane when he heard his name being screamed.

"Noah!"

Sure he was mistaken, he turned anyway as his name was called again.

"Noah! Noah! Wait!"

At the door leading back inside the terminal, Noah saw a man blocked by the agent. It was... *Spiro*?

CHAPTER TWENTY-THREE

Spiro stood behind the petite agent as if her little body was preventing him from passing. Smiling, Spiro's eyes were wide as his arms waved for Noah to see him.

What the...? Was it really Spiro? What was he doing here? Noah stopped. Annoyed that Noah was in the way, the woman behind him huffed as she scurried around him.

Spiro waved again for him, his arms flailing in the air. There was something familiar about seeing Spiro so animated and excited... *déjà vu.* It was the moment he'd dreamt of so many times before.

He'd seen Spiro so excited before, seeing him, finding him, the two of them running to meet one another on a tranquil fishing dock. Noah had it wrong; their glorious reunion was happening on the tarmac against the deafening sound of propellers.

He knew he wasn't getting on that plane, yet his feet hadn't caught up with his brain. No, he wouldn't get on that plane as he ran toward the terminal. His heart pounded, seeing Spiro push past the agent as he reached the door. They sprang into each other's arms, coiling and spinning together.

Spiro's arms wrapped around him, making it difficult for him to breathe. This was the vision he imagined so many times before, the reunion that defined their love. His heart beating against Spiro's chest, their hearts beat as one.

Despite the heaviness in his stomach, emotions swirled through his back and neck, causing his knees to wobble. He didn't fear falling, knowing Spiro held him, held every inch of his body and soul.

"Sir, you're going to miss your flight." The agent tried to speak to him.

There was no flight to miss. He wasn't going anywhere. Noah rested his head against Spiro's heart, his own heart racing. When he pulled back to speak, he was afraid his voice would falter. "Um, um... what are you doing here?"

Bright and gleeful, their eyes locked onto one another. Noah's eyes then took in the rest of him. Spiro had the appearance of someone who hadn't slept in two days. His hair was tousled; his clothes were wrinkled and hung from his body. The normally groomed five o'clock shadow was now the beginning of a dark, scruffy beard.

Out of breath, Spiro rested his hands over his heart.

Noah's anger washed away and was replaced with the need to know why Spiro was here. "What are you doing here?" Noah asked again. *Why show up now? After two days?*

"I can't believe I caught you!" Spiro still hadn't caught his breath. "You're leaving?" His voice shook.

"Well... yes... you vanished... I couldn't find you. I didn't know what happened. You vanished and didn't return any of my calls or texts. I went to your house, the hospital, and nothing; I thought you dumped me, were done with me." Noah was surprised how fast his anger resurfaced.

"I didn't blow you off! My mom, she stopped breathing the other day. I've been in Athens... with her. They flew her off the island that night. I went with her..." Spiro's face revealed his confusion. "You're mad—*at me*?"

"What? Oh my God, is she okay?" Embarrassment stirred in Noah. Spiro's saying that he hadn't been dumped, that Spiro's disappearance had nothing to do with him, but with his mother, caused him to wince. "I'm so sorry."

He wanted to ask about Spiro's mother, but within his clash of emotions, Spiro's excuse hadn't completely dissolved his anger. "And you couldn't call me or text to let me know this?" He crossed his arms.

"I didn't have my phone. When I got home that night and went to my room to grab some clothes, I was planning on driving back to the hotel to be with you. When my theia screamed, I bolted inside the house to see what happened. She and my dad were at my mom's bedside. She'd stopped breathing."

Seeing the distress in Spiro's eyes, the tremble in his voice, Noah felt horrible that he assumed Spiro's disappearance was about him. With the thought of almost not being here to support Spiro, Noah's vision blurred, and his throat clenched as he fought back a tear.

"I went to call you when we were at the hospital, and that's when I realized I didn't have my phone. We weren't there but an hour before the medivac arrived and transported us to the mainland. I just arrived on the ferry from Athens and went straight to the hotel, looking for you. They said you had taken a cab to the airport. I was afraid I would be too late."

Noah hesitated as he stared into Spiro's dark eyes. "How's your mother?" His own eyes filled with tears, seeing the distress in Spiro's eyes and hoping he wouldn't say she had died.

"Better. She still can't breathe on her own. The hospital said she had a lot of fluid in her lungs. She's stable for now."

"Is she going to be all right?"

Spiro rolled his shoulders. "I hope so. Dad and Nina are with her. Thank God for medivac insurance. This happened years ago, the same thing. After that, Nina got what we thought was this stupid medivac insurance thing. It saved her life!"

The gate agent squeezed by them and shut the door leading to the plane. With the outside noise silenced, Noah could focus as he attempted to unscramble all that Spiro was saying and what it meant for them.

Noah was overwhelmed by his emotions, one minute being angry, then surprised and happy that Spiro was here; to anguish of the news of his mother. The fluttering in his stomach felt as if he could vomit at any moment. His wobbly legs suggested he sit before his legs gave out.

Even though Spiro's mother was in the hospital, it didn't change the fact that Spiro didn't care for him as much as he loved Spiro. Out of his love for Spiro, he knew he wanted to support him through this, even if he couldn't have him as a lover. He didn't want to make this moment about him when Spiro's mom was so ill. His throat clenched as he wrestled with the guilt of being concerned about his own needs. It seemed selfish to ask, but he couldn't *not* ask. "You said that you wanted to slow things down with us. What does that mean?"

Spiro released a gigantic sigh as he scratched the top of his head. "The other day, at lunch, when we were talking about me coming to New York, it freaked me out a little."

Noah cut him off. "I would never ask you to leave your mom. I get it now! If you're having fun, if that's all this is, then I should at least know that." Noah didn't mean for that to sound as harsh as it did. His mind was racing; his thoughts, scrambled.

"I never said that!" Spiro's voice raised.

"Then what did you say?" Noah certainly didn't want to put words in Spiro's mouth, especially those words.

Spiro folded his arms as he tossed his head back and forth. He was silent for a second as his eyes held onto Noah. His chest dropped with a large exhalation. "I said... all I was trying to say is, I can't go to New York. My family's here. My mom, my dad, my theia: They need me."

Spiro massaged the back of his neck. "I can't leave my family again. When I told you about leaving Peter and coming home, I didn't tell you the whole story. I didn't just leave him. Peter traveled a lot. He had this black Porsche, a Nine-Eleven. One day, I was behind the wheel of it, and this overwhelming sense of just wanting to die washed over me." Spiro stopped. There was a low groaning sound bubbling from his throat, and a deep frown creased his brows.

Spiro did a quick glance around them as he cleared his throat and resumed. "It was like the car was speeding up all by itself. I could feel my foot on the pedal, but it was as if someone had put a boulder on my foot, and I couldn't lift it off the pedal. I know I had the pedal firmly against the floorboard. I never looked at the speedometer; I just stared straight ahead. I questioned why I was on this earth. I couldn't think of a single reason, so there would certainly be no reason why I shouldn't leave it. I truly think I was committed to dying that day."

Noah gasped hearing Spiro say he was committed to dying. His eyes widened. His jaw slackened as he listened.

Spiro's expression acknowledged Noah's reaction, but he kept talking. "I was on the brink of ending my life, and I got this clear vision of my mother. As clear as day, I heard the words, 'Come home.' As if I had zero control of my body, my foot lifted off the gas pedal and slammed down on the brake. I remember fighting to keep the car under control as it skidded down the highway. I was thinking, *I'm going to die,* and at that very moment, I realized I didn't want to die. I fought as hard as I could to keep the car under control. When the car finally came to a stop, I tried to peel my fingers from the steering wheel. It was as if my knuckles were frozen around the wheel. Behind the wheel, I broke down and cried like I've never cried in my life. Flooded with emotions, I couldn't stop crying. At one point, it scared me, because I thought I was losing my mind."

Noah wrapped his arms around Spiro's waist and hugged him, holding him tight while an announcement over the PA system announced a delay of an incoming flight.

When the announcement stopped, Spiro pulled away from Noah. There was a deep-set frown on Spiro's face as he started talking again. "It was crazy; it was like I had absolutely no control over what my body was doing. I called Nina. I didn't even know why I called her; I just did. She made me promise not to do anything stupid. She came the next day to bring me home. I left everything and came home with just the shirt on my back. I never spoke to him or saw him again."

"I get it; I do. I understand why you can't leave. You don't owe me an apology for loving your mother." Saying it didn't make it feel any better.

Spiro's shoulders slumped; defeat and anguish shadowed his face. "My dad barely makes enough to put food on the table. The money that my paintings bring in helps pay for their medication and doctor bills. Even with Nina helping with the bills, there's barely enough money to go around. But it's more than the money. My father and my theia have given up so much for me. Most of it, I wasted away until a couple of years ago. And my mom," Spiro's voice cracked, causing him to clear his throat. He rubbed his eyes. "When I came home this last time, I made a promise to my mother. I would stop screwing around and be there for them. She's in that bed because of me. The least I can do is take care of her. I don't know how much longer my theia can do it. My dad..." Spiro stopped. He squeezed his eyes shut as he raked his fingers through his hair, pulling it off his face.

Spiro didn't have to say it, for Noah to know what he couldn't say. Not only did he still feel guilty for his mother, but he was also afraid of losing his father. He'd seen how old and debilitated Spiro's father looked. He couldn't imagine how he functioned on a fishing boat day to day. Noah understood it more than Spiro knew. There were so many reasons why Spiro would never leave this island.

"What are we doing? Why'd you stop me from getting on that plane?" Noah's heart was being torn from his chest. He knew what he wanted to hear. He wanted to hear that Spiro loved him, that he was important enough that they could figure out how to make this work.

"When you first got here, I sensed maybe you... I didn't know you were coming. Damn!" Spiro scratched his forehead. "I didn't know what we were doing!"

"What are we doing?" Noah murmured.

"Over the last couple of days, I've had a lot of time to just sit and think. The day you found me, I knew immediately how you felt about me. But I wasn't sure how I felt about you. I was still in shock you were looking for me. I—"

Noah worried where Spiro was going with this.

"You're the sweetest, most gentle man that I've ever known. How can I not love you?" Spiro sniffled as the whites of his eyes turned light pink.

Surprised at Spiro's declaration, Noah was speechless.

"I love you, Noah! I know that, twelve years ago, we said it to each other all the time, but honestly, I don't know if I even knew what love was back then... I don't think I loved myself back then... Did I think about you when I came back? Yeah, I did, but you have to know how screwed up I was back then. I didn't care about anyone but myself!"

Spiro's head shook. "I don't know how people know the minute they're in love. What I know right now is, I can't stop looking at you when you're in the room. I think about you in my sleep! Since you've been here, I've been on a high the whole time, like I'm floating. I've never been happier in my entire life. You're the most sensitive, caring man I've ever met. I love how sweet and naïve you can be. I love planning things for us to do and looking for foods for you to eat that won't make you sick. I love the way you look at me with complete and utter trust, knowing that I wouldn't hurt you."

Noah wanted to tell him it was okay, that he accepted his apology, but he wanted to hear Spiro out instead of interrupting him. Noah had never been in a relationship where he genuinely felt the person loved him as much as he loved the other person. He tried to temper the excitement that Spiro might be the one. He didn't want Spiro to stop talking.

"I didn't get it until I was sitting in the hospital room with my mom, thinking we might lose her. How there was so much I wanted to tell her, that I couldn't see the world without her in it. And with all of that, I never stopped thinking about you, how much I was missing you. Even with her in the hospital, I was thinking about you and how to get back to you. Feeling guilty that I was using Nina's arrival as an excuse to come back here and pick up clothes for my dad and I, I knew I was trying to get back to you. I didn't know you were about to leave. I can't believe I almost missed you. It would have killed me."

Spiro pulled Noah to his chest. Without resistance, Noah fell into his arms. He cupped the back of Noah's head and kissed him.

He didn't think twice about kissing Spiro in front of the few people in the terminal. He wanted to wipe the sorrow from Spiro's face; he needed the agony embedded deep within both of their stomachs to go away. What he needed was to be whole with the man he loved. Softly, he kissed Spiro, feeling the dryness of his lips, his warm breath as their lips met. Noah released a faint moan. Pent-up emotions melted away as his head began to swirl.

When Spiro pulled back, it left Noah lightheaded and dizzy. He opened his eyes, seeing the magnificent greens and browns in Spiro's eyes staring at him, eyes that pleaded for his understanding.

Noah swiped at his mouth, clearing the moisture from his swollen lips. "I love you." Noah's voice cracked.

"And I love you." Spiro laid another soft kiss upon Noah's lips. He dropped his arms to his side and clasped Noah's hands. "I came back to find you. I swear I did, but... I have to go to the house, get our clothes, and catch the afternoon ferry back. I don't want you to go home, but... I have to go."

"Then I'll go with you. I'll stay. I'll get a hotel in Athens. It will be fine."

"Thank you." A slow smile emerged as he glanced at his watch. "Come back to the house with me... to my room. The ferry doesn't leave until one-thirty."

Noah knew what Spiro was proposing, and he wanted the same. He nodded before kissing his lover one more time, ensuring that this moment was real.

CHAPTER TWENTY-FOUR

"Oh, my God! It's burning up in here!" Spiro's breaths were short as he gasped for air. Panting, he rolled off Noah and onto his back. He freed himself of the condom and tossed it in the trash beside the bed.

Morning sex was the best, even if their tiny hotel room in Athens had a bed that was too small for both of them. He wanted to blame the temperature of the room on the warmth of the morning sun casting its rays over the massive Parthenon's ancient ruins and into their room, but he knew it was Noah that had his blood pumping.

For the last week, they'd been staying in a small, old hotel in the heart of Athens, a block from the hospital where Spiro's mother remained. In seven days, this was the first day the two had slept in past ten o'clock.

Spiro ran his finger up Noah's moist stomach as his breathing leveled out. "After I come back from the hospital this afternoon, what do you want to do?" What he was trying to determine was if, this afternoon, if the timing was right and he had the courage, there was a small matter he needed to discuss with Noah. The lack of a response from Noah caused Spiro to look at him. "You okay?"

"Mm-hm." Noah wiggled against the mattress, pressing his bare ass into the bed. "You leave me breathless, is all."

"Well, I'm glad you like it." Spiro leaned over and gave him a kiss. His eyes fell to his beautiful lover, paying close attention to the new super-short haircut Noah got yesterday. He rubbed his hand over the soft hair that covered Noah's scalp. It warmed his heart to see Noah so comfortable in Athens, by himself, venturing out and finding, not just the barbershop, but an internet café from which he could work.

Noah's liquid-blue doe eyes stared at him. There was a softness in Noah's eyes after making love that conveyed his total and complete satisfaction. How could he not be in love with this man?

"I think I want to check out the Temple of Olympian Zeus," Noah said.

An idea stirred in Spiro as he sat up and then stretched across the bed to open the window. "Okay. That's right down the street from the Olympic Stadium. We can go to the Temple first, have lunch, and check out the stadium." What he wanted was to take Noah to a nice lunch, but there wasn't money to do that.

Earlier in the week, they'd visited the Acropolis, the Parthenon, the old Acropolis Museum, and the public market. He didn't like Noah paying for everything, so he got creative by choosing places that were free or cost little for admission. The city was rich in historical sites to visit on a limited budget, and the warm days couldn't have been more perfect to walk the large city.

"Do you know that it took almost a thousand years to finish the temple?" Noah rolled his naked body over and grabbed the shirt he'd tossed on the floor last night. He used the shirt to wipe his abdomen dry.

Spiro admired Noah's pale ass as he reached for his shirt. "Well, actually, they never completed it." He laughed under his breath on how cute Noah was, telling him facts about his own country's history. He still wasn't convinced that he could be this lucky in finding someone who adored him as much as Noah did.

Noah dabbed the shirt across his smooth belly until he was dry. He tossed the shirt back down on the floor. "Any word yet on when your mom will be released?"

"They said they wanted her breathing to get stronger without the machine." Spiro shrugged. "Maybe another week."

Noah smacked his lips as if loosening his jaw before talking. "Yesterday, I ran into this cute little boutique hotel. I went inside and asked if they had any rooms available. She let me check out one room. Since we'll be here most likely another week, we should upgrade to a better hotel."

"What's wrong with this room?" Spiro asked. It was bad enough that Noah was footing the entire bill for this room; how much would a bigger room cost? There was nothing wrong with this room.

"The other room has a shower big enough for two." Noah grinned.

Spiro's initial impulse was to argue this. Noah had gotten their current room for him and Spiro, as well as one for Nina the night they'd arrived on the mainland. Originally, they'd also gotten a room for Spiro's father. Since he refused to leave the hospital, much less his wife's side, the hospital rolled in a reclining chair he could sleep in and they let that room go.

"I need a desk I can work on. This room is too small," Noah complained.

Spiro didn't see anything wrong with the tiny room. Sure, it was a mess. Their dirty clothes were tucked in the corner, a six pack of bottled water and snacks lined the wall beside the bed, and it smelled like sex. "Okay, if it's something you need and you're not doing it because you think it's something I need, I'm okay with you spending the extra money."

He didn't let on that he was still thinking of the shower being big enough for two. A bigger bed would be nice. He'd been spoiled by Noah's room back on the island.

"I'll go by this morning and move us. I'll text you the address. Should I get one for Nina, too?"

"I don't know. I'll ask her when I see her later. She was talking about heading back home the other day." Not having Nina on the opposite side of their wall when they were making love would be nice. It was bad enough that the bed squeaked and the headboard thumped against the wall during sex, but several times, he had to put his hand over Noah's mouth to muffle him as he orgasmed.

"How's your dad doing?" Noah asked.

"My dad's hanging in there. He hates the hospital, the food, staff coming in all day and night. He's protective of Mom. I know he's ready to go home."

"Has he always been like that?"

"A homebody?" Spiro crawled out of bed and stretched. The tiny space between either side of the bed and the wall was barely enough room to walk.

"Protective?"

"Yeah, I guess. We've never talked about it, but I think he blames himself for what happened to her. If she'd listened to her parents and never married him, she would have had a better life... you know." Spiro winced as he pointed to himself.

Noah's eyes followed Spiro's naked body as Spiro went into the bathroom. "Are you getting ready?" he asked Spiro.

"Yeah. I want to get to the hospital before her doctors come in, so I can hear what they say. My dad sometimes screws it all up."

"Okay." Noah laid back down in the bed.

Spiro shouted from the shower to Noah. "I forgot to tell you last night; Nina found another job! One of the waitresses at this restaurant over in Kontopouli quit, moved back to where she was from! Nina is friends with the owner, who knew that the gallery was closing! Offered her the job!"

"Kontopouli? Is that the little village near Kavirio, where we had lunch in that cute little central square in the middle of town?"

"Yeah, exactly! The restaurant is right there, in that square!" He turned his back to the showerhead and allowed the water to cascade down his neck and back, rinsing the soap off him.

Although the owners of the gallery told him he and Nina could take as much time off as they wanted until the gallery closed next week, if he wasn't there, he wasn't making money. He needed to find work soon.

"Well, that's good. Has she been a waitress?"

"Yeah, before the gallery hired her. That's what she did! She's not going to make what they were paying her at the gallery, but it's something!"

The gallery's closing sucked in more ways than one. Without the gallery, he had nowhere to sell his paintings. He would be back on the pier with his paintings, trying to sell them to the tourists as they walked by. Before Noah's arrival, Spiro was hoping to catch up on some of his own paintings. He hadn't gotten to several paintings near completion, and now there was no money for supplies to finish them even if he wanted to.

Out of the shower, Spiro stepped back into the bedroom. Noah was propped up against the headboard, staring at his laptop. "Working?" Spiro asked.

"Yeah, I have a site down, and I can't figure out what happened." Noah's thin, long feet wiggled at the end of his crossed legs, stretched out across the bed.

Spiro's eyes followed up his lean frame to his bony collarbone. He knew how Noah felt about his body, yet he was perfect to him. Body type had never been a factor in who he dated; it wasn't important to him. But he loved everything about Noah—his body, his hair, his big goofy emoji-like smile, the gleam in his eyes when they were together.

Noah looked over the top of his laptop at him. A tiny smile formed at the corner of his mouth as their eyes met. The coy smile that Noah flashed sent a surge of desire through him. He was so in love; how could he have not realized it?

****

It was late afternoon when they arrived at the Panathenaic Stadium. The normal street peddlers were out, standing by the entrance waving tee shirts, tiny Greek flags, and other cheap trinkets they sold to the tourists. Spiro paid the five euros for entry before Noah had a chance to.

After several selfies of themselves with the gleaming white marble hairpin-shaped stadium behind them, they climbed the steep marble steps to the top row, where they had a view overlooking the city.

"I can't believe I'm standing in the Panathenaic Stadium! This place is so freaking huge." Noah's excitement was twice what it was in the Temple.

"Did you know that it's one of the oldest stadiums in the world? They built it way back in, like, 144 AD to host the Panathenaic Games."

"Oh, no! I had no idea!" Spiro laughed as he shook his head at his dork of a boyfriend.

"Then, did you know that the athletes used to compete in the nude back then?" Noah read from the small pamphlet they received with their ticket as he sat on a slab of marble. "It says that they also used it for the first modern Olympics, back in eighteen ninety-six."

Spiro had been here countless times; it no longer held his interest. But feeling Noah's excitement was as if they were both experiencing it for the first time. With a few people wandering below them, they had the entire section of marble seats to themselves.

Sitting side by side, Spiro took Noah's hands. His heart pounded at what he was about to say. "I want to ask you something."

"Yeah..." Nervousness shadowed Noah's face.

"How did you know you loved me?" Spiro took a big breath and exhaled some of his nervous energy.

"Well..." Noah crossed his arms over his chest. "You remember back when we were in New Hampshire? It was the first time we talked. That morning, you and Eros were working on the dock. I'd asked you guys if you could help me get my boat down off the wall in the boathouse. It was the way you looked at me that morning. We didn't talk, other than you introducing yourself. But your eyes, they bore into my soul. I was so nervous to talk to you, but it was like I had to. I orchestrated that whole meeting. I knew that day I loved you. I didn't know you, but I knew I loved you."

Spiro listened, trying to recall that day. "Oh! But do you remember what had happened before that?" The day was suddenly crystal clear.

Noah cocked a brow. "No. What?"

"I first saw you up on the porch, before that. I had walked up to the house to get something, and when you saw me, you took off running into the house."

Noah covered his face with his hands as he let out a scream. "No way. How do you remember that? I remember that now. My hair was uncombed, and I think I was barefoot and... Oh, my gosh, I was so embarrassed that you saw me."

"I remember back then you were so sad," Spiro said.

"I was. I guess, most of my life, I've been insecure. It was important what people thought of me: Did they like me? Why didn't they like me?" Noah squeezed Spiro's hand. "Having you there that summer, with you, I wasn't this dweeb anymore. Until then, I was like invisible to the world. No one looked at me the way you did."

"That's funny you would say that, because that's how I feel about you today. With you, anything is possible." Spiro remembered that, back then, he was nothing but a ball of rage. Noah was so easy to be around. Noah required nothing from him. He remembered Noah having a calming effect on him. He wasn't so mad at the world when Noah was around.

Noah brushed his fingertips over the backside of Spiro's hand. "It devastated me when you left. It was as if my soul had been ripped from me, and I was this hollow shell left behind. For a week, I cried myself to sleep. For a long time, I could still see you and feel you. My dreams of you were vivid. Over time, the dreams occurred less, and I'd go longer periods without thinking of you. But I never forgot you. I used to think, maybe the day would come that I'd no longer think about you, but that day never came. I guess that's how I knew I loved you."

Spiro recalled seeing Noah standing across the street the day they found each other. That rush of adrenaline through his body threatened to topple him, and there was an argument in his head that what he was seeing wasn't real. This should have been his first clue he loved Noah. There were some days Spiro still didn't believe he was that in love with Noah. His pulse quickened as the tips of Noah's fingers lightly touched his arm.

"It's weird how you can go from not thinking about the existence of someone to being completely infatuated by them and wondering how the hell you lived without them. I used to question how someone knew if they were in love. I should have known I was in love with you from the moment you showed up that day." Spiro paused as he collected his thoughts. "Around you, it's like I'm drunk. You make me dizzy all the time. I have to tell myself to breathe when I'm looking at you."

Spiro took Noah's hand and clasped their fingers. "Having you here, it's like a dream, and I'm afraid that any minute I'll wake up. You excite me. I love that you're trusting and sweet and uncertain about your place in the world. I love every moment I am with you. I want to be the man you deserve... I know I said I couldn't move to New York... but..." Spiro hesitated with his real question, where all this was leading up to. "But I can't imagine you leaving, being without you... Would you consider moving here? I mean, to Lemnos?"

Noah was expressionless as the color drained from his face. "You mean, like, move *move* here?" He murmured.

"Well, yeah. You could stay with us. Theia would love another mouth to feed." When he first came up with the idea, it sounded like he was offering something less than what Noah had back in his life in New York. But then, he realized what he was offering Noah was himself.

It was he who Noah had come so far to find. Noah had left everything to find him. He deserved to have the one thing in his life he wanted, and Spiro was fortunate enough to be able to give it to him— something no one else in the world could offer Noah. That was himself.

Nervously, Spiro rambled. "It's up to you, but you could keep your apartment in New York, if it makes you feel better. But I want you here, with me. You're the most amazing thing that has happened to me! I still can't believe—"

"Okay, okay, stop!" Noah cut him off. "How long are you talking, me staying here?"

Spiro barely let Noah finish his question. "Forever! I want you with me forever. I never want to be without you. Can you run your business from here?" Spiro asked.

"Well, yeah, I could..." This was everything Noah ever wanted to hear yet, now, he couldn't believe he was actually hearing it.

"Okay, then let's do it! I want you here forever!"

The color in Noah's face returned. Their eyes locked on one another, neither willing to blink. Their lips met, first with a light, tender kiss, followed by a second one. Noah's hand gripped Spiro's back as their kiss deepened.

Noah pulled away first; however, neither blinked or looked away.

"I love you," Noah whispered.

"I love you, too." The warmth in Spiro's chest, the sparks shooting in his head confirmed he wasn't saying it because Noah said it first. He was saying it because it was true.

CHAPTER TWENTY-FIVE

With Spiro's mother released from the hospital, they had all returned to the island two weeks ago from Athens. Life for Spiro was anything but normal. His days had been chaotic and filled with emotions.

Three days ago, he'd started his new job on the docks as a mechanic working ten-hour days. He woke every morning beside Noah, in his own bed, his room, in the house where he was born.

He was honored that Noah had chosen him. He proudly introduced Noah as his boyfriend to his friends, none of whom had any idea such a love ever existed in Spiro's past, until the day Noah showed up on the island. There was never any reason for Spiro to dredge up a life that was no longer his... until now. All his friends spoke English and welcomed Noah immediately into their lifelong brotherhood.

At home, Spiro warmly translated every conversation between Noah and his Theia Kyra, his dad, and joyfully, to his mother. Having Noah in the house with him was a life he never envisioned for himself, and now he couldn't envision living without Noah.

The night Noah and Spiro face-timed with Rodney, all three were speaking English, but Rodney and Spiro barely understood each other. It was Noah that had to translate Rodney's threat to Spiro, that if Spiro hurt his best friend, Rodney knew people that could reach his entire family in the dead of the night.

This evening, he'd come into the house after work, and after saying hello to his mother, he found his Theia Kyra and Noah in the kitchen. Noah was standing behind the small, frail woman, who was sitting in a chair, staring at Noah's laptop screen.

"Hey, babe!" Noah straightened as Spiro kissed him.

A whiff of his theia's legendary Lamb Stifado drew him away from Noah's soft lips. He glanced over at the big pot sitting on one of the gas burners before looking down at his theia. "What's going on with you two?"

"I'm showing her your website."

Spiro leaned over both of their shoulders to take a closer look. "I thought maybe you were teaching her how to play chess on the computer or something," Spiro joked.

His theia's petite hand cupped the add-on mouse beside the laptop and navigated over his pictures. Like a pro, she clicked on each one to enlarge the photo. A tiny chuckle escaped from Spiro as he shook his head in amazement.

Noah looked up at Spiro. "I wouldn't dare. She's a lot smarter than you. I would probably lose against her."

"Keep talking; your day will come. I'll get you in checkmate one of these days. How'd Mom do today?" Spiro asked as he lifted the lid to the pot on the stove. He took a big whiff, savoring the sweet cinnamon aroma of the stew that had been simmering for hours.

"She had a good day. Dominic stopped by a little while ago with her medication that came in today." Noah paused as a smirk surfaced. "You didn't tell me that Dr. Dominic was a hottie! He rocked the hell out of that man bun!

Spiro shot Noah a look. "He's married... with three kids."

"Damn, I guessed that one wrong," Noah joked.

Not entirely, but Spiro didn't want to talk about how confusing Dominic's life was. "Any spasms?"

"No. She's been comfortable all day."

"Good." It brought Spiro comfort to know that Noah was at the house with her during the day. Knowing there was now a pair of eyes watching over his theia and his mother was reassuring. He turned to his theia and conversed with her in Greek. The two talked for several minutes as her twisted, arthritic fingers pointed to the screen.

"She likes you. A lot." He bent over and kissed the top of Noah's head. "I'm going to jump in the shower and get cleaned up before we eat."

He kissed Noah once more before exiting the kitchen back door toward their room. Before leaving the dock each day, Spiro tried to clean his hands, arms, and face as much as he could before heading home, but without a shower, there was only so much he could do.

He knew Noah didn't care about the dirty grease that stained his fingers, but Spiro did. The last thing he wanted was to be an embarrassment to Noah. In his room, he took off his dirty clothes as he examined his current work in progress that they were working on last night. It was the re-creation of the painting of Noah he started several years ago. He'd never finished it and instead tucked it away.

A week ago, while Noah was going through the stacks of unfinished art in their room, Noah unearthed it. Spiro had forgotten about it. Now, he saw how flawed it was. In fact, it was all wrong, everything about it, the angle, the shape of Noah's face, the light in his eyes. Noah was sitting for him in the evenings while Spiro redid it. Maybe they could work on it some more this evening.

Spiro smirked as he took one last look at the painting before grabbing his towel and wrapping it around his naked waist. He was starving, and the sooner he took his shower, the sooner they could eat.

Within twenty minutes, Spiro was showered and walked back into the tiny kitchen. He was shirtless and in a pair of white nylon gym shorts. Noah's eyes fell to the inked art that covered Spiro's bare chest before lowering down below his waist. His heart skittered, seeing that Spiro was visibly commando under his thin shorts.

"My parents would have a heart attack if I tried to walk around the house like that!"

Spiro stopped and looked down at his own body. "What?" His nose wrinkled, as if he was confused.

Noah looked at Kyra, who had her back to them as she spooned their dinners into bowls.

"I can practically see right through your shorts!" Noah knew he could be frank, since Kyra didn't understand English.

"No, you can't." Spiro took a seat at the kitchen table and then leaned over and kissed Noah.

Noah released a moan. "I want to take you back to the bedroom right now." His groin stretched out his pants.

Kyra placed Spiro's dinner in front of him first. She returned to the stove and retrieved Noah's. He and Noah sat at the table while Kyra and Spiro's father sat in the living room with their TV trays on their laps as they watched television.

"I can't believe you're going home in the morning."

"Me, either. Trust me, I don't want to. I wish I could have applied for residence here instead of having to go back to do it."

"It just seems as if you're supposed to be here, like this is already your home. Earlier, when we were talking about Mom, I know you're not here to babysit them, they're not your responsibility. But, just knowing that you're around, in case something happens, is such a relief." Spiro savored the hint of cinnamon in the tender piece of lamb he popped into his mouth.

"It's not a big deal; I enjoy them." Noah sipped the warm broth, which was his favorite part of the meal.

"I know, but I don't ever want you to think that it's your responsibility to care for my family."

"Well, one day, they won't be just your family; they'll be mine, too, hopefully. I love your family." Noah saw the whites in Spiro's eyes turning a light pink.

"I'm just so afraid that she's going to die." Spiro nodded.

"When that day comes, her death won't be your fault. None of us are spared from dying. Your mom's a fighter. Look at her, all that she's been through, and she just keeps fighting. What happened to her is not your fault. My own experience with losing Nathanael taught me that not everything is our fault. For years, I couldn't understand why Nathanael was taken from us. I still don't get it, but from his death, I think I have a better understanding of how you feel about your mom. How can we not feel responsible? I used to tell myself that if I had waited ten minutes before I told my brother what had happened, he wouldn't have been on Fifth Avenue at the same time as that bus."

Spiro didn't see where Noah was going with this, since what he said was true. Had he waited another couple of minutes, things could have been different for Nathanael.

Noah continued talking. "With my years of counseling, I know you want to accept one hundred percent of what happened. I know I did with Nathanael." Noah paused long enough to clear his throat. "You said your mom was a diabetic all her life. Your dad knew it; the doctors knew. Everyone made choices along the way, knowing the risks... that is, everyone but you. You're the only one that didn't have a say so in the matter. How is that fair to you, for you to decide that the blame is all yours?"

"I never thought of it that way." The muscles over his eyes swelled at the realization that there was nothing he could have done. He would have thought it would have been freeing to hear it, but it really did do little to change anything.

Noah rested a hand on Spiro's thigh under the table. "As bad as it was to lose you years ago, this here, what we have now, I couldn't have asked for more. Maybe if Nathanael was still alive, I would've never met you. Had your mother not been sick, you may have never gone to see Eros that summer. We're both survivors of survivor's guilt. It's one of the things that connects us, that deeper understanding of loss and guilt."

Warmth spread across Spiro's chest. Yes, they were connected. Hearing Noah say it explained so much about why they got each other from day one. He couldn't take his eyes off Noah at the realization that this man loved him, understood him, and would be in his life every day.

"I know your mom is still alive and Nathanael's not, but I can't think of two people in the world that someone could be as close to as their mother or their twin. I see you with your mom, how her mood changes the minute you walk in the room. I don't even know how she knows you're there sometimes, but she does and you make her happy. I see the amazing love you two have for each other. It's pretty damn special. That's kind of why my relationship with my mother hurts so much."

Spiro let out a harsh breath. "Our mothers, in different ways, are our triggers."

"Exactly." Noah squeezed Spiro's thigh. "Seeing your mother every day, you look at her as something you did. My mother has shut me out, blamed me for Nathanael's death, and has never stopped punishing me. She can't look at me without blame in her eyes. I see it every single time we're together, no matter what we're doing, that moment she looks at me and realizes that I'm not Nathanael, that I'm Noah, the person who killed her son."

Noah's words raised the hair on the back of Spiro's neck. He saw the pain as it crossed Noah's face, deep within his eyes. Spiro knew the look. It was the pain Noah possessed when they were kids. Those days now fresh in his memory, Spiro remembered being jealous of Noah's life back then. Spiro hated his own life that summer, thinking how much he'd screwed it up. There was so much that Spiro didn't understand back then, but Spiro understood it now.

The one thing in his life that he'd always had and never questioned was the emotional and moral support of his family. Something Noah never had with his own family. A lump formed in Spiro's throat. He would gladly share his family with Noah, an emotional support system that had stood the test of time. Next to his own love for Noah, he could think of no greater gift that he could offer Noah. There was a long pause as they sat there.

"I'm going to miss you so much while you're gone." Spiro's voice was brittle.

"Me, too. This is something that we both have to work on, and we'll do it together."

"How long do you think it will take before you can get back?"

Noah shrugged. "Not sure. I really don't understand it all." Noah hesitated. "But... I have an idea, something I've been thinking about." Noah swallowed a tender piece of lamb. "Be open, and hear me out."

What on earth was Noah about to say now? It was one of his favorite things about Noah; his imaginative mind never seemed to stop.

"I was thinking of opening up an art gallery here."

"An art gallery?" Spiro lay his spoon on the table before sipping his iced tea. "Here?" Spiro questioned.

"Yeah. On the island. A real one, but with your art, a real art gallery. When I was looking on the internet about visas and how to apply for residence, I read where, if I'm investing in your country, like buying a house or opening a business, it's easier for me to get residence." Noah lay his spoon down as well. "An art gallery would be perfect—not like the gallery you and Nina were running, but a real studio. There's nothing like it here. We can have you as the primary artist with your work always on display and maybe every six months host another artist along with you, giving them a place to showcase their work—none of that crap you hate that's mass produced, but real paintings."

Shocked with what he was hearing, Spiro was not just intrigued, but scared of it. He never dreamed of having his work displayed in a real gallery. He questioned if he was really that good. Thoughts raced through his head as he drew a breath. "You know, years ago, when I was younger, I would have just said sure, why not? But that's not me anymore. I haven't been that person in a long time. Now I avoid making those rash decisions. In the past, they got me into trouble. I don't do change for fear it will be a mistake. I have a family to think about now. What if it doesn't work?"

Noah nodded. "I don't have the answer to that, and I get that you're scared." Noah's face sobered. "The one thing I've learned from you is not to fear failure so much that I refuse to try new things. I was shaking in my boots that day at the lake when I introduced myself to you. You don't think I was scared to get on a plane and come here? This whole business thing, I'm not trying to do it to make you famous or rich or anything like that. It's a plan for us to be together." Noah stared at him.

Spiro tried to hold a neutral face, but the more he let Noah continue, the more the excitement grew in his soul.

"Your work needs to be seen by the world. I know this could work! We can do something like the nice stores on Fifth Avenue in New York." Noah's hands became animated as he continued. "All you have to do is paint and keep my inventory up. Nina and I can run it. Nina can do the day-to-day stuff like the manager, and I can handle web stuff and marketing."

"And where would we get the money for something like this?" Spiro was ninety-nine percent sure he already knew Noah's answer, but he had to ask to tell him no.

Noah held out his hands as if telling him to slow down. "Hear me out before you tell me no. I don't want to be apart from you again. I love you. There's no reason I need to keep my apartment in New York. If I sell it, I'm sure I could get at least a million and a half for it."

A million and a half? Did he say he owned an apartment worth a million and a half dollars? Spiro was sure he must have misunderstood him.

Noah talked faster. "I can continue running my web business. God knows, this island could use a good web designer!" Noah's face was lit with excitement.

How could he say anything but yes to Noah? Not because he wanted his own gallery, but because Noah wanted it. He couldn't wrap his head around putting something like this together. "Why would you do something like this for me?"

"I'm not doing it for you; I'm doing it for us, all of us, our family. I believe in you, in us, in this."

It wasn't the answer Spiro imagined him saying. *Because I love you, because I need more to do, because it would be cool*, but not because he believed in him. No one ever said they believed in him; he'd done nothing for anyone to believe in.

"What do you mean, by having other artists?" Was he seriously entertaining this crazy notion that his boyfriend was trying to sell him?

"You know, like an exhibit or showing."

"Do we have to pay them?"

"No! The artist makes money on what they sell! The beauty in it is that we also get a percentage of whatever they sell."

"So, like other artists on the island?"

"No, baby! Way bigger! From other islands, the mainland, from the States, whoever we want to show. It doesn't have to be paintings. It could be sculptures or anything else."

"I can't have you using your money. What happens if it doesn't work?"

"You make it sound like we won't sell anything. Honey, it will work! Just say yes! It will work, I swear! All I need you to do is paint, paint your ass off every day!"

Spiro wasn't that keen on having to rely on the tourist industry to survive. It was risky, and he didn't do risky anymore. "Maybe during the high season, but what about the rest of the year? The island empties out by December." Spiro shook his head. He couldn't believe he was agreeing to this.

"That's the beauty of working with me. We won't depend on foot traffic or whatever time of year it is. With the internet, you're going international. I can sell your art via the internet to anyone in the world, three hundred, sixty-five days a year."

Spiro would love nothing more than to replace the dirt and oil on his hands with paint. "When do you want to do something like this?"

"I'll call Rodney. Once I tell him I want to sell the apartment, he'll buy it so his lazy ass doesn't have to move!"

Spiro pushed down a lump in his throat. He'd say yes; they would open their own business. He'd be a real painter. But first, he had to get through Noah not being here. Would it be weeks, a month, several months? He didn't want to go a single day without Noah. It was hard enough leaving for work in the morning, knowing he wouldn't see him all day. His stomach tightened as his skin prickled. He rubbed the back of his neck, trying to reduce the tension that was building. He'd never been a dreamer, and now his entire future was nothing but a dream. He didn't scare easy, but dreaming scared the shit out of him.

CHAPTER TWENTY-SIX

Two days before Christmas, Upper Manhattan had been covered in a fresh layer of snow from yesterday's storm. Bundled in a shirt, sweater, and jacket, Noah stripped off his wool jacket and hung it on the back of his chair. He'd arrived at the restaurant twenty minutes early, coming directly from his interview on the other side of town with the Greek consulate. Until now, he didn't realize how much he hated these wintry days of bluster and ice. Noah could go a lifetime and never see snow again, and now that Rodney had purchased the apartment, that was exactly Noah's plan.

This afternoon he was meeting his parents for a late lunch. He planned on telling them he was moving to the other side of the world to be with the man he'd been in love with for so many years. With a little time to kill, he dialed Spiro's number.

After two rings, Spiro appeared on his screen. "Hey, babe. What's going on?"

"Just sitting here, waiting for my parents to show." He adored looking at Spiro's big, beautiful hazel eyes and thick brows as he stared at his screen. Since being back in New York, for the last two months, he and Spiro face-timed every day.

"Oh, the dreaded lunch. I wish I could be there with you to support you."

"After I tell them, it's not support I'll need; it's a drink. Are you at Mateo's?"

"Yeah, Andy's here, and Dominic just came in."

"What movie are you guys watching?"

"When the City Dies."

"Never heard of it."

"It's an old movie. This week was Dominic's pick. He loves the old Greek classics."

"I bet he does. He better stay away from mine."

"Is it still snowing there?" Spiro asked.

Noah could see that Spiro had walked from Mateo's small living room and was now in the hallway. "Not at the moment, but it snowed all day yesterday. There's another storm coming in later this evening."

"Are you excited about Christmas?"

"You know, I'm not. My aunt and her husband are coming in from South Carolina. Rodney's still in Dubai. I know it's in two days, but I'm not going to get what I want for Christmas, so I don't care."

"Ah, babe, it will be fine. Are you still going to your parents' for dinner?"

"Do I have a choice? Is Theia Kyra still baking?"

Spiro laughed. "Yep. She's been baking kataifi and baklava all day."

"What's she cooking for Christmas?"

"The usual. We'll roast a lamb. Her spinach and cheese pie. Probably vegetables. Christmas morning, Nina will make theeples for breakfast."

"What's theeples?"

"It's like a fried pastry."

"Oh, my God. You're killing me." Noah wasn't sure if it was the food that sounded inviting or the fact the Papadopoulos family would all be together in that tiny house, laughing and being thankful for life. "What did Mateo bring tonight?"

"He made some kourabiethes and melomakarona."

"What's that?"

Spiro turned his phone, showing Noah the Christmas cookies that Mateo had made. "These are kourabiethes." He pointed to the round, shortbread cookie made with toasted almonds buried under a ton of confectioner's sugar. "And these are my favorite, melomakarona."

Noah stared at the beautiful mountain of cookies on two big plates. "What's in those?"

Spiro picked up one of the cookies. "They have cinnamon, cloves, and orange. After they're cooked, Mateo dips them in syrup and then rolls them in nuts."

"Are you guys going to eat all those cookies!"

"No problem." Spiro plopped the cookie into his mouth.

"Geez, I should've just flown back this week. I love you so much." Even though Noah couldn't eat most of everything Spiro talked about, the joy surrounding all of it, the sharing, the celebration, the coming together that was attached to it, was so warm and inviting. It was a life waiting for him on the other side of the world.

"I love and miss you, too, babe. Hey, how'd your interview go this morning?"

"I don't know. My lawyer said it was fine. The lady at the Greek consulate was acting as if I was some kind of terrorist trying to get in or something. She grilled me with a ton of questions. I was there over an hour."

Spiro laughed. "Don't worry. They want you to come. It's an act, and more about their pride. Like you don't know our economy is shot out. We need your dollars to help stabilize our economy."

"Yeah, that's what my lawyer said, too. They asked for a ton of information, bank records, proof of healthcare, and all kinds of other stuff."

"I can't believe you need a lawyer for this."

"Everyone said that it would go easier if I had one." Noah looked up as the waiter stepped up to the table and stood. "Hold on." Noah gave the waiter his attention.

"Sir, may I bring you something from the bar while we wait for your other guests?"

"No, but I'll take a hot tea, please. The white jasmine. I'm a little early. They should be here soon."

The waiter nodded before leaving.

Noah returned to his phone. "The lawyer said now we just have to wait and see. I just want to make it back before your birthday." February twentieth seemed a lifetime away. "If I can't get it approved before then, I'm just going to come for a visit. There's no need for me to sit around here and wait."

"Do you think it will take that long?"

"We don't know. My lawyer said that, because I'm applying as an investor, it should go faster. Did you look at any spaces today?"

"Yeah, me and Mateo looked at a space I think would be perfect. I asked the agent to send you the information and pictures on it. It's on Athinon Avenue."

"Oh, that's the nice street that I like. Does it need much work?"

"I don't know. It used to be a woman's clothing store. It's empty. It might be more than you want to spend, though."

"How much?"

"Take a look at it first before I tell you. I want you to see it first."

Noah shook his head at his little worrier. If he left it up to Spiro, they would run the gallery from the back of Spiro's house. This was another reason he needed to get back to Lemnos. "Okay. What's going on with Theia Kyra's house?" Theia Kyra's house that Eros never completed was Noah's other investment. Noah was using the proceeds from the sale of his apartment to finish her house.

"Nothing. The guys haven't started yet."

Noah tried not to roll his eyes. When he purchased the house from Theia Kyra, he intentionally overpaid for the property. In his mind, Noah needed to pay some sort of restitution for what his parents had done so many years ago to the Papadopoulos family. He hadn't told Spiro yet, but his intent was to sell it back for one dollar to Theia Kyra when the house was finished. The house belonged to the Papadopoulos family, not him. In a game of musical chairs, he and Spiro would move into the new house, Nina was taking Spiro's old room, and Theia Kyra would have a bedroom to herself.

Noah was about to ask Spiro how his mother was doing when he looked up and saw his own mom coming into the restaurant. In her hand were three wrapped boxes. His dad wasn't with her.

Noah drew a breath. "Okay, my mom just walked in. I love you!" They blew each other a kiss as Noah's mom arrived at the table.

"Where's dad? Parking the car?" Noah asked.

"No." She placed the presents in one of the empty chairs at the table. "He sends his regards; he was called in for a consultation. He won't be joining us."

Noah knew his dad was avoiding him, her, or both. "Who are the presents for?"

Noah's mother draped her coat over the empty chair. "Those are Rodney's."

"What'd you get him this year?" He didn't figure that they were for him, since he would be at the house on Christmas.

"I was in Williams-Sonoma the other day and found this great Indian-ish cookbook for him, and Barneys had these gorgeous alpaca wool blankets I fell in love with. Be careful with the small box. It's a candle. I know he loves burning candles."

Noah was sure Rodney would love it all. The reality that he was moving away from Rodney was more difficult than leaving any part of New York behind.

The waiter arrived with Noah's hot tea. "Good afternoon, Ma'am. Are we still waiting on one more person?"

"Oh, no. It'll just be us." She answered without giving the poor guy even a glance.

Noah watched as the waiter retreated to the kitchen. Without his dad, telling her that he was moving would be easier. He got a little joy knowing that her telling his father the news would likely cause her anxiety.

During their meal, their conversation centered on the holidays and work. When Noah was done with his salad, he lay his fork down, not being able to hold off telling her a minute longer.

"Mom, you remember that guy Eros, that used to work for Grandma up at the lake house? What happened to him?"

Noah's mom held off putting the bite on her fork into her mouth. "Why are you asking? Or is this something you already know, and you're looking to see what I'll say?" She shot Noah a venomous look, daring him to challenge her.

"Who fired him, Grandma or Dad?"

Noah's mom placed her fork on the edge of her plate. "Neither. Your grandmother had called me, and I made the decision that he and the boy needed to go."

"Was it because of what Chris Alperstein saw in the boathouse?" Anger spiraled from the pit of Noah's stomach.

"Yes! Eros should have known better than to have that boy on the property. We should have had him arrested for what he did to you."

"He didn't do anything to me!"

"I'm not going to argue with you here."

"I can't believe you guys just fired him. He worked for you guys for years!"

"Noah, the man was getting old. He was a liability on the property. It wasn't just about the boy; it was time. Your grandma was talking about selling the property. Your father and I hardly ever made it up there anymore. Noah, why are we talking about this?" She met Noah's unrelenting stare.

"Did you know he died a year later?"

Noah's mom leaned back in her chair. "Yes... his sister called your father."

"And?" His eyes flashed with anger. She talked as if there were no consequences to their action. There was an entire family that relied on the money Eros sent back to Greece.

"And? And what? What are you asking?"

"I'm not asking anything! I want you to know there was an entire family depending on his money—a woman that was sick, that needed medication—medication they couldn't afford without his money."

Noah's blood boiled with fury, thinking about how his family did wrong to the Papadopouloses, the man that he loved, the man that loved him. The Rothenbergs had royally screwed the Papadopouloses, yet they welcomed him with open arms. Being there with them, they never once showed any animosity toward him.

Riddled with guilt, he wasn't sure how he could ever face them again, knowing what he knew now. He rubbed his forehead. Baffled, this wasn't even what he was here to talk about, but it sure made it easier to say what he wanted to say now.

Noah leaned back in his chair. "Well, I know you're not going to ask about my trip, and that's fine. Today, I had an interview at the Greek consulate's office. I applied for a visa and residence in Greece. I'm moving. I sold the apartment."

The color drained from Noah's mother's face. "You're moving to Greece? May I ask why?"

"Mom, you know why. If you want to talk about him, then I'm open to it. I'm in love with Spiro Papadopoulos, and I'm moving there to be with him." Noah stopped as the waiter appeared and asked if he could clear their plates.

With the waiter gone, Noah waited to see if his mother would continue the conversation. Her silence spoke volumes to him, revealing something about her that he'd missed all these years. He'd had an epiphany. For so many years, he thought her refusal to talk about his sexuality was about his sexuality, but it wasn't. It didn't matter if he was in love with a man or a woman; his mother was incapable of being happy about anything. She likely had been unhappy her entire life. It was an emotion she never inherited and was incapable of feeling. None of this had anything to do with him. Sadness washed over him, realizing that those things in life, like falling in love, getting married, the birth of a child, brought her no joy. How sad that she lived such an existence. There wasn't anything to say once he realized this.

They sat through the bill being paid, and afterward Noah stood first. "I'll see you on Christmas. What time do you want me at the house?"

His mother remained seated as her head shook. "I don't know. Your aunt should be there around noon. Dinner's at two."

"Okay. It will be nice to see Aunt Carrie before I leave." Noah leaned over and kissed his mother on her cheek. He felt her rigidness, but that was her problem, not his. "I'm going to head out before it starts snowing again." He started to walk away.

"Noah..." His mother called to him. "Don't forget to take Rodney his gifts."

EPILOGUE
June 10th

This afternoon, the Aegean Sea was like a warm bath. The buoyancy of the water allowed Noah's body to float effortlessly on the surface as a sunray warmed his face and stomach.

This beach, it was the beach Spiro had taken him to when he was just eighteen years old. That summer day, so long ago, they were just two boys sitting in his granddad's Lincoln with dreams and ideas. It was now also the beach they shared on their first date when they were reunited. Other than being in Spiro's arms, this beach was Noah's favorite spot in the world.

Although it was only three o'clock in the afternoon, this was the best birthday he'd had in years. This morning, he was awakened with birthday pancakes, ham, and coffee, served to him in bed. Although Spiro claimed he'd cooked it, Noah had his suspicion that Theia Kyra had a least a hand in his success. He'd had very few problems adjusting to the island's daily Mediterranean diet of mostly fresh veggies and seafood. Even the feta in small doses was doable.

Before breaking for mesimeri today, he and Spiro spent the early morning at the gallery with a professional photographer and a very pregnant Nina. They were photographing all of Spiro's art for the gallery's website. The gallery's grand opening was less than thirty days ago and had been a huge success—success not in the monetary way, but in that it actually happened. When Noah returned to the island back in March, he was caught off guard on how slow construction worked on the island. Everybody's attitude, including Spiro's, was *Stop worrying. It will get done.*

But Noah was a New Yorker and not that laid back. The slow pace and lack of materials on the island that they needed to furnish their first-class art gallery sent Noah into an "I'll-do-it-myself mode." He and Spiro worked long days, with countless trips to the mainland for supplies. If he waited for everything to be shipped, he would never get it on time.

The progress on Theia Kyra's house wasn't much different. Frustrated on how slow things got done, it had been Spiro that had stopped Noah from going off on the lackadaisical construction crew. These four brothers seemed to want to set their own hours and days they'd show up to work.

As the ocean washed up and around Noah's face, he felt a surge under him right before his body was grabbed and pulled underwater. If it wasn't for the fact that he couldn't breathe, he would have stayed in Spiro's arms under the water. Rising to the surface, he gasped for air as he spit water from his mouth.

"Oh, no! Not again!" Spiro laughed.

Noah knew what he was insinuating. He wasn't going to throw up. When he collected his breath, Spiro swam closer to him.

They played in the waves about ten yards from the shore. They let the warm water tumble over them as an excuse to be close, to touch, to feel the other's fingers brush against their skin. Wrapped in a mutual embrace, Spiro's slick skin rubbed against Noah's, sending a surge of desire through him and giving him tantalizing ideas.

From out in the water, Noah could see Nina and George on the beach, sitting on a blanket. George had a hand and ear pressed against Nina's very round bare stomach. Watching them, George and Nina reminded him of his first date with Spiro, when it was he sitting on the shore, completely enthralled by his lover.

George was clearly in love with her and had asked her almost every week to marry him. Nina refused him every time, saying that having a baby was not a reason a woman had to marry a man. He doted over her constantly, as if she'd go into labor any minute. Noah was happy that he'd made it back before the birth. This child would be the first in the family to never know a life without Uncle Noah. He would be just as much a part of the child's life as Spiro and the rest of the family. The Papadopouloses, all of them, were his family.

Noah was deep in thought when Spiro came from behind him and wrapped his wet, slick arms around him. "What are you thinking about?" Spiro's wet lips kissed Noah's neck.

Wet and warm, Spiro's lips were like a drug, a drug that made his entire body tingle. "My brother, my parents." Noah murmured.

"What about them?"

Noah closed his eyes and took a second to embrace the warmth radiating from Spiro's body. He knew this was love that he was feeling.

"When Nathanael and I were little, for our birthday, my mom would take us to Central Park to ride the merry-go-round and eat hot dogs. I remember one day riding the horse behind Nathanael. As the merry-go-round went around and around in a circle, I kicked and kicked that horse, trying to catch him."

Noah chuckled under his breath, realizing how stupid it was, thinking the distances between the horses could change. "Anyways... I remember every time my horse would go around to where my mom was standing, she wasn't even looking at us. She was off on her phone. Every time I went around, I looked at her, hoping she was looking at us." Noah felt the swell of emotions in his chest, which forced him to control his breathing.

The waves had knocked him and Spiro closer to shore, enough that their feet could reach the sandy ocean bottom. Spiro pulled him closer to him. Noah wrapped his legs around Spiro's waist and his arms around Spiro's neck and shoulders. They exchanged a light kiss as Noah savored the wet coolness of Spiro's lips.

Noah continued his story. "I don't know how many times we'd gone around when I noticed every time we came around to where Mom was, Nathanael started making these goofy faces at her or do something stupid that would make me laugh at him. I had completely stopped focusing on what she was doing and the sadness of her not paying attention to me and was focused on Nathanael being silly. I'll always remember that day because it was the day I realized the connection we shared as twins. He totally got me and was always there for me."

"How old were you guys?"

Noah thought for a second. "I don't know, maybe around eight or so. I can't believe I wasted my whole life trying to get them to see me."

Noah's epiphany about his mother was like a rebirth for him. Understanding who she was freed him from his struggles with her. What she did or had to say no longer had the same power over him as it once did. He'd stopped holding her accountable for something she was incapable of doing, and that was being happy in this life or sharing in his.

Although his relationship with his father was not as easy to define, Noah could see that his father's issues were also more about who he was as a person than who Noah was. His father was a deeply disturbed man, the classic definition of a narcissist.

Noah stared at Spiro, taken in by his beautiful wet hair, dark eyebrows, and gorgeous hazel eyes. Spiro was the only other person in this life besides Nathanael that he loved to the depths of his soul, so much that it was indescribable. He was about to say something when Spiro spoke.

"Happy birthday, Nathanael!" Spiro said as he looked up toward the sun. "Thank you for sharing your brother with me. I promise, I'll take care of him."

Warmth spread through Noah's entire body as his heart melted, knowing just how much Spiro got him, and had always gotten him, from the first day they met. "God, I love you!"

Spiro squeezed Noah tighter. "*Méra me ti méra, aftó pou epilégete, ti skéfteste kai ti kánete eínai poios gíneste.*" He then delivered a light kiss to Noah's bottom lip.

"I'm still working on my Greek. I have no idea what you just said." Noah couldn't help but smile as Spiro's tender kiss warmed his entire neck.

Spiro chuckled. "It's an ancient Greek quote from Heraclitus... 'Day by day, what you choose, what you think, and what you do are who you become.'"

Noah pondered what Spiro had just said. Not only did that fit his parents and their life of misery, it had almost taken him out. Noah knew he would never settle for bits and pieces of love to be doled out to him again. Spiro loved him unconditionally, something Noah at one time didn't even know existed.

Noah's heart swooned. "Babe... I think you finally put me in checkmate." Joy bubbled up in him, knowing there was nowhere for him to go. He would stay in Spiro's arms forever if he could.

Checkmate

About the Author:

Bryan T. Clark is a multi-published award-winning author of gay romance, and contemporary books. In his early life, Bryan learned that he was different from everyone else in his world. As a young African American boy, he was the second to the youngest of seven children. Long before hormones kicked in and the realization of same sex attraction, it was his light skin and blond hair that made him different from those around him. Teased within his own race for being lighter than everyone else, the kids on the playground called him "Cornbread".

As a writer, Bryan has taken back the power once given up to those schoolyard bullies. He is committed to bringing his readers stories of real life, with multicultural characters, riveting plots, and where the underdog always wins. He is the founder of Cornbread Publishing: the name empowers him and is a constant reminder that life can have a Happily-Ever-After.

Born in Boston, Massachusetts, Bryan and his husband of thirty-six years have made their home and life in the Central Valley of California.

Thank you so much for reading *Far Away* and I hope you enjoyed it. I would love it if you would consider leaving a brief review on Goodreads or wherever you find your books, or any author boards or social media groups you belong to. Your review may help other readers discover their possible next read. Thank you again, and wishing you many more Happily Ever After's.

Website: http://www.btclark.com/
Facebook: https://www.facebook.com/btclarkauthor
Instagram: https://www.instagram.com/romanceauthor/
Goodreads: https://www.goodreads.com/author/dashboard
Twitter: https://twitter.com/BryanTClarkx2

Read more from Bryan T. Clark

Escaping Camp Roosevelt
"He's a bad boy—cocky and damaged. So, why can't I stop thinking about him?"

Broken Dreams
Sociable and unselfish, eighteen-year-old Tucker Graves loves two things—his darling little sister and the thrill of playing baseball. He never dreamed that he'd be homeless, but after a series of misfortunes, his life is nothing like he could have possibly imagined. Shocked and shattered, Tucker, his mother, and his baby sister now must brave the dangers of a dilapidated homeless encampment called Camp Roosevelt.

A Wounded Heart
Homeless since the age of fourteen, Dancer has mastered the tricks of living on the streets as a sex worker. The quiet, reclusive, and calculating ways of this twenty-year-old, green-eyed Adonis help him to survive. He hides his emotional scars from the world by interacting only with his clients, whose occasional bizarre requests he reluctantly fulfills. Dancer's past has taught him to trust no one.

A Second Chance
When Tucker and Dancer come face to face on a stormy night, having been thrown together under the same roof, Tucker brings out a feeling in Dancer that he didn't know still existed in him—desire.

Neither man can deny the attraction he feels for the other. But some scars run deep, causing both Tucker and Dancer to question whether falling in love is even possible, especially when survival is on the line.

Bryan T. Clark

*** *One hundred percent of the royalties from the first year of Escaping Camp Roosevelt's publication was donated to the Larkin Street Youth Services/Castro Youth Housing Initiative. The CYHI provides transitional housing in the city of San Francisco, California, for LGBTQ youth experiencing homelessness. Fear of being raped, abused, or murdered should not be a part of anyone's youth.*

Diego's Secret
International Book Awards Finalist for 2019 LGBTQ FICTION

Diego Castillo struggles daily under the weight of his secrets. Not only is he in the US illegally, but he's also forced to hide his desire for other men from his brothers. Lately, the only time he can really be himself is when he's with his landscaping client, Winston—a man as beautiful as he is intimidating. They come from two different worlds, but in Winston he senses a vulnerable kindred spirit, and even though getting involved could uncover Diego's secrets, putting his entire family at risk, he's powerless to stay away.

Winston Makena is suffering, too. All his millions can't buy a minute's peace from the crushing grief he's felt since his husband's death. The only relief he finds these days is when he's with Diego. Despite their differences, Winston finds himself inexorably drawn to Diego's honesty, kindness, and gentle soul. But he can never truly love again... can he?

It's not long before Diego and Winston's clandestine attraction grows into something much more complicated, and as cultures clash, misunderstandings mount, and secrets loom, they're left to wonder if the cost of following their hearts is more than they can ever pay...

Come to the Oaks
Winner of the 2017 Rainbow Award for BEST GAY HISTORICAL

LAMBDA Literary Award Finalist for 2017 BEST GAY ROMANCE

In 1845, as America is drowning in its own racial conflict, in a time when forbidden love has to remain a secret, can two young men find love when one has everything to lose, and the other has nothing?

For Tobias, a young African man, life has ended before it began. Snatched abruptly from his homeland and enslaved into the Antebellum South, grand homes and majestic oak trees meant little to him. Now he is considered the property of other men, but his spirit would not be broken.

The awkward Benjamin Nathanael Lee lives a privileged life. His father owns the largest tobacco plantation south of the Mason Dixon line. Ben wants little to do with the harsh realities of running a plantation—that is, until he meets Tobias, the one person that changes everything for him.

Wealth, greed, and power brought them together. The same now threatens to separate them forever. The two men are on the verge of losing the one thing that matters: their love for one another. Against the odds, they steal off and embark on a journey to find freedom: the freedom to love one another and to live a life without the chains of slavery.

Come to the Oaks is the tale of a forbidden romance—a love forged by two young men as they journey through a land that is tearing itself apart.

Before Sunrise
USA-Today LGBTQ BOOK OF THE YEAR
*Bryan T. Clark, has again masterfully crafted a romance where the fine line
between right and wrong must be resolved for love to survive-USA-Today*

Just Before Sunrise, as the fog lifts from the pool, the light reveals the tapered backs of male swimmers in Speedos concluding their morning workout.

Nicky O'Hare, a promising freshman recruited to the Tampa Bay University swim team, shows promise both in and out of the pool. The lean Irish kid with the 'boy-next-door' good looks from Brandy, South Dakota, is likely the most talented swimmer on the team. Ready to experience all that college life has to offer, Nicky has even put finding a boyfriend on his wish list.

Coach Phillip Silva, a former Olympic swimmer with a once-impressive swimming career, has recruited Nicky as part of his mission to rebuild the University's failing swim program. Focused on the upcoming season, Phillip's real challenge will be keeping his secrets and demons submerged below the surface.

All seems well until one night when Nicky and Phillip end up at the same Fourth of July celebration. With fireworks in the sky, the hot and humid night reveals the attraction between the two. But can these boundaries be crossed? Suddenly forced to reevaluate his life, Phillip is met with the moral dilemma of discovering true love with the University's rising star.

Before Sunrise presents a story of friendships, love, complicated relationships, and deception, woven into a hard-earned happily-ever-after.

Ancient House of Cards

Sebastian Morales is smart, gorgeous, and has just turned 30. He is also one of the youngest priests to be assigned to the sleepy little town of Morris, Colorado, nestled just below the majestic Rocky Mountains.

Born in a remote village in Spain, Father Morales's life had been perfectly scripted as he obtained his dreams. Now in America, he is tasked with revitalizing an aging congregation. The job seems easy, until he meets Ian Stephens. Ian is troubled, good looking, openly gay, and trapped between his own dreams and the responsibility he feels for caring for his aging mother.

Escorting his mother to Sunday mass one morning, Ian's and Father Morales's lives intersect, changing both forever. Ian believes he has seen something in the Father's eyes that morning—a spark, an intuition—or was he just fantasizing about the seductively alluring priest?

Ian is willing to risk it all in order to find the answer, in turn feeding his own sexual desires and causing boundaries to be questioned by everyone.

After an unforeseen yet unforgettable kiss between the two men, will an Ancient House of Cards be toppled when they are faced with the moral dilemma that neither of them can escape?

www.ingramcontent.com/pod-product-compliance
Lightning Source LLC
Chambersburg PA
CBHW070845250626
47159CB00003B/936